CONTRABAND

Also by George Foy
and published by Bantam Books

The Shift

CONTRABAND

George Foy

BANTAM BOOKS

LONDON • NEW YORK • TORONTO • SYDNEY • AUCKLAND

CONTRABAND
A BANTAM BOOK : 0 553 50629 3

First publication in Great Britain

PRINTING HISTORY
Bantam edition published 1998

Set in 11/12pt Joanna by Falcon Oast Graphic Art

Bantam Books are published by Transworld Publishers Ltd,
61–63 Uxbridge Road, London W5 5SA,
in Australia by Transworld Publishers (Australia) Pty Ltd,
15–25 Helles Avenue, Moorebank, NSW 2170,
and in New Zealand by Transworld Publishers (NZ) Ltd,
3 William Pickering Drive, Albany, Auckland.

Reproduced, printed and bound in Great Britain by
Cox & Wyman Ltd, Reading, Berks.

For Kitty Foy

Acknowledgments

Thanks to Dan Burke, Pete Sessa, Gin Ryan, Fred Barthet, Jean-Francis Perrot, the Writers' Room, John Stearns, Jeff Kaufmann, and Tom Cook for their help on this book.

1

'A sort of lewd people called smuckellors,
rarely heard of before these late disordered times,
who make it their trade . . . to steal and
defraud his Majesty of his Customs.'

Royal proclamation, Westminster Palace
9 August 1661

The pilot had been on the run for almost twenty years
before anyone realized, much less did anything about
it.

The first murmur of pursuit came faint and abstract
as the sound of strangers whispering in a forgotten
language in another room.

It happened on an autumn Sunday in a village
eighty-five miles up the Rio Chingado, in the corner
of South America where Brazil, Colombia, and Peru
are stitched together by rivers.

The pilot was sitting, waiting for cargo, on the
porch of a tin-roofed hut. The hut hung over the river
on long thin stilts. It smelled of coffee and minerals
and rot. The hut belonged to the Brazilian, who
always sat in the corner behind the weighing table. If
you came in without knowing he was there, you

might not see the Brazilian, so still was he, so much a part of the jungle gloom inside this corrupted structure.

A board of green wood linked the hut to the river-bank. The Cayman came down the plank like a ballet star, toeing delicately in soft gaucho boots. He peered behind the weighing table, noting the shine of metal and how it was reflected in the Brazilian's eyes, apparently without reference to light.

'T'ree tolas,' he said. With one hand he lifted a cellophane bag against the window, against the canopy of fattened trees overhanging the river.

The Cayman's other hand gripped a two-foot-long glass jar. It was an old-fashioned specimen bottle with a bell-shaped end, of a type that might have been used one hundred years earlier for experiments concerning phrenology and the seat of intelligence. Behind a ceramic stopper, the glass was full of long and curled silver. Two copper wires twisted out of the ceramic. 'No fuck conmigo, man,' the Cayman went on, 'dis t'ree at *least*.'

The Cayman was fat and gray; fever had leached color from his skin the way rain leached the forest's meager topsoil when the lumbermen had been and gone. His eyelids had folds so that when he blinked, three different cowls had to be moved in sequence to cover and uncover his pupils. A grimy mauve waistcoat failed to close over his large belly. Sweat dripped from his belly button, darkening his loose pants. It looked like he had pissed himself.

The Brazilian was thin and taut as piano wire. He kept on spooning gold dust from a small gourd to an even smaller bronze scale. Kerosene lamps wrestled the jade gloom. The gold took this light, broke and

12

yellowed it, played it against the brass weights.

Smoke from the steam pumps of the emerald mines upstream formed parentheses around the hut. The tin roof cooled the air's vapor, condensing it into water that dripped steadily on the floor.

Clouds rubbed bruise marks into the jungle shade. A gunboat churned grayly upriver, radar turning in circular, arachnid alert.

The Cayman spat into the river and picked his way over soft planks, through the riverside door, to the porch at the shack's far end.

The pilot did not look up. He stuck the second finger of his left hand in a mug of *tinto*. He squinted through black glasses toward his float-jet where it crouched warily among the tendrils of smoke and the coiled black muscles of the river, rocking slightly in the gunboat's wake.

The Cayman leaned forward, almost touching the pilot's ear with his lips.

'Bokon Taylay. He look for *nosotros*,' the Cayman whispered.

The pilot lifted his finger out of the coffee. The movement pulled sweat from every pore in his body. The boil in the pulp of his finger was plummy and taut. He stuck it in an adjoining cup of *cachaca* rum, and winced.

'Go away, Fawcett,' he muttered.

Upriver on the same side, an ancient paddlewheeler lay half awash, braided to the bank with vines. Indios had slung hammocks from brass fittings in the saloon. Even from the hut you could hear their guitars rub, like rough tools scraping music from the substance of the jungle itself.

In the trees overhead, bearded monkeys flung

13

papaya rinds at each other. The trees' roots were lean, and white from lack of sun. They touched the fallen rinds and closed on them, seeking food.

'My last two cargoes, Bokon take.'

'You're breakin' my heart.'

'Bokon Taylay, he get everybody now. *Tu sabes?* He know de code. He know de *dance.*'

'I told ya. No.'

The Cayman smiled sadly. No man trades for love, he thought. It was as close to an article of faith as he possessed. He shifted the glass jar from left hand to right, and reversed the procedure for his bag of gold.

'Fifteen tolas,' he said. A tola was a wafer of gold, 3.75 troy ounces in weight. 'Is K-Y, man. For dis you run only twelve bale of jisi. Next run, you bring Deutschmark. Or maybe you wan' jive wi' my *pescado?*'

'Your fish don't bother me.'

'Escuchame.' The Cayman leaned close. 'Listen.' The jungle had rotted his insides first and his breath smelled like mulch.

'If you don' help, my cargoes no run. If cargoes no run, my Indios no manjay.'

'I got too much weight already.' The pilot spoke too loud. He did not want to think about the Indians. 'An' I'm down with a tailo, for this run. So forget it.'

A raindrop the size of a walnut cracked into the water. A gun coughed from the Brazilian side of the Chingado. A soldier came out of the frontier post and stared through night-vision goggles over the dark water. It was two in the afternoon.

'Dey sell their M-2s. Can't buy bullets. Already dey go back to blowpipes.' The tone was full of hurt, but the Cayman's face was rejigging itself in different directions – a curious sequence where the eyelids slid up, one after the other, and large cheek muscles hauled plates of fat out and up to reveal sharp teeth – a smile. His pupils narrowed. He jammed the bag of dust in a pocket of his waistcoat. The pilot dropped his right hand toward the switchblade in his boot, but the Cayman was quicker. He grabbed the glass jar with both hands and shook it very hard in front of the pilot's face, the wires almost touching his nose.

The jar exploded in a convulsion of finned and rounded silver, turning, twisting, folding. In the vortex of spasms you could catch a freeze-frame of Horror, its ratchet mouth and chainsaw teeth and psycho eyes.

The pilot backed away from the electric eel and the sparking wires that conducted its fury. His chair tilted. The doubled pressure under the back legs finally tore the soggy fibers of the deck planks, and the legs broke through. The pilot toppled backward, without hope or possibility of saving himself; fingers spreading in a prayer for flight, he rolled straight over the edge of the deck, into the arterial river.

The Chingado was hot as blood, thick as gruel, the color of double-strong espresso. As the water closed over his head and leaked through his lips the pilot thought he could taste the whole history of its run; the flatness of Cordillera snow, the grit of stolen soil. Lime of murdered Indians, of poisoned jaguars. In his mouth he knew the death of peasant squatters who wound up tied hand and foot in the Chingado's middle stretch. He knew the quickness of alligators and blue piranhas and coral snakes, and the tiny silver fish that swim up your asshole and wedge themselves with hypo spines against the pink coruscations of your tripes.

He shot out of the water faster than a panicked porpoise. At the top of his arc he wrapped both arms around one of the hut supports. With elbows and knees he tried shinnying up the pole toward the broken deck. Algae grew green, inch-thick on the support, and for every upward thrust the pilot lost almost as much ground as he'd gained, so that at the end of two minutes his ankles still hung in the umber water.

The Cayman and the Brazilian stared over the edge of the deck, watching the pilot struggle among the fumes of mingled rivers. The Brazilian was laughing so hard he vibrated like an instrument and had to be held up by the fat man.

The clouds released their water. The opposite bank disappeared behind metallic folds of rain.

On the paddlewheeler, the guitars had stopped, or maybe it was just that the noise of rain overpowered their soft rhythms.

In the forest behind the paddlewheeler an Indio wadded a dart, and lifted his blowpipe toward the invisible sun. The Indio belonged to a tribe that thought they were parrots. He wore yellow feathers around his neck to protect himself from humans.

'I will radio to Chico Fong,' the Cayman shouted. 'He will make you take my jisi.'

'Rot your balls,' the pilot screamed. 'You did this on purpose; you knew I hate getting my duds wet, ah you scum!'

But the pilot's anger was largely chemical and soon faded. When it was gone, he hung on to his pole, wondering when the two would get over their giggling long enough to throw him a rope. He wondered, also, how to prevent the Cayman from getting in touch with Chico.

16

Wondered who in hell 'Bokon Taylay' was.

It was his last trip to the Chingado, the pilot decided. He hated places with no horizon.

The Indio's dart found its mark.

A baby monkey fell with no sound while its mother screamed from above.

17

2

'The airplane is doubtless only a machine; but
what a fine instrument for analysis!'
Antoine de Saint-Exupéry
Terre des Hommes

A chapter called 'Sit On My Interface' in the 14th
edition of *The Freetrader's Almanac and Cookbook* (Charras
Press, Boulder, Colorado) – better known as the
'Smuggler's Bible' – includes the following advice:

> The freetrader should always jive on the bound-
> ary layer between earth, air, water, and space.
> Interface like a beach, a storm front, a dewpoint;
> this is the space where different kinds of waves
> meet, flirt – and zoom-zoom into craziness,
> because it is the nature of a wave to believe it is
> unique. This is the space where matter splits
> from form, because the FORM of a wave is what
> holds it together. The weird trips of turbulence
> or surf offer the same opportunities for chaos
> and catastrophe as a human frontier. Chaos and
> catastrophe are the freetrader's homeboys,
> because the instruments of the Man can ride

only one wave of reality at a time . . .

Practical applications of boundary-layer travel are numerous, especially if you want to evade visual and electronic surveillance in heavy crisis situations. They include dewpoint (fog), surf (small boat landings), saline layers and SOFAR (submarine operations), the Great Red Spot of Jupiter (radio transmissions), storm fronts (aviation, marine) . . .

The pilot folded his hard-copy of the Smuggler's Bible and stowed it in his chartcase with one hand while with the other he touched the control column, feeling the autopilot adjust as it kept his aircraft hurtling over the western Atlantic, dead in the lane where night and water stretched invisible fingers toward each other and danced briefly, like shy kids in white gloves, wherever wind rubbed, and fog precipitated, and waves built – never quite mingling.

In the narrow windscreen, at forty-five feet of altitude and 320 knots of speed, the effect was hallucinating; worm after parallel, broken worm of white spume ripping out of the blue-black nothing of time unspent and distance-not-traveled, strobing almost quicker than the mind could grasp between dark sea and invisible night, to vanish one splinter of a second later under the nose-antenna of the jet.

The deflectors barely managed to keep his windscreen clear of salt spray. The squirts of rain-repellent only smeared around salt left on the glass. That same spray must be soaking the turbine blades of his two Pratt and Whitneys. He would have to take the crate in for overhaul as soon as he got back to Newark.

The pilot switched off the chartlight. The

19

Smuggler's Bible came in CD-ROM form but you could not fool around with LCDs and keyboard at this speed and altitude. Luckily Charras still printed hard-copy for Darkworld use – for places, in what was once called the 'Third World,' or the Third-World-like areas of richer countries, where freetraders tended to end up. He had taken a risk reading hard-copy at this altitude but the Smuggler's Bible, if you ignored its weird pseudo-religious side, was full of vital info. It carried timetables for satellites, navigational listings from the Air Almanac, and microcharts of air routes with plastic magnifying pages attached. Also, the 'Interface' chapter ended with a list of the Bureau of Nationalizations' Synthetic Aperture and phased-array radar frequencies. The Synthetic Aperture radar was mounted on modified AWACS that BON was flying on the Exuma-Brownsville axis. Phased-array was what the new high-endurance cutters were carrying. Therefore the risk was necessary.

Only SA and phased-array radar stood a chance of touching a jet this low, and even that was a small threat.

The real danger lay in this kind of flying; the dearth of altitude protecting him from normal radar left him no margin for error if something fucked up. And his reaction time was dragging.

He'd been flying for thirteen hours, with one break to refuel at Duncan Town, in the Jumentos. It had not been much of a rest. He'd had to keep the engines whining while the plane floated at a broken dock; playing guard at the door while the Santa Martans and Guyanans aimed lusting eyes at his plane.

They were dangerous, these Santa Martans and Guyanans of Duncan Town; men with razor smiles, falsely loose gaits, and eight generations' worth of natural selection in the Caribbean piracy industry coursing through their veins. In cooperation with the Organizatsni they recently had taken over all the coke and smack traffic in the Northeast. They'd achieved this by blowing away their opponents, as well as their opponents' families and third cousins and casual acquaintances and hairdressers, spreading carnage among the ports and airfields with Ingrams and M-16s and Roland anti-tank weapons. Thus the square-up smugglers – the ones who ran grass and gold and memory and stayed away from blow and Downtown – the square-ups kept a wary eye on them in case they got greedy for the rest. And so it was that the pilot had fought to stay alert for a total of an hour and twenty minutes while the dangerous men smoked spliffs around patched and leaky hoses full of warm Jet-A; while the moist tradewind blew salt, crab skeletons, and bat guano into the delicate spinning whiskers of his turbines.

The pilot's eyes flicked automatically back and forth between the windscreen and his crucial sets of data; horizontal attitude indicator, gyro, vertical-velocity (windscreen); sat-nav, engine pressure ratio, first-stage compressor rpm (windscreen); fuel flow, air-speed, countermeasures readout – and back to the windscreen to resume the cycle.

The pilot felt like the sheer torque of this work had altered him into a weird organism, half-blood, half-capacitor, specialized in the feedback between flight and darkness.

The autopilot was coupled to a Sperry Terrain-Following-Radar, which was how it could handle the plane this low – but the TFR, liberated from a mothballed B-52, was old. Even with new TFR you were supposed to be right there, because if the unit malfunctioned, even briefly, you would have maybe half a second to correct the error before the waves smashed plane and pilot to a million separate pieces.

Anyway he needed the discipline of sheepdogging the auto, to stay alert. The boil he'd got on the Rio Chingado had abscessed, he could feel his body temperature rising; and while his specialized hands and eyes could cope with reflexive supervision, the resulting fever made his mind wander.

Sometimes he saw shapes rushing out of the night; snowy mountains, lace curtains, buildings of wedged glass that had no place in this part of the Atlantic. At other times the illusions were more disturbing, and the forms of extinct birds, striking fists, and choirs of blonde women clad only in turquoise ribbons, had he actually been flying, would have affected the soft touch of his hands, putting him perilously close to the snapping spume beneath him or the questing electronic waves above.

The pilot, looking for solid images, checked his reflection in the side window. The features were strangely young; upturned nose, freckles; faraway and permanent grin crammed angular and Norman-Rockwell-ish into the leather World War I flying helmet that he'd modified to take audio from the countermeasures pak. It was the face of a slingshot sniper, an apple thief, someone who trafficked in fire-crackers and baseball cards. A boy who stuck moths down girls' blouses and filled his pockets with string or the dried skins of tree frogs. Even the glitter of headache, the blackened eye-sockets of fatigue could not put age on him.

The pilot winced. He did not care to look fifteen. It made clients think maybe they could get away with things.

(*Like Poop-face Provenzano had gotten away with things.*)

The pilot checked the plane's trim, reflexively, while the memory jimmied its way into the front of his brain.

The thing with Poop-face happened in the days before the pilot learned to fly, when he had quit Trout River Voke because he was so goddam sick of being young, and in school, and in upstate New York. All he'd wanted to do in those days was go fast. The destination didn't matter, it was speed alone that counted.

He'd spent days following the downhill speed-skiing circuit, training to be one of those human bullets in stretch kevlar suits locked onto ten-foot boards.

He'd watched hours of Sunday television to catch the scant coverage of luge, or motorcycle rallies, or Open Offshore Superboat racing in the deceptively smooth swells off Florida.

Superboats, the young pilot had decided, were the best. The V-hulls were huge, sharp, dangerous as the water they moved upon. They mounted two, three, sometimes four turbocharged engines of up to eighteen hundred horsepower apiece. They thundered over the ocean at speeds close to 150 m.p.h. and spent as much time in the air between waves as on the water. Their drivers wore oxygen equipment to filter out the engine gases, and water-cooled suits; they sat in airtight one-piece titanium ejection pods built for fighters. The pods were supposed to protect them in case the boat flipped, or burned, or sank. In practice, the pods just broke up, melted, or went to the bottom with the rest of the boat.

One day the pilot told his parents he was going to South Florida to work on the superboat circuit and become, eventually, a racer.

'What part of Florida?' his father asked.

'It's a circuit, Papi,' the young pilot answered. 'Lauderdale, Miami, the Everglades. Key West.'

His father reflected a moment.

'You got the Apalachicola Northern Railroad, the Seaboard Coast, the Florida East Coast,' said Roman Marak. Roman had worked on railroads all his life, and tended to define issues by what trains ran, or had run, in the area. 'Also, you will be near Cuba, the Bahamas, Jamaica, if you get into trouble.'

Even at that time Roman Marak was fairly certain his son would wind up with uniformed men at his heels.

'I'll pack your swimsuit,' his mother said.

So young Josef Marak – he was seventeen then – collected his savings from the Oneida County Savings Bank, and an Amtrak ticket from his father, and boarded a train going south.

He showed up in Everglades City eight days before the Everglades International Open Ocean Superboat Challenge Cup. For five days he was abused, laughed at, and sometimes propositioned by overweight, loud, foul-talking men in greasy overalls. For five nights he slept under a tarp in a mechanic's pit that smelled of oil, whiskey and semen, in that order. On the sixth day Cal Bigbee – the biggest, loudest, foulest-talking man of them all – took pity on the Yankee kid with the funny accent and hired him on a temporary basis as coffeeboy and grease-monkey for the Miss Slew/Rebel Beer hydroplane racing team.

24

The pilot was good with his hands. More importantly, he loved machinery; loved the way it rumbled, interlocked, even 'thought' in that honest, gleaming, step-by-step way machines had. The tight tolerances of superblower flanges rang like crystal in his brain. He adjusted them carefully, sensually, by feel, like playing an instrument. The clean balance of nitrated clutches, the smooth conjunctions of lubricant seemed to him the poetry of matter itself, the push-and-pull of atoms translated to heat and steel specifically for the religious devotions of man. After nine months on the circuit he could fine-tune the fuel injection on a fourteen-hundred-horsepower Statkus-Chevy as well as Cal Bigbee. After fourteen months Cal let him ride as driver, then throttleman on the *Miss Slew*.

'V-hull racing,' Cal used to tell him reassuringly, 'it's just like handlin' a woman. Y'all got to go so fast you're ready to explode with every cross-wave. But at the same time y'all got to go just slow enough that she don't blow up on you – keep her turbo and water temp and oil pressure just south of red-line the whole way.'

On his third race the pilot pushed *Miss Slew* at an average speed of 139.74 m.p.h. over a 115-mile course. He won the heat on a red-hot bearing that burned the boat to the waterline ten minutes after he crossed the finish line.

Cal Bigbee knocked him off the dock by way of firing him. Poop-face Provenzano found him sitting on the dock that same night, drinking Rebel beer, nursing his bruises. Listening to the pelicans splash and croak.

Poop-face had no nose to speak of. He was weedy

and dressed in Kmart 'Windjammer' shorts and a safari jacket he thought made him look like Gregory Peck but in fact made him look like what he was, which was a geek.

'You wanna drive superboats?' Poop-face asked him.

'Who's gonna hire me?' the pilot asked sadly. Rebel beer was making him morose. 'After I burned Cal's boat.'

'Might know some people,' Poop-face offered.

'Nah,' the pilot answered. 'I'm thinking of learnin' to fly. I'm sick of fuckin' with machines only spend half their time in the air.'

'Fifteen thousand dollars a run,' Poop-face said softly.

'Sens'?' The pilot had been around South Florida long enough to know what was going on.

'Hunnert bales of Guajira.'

Fifteen thousand bucks would pay for flying school, qualify him on small jets, maybe leave a little left over, the pilot thought.

'For fifteen grand, maybe I could fuck around a little while longer,' he told Poop-face.

Poop-face showed him the craft. It was a former circuit tunnel-boat, a catamaran-planer with twin turbocharged Lycomings, rigged for single-handling. The pilot found out later what everyone on the water-front knew all along, namely that the boat was so old it had two chances in five of surviving the 320-mile round trip to Mangrove Cay. Also the going rate was $25,000 for a hundred-bale run where the cargo would bring in close to a million dollars on the street. However in the beginning the pilot did not know any better and in due course he drove the boat carefully through the loud warm waters to Andros, and then back in a screaming, spine-telescoping rocket-ride over the odd-shaped swells and the startled dolphins, trying to keep the craft somewhere near stable at 95 m.p.h., skimming her like a fiberglass frisbee from the cracking slope of one wave to the ragged crest of the next; betting on luck and reflexes and good night-vision, waiting for the engines to rip out of their cracked supports or crush the craft like a Christmas ornament against the cement sea; looking for cutters and the slow boats of Customs under the great devil's temple of the tropical night—

A hint of green and white in the corner of one eye and the pilot stabs down with his right foot, yanks the control column back and right with the left hand while his right mashes the thrust levers forward for maximum power, the ancient Citation-C slewing to the right in a 375-knot banking climb that brings it over the deck of a light Panamanian crude carrier with a good twelve feet to spare.

The tanker was gone – smeared yellow decklights, bow wave, rusting pump system lost under the plane's right wing.

The pilot's fingers trembled as he adjusted the ECM-pak to include marine frequencies. The ECM-pak was an oversized laptop that plugged into the electrics of whatever mode of transport you were riding in. It included a jammer, a communications scrambler, wide-spectrum scanners, a satellite navigation system, a single-sideband transceiver, along with software that tracked radar and other electronic traffic in relation to your own position.

He brought the plane steady at forty-five feet and

checked the sat-nav readings, and the chart. He should have remembered the Ambrose shipping lanes. If you flew at sea level, it followed that ships were going to pose a collision hazard.

Squawks, yammers, and curses in Portuguese and Spanish perkled from the back of the plane as part of the cargo woke up.

The pilot carefully adjusted the trim, seeking a hint of nose-heaviness. He checked the ECM screen, but no radio input was visible in the short-range; the tanker had been asleep, or indifferent. More likely, he was washing his tanks into the cleanish brine and did not want to disturb the authorities at this point.

The pilot blipped on the weather radar to check he was still shadowing the north-south axis of a frontal system that would track him nice and discreet over the coast at Deer Isle, Maine, in 50.6 minutes. He recalibrated the TFR against the radio-altimeter and the horizontal indicator, and brought the jet up to sixty feet. This altitude would increase the danger of being spotted but it was an acceptable risk. The Smuggler's Bible said all AWACS were down for another thirty-two minutes in this sector. He allowed himself one final glimpse at the invisible horizon. Then he went aft.

The most important cargo needed little space and no maintenance. It consisted of three fiberglass suitcases crammed with rough Sierra Parima emeralds, strapped into the last remaining seat of what had once been the passenger section; also, one medium-sized, Tienshan-built refrigerator, bolted to aluminium rails on the deck and hooked up to a bank of truck batteries behind.

The emeralds were valuable enough, but the

refrigerator was beyond price, for it contained 4,082 cultures of pirated Korean aminochips. This was enough to start your own live-semiconductor factory. Theoretically, with your own factory, you could bust wide open TransCom's monopoly in the field of organic microchips. It was a modern version of printing your own money, the pilot thought.

The less valuable part of the cargo filled four-fifths of the cabin space with flapping, stale smells, and blinking brass-colored irises. When he switched on the emergency lighting it once more took up the chorus of shrieks and catcalls with which it had greeted his jump over the Panamanian tanker:

'*Ay! Ay! Ay mi vida!*'

'*Vaya al infierno maricon!*'

'Hegel, *apostata!*'

Twenty-five Spix's macaws gawked, perched on one leg, cocked heads, shat, fluttered, bitched, and rubbed their bills against the cage bars; twenty-five living tapestries of feather and bad temper, three feet long from beak to tail, held together by the rules of flight and the harmonics of color; dark indigos, dovegrays, a play of olive and aqua under the dim cabin lights; twenty-five pampered and restricted fowl with a black-market value of seventy thousand dollars apiece in New York, and twice that in Frankfurt.

The pilot smiled. He thought the birds were the most beautiful things he had ever seen. It made him feel good to run this kind of cargo. For the sixth time since he'd left the Rio Chingado he checked their food. He refilled their water, adding a few drops of vodka from a flask in his flying jacket to put them back to sleep. Working fast, he uncoiled a hose, went back to the cockpit, cracked the copilot's window, fed three feet of hose into the jet's slip-stream and, using the tube's other end like a hoover, vacuumed the worst of the shit from the parrots' pens. Talking to them in adult tones.

As he worked he pulled out a half-gourd of coca leaves he had bought from the Cayman. He stuck three fingers-worth in his mouth, with a dusting of lime powder. Chewing the mixture would keep him awake, gently buzzed, without the ragged edge of straight perica.

The ECM alarm beeped in his headset.

Dropping the hose, the pilot ran back to his cock-pit.

Two minutes before the ECM display had been quiet; he had seen eighteen narrow yellow lines only, indicating the tanker's short-range radar, fourteen commercial flights, and the faint touch of air traffic radar from FAA's Westbury Tracom Center as well as JFK and Tweed-New Haven.

Now, all of a sudden, thick tracks of cobalt domin-ated half the screen; three different vectors denoting strong radar, behind, above, to the right.

Adrenaline ran over fever, headache, fatigue. The pilot switched off the autopilot and slotted straight into reflex.

3

'The Manila revolt gave BON bureaucrats the
chance they'd been looking for. Though the node-
rebels didn't nationalize shit, they did back up the
takeover of Chevron and Weyerhauser orgs by local
employees, at a price the oil and lumber honchos
did NOT dig. This was termed nationalization,
back in Washington, and it made the Bureau of
Nationalizations the point organization to zap these
node upstarts in the balls. The enabling regs, it
turned out, put nationalization and smuggling in
the same legal dope-bale. Evidence suggests the
hungry lawyers of BON may have brewed this
power-play for some time . . . In any event, when
the Manila intervention went off cool – thanks to
the far-out intelligence at BON's disposal – BON
was in a position to corner the market in all extra-
national law enforcement.'

Hawkley
The Freetrader's Almanac and Cookbook
(Appendix 'F')

The pilot gooses the ECM-pak's audio, jams the
thrust-levers to ninety percent.

He pushes the controls forward to bring the
Citation back down to forty-five feet – the waves
reaching for him once more, lethal, loving.

'— late, asshole.' The programmer of the ECM-pak is a friend, but the recorded profanity sits ill with the situation. 'Attack radar, look-down shoot-down, three contacts, 193 degrees, 301 degrees.' There are two more sets of readings, two numbers each. The second number is a vertical bearing.

The pilot pulls in the vacuum-hose, closes the co-pilot's window. The cockpit noise dims to a rushing hum. To the west, the front's cumulus clouds rise like great circular castles into the purple night. Their insides glow with lightning.

He jinks left, pulling up a hair. The readout shows the targets shift with him.

'A-6 Vikings. Two contacts. Mark-Seven Predator, one contact.' The Predator is a UAV, an unmanned observation aircraft piloted from a VR terminal on the ground up to three hundred miles away.

'Predator switching to pulse. Evasive action, evasive. Move it, motherfucker.'

Vikings. The pilot winces a bit, though the shadow associated with these planes has hung over his mind since Rio Chingado.

Vikings means BON, for only BON flies these all-weather surveillance interceptors.

BON means the Bureau of Nationalizations of the Joint Committee on Intelligence.

It has only been sixteen months since BON was put in charge of specific activities of the NSA, DEA, Coast Guard, Air Force, and CIA aimed at elimination of, not only smuggling, but any offshore action that subverts the US-EC share of Darkworld trade. However BON's bureaucrats have been so thorough in their takeover that their acronym is now used officially on patrol and interception craft.

They have done their job so ruthlessly that the jets, high-endurance cutters, and internment camps of BON have come to equate with disappearance in the minds of those who try to subvert its shadowed force.

The pilot tunes the ECM's radio scan back to aviation.

'—IFF,' the voices are calling. The voices are evil by default, there is no feeling in them, one way or the other. Automatic-cool. 'Unidentified aircraft, Montauk sector, United States BON patrol, identify-friend-or-foe.'

No time for useless questions, like how in hell did they find him so quickly when he was only sixty feet from the waves for maybe a minute and a half and there are no theater-control aircraft over this sector for another twenty-six minutes?

The pilot hits his own pulse radar. It shows the BON jets at 8,200 feet and closing. The thick cobalt lines converge on a green dot marking the Citation. The cobalt shimmers, turns briefly pink, goes back to cobalt.

When the line turns solid red it will mean the Vikings have locked on their target.

He asks the ECM to jam the Vikings' attack wavelengths. The Vikings counter immediately by using jump frequencies. Then they jam his own radar. These boys are good.

He bounces the throttles against their stops but the Vikings are new and his Cessna is old and weighed down with her Dornier-Akai floatgear.

'—required to consider this aircraft hostile.'

The pilot flicks on the ECM's chart display. The sat-nav puts him thirty-seven miles from the Connecticut coast, twenty-eight miles from Montauk. So little

cover here. He can dogleg back to JFK, and its rat's
nest of air-traffic patterns. Or he can aim for the
storm front, three miles to his left, in the hope that
lightning and sheet rain will confuse the Vikings'
radar, giving him a chance to lose himself higher up
the dense commercial traffic of the Northeast
corridor.

'The freetrader should always jive on . . . the
boundary layer.' The words of the Smuggler's Bible
come back to him like a curse. The Bible is OK but at
times like this its hipster groove, its use of Lingua,
make him feel lonely – as if danger immediately puts
him out of the reach of the conceits and theories of
normal men.

He pulls the plane up and left, climbing toward the
storm, and catches a glimpse of one of the Vikings'
navigation lights blinking tiny against vague stars, out
the side window. Still much higher. The second
Viking transmits from behind: 'Be advised I am
authorized to interdict. Repeat, I will interdict if you
do not respond or change course away from US
airspace.'

One of the cobalt lines turns red, and pulses.

'Lock-on,' the ECM informs him. 'AMRAAM,
infrared targeting, fifteen seconds. Good luck, butt-
brain.'

The first lumps of turbulence hit. Rain makes a
million silent cracks on the windscreen. The Citation
will never reach the clouds on time. Impulsively the
pilot flips a red cover and hits the button underneath.
A series of explosive bolts on the plane's belly blasts
off welds on the huge aluminium sled and the smaller
wingtip floats that allow this jet to land on water. The
Cessna bucks violently, rears forty degrees, aims at the

34

stars, wings left toward the black waves. The pilot fights hand-to-hand for control. Wrestling rudder, elevators, trim tabs, he evens out the plane's flight. Airspeed climbs ninety knots and he veers the jet suddenly to the right, into the path of a small outrider of cloud. Vapor streams, the Citation breaks free; then plunges without fuss into the main storm front.

On the ECM display, the second cobalt line goes the color of well-oxygenated blood.

'Circus Two,' one of the BON pilots says, 'commencing attack pattern.'

The pilot jams the levers to full thrust. He pulls the plane into a steep climb, aiming for the deep blue phantoms of electricity inside one of the storm cells.

'*Pendejo!*' One of the macaws is so loud you can hear him even over the turbines. '*Pendejooo!*'

'AMRAAM, fuckface!' the ECM snaps. 'Drop flares. Drop flares!' Burning flares would confuse the Vikings' heatseeker missiles. But the Citation has no flares.

The oil temperature on the port engine shudders into the red zone. The Citation was not designed to run at full speed when it was new. It is now sixteen years and eighteen thousand hours of engine time older, and anyway the pilot has unhooked the governor so he can run the engines twenty or thirty percent over TSO.

'*Missile closing; evade, evade!*'

Air buckles and breaks around the plane. The pilot is throwing it from side to side but the storm is gaining control and throwing the jet around far more radically than he can. Lightning spiderwebs the dark. A splayed brush of flame tears past the cockpit. The missile disappears in the cloud, searching for the

35

greater heat, leaving everything yellow in its wake.

The pilot's guts heave. He pulls back on the thrust levers. Eleven thousand feet, and lightning has killed the gyro, but the display still shows cobalt, and close radar activity.

The Smuggler's Bible update on CD-ROM includes software based on nonlinear equations – period-doubling, fractal-progressing. Supposedly, that software can be hooked to your autopilot to blend you like a major chord straight into the harmonics of a storm-cell such as this. However, the update had not arrived by the time the pilot left for Rio Chingado and for now the pilot is lost.

Twelve thousand three hundred feet. Electricity cracks the clouds again, lifts them like a can opener. The lightning spreads, claws closer, it is all around, it holds the plane in crooked blue fingers. A weird green haze grows from the wings. 'Fuck!' shrieks the ECM-pak as its circuits cook. The circuit breakers flip, the display goes blank.

Abruptly the plane drops like someone yanked the sky from under it. Lacking bite, the wings tremble and pull to the left in the opening steps of a stall.

The pilot pins the control column forward and left, and knocks the thrust levers wide open again.

Now vacuum is king. The Citation is dropping belly-first into a pit of flashing violet nothing, lined with the striations of clouds. The striations resemble geological deposits. With every bolt of lightning the bands light up like neon signs, glaring every shade of pink and blue known to the universe.

'Hegel *nao vede*,' yells a macaw who was once owned by a Jesuit in Belem.

'I shoulda given 'em more vodka,' the pilot thinks, irrelevantly.

Seven thousand eight hundred feet.

Turbines screaming, the plane accelerates through a movie of rose, sapphire, turquoise, lavender, carmine, midnight blue. The noise is terrifying; scream of engines, bang of windshear, the maddened baying of airfoils. The pilot keeps the control column down and left, bouncing against the straps of his seat belt, sweat shaking off in every direction, but the plane is only half responding, the nose is still cocked up, it's falling more like a rock than a flying thing. If he ever comes out of this stall he will never, ever again take the governor off a Pratt and Whitney 545. Never chew coca, never run parrots.

Six thousand feet.

The weird light has grown. It has become a uniform green-silver haze. The haze seems to take root in everything it touches, silver-green tendrils reaching into the core of matter, into the aircraft's wings, into the walls of this canyon in the sky, where it pulsates like some radiation of evil.

The buffeting gets worse. The wings will fall off, the whole fabric of the Citation will give if this goes on any longer. A bell rings; the left engine's oil pressure is down. The pilot starts to laugh. Everything is so absurdly out of control, it seems the only rational reaction.

But, at last, the plane is starting to respond. The nose drops, the control surfaces bite. The Citation twists viciously, into a dive. The pilot pulls back, seeking horizon. The nose comes up twenty degrees from the vertical. Strands of black cloud reach for the plane to grab it back into the heart of the weather.

Four thousand five hundred feet.

There is a christly almighty bang. It feels as if the plane has hit a wall of very thick rubber. The macaws are shaken so hard they shut up—

Then he is through. The wings are lifting again. The silver-green haze is gone. He pulls the plane back into level flight; it responds mushily, as if cotton filled the spaces in the hydraulic pistons, and between the miniature jewels of microcircuits. He throttles back to cruising power. The fire alarm trumpets doom in the left turbofan. The pilot shuts it all the way down. He lets loose the left extinguishers, and cuts the alarm.

The ECM-pak repeats, 'Fuck, fuck, fuck, fuck,' monotonously in his headset. He shuts that down too. He is blind and deaf to radar now, but there is peace in this fact. If the AMRAAM comes he will not know it, except for the briefest awareness of flame, and pressure.

Lightning winks and pulses in the contusion of sky, but its flash is suddenly thin.

The front is behind them.

Four thousand feet below and three miles ahead, gold streetlights mapped out the herd instincts of humans against the more complex parameters of the coast.

A plane appeared from a rainsquall a mile away, a little lower, to the south. The pilot jerked, then relaxed; it was a commercial airliner, a turboprop, Dash-7 by the high wings, losing altitude for an approach to— He had no idea where.

The pilot flicked on the chartlight and picked up the Smuggler's Bible, opening it to the Newark-Logan chart. The sat-nav, the gyro unit were both locked into the dead ECM. It would take too long to switch the pak's circuit breakers back to 'on,' and then reboot the system.

He looked at his watch.

He estimated nine minutes flight through the storm, at an average 225 to 275 knots. It felt more like two hours. He must have been heading dead north, when he was heading anywhere, to hit the coast this soon. Montauk was too small for Dash-7s. New London, or more likely Providence.

He looked at the chart again. He thought there was no way he could have covered the fifty miles to the coast in that time, even at maximum speed.

But the yellow tracery was below him now, and this was not Suffolk County.

The Smuggler's Bible says;

There are two goals the freetrader seeks in the interface. Uno is evasion, because the boundary layers royally shine on the forces of the Man. Dos is even more cool. Because the craziness of this space puts in doubt our oh-so-touching belief in the togetherness of matter and wave, and in this Nirvana of cosmic potential, the free-trader may be able to focus the power of his imagination – the part of the brain that makes the leap between wave and matter possible in the first place -- with mind-fucking results in camouflage, evasion, and speed.

'Bullshit,' the pilot grumbled to himself, as the oil pressure alarm for the right turbine started to shrill—

* * *

Time, which was just getting its breath back, stretches like a Slinky once more. Options fade. With the jettisoning of the float-tank, the Cessna has become a land bird. The pilot drops the nose, speeds up a hair. He cranks in thirty percent flaps and slots himself fifty yards behind and a little above the Dash-7's broad tail, well outside the scan of collision-avoidance radar. He throttles back and follows.

He used to run a 'dummy' a few years ago when he flew into South Florida. He hired another pilot to fly out of Lauderdale, legally, and circle an Aerocommander ten miles offshore at seven thousand feet. At an appointed time the pilot, flying below radar from the south with his plane's transponder shut off, would climb fast to seven thousand and slip right behind the Aerocommander. To any radar — even AWACS — the two planes were now one and, since the Aerocommander was tagged and identified, they could fly back into Florida unchallenged.

With any luck, the same thing will happen here. Air traffic control at TF Green Airport will read the two planes as a single Dash-7, and dismiss any earlier readings as ghosts.

Watching the right turbine oil pressure drop. Crabbing the Citation on one engine over the De Havilland's propwash.

Narragansett Bay snakes and narrows to the right. Lights thicken around its course. The Dash-7 curves northeast to approach Green from that direction, into the prevailing southwest wind. The strange skyline of Providence brightens and dims, abnormal EKG of city streets through the smog. A sign blinks green; even at that altitude the words are legible. 'ZERO COLA,' it says, 'NOTHING but GREAT TASTE!' The pilot examines the chart again, looking for a secondary airport where he will stand a better chance of avoiding questions from men in suits. The abandoned Navy yard at Quonset Point has an airfield. 'Emergencies only,' the notation on the chart says. They are six miles from Green.

Now the right oil temperature sweeps into the red zone so fast he can see the needle move. The fire alarm for the right engine glares at him.

The pilot throttles back to minimum speed. He can no longer keep up with the turboprop. With one finger he wipes sweat from his forehead between helmet and eyebrows. Then he peels off left, away from the massed glows of Providence and Cranston and their connective tissue of road.

The plane loses altitude. The bay shows up again to his left; flat gleam of reflected light cluttered with black gridwork of old pumping stations, railroad workings, oil tanks, a hurricane barrier. To his right now, headlights crawl like bugs along a beam. A six-lane rises on ornate supports, arching one hundred feet into the smog as if repulsed by what lies below. The pilot gets a sudden flash of Carmelita, with her mouth slightly open and surprise in her eyes, the way she looks when she is just on the point of coming; as if everything is about to fall apart, and gravity no longer works. He might never make love with her again. This does not seem to matter as much as it should.

The Citation drops faster. He will never make the disused airfield. Bluish security lights define broken-down hangars and gantries and, in their midst, flat tracts of gray. Marshland, between slime and the river.

41

If he can land on one of those tracts, the pilot thinks, he might just get away with it. More soft gray appears, dividing a line of jetties, the four giant concrete vents of a former ammo dump. Far ahead, the long slow arc of the New Davisville Bridge lifts a string of orange lights to the sky, like a woman offering an amber necklace to her lover.

He shuts down the right turbine and hits the extinguisher. Adding an extra forty percent flaps, he aims for the gray. He is losing altitude fast. Radio towers loom from nowhere, on the right. They miss his right wing by a bad joke. He can see the dark channels in the marsh now; can pick out clumps of reeds, pilings, abandoned barges; scattered among them, the ragged scarlet orange of marshfire. The sweat soaks his armpits, drips off his nose. There is too much relief here. He should go for a straight water landing but he has no altitude. The stall alarm buzzes. Options gone, he pushes the nose down a little, ekes left, and lets her settle quickly toward what looks like a long bank of cattails with only a couple of black bits of solid piling or other junk to rip into her tender belly . . .

The old Citation hits the marsh perfectly. It's as if she knows it's her last landing. The cattails sit on a bed of saltwater and mud as well as avgas, dumped hydrochlorines, and old rocket fuel from a long-abandoned BOMARC missile site. Inky liquid smashes over the windscreen. The pilot is jammed forward against the instruments. It feels like a six-hundred-pound weightlifter is ramming him in the small of the back. A couple of bangs, insanely loud, against the fuselage; a howl of friction and tearing molecules. For what seems like minutes, every bump and crevice of the dead marsh adds its instrument to the continuous symphony of destruction playing on the plane's aluminium skin.

The aircraft leans right. The right wing trips in the sludge. The Citation slews in that direction, stemming up a tall roostertail of water, shit, and debris, and skids to a soft halt about four hundred yards from where she first hit the marsh.

'Coño.' One of the macaws speaks in wonder.

There is so little sound now. Only the hiss of water where it touches hot turbine, and the gurgling of mud, and a trickle of Duncan Town jet fuel.

The marsh feels the intrusion.

The marsh is still alive – almost, barely, all the close words.

Once it was quick and vigorous. It was part of a single organism made of thousands of such marshes from Canada to Florida. It formed part of an unbelievably complex and rich stew of nutrients and heat and fast reactions, brimming with sex, sex and more sex; sex of algae and noctiluca and fiddler crab; sex electric and blue, or sex small and armored, or sex tiny and jelly-like, or tall and gawky and top-of-the-food-chain – a whole universe whose fuel was sunshine and whose product was change. A powerful, subtle, benign monster that created, maintained, and protected a gene pool for half the living creatures of the Atlantic.

But that was long ago. Now the marsh has changed. Twisted by the abuse of men, it has turned evil. Like a spider. The foul water is its poison; the web is its grasses; the mud is its cocoon. It palps its latest prey with liquid fingers. Long, cool, heavy –

smooth. Already the mud settles below, the reeds drift in from the side. In a few weeks the Citation will be part of the bay's mutated agony. By the time spring comes, it will be gone . . .

44

4

'It is interesting also to note that stories about
smuggling flourish in proportion to the intensity
with which the attendant laws are enforced and
the severity of the penalties attached to them.'

Horace Beck
Folklore and the Sea

The main door was jammed and it took the pilot
fifteen minutes to pop the emergency exit. It was a
rough fifteen minutes because he kept expecting the
Jet-A to ignite and roast him like a Thanksgiving
turkey; but the extinguishers had done their job and
nothing happened.

When he finally got his head outside, the sky to the
east was free-basing blue.

Smoke from marshfire drifted through the reeds.
There was a smell of ash, and things dying. The
bridge approach highway exhaled endlessly, above
and to the west. Trucks shoved headlights into the
sky.

The pilot stilled the tremble in his fingers.

Inside the cabin, the emergency lighting cheaply
rationed out its pink glow. The refrigerator had

sheared right off its rails on impact and burst open like a rotten mango. Little cone-shaped glass vials full of cryoliquid lay all over the cabin floor. A number of the vials had broken, exposing the tiny spinach-green root network of their individual plants. The plants contained forty-two million potential analog switches per ounce, which was not far from the density of the human brain. Each looked like a dot of green lichen and smelled like old broccoli.

The pilot broke the seal on one of the fiberglass suitcases. Here was green of a different order. The emeralds were raw, uncut, lined up in foam and odd sizes, but even in the battery light they smoldered with a sallow flame that promised the blooming of a thousand more greens once the random insults of geological time had been burred and polished away on 47th Street.

The aminochips were a loss, the pilot decided. With luck he could save the emeralds. There was only one thing he had ever really wanted to do with the birds.

He went back to the cockpit, unplugged the ECM-pak from its jacks, and folded it shut. Locked and slung by its leather strap over one shoulder it looked like a plain aluminium suitcase, much dented by travel, colorfully spotted by stickers from hotels, and Darkworld airlines. He slung the chartcase, containing the plane's false papers and the Smuggler's Bible, on his other shoulder. In the cargo bay he unbuckled the straps securing the macaws' cages against the bulk-heads. Broken vials crunched beneath his workboots. The smell of broccoli grew downright offensive. One by one he dragged the coops to the door and out onto the slippery wing.

The birds smelled the cold air, the sick grasses, the dead water.

'*Cabron*,' one of them muttered.

'Hegel, *Diablo*,' the Jesuit bird answered sadly.

'Evade, missile closing,' commented a third.

'I'm sorry 'bout this,' the pilot told them. 'I don't like Davisville, either, but it's the best I could do.' He opened the cage doors wide.

The Jesuit bird was the first to move. It shuffled sideways through the canted flood of birdshit, organochips, sawdust, puked sunflower seeds. Swayed on the cage's sill. Still woozy from vodka, it hopped out on the wing, and fell flat on its beak.

Another macaw followed its lead, then another. Finally they were lined up like the Supreme Court; hung over, shortsighted, still pompous in their gaudy robes.

The pilot was never sure which went first. All he knew was that one of the Spix's macaws suddenly spread its wings and even in the half light between neon and dawn it looked as if all the complex forces of spring shone from its feathers. It took off, without hesitation, straight up, and disappeared over the reed horizon.

The rest followed hurriedly, afraid of being left behind in this cold and smelly swamp. As they left, one by one they subtracted every shade of green and blue so that when the last macaw was gone there was nothing but gray and brown and darkness left in the marsh, with the crackle of fire to the north and sulfurous sodium lights to the west and the sullen sharpening of smog to mark where the sun was trying to climb hand-over-hand out of Massachusetts.

For a long time the pilot watched the curl of smog

47

and smoke into which the birds had flown. A slim figure in a World War I flying helmet and two shoulderbags, standing against the soiled dawn.

He was still watching when a voice behind him said:

'Palm Beach, Nantucket, da Marsh.'

The pilot's muscles froze.

'Me say befo' time, Smegs, soon come pezzo-grossos in Boeing, tourism, sure thing.'

He forced himself to move as slowly as swaying grasses. Checked his chartcase and ECM-pak were still firm on his shoulders. Then swung to face the voice.

At first he saw nothing but bulrushes, cattails. After a couple of seconds he picked out a pattern, then three, seven. The shapes were human, but not right. Even in the gloomy dawn he could see that.

One of the faces seemed to sag to the left. An arm was thick and crusty with burns.

A leg jointed in mid-thigh.

The shapes all wore tall rubber boots, and jumpsuits, with dark blankets covering the shoulders. Crooked sticks hung at their elbows. Clothes, boots, flesh were all stained black with smoke and muck. Their heads were completely bald.

Jumpers, the pilot thought, and reached toward his right boot.

No one knew where the Jumpers had come from.

All the pilot knew was this:

Once upon a time, the real estate divisions of large organizations – certain banks, investment groups, the Gambinos – became aware they had run out of space, for they had covered virtually every piece of developable waterfront with their resorts, their condos, their

Kmart Colonials. The only waterfront left lay in the salt marshes of the East Coast.

So they started filling in the marshland.

The federal government, responding to a passing environmental guilt, put a brake on the filling.

The organizations, to show who was boss, brought in the Jumpers.

The Jumpers were the id of industrial America, the toilet fixation behind the junk-bond markets, the despised and essential sewermen for a society obsessed, one way or another, with the production and hoarding of shit.

More specifically, the Jumpers dumped poison. You sent for Jumpers when a rod of fissile jammed in a hot reactor core and you couldn't pull it out by normal means. The new Mobs — the Netas, the Guyanese, the Spirit Knife-Organizatsni compact — all hired Jumpers whenever they had to dump chemicals so illegal, so perilous that even their own scum wouldn't touch them.

The Jumpers didn't mind the danger. They had grown up toxic. Many of them were children of the first poisoning grounds. Their parents had settled in places like Love Canal, the Nevada test zone, the bayou dumps. They had worked at TMI and Millstone One. They'd been vaccinated with hazardous waste. Because of this they had no hope, they were beyond despair, their pride was the pride of zero. In fact they adopted a kind of reverse chic out of toxicity. They alone had the courage to handle what everyone else feared to touch. They entered reactor cores with torn suits and when they came out proudly nailed the maxed radiation discs to the plastic walls of their trailers and cabin cruisers. They competed to dump the used needles, the white urine, the slivered yellow tumors from the stigs clinics, the Plague hospitals; burst-plopping the biohazard at night into the frail wetlands of Wilmington, Port Elizabeth, Quonset.

The Jumpers lived where they dumped. They had come to resemble their habitat, and vice versa. The Jumper's Hell was of one dimension, where variety was the first casualty and all difference was twisted. It was a hell of smoke and tar and blackest acid, where the chemicals had soaked in so deep that they burst into flame on their own, feeding on lifeforms they had already killed, glowing forever underground, underwater, under the sickened grasses.

But something was new here — and this was something the pilot did not know. Something was changing in this place. Hell was being, if not attenuated, at least given a vector.

For a prophet was coming from the Marsh. Soon from the ranks of the already-dead would rise one who had been buried, and changed, and lived. And for him to rise in a suitable manner was going to take scratch, and lots of it.

For this reason, the Jumpers wanted the fallen plane.

5

Boarding Party Pissaladiere

Five cloves pre-chopped garlic
extra virgin olive oil
1 pound pre-chopped onions
jar of anchovies
twenty Kalamata olives
pizza dough

Prepare dough ahead of time. Keep cool in ice
chest. As soon as you grok the cutter – as soon as
you hear the first off-key transmission – break out
onions and garlic. Immediately heat olive oil in
large skillet and sauté chopped onions with lots of
pepper, sea salt, thyme, and rosemary, adding
garlic later. Keep cooking till smell fills boat and
onions are mostly done. When the BON boarding-
party launches its inflatable, add garlic. Spread
dough in 8x10-inch pan. Puncture with fork.
Spread onion mixture and cover with anchovy
fillets and sliced olives. Cook in 360-degree oven
for one half hour. The smell of onions, garlic, and
pepper should be enough to keep BON search-dogs
from sniffing out any well-wrapped weed. After
boarding-party has left, cut into small squares and
serve with dry white *Côtes du Rhone*.

Hawkley
The Freetrader's Almanac and Cookbook

The pilot thought of what he knew of all this as he watched the Jumpers. He was not reassured. These people had nothing to lose and they would kill strangers for the fun of it.

The one called Smegs had no right hand. He pushed the reeds aside with his left arm and said, 'For why you groundin' Boeing in the Marsh, amigo?'

'Meltdown, mon.' The pilot reverted automatically to Lingua. Lingua was the jive of the streets, of the black market. It was the language of Darkworld. 'Me losin' bullgine high-up.'

A couple more Jumpers squelched out of the spartina. One of them was the sag-faced man; now the pilot could distinguish the tumor, like a huge brown crab under the skin, stretching his chin and cheeks.

The stick-like objects were luparas, sawn-off automatic shotguns, slung from the shoulder on harnesses made from old inner tubes.

'Freeze wid da shiv, babe,' one of them warned. It was a woman's voice, though the face was black and flinty, the scalp smooth as the rest.

The pilot straightened. Workboots, it seemed, were not the place to hide a switchblade.

The Jumper with the sagging face moved. The barrel of his lupara made a circle and appeared in his fist, pointing at the pilot's stomach.

'Okay, slimeball,' he said. 'Gracias for the Boeing. Now git—'

A battering of air behind the pilot interrupted his words.

The eyes of the one-handed Jumper, the one called Smegs, grew big as dollar-coins.

The pilot felt his guts sink. He turned around to see

52

the macaws shining in the upper sunlight, dropping toward the plane, greens first. They were coming home, he thought irrationally.

'Funny pigeons,' the tumor man said, and aimed his lupara at the lead macaw which was helicoptering in for a landing on the Citation's canted tail.

'Stop!' the pilot shouted, raising his arms in protest toward the Jumper, certain there was no hope. What difference would one more small death make in this wasteland; but support came from an unexpected quarter.

'No shoot, bro'.' Smegs was looking at the tumor man. His shotgun had come off his shoulder; with his one hand he held the butt against the joint in his thigh, pointing in the tumor man's general direction.

'*Que?*' The tumor man's mouth hung open.

The woman pushed forward. She stepped onto a rotten piling to gain height.

'Who the capo heah? Doctor Filth, is who, pizhdal.' Her mouth smiled toothless. She pointed at the tumor man; Doctor Filth.

'Toad's right.' Another Jumper stepped out of the lee of a junked Yugo sedan. This one wore a bandanna over his bald skull, and a ripped jumpsuit. Open sores wept redly down his chest.

'So fuck you, Smegs,' Doctor Filth grunted. He jammed the lupara's sights against his tumor, squinted down the short barrel, and fired.

The blasts were huge, and double. The air sang with concussion. The pilot spun around.

A cloud of bright feathers hung in the smoke, and drifted down a ray of dawnlight toward the mud. 'Oh, dag,' the pilot said, certain it was the Jesuit bird.

He swung back toward the Jumpers, his face emptied by anger — and choked.

A half-dozen luparas were leveled in every direction, at him, at other Jumpers. They had all hit the deck with luparas aimed from the shelter of cattails, from the wrecked Yugo; Mexican stand-off of double-ought buck and one Jumper torn backward against a rusted barrel embedded in the muck, a can with many red markings and the words 'DANGER' and '2, 3, 7, 8 tetrachlor . . . P-dioxin' showing even through the corrosion; the Jumper half-sitting against the barrel, kicking absentmindedly, blood crawling down the metal, turning the rust black, making streaks in the gray mud — the tumor surgically removed along with the rest of his face.

'*Capish*, Toad?' the man called Smegs yelled at the woman. 'Doctor Filth no problem nah.' He poked the barrel of his lupara at her.

The pilot scrambled up the fuselage. The rest of the macaws had split with the shooting. He could not see the dead bird. It had been blown into the high grass.

Smegs got to his feet. He broke the lupara, slipped another round into the magazine, hung it over his shoulder. His one hand, using the double-jointed thigh as fulcrum and friction-hold, worked as fast as two. He moved with a curious, sliding gait, into the filling stinking canyon where the jet had landed. He picked a bright jade feather out of the black water. He stared at it for a minute, then looked up at the pilot, his face distorted in rage.

'Mira what you done,' he screamed. 'You happy now?'

The pilot looked around him. The rest of the Jumpers had got to their feet and were watching him

54

carefully, their luparas still pointing at each other. All except for Toad, who leaned her shotgun against the barrel, and kneeled by Doctor Filth's side.

'Me just take bindle,' the pilot croaked. He cleared his throat. 'Just three cases—'

'*Cabron!*' The Jumper with the weeping sores spat the word out. He brought his shotgun up so the barrels yawned emptiness right into the pilot's eyes. 'Git-go! Chop-chop! *Andalay!*'

The pilot paused, a beat. His head was light, his eyes burned. The fever was gaining on him.

He kneeled to touch the plane's cold aluminum. A farewell feel-up.

Then, discreetly checking that his ECM-pak and chartcase hung solidly on the shoulder, he slid down onto the wing on the far side of the aircraft, and stepped carefully into the marsh, into the spartina and bulrushes.

The footing was uneven, soft. The mud burbled around his boots, letting go of a billion tiny corruptions.

He took another step. Foul liquid slopped over the tops of his workboots, and he grimaced. Already the Citation was half hidden in the reeds.

Behind him, Smegs had climbed to the top of the fuselage, still holding the macaw feather between index and thumb.

'It's what you get,' the Jumper shouted at him. 'That's what you get.'

As he sank deeper into the reeds he could still hear Smegs shouting after him.

'That's what you get,' Smegs was screaming, 'you bring something *pretty* into da Marsh!'

6

> 'The smuggler needs a forwarding office he can
> trust, with a shit-hot beeper system. He needs an
> online privacy service if he's going to do any slip-
> 'n'-slide through the 'nets. Good forwarding and
> privacy services will not only warn him if things
> melt down, they will also provide an airlock
> between the freetrader and all the jive of the out-
> side world.'
>
> Hawkley
> *The Freetrader's Almanac and Cookbook*

When the pilot got back to the City he went straight
to his apartment on the ninety-sixth floor of the
TransCom Building.

He plugged the ECM-pak into its recharger, and
flipped the circuit breakers back to 'on'.

Then he got into his bunk and let the fever take
him, shake him, and scour him out.

The apartment was not legal. It was actually a
lounge, bathroom, shower, and kitchenette area built
for the twenty-four-hour technicians who had once
worked a TV studio under the building's pointed
spire.

The TV people had worked for the TransCom

broadcasting system. When TransCom merged with X-Corp, and all their programming was diverted into X-Corp's high-speed B-Net cable system, the studio shut down. The TV broadcasting antennas were removed. Automatic microwave cellphone transceivers and airconditioning ducts were installed in the studio's place. The door to the lounge was blocked. Everyone forgot about the space except Obregon, the building manager.

Obregon opened a secret entrance through the airco. He made up new building plans, removing all trace of the lounge, and put the space on the market as a one-bedroom apartment.

The place was perfect for the pilot. Like the pilot, it did not officially exist. Like the pilot, it required a fake ID; whoever used it had to be 'hired' by Obregon as a part-time security guard to account for his presence in the building.

The place also suited the pilot for personal reasons. Its narrow windows faced east and south. They went halfway around the base of the spire, and gave it the safe, watching feel of a large cockpit.

The spire was protected by mythic creatures, ten-foot-high griffins, gargoyles, serpents, and dragons cast of stainless steel by the Krupp works in Essen, Germany. These creatures appealed to the pilot's deepest identity, for his parents were Czech, and had raised him on middle European folktales; myths where dragons and griffins ruled the earth, and men never asked themselves what they were going to do with their lives, or should they go to Wharton and study business telecommunications, but instead got on with the business of hunting down and wasting monsters as soon as they were old enough to lift a sword.

Now, lying on the couch, level with the windows, the pilot thought he saw these stainless steel creatures move, and flex, and take off in slow silent flaps of horned wings.

In his hot mind he followed them; cruising the canyons of liquid-crystal and light; patrolling the metalled rivers; sending their hungry shadows over the microscopic beings that jaywalked, hailed cabs, and ran crazily to predictable rhythms.

Sometimes (he imagined) the griffins would stoop, dive to pick up some junior vice-president screaming from the pavement, haul him up to a corporate cornice to peck out his liver while dozens of floppies containing focus-group reports and marketing forecasts spun away cleanly in the wind.

The fever hallucinations bled into each other. The dragons turned into pigeons, the pigeons into brightly colored macaws, the macaws into alloy airplanes shaking themselves to death at eleven thousand feet while the instruments dissolved into green-silver cloud and the controls came apart in his hands.

But above and behind the fever-dreams hung a new and constant awareness; someone, behind the clouds, behind the blank windows, watching; someone with no face and all frequencies. Someone who knew who he was, and where he was going, despite all the tricks and cunning and electronic devices the pilot used to hide himself.

There were periods of waking and lucidity. During such periods, the pilot drank Letuva vodka, popped tetracycline, and reread his favorite books, volumes by Antoine de Saint-Exupéry: Night Flight and The Little Prince.

Even when he was asleep he kept the ECM-pak on,

hooked into one of the spire's disused antennas. Listening through his flying helmet to cop cruisers, airline traffic, the occasional terse cipher from BON transmitters at the old DEA Central on West 57th.

Sometimes he switched the pak to one of the Wildnets, going through a cellphone link, through a privacy service in Reno, and finally into one of those systems of SAPs – Secure-Access Providers, with their Fedchip transponders illegally disabled – that people said were too fast, too scrambled, and too numerous to be broken by NSA software in the short time they'd have to do it.

At the top of the ECM screen the vast background traffic of the Web hung like a multicolored, pointillist sky in which every molecule of air represented both one site, and the dendritic threads linking it to other sites; all pulsing, contracting, expanding, undulating, like something alive and huge.

But he did not surf upward, into the Web. Instead, staying below, among the SAPs, he set the parameters to traffic and visual scan, keeping an eye on Usegroup sites where freetraders hung out to exchange contacts or gossip.

The green lines on his display indicated heavy back-and-forth traffic. The black signified one-way messages, unanswered or unanswerable.

Maybe it was his mood, the somber brain-chemicals of sickness, but the Wildnets seemed to the pilot to be heavy on the black side; the intricate flowers and tapestries marking free-trade data streams resembled those dark jellyfish that live in chasms in the southern Atlantic, linking up with tens of thousands of their like to form a wall of soft, somber, translucent tissue; pulsing, growing, weaving their inky tentacles around the fragile green.

He switched off traffic-scan after a couple of minutes. As a matter of principle he did not believe in unbreakable security, especially in a medium as wide-open as Wildnets. One-point-four minutes, the Bible said, was the minimum time needed for trace on a nonsecure channel. Anyway, he could barely keep his eyes open that long.

Once a day Obregon brought him food from the take-away Cuban-Chinese restaurant on 28th Street. The body battled infection on fuel of pork chow mein, Habana-style; fried plantains, duck sauce.

The abscess in his finger spread pink pressure to his knuckles. On the third day, it burst, releasing clear liquid and two clusters of tiny, translucent grapes. He recognized the larvae of the Amazonian chiggoe fly, and washed the wound out in Letuva.

The fever broke on the fourth night in a dream of hedgehogs. When he woke up, Obregon was standing at the windows, watching morning traffic loose smoke on the East River bridges.

'There's a three-mile pile-up on the BQE,' Obregon announced in a tone of satisfaction. 'Truck bomb, again. Chihuahuan Adornista Faction, again.'

Obregon was thirty-five. His features were sharp and handsome. His hair was spiky, like short feathers trained back over his head. He looked like a hawk as he squinted over Brooklyn.

'Traffic's backed up on the Battery Tunnel approach all the way to the Schermerhorn Street exit.' He adjusted earphones that led to a pocket radio.

Outside, the quick thunderheads of an ozone shower washed a single skyscraper in vertical fingers of rain.

The shower was one of a million tiny pockets of precipitation that came into being around the time accumulated chemicals from aerosol deodorants started to eat at the earth's protective layer of ozone.

At the same time, industrial pollution was accumulating carbon dioxide in the atmosphere. In a process not yet fully understood, this caused the plankton in the world's oceans to store up nitrogen. When a lens of ozone depletion passed over a plankton-rich stretch of ocean, the tiny creatures released nitrogen, which formed clouds – short, round balls of precipitation, dispersed by the wind, that appeared out of nowhere, dropped a handful of raindrops, and scudded off quickly somewhere else.

The pilot looked at the dragons and griffins outside his windows. They crouched absolutely motionless. Soot dulled their gleaming eyes. The pilot admired how well they concealed their capacity for flight.

'What time is it?' he asked Obregon.

'Eight thirty-seven.'

'What day is it?'

'Thursday.'

The pilot sat up. His muscles were weak. His brain felt like it had been sluiced down for days at a time in a great waterfall; very clean and pink and delicate.

The room was filled with empty vodka bottles and lozenge-shaped boxes that once held Cubano-Chino food. Sharp darts of light bounced around the curved walls.

'Your forwarding service beeped. I called 'em up,' Obregon continued. 'They said Chico Fong wants to talk to you.'

Shit, the pilot thought. He did not want to talk to Chico Fong.

61

'When did he call?'

'Yesterday. Carmelita, too.'

'You call back from here?'

'*Seguro*, man. But I use a privacy service, like you tole me.'

'Payphone's better. Some of those local services—'

'*Fresco*, babe.' Obregon was standing on tiptoe to look down at the near streets. 'Man, they double-park up and down 27th again. They gonna get towed, I give 'em eight minutes, you watch.' He chuckled happily.

Obregon was the only person the pilot knew who was truly obsessed with parking.

The obsession made sense, because it was built on a worldview; for Obregon, who also loved New York, actually took pleasure in New York traffic, believing it to be the City's truest vital sign, its very breath and systole.

Obregon had driven to New York in 1996, on a three-day visit to see a girl he'd met on the beach in Seagirt, New Jersey.

He got in on a Monday night, and found a whole metropolis sinking like the USS *Hornet* under wave after wave of Kamikaze automobiles without enough parking spaces for even the women and children.

In panic, the Board of Estimate earlier had divided the streets into areas that were off-limits to parking half the time. The net result of this action had been to turn the average Manhattan driver into a psychopathic beast, a vehicular saurian equipped with airbags and five-hundred-cc pistons and aerodynamic armor, ready to claw and stab over the last square millimeter of curbside territory.

In the midst of the carnage Obregon sailed in

blithely to slot his ancient Mercury under the nose of a snarling local turbo job right in front of the girl's building.

A sign told him the space was good till Wednesday morning, when any car in it would have to be moved, between the hours of eight and eleven, so machines could clear out the gutters.

'Wow,' the girl commented admiringly. 'Right in front of the building? That's unheard of.'

That Wednesday, after moving his car for the sweepers, Obregon found another space, on the same side of the street. The space was good for another two nights.

When he gave her the news, the girl told Obregon he was the luckiest man she had ever met. She kissed his neck, and asked him if he could stay forever.

On Friday, he found a space that was good till Monday. On Monday, the day he was supposed to go home, his old space in front of the building fell vacant just as he was finally getting ready to depart.

Obregon was Cuban. He believed in luck, and the importance of playing out a winning streak. To break it flew in the face of chance and all associated saints. He put his car in the vacant slot, and stayed on in the City.

The lucky streak outlasted his vacation, so Obregon got a job. It outlasted the girl, who got sick of him hanging out her windows, checking on traffic; so he rented his own apartment. It even outlasted the Mercury, which was stolen from a parking space (good for another thirty hours) by a person from Brownsville, Brooklyn. But by that time eight months had passed, and Obregon had become part of the City's rhythms, and had no need of a car in any case.

'You gonna marry her?' Obregon turned toward the pilot, carefully patting his oiled hair.

'Who?'

'Carmelita. Who you think?'

'No.' The pilot waved wearily. 'It fucked up. Last month. Just friends, now.'

Obregon's face dropped. His hands fell limply, in a caricature of distress. 'Man, I'm sorry,' he said.

'She said I was too hungry, for her taste,' the pilot went on, watching four 777s and an Airbus chase each other slowly down the spiral over La Guardia. 'I wonder what she meant by that?' But Obregon was staring at traffic again.

'Look at that,' he burst out, 'look at that!' He whipped out a pair of Spetsnaz binoculars from under his uniform jacket, and focused it to the east. 'Breakdown on the FDR. Cars backing up to the UN.' He cruised channels on his pocket radio. 'None of the eye-in-the-skies got it yet.'

The pilot switched the ECM to cellphone, punched in the privacy service, ran his fake UCC-card through the scanner.

When the tone came, he punched in Carmelita's number.

Her machine answered. It said she could not come to the phone right now. It offered to trade information on the caller for a return call, later in the day, from the girl herself.

God peeked out of his box under the window. God was the lounge's longest-serving tenant, a small, brown, long-haired Norway rat with dark, wise eyes and a look to him that said he was surveying the world he'd created, and finding it acceptable, with a few minor corrections to be made later. He skittered over to investigate the remains of the pork chow mein.

The pilot punched PC's number. PC should know where Carmelita was, but the machine there said he was out for a few minutes.

Carmelita's mother's phone was disconnected. He called the forwarding service used by her brother Roberto and got a recording that said the line was 'temporarily out of service.' Finally he phoned the Go-Go Emporium in East Orange, where Carmelita worked weeknights.

'Bitch din' show up for her set,' the manager there said. 'You see that bitch, you tell her get her ass ovah here fast, she wan' her job.'

'Go fuck yerself,' the pilot told him.

Vaguely worried now, he took a shower and got dressed. He made a cup of coffee, with lots of sugar added for energy, and drank it. He put God in an inside pocket of his City overcoat, slipped through the airco ducts, and took the elevator to the outside world.

The minute he stepped out the glass doors of the TransCom Building and felt the cold smoke on his skin he knew it was too soon.

It was not the fever, he thought. It was more the overdraft of stories that had galloped through on hot midnight horses. He had an idea dreams were the brain's way of breaking down, digesting, balancing the too-strong forces of perception, and as such they usually were a good thing, but this time he'd had too much. His mind was reamed hollow from their passage. Any input now was like eating cold pizza on an empty stomach. He went to the garage nonetheless, got out his Yamaha, roared the bike slowly up the ramp, and turned west on 27th.

Men staggered from the steaming asphalt. They wore two or three golden watches on each wrist. Cellphones occupied their ears, cellphone throat-mikes their jaws, notebook computers their fists. They talked without pause, surfing from link to link, drunk on schedules.

Their wives, lovely and fit, learned Hausa to communicate with the baby-sitter, discussed personal Websites over diet lunches in Tibetan restaurants, newly fashionable in the City.

Kiowa helicopters stuttered over the rooftops, sniffing for Chihuahuan terrorists.

A trio of young derivatives analysts, wearing the Maine hunting boots and button-down oxfords of the Manhattan Safety Volunteers, pulled a Tele-DysFunction victim to the pavement. The tee-dee, festooned with dead radios, screamed 'Gilligan! The Skipper! *Gingerrr!*' repeatedly – for TDF, a serotonin imbalance apparently triggered by excessive exposure to electronic media, had as primary symptom an obsession with schlock television.

The volunteers, vowels cracking angrily, loaded him into a brown Swedish station wagon.

Next to the Plaza, police were setting up tollbooths at the entrance to Central Park.

Two years before, the mayor had hired a Minneapolis think tank called The Omega Corporation (once known for its Cold War disaster assessments) to exploit New York's advantages in name recognition and communications access.

The Omega Plan, as it became known, had been activated three months ago. It called for turning

66

Manhattan south of 110th Street into sixteen 'theme development sites.' Towers full of expensive offices would be designed around motifs from Europe, Russia, and East Asia, as well as the Liteworld enclaves of South America and Africa. More specific themes from popular B-Net dramas also would be featured. Cafés, restaurants, VR arcades, communication centers, all would favor the theme in vogue in that sector.

The sectors, of course, would turn a profit. New co-op complexes in the general shape of Schonbrunn Palace, the Taj Mahal, or Tara were sold out the day they went on the market. Already Bambi-42nd Street, Zabar's-Old Vienna, and Hampstead-TriBeCa were charging steep admission to their daycare, parks, and playgrounds.

Because of the tax breaks involved, the City did not make enough from the plan to fix the streets, or hire sufficient teachers, or pay the ones it did hire.

Outside the moats of Manhattan, the Projects smoked with arson.

On Central Park South, in the middle of the crowds and cold wind, a smell of life and fields. God, smelling horseshit, poked his thin nose around the pilot's collar and twitched his whiskers. The pilot cruised his motorbike slowly down the line of horse-drawn tourist carriages, looking for the Appaloosa with the black-rimmed eye, and the brown-and-white brougham Carmelita drove for a living. Neither was present.

He headed west to Tenth Avenue, steering carefully around potholes. Some of the holes were the size of small cars. A few even contained small cars, trapped like mastodons in a pit on some callous rush hour, abandoned an hour or a month ago by despairing owners.

The abandoned cars now served as shelters for men and women who could not afford theme-area rents, humans trapped like the cars down a hole in the infrastructure that was simple to fall into but near-impossible to climb out of. Thus it was not uncommon to see smoke from cooking fires, and makeshift cardboard tents sticking up like the sign of underground armies from a half-covered pit in the middle of the street.

The pilot stopped to buy a bag of carrots from a Korean, then motored slowly to the hack stables over the Lincoln Tunnel.

An ancient Jamaican groom pulled him over by the gate.

'What you got there, mahn. A rat?'

'You see Carmelita Chavez?' the pilot asked the old man, stuffing God's inquisitive nose back down his pocket.

'You can't breeng anyting in here, 'specially not rats. We got too many already.' The Jamaican wore a wool cap. His hands were twisted like mangrove roots.

'Okay, you keep him.' The pilot put God on the guard's desk. The Jamaican leaped back, yanking a .38-caliber revolver from his jeans.

'Tekk heem out,' the old man threatened. 'I keel the rasclout.'

'Look,' the pilot said, 'he's a good rat. He even does tricks.' He tickled God's belly and the rat rolled over on a hard-copy of the *Daily News*, grinning like an idiot.

This was, in fact, his only trick.

The pilot went through the doors and walked in a maze tunneled through ancient wood by the hooves of ten thousand long-dead horses. Lights were few, bare, and feeble. The beams apparently were held up by a century's worth of caked manure. He found the Appaloosa in a stall full of Titian shadows and old hay. He rubbed her felt-tipped nose, patted her black eye, fed her the smuggled carrots.

When he came out, the Jamaican was sitting back in a corner of his cubicle, his .38 still aimed at God.

God sniffed without much enthusiasm at the remains of a tuna sandwich in a drawer of the cubicle's file cabinet.

'Heem lookin' at me funny,' the old Jamaican said.

'How would you look at him,' the pilot answered, 'if he was holdin' a .38 on you?'

The pilot had a theory about God, and how people reacted to him.

He had noticed how, near the turn of the second millennium, humans were romanticizing creatures that lived in wide-open spaces, even as the corporations they worked for destroyed those open spaces forever, sending the romantic species into extinction, or zoos, thereby.

He knew that, because the big corporations required a dense and dependent labor pool, the humans themselves spent their lives in tight unhappy spaces near their workplace. The humans did not know for sure why this had to be so. All they could do was protest, by purchasing things they did not need, or withholding touch from their kids, or smoking jisi yomo, or demonstrating in support of romantic, extinct animals.

But the romanticization did not extend to all animals. Far from it. In fact, it seemed to go hand in hand with a growing hatred for the creatures that had managed to adjust to man's ravages; the coyotes who were infiltrating the suburbs; the raccoons who raided the stacked garbage; the congeries of crows living in City buildings; the peregrine falcons who built nests on tall towers and filled the ledges with sun-dried pigeon guts; the rats who dominated the City's dead spaces and forgotten tunnels; the varieties of cockroaches that dwelled in the cracks everywhere and between.

The humans said they hated these animals because they posed a health hazard, but in fact the animals were no dirtier, or cleaner, than they. The pilot believed the real reason was jealousy. Because the big corporations could not control the rats and roaches as they did the humans; because the crows in the water-tanks and the raccoons in the disposal areas and the coyotes haunting the City parks managed to live better in this metropolis, and with more freedom, than the humans around them.

When war came; when the third- and fourth-level pressures finally crushed the eggshell structure of the communications economy; when the tanks finally rolled and the missiles finally flew – then the rats and crows, the coyotes and raccoons and roaches, would inherit the poisoned cities. They would take over the humans' apartments, they would play among their femurs. They would uncover the relationship between the computer and the microwave. They would program the VCRs to nature shows and cooking channels, they would switch the trash compactor on and off for fun. It was this prospect, the pilot felt, that fueled the humans' hatred, and kept the sales of pesticides high and climbing.

The pilot got hold of PC in the late afternoon.

PC's real name was Fred Rosenbaum. The nickname 'PC' stood for 'Party Connection.' He acquired this name by functioning as a living network, an organic hotline relaying news of every bash, waltz-mosh, and Shift-shin rave going on in the New York metropolitan area, getting the word to his friends via e-mail and B-Net cables.

PC had started in his avocation when he decided that the odds against meeting the woman of his dreams in chance social encounters were pathetically long. The logical way to shorten the odds was to find out about, and attend, every party likely to attract women. PC had made this calculation two and a half years before. He had dedicated his free time to the pursuit ever since.

'I wish the fuck I did know where Carmelita was,' PC said. 'I got her a job at the White Angel's waltz-mosh tonight. If she doesn't show up, I'm gonna look like an asshole.'

'Too late,' the pilot said.

'I don't need this. I don't need comments like this.'

'She blew off the Go-Go Emporium last night,' the pilot said. 'I talked to the manager. And she always keeps fresh hay in the Appaloosa's stall . . . but today the hay was old.'

'Come to the party,' PC said. 'Maybe she'll show up. You know the scene,' he continued. 'It's costume, which means black cloak, long teeth, with that crowd. You should fit right in,' he added. This was his way of paying the pilot back for the 'asshole' comment.

71

After the pilot hung up he played with the pay-phone for a few seconds, putting off the call to Fat Chico Fong. The tai-lo was going to be upset, because of his lost cargo. Also, the Cayman had threatened to contact Chico, claiming the pilot turned down extra cargo; and if he'd done as threatened it would not improve the tai-lo's mood.

When Fat Chico got upset he always got heavy.

Normally the pilot did not pay much attention to the bluster of people like Fat Chico but today he lacked the energy to deal with it. He swiped his card through, got a machine at the tai-lo's number.

He left a message.

On his way home he stopped by the forwarding service to pick up his mail.

There was the usual backlog of *Aviation Week*s and *Smuggler's Gazette*s. The *Gazette* was the update to the Smuggler's Bible, published in both hard-copy and CD-ROM. The pilot noticed the *Gazette* CD with the harmonics program had finally come in. There was also a small, unmarked cardboard box with a Texas postmark containing a half-sucker the pilot had ordered two months ago, along with a batch of floppies. When the pilot got home and opened the box he found, embedded in the styrofoam peanuts, what looked like a big pair of graphite sunglasses, shaded indigo on top. A jack protruded from one earpiece.

On the ECM, the pilot booted up the first floppy and loaded a conversion program. He punched in passive-radar, fitted the half-sucker over his eyes, and moved the small joystick to the left of the pak's key-board.

The top half of the sunglasses blossomed with an array of lights; blue dots, pink squares, lines connecting the shapes. In between, clear space only. The display was in 3-D, and that was the point; it felt as if he could walk in that space, among those patterns, touching them with his fingers, pulling them into curves and altered webs. When he pushed the joystick forward, he did move, in fact he flew, zooming behind the connections, hovering to pick up info on the different targets identified by the ECM.

'DX, trafrad, 015,218.' The info came in little boxes outlined, for some reason, in a delicate pink.

'PD, trafrad, 112, 42. UAV, suvrad, 125, 088.'

The last contact was an unmanned surveillance aircraft to the southwest. The pilot turned and lifted his head, peering through the clear bottom half of the glasses out the windows of his spire, but saw nothing. BON, or the cops, often flew UAVs over Brooklyn, sniffing for fortified apartments out of which the Guyanans or the Rwandans traded their ice and smack.

Then he removed the half-sucker, and put it away.

He thought, if he'd had all this equipment last week, he might have saved the Citation. The thought got him completely depressed.

To kill that mood, he opened the letter from his mother, long pages in Czech about how the chickens and dog and cat were doing, and how much food she'd laid in for the winter.

His parents had seen their homeland invaded four times in thirty years from varying directions. Now they lived in a wonky-jawed old farmhouse smack on the New York-Quebec border, from which they figured they might see the next one coming.

The pilot dozed, and read about his father's conjunctivitis, until it was time to go to the White Angel's.

7

'Let me taste your neck, darling. It's so white.'
Amy Dillon, as Ilona, in *A Hunger for Blood*

The White Angel held court in a pink mews house off MacDougal Street. The house had a cobblestone forecourt, iron gates wrought in the shape of exotic plants, and magnolia trees that she always festooned with dead Spanish moss and Christmas lights for parties.

The pilot liked the Christmas lights. They reminded him of stories about Victorian families who drove home through the snow in sleds, horses neighing in the sharp wind, harness bells jingling, stars bright as polished pins; back to fond servants, guiltless silver, the smell of eggnog, the toys made of painted wood – easy myth-time of industrial man. He parked his old 650 between a Bavarian car and a car from Sweden. He stood in the dappled light of the magnolia for a while, sipping vodka from the silver hip flask, watching the glowing windows for a glimpse of Carmelita.

A constant stream of taxis and limousines schmoozed up to the gates. They dropped off passengers in a sequence of chunky slams, leather footsteps, and light remarks. Car helmets were casually tossed in a box by the door. The passengers wore long black cloaks. Their faces were powdered white, or covered in polyester fur, artfully pasted and combed. Hues of lipstick never before seen in nature smeared their lips. Occasionally, a pair of three-inch incisors, molded in enamel, stuck out from the corners of a mouth; some of the hands wore real wolf claws, unbelievably expensive, glued to the fingernail.

At the door of the town house a wispy man in a lavender cloak checked invitations printed on Amalfi paper.

A street person, a tee-dee, followed one of the limos to the door, staring through the smoked windows at a VCR showing music videos. The lavender-cloaked man got ready to warn him but when the limo moved off the tee-dee followed, eyes still fixed on the screen, hands fumbling at a dead Walkman, shuffling his blown-out Nikes.

The pilot sighed. He removed his City coat, took a cloak out of his saddlebag, and put it on. He scooped God out of the City coat and held him up to eye level.

'I'm gonna need somebody to talk to,' he told the rat. 'Try to stay sober.'

He stuffed the rat gently in the cloak's pocket and, clambering over a low wrought-iron fence, made his way to the back yard.

Unemployed actors were replacing empty crates of Doyen-Kruyff champagne with fresh ones and dumping bags full of half-eaten canapés into metal bins by a brick wall. When no one was looking, the pilot walked to one of the trash bins and leaned over it, dragging dramatic retching sounds from his vocal chords.

A thespian with great hormone confusion asked him a question that had no logical answer. The pilot pretended to wipe his chin on his cloak. He mumbled something about the bathroom. The actor flicked his fingers, shooing him through the kitchens and up the back stairs.

The upstairs consisted of one enormous room with artists' sky-lights that could be opened by electric motors in hot weather. The room dripped colored candles, sweated crystal and diamonds, swam in music and forced chatter. A fire snapped in the chimney. Tables twenty feet long creaked under silver-plated trays full of rich and thickening sauces. A sideboard steamed with cartons of Tibetan food, gloppy but rich in cachet. A swing seat stood on trestles in one corner. Six-foot-high VDTs mounted in three corners of the room showed sliced episodes of the latest fad series, a weekly drama entitled *Real Life*.

In one corner, wedged on couches provided for the purpose, guests wearing the doglike face-suckers of full VR moved their limbs slowly, together, like pair-swimmers, in rhythms that matched those displayed on the TV screens.

Every other square inch of space was filled with people in white faces and Nosferatu fashions.

The pilot snagged a glass of champagne from a tray carried by an unemployed actress in Romanian peasant dress. He wondered why, whenever the White Angel held a costume party, everyone dressed as drinkers of human blood and eaters of human flesh, or their prey. The answer was obvious, but it was precisely the obviousness that bothered him.

He drew the cloak tighter around his neck and walked around the room. On a stage to one side, a

Shift-shin combo wailed. A thin pale man blew on didjeridoo and thighbone trumpet. A Mongolian breathed mouth-music, a black man with a bored expression laid down a George Collins riff on bass, and a black woman who resembled him sat at the mainframe, sampling Lamont-Doherty recordings of surf and underwater eruptions into the overall beat.

A bamboo cage six feet high stood next to the thighbone player. The cage was empty. The pilot assumed it had been intended for Carmelita.

Bubbles tickled inside the pilot's chest. The bubbles stemmed from something other than carbonated wine. She hadn't pulled this stunt in a long, long time.

God stirred uncomfortably. He had sensitive ears, and the Shifta-Shinjuku sound was heavily amplified. The pilot found a delicate marble staircase with banisters made of alabaster figures; succubi, incubi, little sculpted naked putti. He went back downstairs, looking for what the party had to sell, because every party had something to sell, whether it was a physical product or an image, an idea the giver wanted his guests to take away with their coats and hangover and heartburn; even a debt, in payment for another sale, at another party.

The product of this party, the pilot knew, would be very clear, green like the inside of dandelion stems and crystalline. It would come in small, delicately folded spills of turquoise wax paper. It was, in two words, jisi yomo. The White Angel was the largest purveyor of the South American stimulant for the City's Safe People; its young, wealthy, and bored; and she sold her wares at parties like this one, in bedrooms with gilt-framed mirrors, in bathrooms with upholstered chairs.

The White Angel herself sat in a wicker throne near the staircase, attended by tall homosexuals. She looked hard at the pilot as he walked by. She was trying to figure out where she'd seen him before, who he came with, how much money he had, what he had to hide, what he was ashamed of, how much she could sell to him, how much she could sell him for, how she could find his darkest secrets and use them in ways that suited her purposes.

The White Angel's name was Evangeline Morgan. She came originally from Alabama, like the song, but with no banjo on her knee, and no monkey on her back; only a scarlet damage somewhere deep, as well as an honest desire to flee the damage, and a kinked need to drain it by passing it on. She had plenty of tunes to play, and an eye for making people dance.

Evangeline was five feet high, and weighed 320 pounds. She had a laugh as deep and rich as chocolate fudge, a tight smile, and the sharpest, meanest eyes you ever saw.

The sharp mean eyes met the pilot's. She saw the search in them. None of her guests ever searched for anything, except jisi.

'Keep a tail on that square-up,' she told one of her bodyguards. 'Shake him down when you get a chance.'

The pilot spotted the bodyguard on his tail. He slipped through the kitchen into a bathroom, locking the door behind him. From the bathroom another door led to one of the bedrooms.

In a corner of the bedroom a 68-inch TV showed lively reruns of UAV footage from last year's occupation of Silesia. Tanks exploded in bright fire-balls. A missile's camera dove on a bunker full of Polish soldiers. The lens was so sharp you briefly could see faces inside the gunports as the missile accelerated until it all disappeared in white heat. German troops, smiling, waved EU flags.

The attached face-sucker hung, unused, on a nearby stand.

In the opposite corner, a New England girl who made a living out of being the daughter of a US senator talked to a Southern girl who made a living out of being screwed up from inherited wealth.

'I drank my own urine in Bhutan,' the rich folks' daughter sighed. 'It was bitter. But it completed the cycle I'd started so long ago. You know?'

'The world I love is doomed,' the senator's daughter sobbed, dabbing greenish powder on her gums. 'Who's going to care for Jennifer Bartlett when the bombs fall?'

'That's why I lived in Mumbai,' her friend moaned. 'Everything has already *happened*.'

'That's why I'm an actress. Because to have all roles is to have none. It is the identity of zero,' the senator's daughter countered.

'I've been fasting for three weeks,' the rich folks' daughter shot back. 'I can taste our deaths on the wind.'

A British woman who made a living out of having been a rock star twenty years before, and the man who made a living off of her, strode into the room, pushing the pilot from his place at the door. The senator's daughter jumped off the bed, wiping her teeth.

'Christine!' she shrieked. Utter sparkling delight

had replaced the despair in her tone. 'I was just thinking about you!'

'Her name's Claudine,' a voice came from under the bed, 'but she'll talk to you anyway. It's as close as she can come to suicide without actually doing it.'

Everyone looked at the bed. A man who called himself a prince, though his dynasty was founded by brigands and murderers and whose grandfather in any case had been thrown out of his country by angry iron-ore miners eighty years previously, took from his cloak pocket a large plastic decal with the family coat-of-arms, a black, two-headed duck, engraved on the front.

'I stick this on every helicopter in which I ride,' he confided to Claudine in Italian. 'Women adore it.'

'Where's the jis'?' Claudine said in a voice like busted cola bottles.

The rich folks' daughter, suddenly coy, lifted a glass tube with the clear round mixing bowl attached. In the relative silence that followed, the sound of sucking, and compressed gas, was loud.

The pilot walked around the bed and looked underneath. There was very little light but he could just make out the features of the man lying in the spidery gloom.

'Oh, it's you,' PC said. 'Nice cloak.'

'What are you doing under the bed, PC?' The pilot found a chair. He was feeling light-headed. Ghosts of fever still hung around his brain. The skunky smell of jisi yomo made his nostrils ache.

'Figuring out how to accept decay gracefully,' PC said, 'like the rest of the phonies around here.'

The jisi yomo ran out. The rest of the phonies left, seeking another source.

'I don't understand.' The pilot's voice was puzzled. 'I thought, I mean, well, it's a *party*, PC! You need more champagne?'

'Of course I need more champagne.' There was something wrong with PC's consonants. They were mushy, as if he had too much saliva.

'You want I should get you some?'

'No,' PC mumbled, sliding from under the bed and removing a denture of werewolf teeth from his mouth. He stretched his lips first one way, then the other.

'Come on,' he continued. His words now were more distinct. He lifted the cloak from his left wrist where three genuine Vacherin watches furnished time and altitude in sixty major cities. 'Something happened, we have to talk.'

'It started a month ago,' PC explained a few minutes later, after they had snuck a full bottle of Doyen-Kruyff from the kitchens. They were sitting in a balcony recess now, half hidden by red brocade. Vampires clotted around them, drifted apart, clotted again, sniffing discreetly. A werewolf unfolded his hands, while another helped open his cloak. All stared in admiration at the black splotches in the palms and above the heart that marked the first stages of stigs. Evangeline's bodyguard floated through the crowd, searching for the pilot.

'Everything seemed fine,' PC went on in a bemused tone. 'I was meeting fifteen women a week. That was a perfect average. They were lovely, smart, talented. And I suddenly realized I wasn't having any better luck than in the old days, back when I was just meeting seven, or four, or two.'

'What do you mean, luck?'

'You know.'

'Would I ask?' The pilot cut up some shrimp canapés with his switchblade and fed them to God. He gave the rat a glass of flat champagne to wash it down with. The rat stuck his nose in the bubbly and sneezed.

'I mean, I couldn't feel enough for them. There was always something wrong. I dunno. Zoe, in September, she was too bright. She knew it, too, talkin' with her was like a constant chess game. Denise in early August was real quick, but she had this big sadness inside her she had to protect, she was like juggling razor blades. Late August, Tareesha, what a sweetheart, she was so easy to be around even though she's mostly bone tired, doing a first year internship in, like, pediatric oncology, but there was this thing about her chin, I dunno. Finally I got upset about this. I mean, two and a half years, man, I'd met over two thousand eligible women, and always something wrong, where does that leave the Plan? So I played my desperation card. I went to a private dating service. Not online, you know, you had to go there, actually talk to them — the real thing? In fact, I went to four of 'em.' PC refueled with champagne.

'They were real high-tech, and private, and super-expensive,' he continued. 'Fresh-cut orchids, mahogany desks. You know. Elegant ladies in Italian shoes to do the interviews. Pimps of the cyberdude, Jack, Madams of the lonely. That's me, the new man, emotionally sterile outside the 'nets, the rave scene . . . They were complete as hell, too. You got up to, like, 450 different parameters. Hair color, maybe whether your potential partner likes olives, what she thinks of Adorno, whether she knows who Adorno *was*. Sexual

82

tastes, even, I couldn't believe the variables. VR run-bys, the works. I scanned 832 women and that was *after* preselection. They had pheromone samples, favorite perfumes even, my nose burned, after. I was a problem client. And you know what I found out, from all of this?'

'No,' the pilot said. He was looking between the marble columns of the balcony, watching the body-guard, scoping the crowd in case Carmelita showed up.

Roberto, he thought suddenly. Her brother should be back from the last job by now. That meant he was probably hanging out in the Weather Café, over at Newark, as he did after most flights. Roberto would know where Carmelita was.

'I found out I didn't *know* what I wanted.' PC waved his champagne glass so hard it sloshed. 'No, that's not true – I found out I wanted too much. It was im-possible! I wanted the perfect woman, or else I wanted women who weren't perfect, but in *specific* ways. I wanted one woman, I desired them all. I needed one woman to share my bed, my life, my automatic tsampa machine – but still I wanted the thrill of meeting someone new every week. Someone – you know – that look, that fractured instant, that little shaving of a glance, that eentsy-weentsy spark of curiosity, in the eye, you know? You've seen it, it's happened, like, a head turned as the bus goes by, a look that lingers one ten-thousandth of a second more than it should in that situation. I wanted—' PC's voice was getting louder, the color in his cheeks was high '—to fall in love with someone, man, but what I'm really in love with is so hard to define, it's so small, like slivers, like bits, almost geological tests or, or core samples of woman; you know, woman with a capital W, all the little crumbs and details, how she shakes her head to clear the hair from her eyes, the way she stands straighter when she's angry; the little thrust of her hips when she's buttoning jeans that are too tight (Amanda did that); or the kiss of her fingers on a glass; or the arc between her ribs and that extra swell above her hipbones, you know, the subcutaneous fat that's for keeping babies warm; the taste of her, between her legs, like lemon and fresh scallions and coconut milk and mineral spring water, and there's a touch of boiled cinnamon and alfalfa honey added, just a touch (especially Zoe); the color of her inside, like that coral glow in the deepest part of the perfect spiral inside a conch shell; the lift, the balance and weight in her breasts; the way she curves her movements, man, like a half-zero, instead of cutting them like we do, the—'

Swelling commotion on the floor below interrupted PC's monologue. Cloaks fanned away from the swing seat as vampires rushed from every direction to gape at Claudine. The ex-rock-star was sitting in the swing seat, still as a fireplug, her eyes wide open, her fingers locked iron-tight around the stem of a champagne glass.

'But I *knew* it was pregnant,' a voice from the TV complained.

The face-suckers moved backward, each recoiling in a different direction from the horror that filled their vision.

Someone picked up an empty jis' works off the floor. A fat Dracula checked Claudine's throat, drawing caustic remarks from the multitude. 'It's okay, she's got a pulse,' he announced, and pulled a stethoscope from his pocket.

'Then the merger's off,' the TVs replied.

The vampires drifted away, vaguely disappointed. A woman pulled out three cellphones and handed them around, rattling off the numbers of detox centers. The senator's daughter talked brightly with the son of a top memory-broker. Death intrigued her, she said. It was the esthetic of vacuum, it was the opposite that defined creation. Where would art be without the counterweight of absence? The broker's son fingered his watches. She drew her cloak around her mouth, hamming it up for a photographer from *Shadow*, a magazine that published articles exclusively about people who derived fame from their association with others.

'Wondered when Claudine would freeze out,' PC commented. 'That jis' is fresh as I've ever tasted.'

The pilot tilted his head back. Champagne coursed in his brain through channels the fever had cut. When he opened his eyes he noticed a painting on the far wall, over the banister.

It showed a nineteenth-century amusement pier, the old kind, a good mile long, filled with cockle stands, penny arcades, and merry-go-rounds. The signs, the flagpoles, the railings were painted in cheerful seaside candy-stripes of cream and light blue and red and yellow. It was the kind of place that was soaked in summer, the way popcorn was soaked in butter, a place where the sun always shone and little girls wore straw hats with ribbons; the type of place where you wanted nothing more of life than what came out of a pinball machine or a slushie stall and everything smelled of salt and warm, tarry wood and toffee apples, and the thought of the day ending was like a pain in the valves of your heart.

But something had happened. The sea had risen, or the land had sunk and this pier was fifty feet underwater. Schools of nacreous fish hovered over an ice-cream stand. Starfish clung to a jukebox. A hammerhead shark nosed through a movie house. Jellyfish floated in a pinball parlor. Above the pier, where soft breezes should have blown, the ocean depths hung, green, mysterious.

'I'm sick of this joint,' the pilot said. 'I'm goin' to the Weather Café. You wanna come?'

'Are you kidding?' PC looked at him in amazement. 'There's still women here I've never even met—'

'You,' someone said behind them, 'let's see your invitation.'

The pilot twisted around. Evangeline's bodyguard stood in a position of challenge, lavender cloak dramatically swept over one accusing arm.

'He's my guest,' PC said, and took another sip of champagne.

'Evangeline's the only one with guests here,' the bodyguard said. He opened his cloak to reveal a .25 Raven strapped like a small pearl-handled tumor beneath his shoulder.

The pilot laughed. He'd had enough champagne to see everything in light pink, and the bodyguard's gesture was pure spaghetti-Western, 'Been-lookin'-fer-you-Cisco,' all dark moustache, carefully aged leathers, nylon tumbleweeds, the ka-chink, ka-chink of Spanish spurs.

'Get up,' the bouncer said, nervously touching the pearl butt with his fingertips.

The pilot narrowed his eyes, still reacting to image. 'I wouldn't do that,' he hissed, cowboy tough. 'I'll edit you, bo-woy, like I edited yer brother; left him all over the cutting room floor.'

'Jesus,' PC whispered to the bouncer, 'don't you know who you're messing with here? That's Crazy Skid Marak, man! I mean he's blown away more Safe People moshes than you've even been *invited* to!'

The pilot stood up. The bouncer gulped. Only last month one of the homosexuals had been wasted by the son of a Neta capo who like many sons of capos was troubled about his own sexual identity as much as he was annoyed by the soaring price of jisi.

The pilot bunched his own cloak over one shoulder. Slowly, deliberately, he reached in the inside pocket, and pulled out God.

'Look out!' PC shrieked hysterically, 'he's got a *rat*!'

The bodyguard jumped back, reaching for his piece. The pilot hopped down the stairs, knocking vampires like skittles. 'That rat's *loaded*,' he heard PC yell, 'he's been drinking all *night*!' People screamed, without being quite sure what they were screaming about. Men dragged women to the floor, throwing themselves on top of or under them depending on taste, courage, and inclination. Evangeline and the rest of her bodyguards were crawling like slime mold in black silk to block the front door; so, shifting direction, he crashed back through the kitchens, into a banquet room, and found himself in the middle of the waltz-mosh, complicated by a game of dwarf-throwing, which he had never seen before.

Two dozen vampires, paired off in couples, swung and dipped in graceful circles to a loud recording of the Emperor Waltz, then, whenever the music crescendoed, slammed as hard as they could into each other.

Loud shrieks and shouts of 'O-*lay*!' rang out when

87

a couple was knocked to the stone floor.

Meanwhile, a man about three feet tall, dressed in a cheap blue size-four suit, with a beard covering his too-big chin, was being hurled, over the waltzers, from one side of the room to the other by two groups of men who were fully grown and well dressed.

'Ouch,' the dwarf shrieked, 'catch my wrist, you idiot!'

'Fore!' cried one of the players, swinging the dwarf like a golf club.

'O-lay!' one of the waltzers howled.

'Shiiiiit!' the dwarf yelled.

The pilot stuck his head through the outer door, and the White Angel, lurking in ambush, slurped her fat arm around his neck and smushed him to her huge tits. 'Gaar,' he choked. She reeked of good brandy, and Lebensraum, by Lanvin. He felt like he was drowning in fascist cholesterol. 'Ovah here,' the woman yelled, 'git him, y'all—'

The yell became a burp as the pilot stiff-armed her in the solar plexus. His fingers sank in at least four inches. She let him go. He ran around her, through the kitchens, the way he had come in.

When he got outside he put God in his pocket, straddled his bike, and kicked it into burbling life.

He roared off through the gate, right-angled west down Waverley, winter trees making Dutch hex signs between the bricks. The cloak billowed black behind him as he rode, like the angel of death come on wings of Plague to mark the streets of Greenwich Village; God cheeping anxiously inside his shirt.

8

'History = Human Weather'
Meteorologists' graffito

The Weather Café took up the higher level of the old control tower in Building 51 at Newark International Airport. It remained open twenty-four hours a day to serve the National Weather Service scientists who staffed the meteorological station in the building's lower portions. It had a fine view of the eastern runways, I-95, and the Jersey marshes.

Sitting inside the Weather Café at night felt like sitting inside a Christmas-tree decoration because its curved art deco windows looked out on a million colored lights; the distant glow of marsh fires, the blinking orange of airport vehicles, the long double strings of blue, yellow, red, and green lights that marked the runways, disappearing to mate with perspective in the distance; the winking red-white navigation lights of the jets, and the bright cones of their landing lights marking out diagonals in the sky.

The pilot nodded toward Lee, the waiter. He took his usual table in the corner. Lee brought him a coffee. The pilot asked if he'd seen Roberto.

'Not for a week, ten days,' Lee said.

Lee was seventy-five or eighty years old. No one knew for sure. He had droopy eyes, a little old-man's belly like a basketball, and yellow-white whiskers at which he pulled while thinking. 'Well, anyway. You wanna special?'

'OK,' the pilot said, and put a twenty-mark note on Lee's tray. The Weather Café was not licensed to sell liquor, but Lee took care of regulars.

The pilot looked around him. There were three tables full of meteorologists arguing quietly among themselves.

The other four customers looked like pilots. Two had chartcases. One wore an airline jacket. All had the squoze-eyed expression that comes from squinting through dark glasses for too long.

The pilot thought two of the pilots probably worked the Trade, at least part-time. They were the age, they had the wariness; most of all they were sitting in the Weather Café, which had a history of attracting the kind of lone long-distance flyers the Trade needed, and used, and threw away like soiled Kleenex when it had worn them out.

The vodka was clean and cold. Lee got only the best, from scammers in the cargo area, square bottles of one-hundred proof with labels printed in Cyrillic. The pilot sipped at his glass, letting the party crank bleed off slowly. It was not only the champagne, the social buzz. He still did not feel quite right. Part of it was the sludge of fever. Some of it was a tinge of disconnection, a hint of being apart, that had started — he was sure of it — in that green-silver fog in the depths of a storm system, and had never completely gone away.

Maybe it was the storm-electricity that had done this, he thought fancifully. Like one of those antique sci-fi flicks where the hero went through a mysterious cloud, of radiation or strange magnetism, and was never the same thereafter.

Or perhaps this was what happened when you came a little too close to death. It certainly set you apart from those who spent their lives diligently avoiding the idea, let alone the reality of final extinction.

All of a sudden the pilot found himself mourning the Citation. He told himself it was a heap, but that only made him feel disloyal on top of everything else.

Ten minutes. Fifteen minutes. A Hawker 550 whined away from the STOL terminal next door. A couple of weathermen came in, got coffee to go, went out again. The pilots sat as still as if they were stuck in the cockpit of a C-119, low on power; flying their drinks carefully around the tables' brasswork edge.

No sign of Roberto.

'None of that pumps in enough variables.' One of the meteorologists suddenly raised his voice. 'Look at that.' He threw his left hand in a loose gesture at a dozen VDTs lined up over the counter. The sets were all tuned to various B-Net weather channels. They featured colorful graphics, mockups of every weather pattern in North America; the sharp-tooth lines of cold fronts, the worn molars of warm fronts, the organic spreading ripples of isobars, the fractal digits of weather radar, with red marking the lowest pressures and chill blues the rain.

'Look at these.' The meteorologist got up and ripped about fifty feet of paper data from one of the

NWS printers humming and zipping to themselves in laser talk in one dusty linoleum corner of the café.

'You tell me,' the weatherman said, 'how even Lorenzian equations gonna crunch all of this, just these numbers we got here, and make sense day to day. Well, they won't.'

The weatherman was tall, and graying, with a big black Groucho moustache. He wiped his hair back with one hand.

'Even Lorenz said so. "Program in every beat of a butterfly's wings, every fart from a bullfinch, every door slammed in anger in every suburban ranch house, and I'll give you an equation that will predict the weather," that's what he said more or less, words to that effect.'

'Take it easy, Dave,' another weatherman muttered.

'But what he really meant,' the gray-haired man said, 'is, This is where the bottom drops out. Fractal progression, my Aunt Fanny. This is the hole, guys, this is the quantum hole, which we don't fuck with. This is where things like ozone showers come from. A trillion-trillion jellyfish reacting to Reddi-Whip cans. And now they tell us they want us to control it. Control the weather!'

The pilot got a feeling of invading someone else's most intimate madness. He looked down at his table. 'The Bridge is the Other Side,' someone had carved on the tabletop. It was a Hawkley-ism, a slogan attributed to the mythical author of the Smuggler's Bible. The carver probably took seriously the so-called rites of navigation woven into the text like Day-Glo thread through a figurative painting. It was not just smugglers, or node rebels; a lot of weathermen seemed to be Hawkley-ites, or at least read the Bible, or subscribed to the monthly *Gazette* and CD-ROM updates.

There was another graffito under the Hawkley-ism. 'Sea Beasts Suckled,' this one read, over an e-mail address. Not for the first time, the pilot wondered why meteorologists were so strange.

A man walked in, dragging a heavy chartcase. The light from the stairwell was behind him and his face was in shadow.

The weatherman walked over to a big glass case in one corner. It looked like a jukebox but instead of CDs contained dust, three powerful fans arranged in an exact pattern, an electric heater, and a scale model of a Missouri farm. The motors whirred, the glass dome filled with blown dust, which began to concentrate toward the base, move in a circle like an exotic dancer, very slow at first, then faster and faster, the circle growing tighter and longer till it became a cone, then a spiral, then a funnel, and finally a recognizable tornado about two feet high, bellydancing to itself over the minuscule cows, trees, and cornfields on the floor of the device.

'We can make toys,' the weatherman said. 'But now they want us to play with the fucking continent. Aerial bursts! Silver nitrate! Ozone machines! Jetstream punches! I mean come on,' the gray-haired man addressed one of the flyers, 'would *you* trust us?' The flyer shrugged.

The 'twister' subsided, dry of credit. Uprooted 'silos' the size of dimes dropped back to earth. The newcomer sat at a table near the back. In the light of the massed TVs, the pilot saw his face. The pattern of expression lit up circuits in his brain. The man's name was Adam Coffin, and they had run a cargo together in a DC-3 a couple years before, automatic pistols to Cap Haitien, illegals back.

The pilot was pretty sure Adam knew Roberto. They both used Newark a lot, often for straight cargo.

Coffin did not look in his direction. The pilot did not look at Coffin. He looked around the walls of the Weather Café. Half of one wall was covered by a cracked and faded fresco painted, two years before he killed himself, by a Russian surrealist named Arshile Gorky. It had been plastered over in the fifties; Lee had found what was left and painstakingly chipped away the plaster with a dentist's pick and a toothbrush. The artwork featured shapes that looked halfway between birds and pieces of sirloin, flapping slowly in a sky that was stripped and banded like geological layers in colors of rose, lavender, sapphire, midnight blue. The pilot had never seen planes like these, but that sky looked familiar as hell.

He drained his vodka and ordered another. Vodka put a nice transparent lid on the buzz of Doyen-Kruyff. When he had finished he put on his City coat, made sure God was comfortable, and wandered over to Coffin's table.

'You got a chart for Jérémie?' he asked Coffin.

'In my truck.'

'Mind if I look at it?'

'Sure thing.' Coffin's eyes were neutral. They avoided the pilot's.

They went down the spiral staircase together, into Coffin's pickup. He turned the engine on for warmth.

Coffin had a small version of the pilot's ECM-pak in a hidden compartment behind the seat. He switched on a white noise generator to block any eavesdropping devices, any parabolic mikes. He turned on

94

a frequency scanner and listened carefully to the chopped bits of transmission on state police, BON, FAA channels, but it was all caretaking traffic; ten-nineteens, stolen cars, route changes. He asked the pilot to open his coat and checked him for wires. 'Still got that rat,' he commented, without smiling. Finally he put on RayBans to stare at the nighttime airport.

'Ain't too cool,' he said at length. He talked in short, punched sentences, the kind flyers used to communicate with air traffic control. 'Split soon.'

'We'll keep it short.'

'Been bad traffic, last few weeks. Too many trips busted. All of a sudden. Everybody lyin' low.'

'I heard something,' the pilot said carefully, trying to remember the Cayman's words, two continents, three rivers, four borders, five days ago.

'Careful time.' Coffin still would not meet his eyes.

'Bokon.' The pilot leaned over to check the dark glasses. 'A lot of trips busted, like you said, because of something, someone called Bokon Taylay.'

Coffin shook his head. 'All I know is, lot of people been nailed. The ones that got out, they say no sign, no warning, no radar sometimes – just all of a sudden, BON Vikings on yer tail. Just like that. It's what we heard. What do you want, anyway?'

'Roberto,' the pilot said. 'I'm lookin' for him.'

'Roberto Chavez?' Coffin looked up. The sunglasses reflected sodium lights from the airline parking lots.

'You seen him?'

'Why?'

'We share a mutual interest in Neo-Platonic meta-physics, is why.'

Coffin nodded. 'I guess you din't hear then.'

The pilot waited. Coffin gripped the wheel as if he wanted to drive off.

'One of the guys I was talkin' about. Wasted. That's what I heard. Overdue on the milk run, Abaco to St Pete four days ago. It's what I been *tellin'* you.'

The pilot felt his chest expand, then sag. Numbness, pressure; too much empathy for the fate of tendon and fluids and quick jags of brain electricity all flying at speeds and heights they were not really designed for.

No sadness yet. That would come later, with the guilt. All he felt now was a clicking into place, because he knew what had happened to Carmelita.

'Dag,' the pilot said. 'Dag.'

'Yeah,' Coffin agreed.

The pilot got out of the pickup, found the Yamaha. Checked God was wrapped up warmly. Put on his helmet, kicked off, and roared, too fast, onto the ramp leading to the New Jersey Turnpike.

The shock from Coffin's words hollowed out space for thoughts to hook up with each other in random ways.

The blurring of road and sky on each side seemed to allow a fudging of memory as well; or perhaps it was the blur itself that reminded the pilot of the huge swirling blue plastic brushes of Krazy Karl's Kwik Kleen Karwash . . .

. . . where Roberto was working the first time they'd met.

Carmelita had brought him to the carwash to meet her brother. She'd introduced her friend by what he did, and Roberto's eyes lit up like Macy's on Thanksgiving weekend. Roberto was twenty. To him, being a pilot meant flying, and flying meant getting out of the boroughs, out of Queens, out of the car-wash, out of the house where his mother beat up on herself the way all the men in her life had beat up on her, so as to stop passing on the abuse to Roberto and his sister.

He wanted just to ride, the first time. The pilot, drunk on the vinho verde of infatuation, took Roberto up to Halifax – square-up tourism flight, high over clouds and ocean. Ten thousand feet up, he let Roberto steer the plane.

The next time, Roberto wanted to learn.

This of course was more of a hassle, but the pilot agreed. He did so partly because Carmelita approved, on the grounds that it might keep the kid out of the local gangs – the Netas, the Latin Kings were expand-ing like wildfire in the 'hood around then. Mostly he agreed because he remembered a similar situation, a few years ago, and a large, smelly, foulmouthed red-neck named Cal Bigbee, and a younger version of himself who would have swallowed hot coals to be given a shot at doing what he most wanted to do.

Teaching Roberto had opened pockets of warmth in the pilot he had not known existed. It had something to do with the kid always smiling, even when he was busting ass to get the navigation right; it had to do with the minor scrapes he got into around the general aviation terminals, and his eyes, which were kind. This affection must have been shared to some extent, for Roberto early on took to calling the pilot 'hermano,' and like all younger brothers, real or honorary, he took advantage of the pilot's indulgence to roughly the same degree that he listened to his life-advice. The pilot was happy to fall for it, to help Roberto out, in half-conscious resonance, in payback perhaps, for his own older brother and the roles they'd both assumed.

In the marshes under the girders of the Casimir Pulaski Skyway now ripping under his wheels at 84 m.p.h. he saw many curtains of smoke and a lot more fires than was usual in these poisoned wastes, but he spared no thought for Jumpers. His mind was spiked on the memories, on the shock from Coffin's words; but the pain was getting too big. Great speed somehow brought time and space closer together, and now to kill the pain he chose to fill every space left with their concupiscence; the clean freezing jag of acceleration, the sharp delight of a ninety-mile-per-hour wind, the great cold slowdown in the molecules of guilt that came in knowing he was going too far too fast on roads crushed and spavined by too many winters, on dying bridges with broken cables and rivets eaten out like root canals. Knowing his life depended on keeping the precise edge of balance, rested on fractional decisions made by some overtime office of the brain shaving a micron electric to the left or right; knowing one atom of overcorrection on handlebar or angle-of-lean meant death or paralysis; speeding toward the place Roberto's sister always went when the world broke down around her.

9

'He who would travel happily must travel light.'
Antoine de Saint-Exupéry
Terre des Hommes

The pilot did not wait for visiting hours to enter Bellevue. He went back to his apartment and returned God to his box. He dug out an old surgical smock and stethoscope he kept handy for these occasions. From the Bedou saddlebags that housed his false papers he selected a UCC made out to someone named Brian Veitch of Northwest Washington, DC. The Universal Credit Card contained the driver's license and social security ID of somebody else, but the credit-chip inside was white money, paid in by the pilot to Riggs National Bank.

He looked around for the clipboard he kept for aeronautical charts. Couldn't find it. It was not in his chartcase, where it should be. Nor in the milkcrates where he kept his Saint-Exupéry, his Pratt and Whitney manuals, his tomes on tidal currents and Usenets and radio navigation. Nor in the Navy surplus duffelbag with his clothes, or in the footlocker with his camping equipment.

He stood in the middle of the lounge, looking around at his scavenged belongings. There was something wrong with this place, the pilot thought; nothing specific; it just did not feel right. For the first time since he had lived here he got a sense of loneliness that the lights of the City, massed outside his windows like the combined engines of some great starship, could not kill.

He'd been living here too long, the pilot decided. It was getting too permanent. He kept all his possessions in travel gear, trunks, boxes and saddlebags, like a nomad, for exactly this reason; like any good nomad he could break camp at a moment's notice. Ditch the expendable stuff and move the survival gear out before anyone had a chance to trap him.

'Never own more than you can carry down the dock by yourself,' the Smuggler's Bible says. 'Never own more than you can stow comfortable and cool on whatever mode of transport you rely on to get yourself out of trouble. This is true of all baggage, both psychic and material . . .'

He found the clipboard under the skeleton of a baby dolphin he had brought back from the Windward Islands. The Hermes A2 thrust chamber solenoids he'd got off a high-tech junk dealer on Canal Street lay behind an ancient linotype keyboard he'd salvaged from the old Brooklyn plant of the Daily News. 'ETAOIN SHRDLU,' the first two lines of keyboard read.

All junk, all expendable. Expendability was the price you paid for mobility. He stuffed the solenoids into a canvas shoulderbag and went back into the night.

No one stopped him at the staff entrance to

Bellevue Medical Center. The guards all worked on their own patterns of recognition and the pilot checked off green on every one; smock, 'scope, pinned ID. Tired face, blank eyes. They went back to their tiny TV screens as the word 'intern' came up on their brain monitors, watching Ned Reynolds anchor wonderfully gory reports on the latest terror bombing perpetrated by the Paquito Munoz Revolutionary Group (Adorno Faction).

The mental ward in Bellevue occupied two new towers that grew like concrete celery from the dirty brick compost of the old complex. The pilot waited at the door to B-29 while a black nurse almost as big as Evangeline turned the locks.

'Who you lookin' for?' the nurse asked him.

'Chavez,' the pilot said, 'C.' He looked up from his clipboard.

'Wha'choo lookin at?' the nurse barked at him. Her eyes resembled a water moccasin's.

'Sorry?' The pilot was taken aback.

'You was lookin' at me!'

'Well of course I was. I was talking to you—'

'You was lookin' at me.' The nurse drew her lips back in a snarl. 'You got any matches?'

'No,' the pilot said.

'Well you caint bring matches into this ward. Just you remember that. Wha'choo got in that sack?'

'Rocket parts.'

The nurse's jaw fell open. 'You think you so smart,' she said. 'You see wha'choo can do with that Spanish bitch. She's in SR-16, with the rest of the gabbers.' The nurse looked at his stomach, checking where to aim the steak knife, should the opportunity present itself, and stomped off.

It was four in the morning but only fifty hours away from a full moon and the orange plastic corridors were full of pale men and women, some in hospital johnnies, some in jeans. All smoked, many paced, a few muttered to themselves. Knots of people from the TDF sub-ward clustered as close as they could get to the televisions, mouthing words the actors spoke.

The pilot found Carmelita sitting at a table in the South Recreation room. The television was on, but she did not watch it and anyway it was hard to see through the tee-dees. He sat down opposite and looked at her for a full minute. She looked back at him as if he were part of the linoleum.

'Carmelita.'

It was always her hair that changed first, he remembered. It went from that deep glossy black, that mixed weave of panther fur and onyx, to stringy matte. Her skin was the color of stucco. Her neck, always delicate but strong and counterweighted on good tendons, now seemed to bow slightly sideways as if unable to support the weight of her obsession.

Doors stood shut and triple-locked behind the irises.

'Carmelita?'

Her fingers made housekeeping movements.

The television showed a rerun of Pain in the Afternoon. Brooke Denali – she played Shana, the wife of Chase MacBride, who owned the Network – had been locked in the refrigerator by Yakusa mobsters looking for a VR porn disk featuring Chase and a Shih-Tsu. Chase's illegitimate daughter Simone, played by Amy Dillon, had been raped by MacBride's intellectual-copyright lawyer, who knew enough to get away with it. 'She's going to be all right,' the TV medic said. 'Trust me. It's her mind that's in pain.'

The pilot suddenly felt the urge to sob. He got up and strode around, slapping his boots from one end of the room to the other, disturbing a man of about his own age who was trying to get across the room without the benefit of either floor or walls or ceiling.

When he returned to his seat, Carmelita had not moved, but a very large, slightly pudgy man in a blue jumpsuit with NASA shoulder patches was sitting and smoking in the chair he had just vacated.

'Rocketman!' The pilot stopped dead in surprise.

The big man frowned. He put a finger to his lips. He checked under the table, under his seat, looked around to make sure no one else was in the room. The man seeking levitation did not seem to count.

The big man's eyes were a very clear royal blue. His nose was large and hooked. His skin was the color of roasted almonds, his hands the size of baseball mitts. The first two fingers and the thumb of his right hand were stained orange from tobacco.

'You bring the stuff?' he asked the pilot, after his security check was complete.

'Right here. How do you *do* that?'

'Do what?'

'Get in here without me seeing you?'

The big man blew away the question with an impatient wave of his hand.

'Hermes A2 hydraulic ram solenoids, modified for RV-A10 missile launchers, it's gotta be.'

'I think that's right.'

'With the Northrop adapter?'

'What the dude said.'

'Aaaah.' Rocketman put out his cigarette. He dug

103

his hands in the bag and opened the flaps wide. He was too polite to examine a gift in the giver's presence and to vent his curiosity he started to jump in his seat. 'Aaaah!' he repeated, and grinned. His mouth was as wide as his hands were big. The smile seemed to bring real sunlight into the saturated neon. Even Carmelita's silence lost weight.

The big man glanced in her direction. He stopped jumping, and the smile dimmed.

'She's been here three days, hasn't said one word.'

'It's her brother,' the pilot told him. 'He's missing.'

Rocketman looked around the room again, then leaned toward the pilot.

'Missing, you said?' he whispered.

The pilot nodded.

'Aaaah,' the big man said. 'I thought it was you.'

'No. I was gone for a while, but I was only a day late, getting back.'

'No,' the big man replied. 'I don't mean you were missing. I meant, you gave her a hard time. That's what she said, last time she was here. You gave each other a hard time.'

'We weren't easy on each other,' the pilot agreed, and reached for a chair.

'I thought that was it.' Inside the bag, Rocketman's hands touched a solenoid lead, delicately, like touching a woman.

'Places,' he said suddenly.

'What?'

'Places,' Rocketman repeated. 'She said that. You was obsessed with places, not people. You think, by changing places, by going different places, you can change things inside you. Crossing borders, she said. That's what your hope is.'

The pilot thought about it.

'Maybe,' he admitted, finally. 'But it don't seem to work.'

'She didn't say it worked.'

They sat in silence for a while. A girl came in and asked Rocketman for a cigarette. He gave her one. She asked the pilot for a light. He gave her one.

'It's almost ready,' Rocketman said finally.

'You got the oxy-alcohol all right?'

'Yeah. There were other bugs.' The big man wiped his forehead with one sleeve as if thinking of the sweat involved in solving them. 'The worst is guidance. The balance is so sensitive. That gyroscope you brought for me is cranky as hell. Not your fault — it's s'posed to be supercooled, and anyway the good ones are still classified. But—' he lifted the bag '—if these adapters are as smooth as they say, it should hook up okay.'

'Great,' the pilot said, not very enthusiastically. 'Listen, man—'

But the Rocketman knew. He picked up the bag, opened it for a brief, loving peek. He went to the door, checked the corridors carefully, left and right — and disappeared.

The door swung to behind him.

The pilot pulled his chair next to Carmelita's. Very gently, so as not to scare or disturb the girl, he put his arms around her shoulders, and laid his head against her cheek.

The girl did not move. Her eyes looked at the sign on the wall.

NO MATCHES, it read.

He hugged her tighter. Her skin warmed against his.

'Carmelita,' he told her, 'I know you can't or won't hear. But there's a chance. A guy I know spent four days in the Gulf Stream, once. On a raft. Roberto coulda been picked up, like that guy was.'

Rocking her softly against the chair's adamantine plastic. Holding a conversation with a memory of her.

'D'you think it's my fault?'

'It doesn't matter, I guess. Whose fault. Even if it does. It's OK not to tell people. As long as you talk to yourself. Inside. Let it balance out. OK? Don't stop communicating, inside. That's what Roberto was doing, you know? Communicating. Same thing. Me too. People try to stop us, stop the words, stop the cargoes. They use borders or taxes or fear, same thing. We all got to fight the fear. We got to keep movin', we got to keep those lines open, those cargoes running, inside, outside. We got to get the pretty things through. Carmelita?'

The pilot hugged her for ten or fifteen minutes, mumbling in her ear, hoping it would soak in somehow.

Pain in the Afternoon was replaced by an enter-news show. The anchor was explaining what people in St Petersburg were wearing now the army had thrown its weight behind the Centrist-Organizatsni coalition. 'Kevlar monkey-jackets are definitely in,' the anchor said. 'Short short leather skirts are out.'

Then he left. The big nurse made him wait another five minutes while she finished a half inch of Zero Cola from the bottom of a can. 'Hope you had a real nice talk, Doc,' she hissed as she let him into the outside.

Carmelita's face played on a screen behind the pilot's eyes while he rode the elevator down Bellevue.

He remembered the way it looked the first time he met her, at a smoky little convention center near Raleigh-Durham where the qualifying heats for the XVIth Annual Miss East Coast Rollerblade-Go-Go Championships were being held.

The pilot had taken a room in the center's motel while he waited to pick up a cargo of tax-free cancer sticks to fly into the (heavily taxed) New York metro area. He was sitting at the motel bar, sandwiched between fake Olde England hie-thee-hither-wench decor and puce recessed lighting, when she first skated in. She wore pink in-line skates with yellow tassels and a loose wool cardigan over her leotard. She stood at the bar, one leg straight and one foot resting on the skate toe, and ordered a shot of tequila. Her face was half scared, half determined. She slugged the shot and choked a little. Then she turned around and skated out – head high, ponytail feathering like a banner – skated out to the main hall to perform.

He was still sitting at the bar when she came back an hour and a half later. There were no skates this time; she had on jeans and a sweatshirt that read 'Life is a Constant Audition.' Her hair was down. It caught the light and sort of rippled. She came in with a gaggle of other go-go skaters but sat alone at a booth, head bent over a colored drink.

She did not lift her head when he sat down opposite.

'Didn't win, huh?' he'd asked her.

No answer.

'What's your name?'

'Fuck off, pal.'

'That's a nice name,' the pilot said brightly. 'Mine's

Joe. People call me Skid, sometimes. Mostly, they just call me "pilot." '

'Lucky you.'

'I fly planes,' the pilot agreed. 'I *am* lucky.' He'd recently done three runs in and out of Barrett Town, Jamaica, fast runs at minimum altitude with no problems. On one of the runs he'd met a Guyanan flyer who had ripped off three Sperry TFRs from McCain Air Force Base, where B-52s went to die. The Guyanan had traded him an entire 464-A unit – radar, feedback computer, servo-gimbals, manual – for five bales of compressed Barrett Town sens'. Once he figured out how to couple it to the autopilot, he'd be able to do more runs, faster, at lower altitudes, than he was doing now. The girl caught his tone and looked up.

'You don't *look* like a creep,' she said doubtfully.

'Ah, you can't tell by the looks.'

'You look young, to be a pilot.'

'It's the freckles.'

'You look normal.' She didn't say it as a compliment.

'That's what they all think, at first,' the pilot replied. 'Even my mother. Then they find out about it. My habit.'

She needed to smile. He could tell she needed to smile, but instead she said, 'No. No,' she repeated, 'I don't want to hear.'

'Celery,' he whispered, 'I eat celery in bed. I keep the salt in the little hollows under my collarbones. I don't have any choice, 'cause of BBL.'

'All right,' she said. 'I give up. What da fuck is BBL?'

'Belly-button lint.'

'Fuckin' ay,' she said. Her smile loosened. When it loosened it took the rest of her face with it. Her eyes turned up at the corners. 'That's not very funny.'

'I didn't *say* it was funny. It's ruined my life.'

'You caught me at a bad time.'

'I'm not fussy.'

'You talk a little funny,' she said, in an accent that owed more to Santo Domingo than to the East Coast of the United States.

'I was born in Eastern Europe. It used to be called "Czechoslovakia."'

'Oh Christ,' she said, and looked around. 'It's just – I don't know. I'm better'n all these bimbos. I was go-go skating when they were still playin' with dolls.'

'They prob'ly don't like Yankees down here.'

She nodded. 'It was the girl from Macon,' she said. She took a swallow of her drink, shook her hair around. 'I'm not so good with blades yet, either. I was better on roller skates. Maybe that's it.

'But you remember my name,' she went on. She turned her eyes on the pilot, a strong gaze, and her voice gathered depth. 'I'm gonna be the best rollerblade dancer on the East Coast. In America. Maybe the world.'

'That's right,' the pilot agreed. '"Fuck-off-pal." I'll watch the marquees.'

The cigarette connect showed up then and the pilot hadn't got much further than finding out she lived in Queens, and giving her his answering service number. But he'd never forgotten the way her hair glinted and her eyes shone when she talked about go-go skating, and the contrast between the memory and the way she looked upstairs in Bellevue made his guts sink faster than the elevator he rode in.

10

'Remember; after Night there is always Day.'
Cubano-Chino fortune cookie proverb

When he walked out the 34th Street gate of Bellevue
two men came up behind him. One poked a roscoe
just under his right ear. The other tried to do surgery
on his left kidney with the muzzle of a sawed-off
twelve-gauge.

'Peace-up, Chico,' the pilot said without turning
around.

'How you suss that, amigo?' one of the men said
in a puzzled voice.

'Just lucky, I guess,' the pilot answered.

'Wise guy.' The man jabbed him with the revolver.
They pulled him with arms and pushed him with
guns to a black limo parked down the street. They
made him sit on a jumpseat between them. Fat Chico
Fong was sprawled out on the backseat, eating a hot-
dog-with-everything. A small Eurasian girl sat beside
him, applying dark-green makeup to her eyelids.

Chico Fong was half Cuban but he looked mostly
Chinese. He was very broad. His chin was very broad.

His chest had no hair and lots of golden chains, and was also broad. He wore a Hong Kong suit, dark glasses, and a toupee that actually made him look older than forty-two.

'Hello, Chico,' the pilot said again.

'Shut you face,' Chico answered. 'The chopper,' he told the driver, 'andalay.'

The trip, up one ramp of the FDR, down another, took all of four minutes. The limo stopped under the Drive, next to a chain-link fence and a couple of trailer offices. 'Eastside Heliport,' a sign read. Early patrols of rush hour made the ground tremble. A tug moved on the silent tide, upriver. Someone died of renal failure in the NYU Medical Center next door. A tall man with an attaché case joined the group as they hustled into a whistling, eight-seat Alouette. The pilot noticed a decal pasted beside the door. The decal bore a black two-headed duck and the words 'Von Ewig-Halssteif/*Am Heuchler Immer Treu.*'

'Hey Chico,' he called, 'why don't you own your own chopper?'

'You wan' me off him?' one of the men proposed, hopefully.

'Later,' Chico said.

'It's a rental bird,' the pilot said. 'I'm *down* with it, Chico. Real class. Tax deductible and everything.'

'I *own* the rental company, asshole,' Chico said, licking onions and sauerkraut off his fingers. 'Brookolino,' he told the chopper jockey.

The flight was shorter than the limo ride. The helicopter crossed the East River at two hundred feet, followed Newtown Creek, turned southeast. Two minutes later it slowed, hopped over a couple of chimneys, dodged a burnt-out office building, and landed, noisily, on the roof of a five-story factory that took up an entire city block. The goons hauled the pilot over the roof tar, down a fire exit, and into a hallway so brightly lit it was blue. The hallway was lined with dormitory rooms. Bells jangled, radios crackled, satvids glowed with the cheap colors of Taiwanese VR serials. A lot of Cantonese men, wiping their eyes clear of sleep, walked around in pajamas and towels. The night shift, just getting off, drank green tea and played mah-jongg in dirty coveralls. No one so much as glanced at the group as it passed by.

There was a familiar smell in the air that grew stronger as they went down another staircase.

The next two floors were taken up by freezers large enough to drive small trucks into. Labels on the doors read waterchestnut, plantain, MSG (liquid), bean curd, mofongo, snow peas, in Chinese characters with Spanish translations underneath. Forklifts backed and whined. An arrow pointed to the 'Seccion Cubano.'

The two lower floors held kitchens, gleaming steel, chopping machines, and one long office where small men at wide desks typed short phrases on Malaysian word processors. 'Fortune cookie department,' Chico told the girl, and laughed. 'We got six writers on payroll. Writing fortunes. "You will live to great age, you get very rich." Hah! Not fockin' likely, my pilot.'

A cargo elevator took them below ground. When it stopped they found themselves on a vast floor filled with gigantic stainless-steel vats, three-foot-diameter pipes, and coiled pumping stations the size of summer cottages. The smell of Cuban-Chinese food was overpowering now.

Chico Fong told the red-sticks to stop beside the

elevator. He stood in front of the pilot, crossed his arms, and looked judgmental.

'You down wit Cubano-Chino food? Hah?' he asked suddenly.

'It's OK,' the pilot answered. 'But, *entiende*. It goes right through you. You scarf a big meal, next thing you know, you hungry again.'

'Very funny,' Chico said and snapped his fingers. 'Spring roll!'

The goon with the pistol scampered off. The one with the sawed-off kept feeling for the pilot's innards. It was a Benelli Super-90, the pilot noticed, the kind with the round magazine like a Thompson. This goon wore a portable CD-player. A tinny sound came from the earphones; the funk beat, earth-rumbles, and weird samples of Shift-shin.

'Can we go now, Chico?' the girl complained. 'You know I'm allergic to MSG.'

'You can't be,' Chico said, without looking at her. 'It's you roots. Even pilot here dig it. What's you numbah-one favorite Cubano-Chino restaurant, my pilot?'

'The Szechuan Bordello.'

'On 28th Street. What you favorite food, hah?'

'They all taste the same,' the pilot answered, just to get Chico's goat, for he liked pork chow mein, Habana-style.

'All taste the same.' Chico said it neutrally. The pilot sighed.

'Number 45,' he admitted, 'on the Bordello menu.'

The pistolero came back with two spring rolls. He offered one to the girl and the tall man. They refused. Chico Fong took both. 'Numbah 45,' Chico mumbled, as he stuffed an entire spring roll in his mouth. 'Andalay.'

They walked for several minutes through thickets of valves and meadows of gas burners. The stainless-steel vats, polished to mirror-shine, rose fifteen feet high on either side. The bodies of five men and one girl swelled from thin sticks to gross proportions then narrowed back in the silver metal as they walked by. Huge fans sucked out steam and air and replaced them with the hum of their machinery.

Eventually they came upon a vat with '#45' stenciled red upon the out valve. Fat Chico led the way up an iron inspection ladder to a small gridwork platform on top of the vat.

Eight thousand four hundred gallons of gooey gray slop burbled and smoked beneath their feet. Their faces softened in the greasy steam. The steam in fact took over. It shot through their nostrils, pumped down their throats, pissed through the fabric of their clothes and streamed into every pore. Each follicle of hair put on a coat of steam. Greasy steam was in the backs of their ears, in the cracks of their ass, under their nails and eyelids. They *were* steam; hot, spicy, pungent.

Fat Chico Fong pointed at the vat.

'Pork chow mein, Habana-style, pilot,' he yelled triumphantly, 'that's you favorite food. Twenty-four long tons, asshole! From here, we pump it to mid-station, then tank truck. We supply every Cubano-Chino restaurant in the Eastern states, all the way to Pittsburgh.'

'Dag,' the pilot said, at loss for words.

'Also sweet an' sour chicharron, number 67; beef with plantain and bamboo shoots, number 12; shrimp lo mein, 48; ropas viejas an' noodle, number 8; diced pollo with mofongo, number 36; you name

114

it, we make it right here in Brookolino.'

'I always suspected something like this,' the pilot said, staring through the steam at the lumps of pork and water chestnut that oozed to the top, waltzed around the interface, then sank into the hot ocean forever. 'So number 45 is always pork chow mein?'

'That right.'

'And number 33 is moo goo squid — all over the States?'

'Yes.'

'Number 23,' the pilot thought back to his favorites, 'paella, bean curd?'

'You got it,' Fat Chico yelled back proudly. Then his face altered. His eyes narrowed like a cat's. 'An' you gonna be part of number 45 forever, pilot,' he screamed, 'if you don' tell me what happened to my cargo!'

'I left you a message,' the pilot said.

'That's bullshit,' Chico answered. 'You tell me plane meltdown, ditch in Rhode Island. Hah! I send redsticks, chop chop. Find Boeing — no *cheung*. Emeralds, eighty-sixed. Reefer full of aminochips, B-'n'-E, empty. Parrots, eighty-sixed. OK, flyboy,' Chico's voice crescendoed to a psychotic shriek, '*Que pasó?*'

'They were waiting over Montauk,' the pilot yelled back, 'BON. Two Vikings.'

'You think Chico estupido, man?' the mobster barked. 'No bullet holes. No rocket marks.'

'The engines caught fire, man. You soldiers see it!'

'My soldiers find firemarks. No find jewelcases.'

'Jumpers stop me, Chico. Luparas all over the place.'

'You take the emeralds, Gwailo moth'fuck! You

chow mein!' He stabbed stiff fingers at the pilot. 'You think Cubano-Chino food go through you? Hah! Now you go through Chinese food! Number 45, Ay-numbah-one, pilot.'

'Christ,' the pilot muttered, and looked down at the bubbling vat. He thought of how many times he had eaten number 45. 'This how you off people?' he asked Chico. 'In number 45?'

'Sure thing,' Fat Chico said. 'Chow mein, baby. Nosy reporters. Guys think restaurant union happening again. Long pig, no problem.' He snapped his fingers. 'You got fifteen seconds to spill where you took the emeralds. Fourteen, thirteen, twelve.'

One of the guards lifted his sawed-off in anticipation. Too high, the pilot thought; the Benelli pulled up like a bastard if you didn't hold it down hard.

The pilot hung on to an iron railing as Chico counted and snapped his fat fingers in time to the count.

He had been close to death before. Once he'd flipped a superboat off Bimini and it had ploughed straight underwater and broken up, almost taking him with it. Another time he'd ditched a DC-4 off Hatteras. Death for sure had skull-grinned over his shoulder while he stalled in that electrical storm, and then pancaked the Citation into the Davisville marshes. But in all these cases he'd been too busy to take much notice.

Here, he was helpless. He had nothing to do. So he worried.

He wondered, for example, how his parents would take his disappearance. They already had lost one son; it sometimes seemed that pain had spaced them out so far they had forgotten about the other. Perhaps they wouldn't notice.

He hoped someone would take care of Carmelita now Roberto was gone. Her mother was useless, far gone into the dog's-eye depths of cheap mescal.

No one had heard from her father in years.

He peered at the Cubano-Chino food through the steam. This was too ridiculous, he thought. No one goes this stupidly. Then he wondered if that's what everybody's last thought was; 'Oh dag I finally fucked up and all I had to do to avoid it was this, an' I don' wanna g-o-o-o-o,' final baby wail, full circle to the first *waah* of disgust and protest from the wrong side of the vulva.

Snap, snap, snap. 'Five, four, three.' The goons pressed harder, watching Chico's fingers, getting ready to bend and pull their prisoner over the guardrail.

'Cut the *shit*, Chico!' the pilot yelled in panic. 'The Jumpers glommed the fuckin' stones! I swear! Offin' me ain't gonna get it back!'

'He's right,' the tall man said, and nudged the goons with his attaché case. Everyone stared at him. 'He's tellin' the truth.'

The tall man was not Chinese. It was hard to tell what he was, especially through the steam. His features were too thin, his eyes too small. He lifted the attaché case and showed Chico a tiny green pinlight set in the handle.

He opened the case. It was filled with memory boards, sound equipment, dials. A little adding-machine printer pipped out a ribbon of paper. He ripped it out and read it off.

'High background noise,' the tall man said. 'Readings ain't exo. But his glottal strain is okay. No laryngeal stochastics. No training plateaus, either.

117

That's what I believe, you wanna know the truth. The plateaus don't lie. It happened like he said.'

'So he's not lyin',' Chico yelled. 'So what? The emeralds, gone. The chips, eighty-six. What the difference? Chow mein!' He snapped his fingers in the pilot's face.

'We can still use him,' the tall man said.

'Fuck,' Chico said, and cracked his knuckles. 'Chewing gum!' The goon with the pistol whipped out a pack. Chico chewed so noisily you could hear him masticate over the bubbling of number 45.

'What you say, Mister Pilot,' the tall man yelled, 'you run a couple cargoes for us, free, no cut, no share?'

The pilot looked at the tall man. Over the pounding of his heart and the buzzing adrenaline in his brain he wondered where this guy came from. The Tongs seldom used people who weren't Chinese, or Cuban, or, more rarely, Viet. Maybe this was Organizatsni talent, the Tbilisi mob; though you'd think they would know the first rules of the Trade.

'You gotta be loco,' the pilot shouted back. He wiped his face. The steam was really getting to him. If he ever got out of this he would smell like number 45 for a week. 'That ain't the way it works.'

The tall man wiped fog off his dials, closed the attaché case.

'You jivin' us how it works?' Chico yelled. 'You jivin' us, here?' He pointed at the vat.

'Nobody takes the rap for busted cargoes,' the pilot shouted at him. 'It's basic. You make smugglers pay if we get busted, or crash, we don't do the runs. We ain't got the scratch to do it any other way. No immunity, no cargoes. It's as simple as that.'

'Then you fuckin' lunch,' Fat Chico shouted happily. The goons moved to handle the pilot again.

'Stop,' the tall man said.

'This Spirit Knife place,' Chico told him.

'But we own half Spirit Knife now,' the tall man answered. 'You know the deal.'

The two looked at each other. In the tension, in the steam, it seemed to the pilot neither of them had eyes anymore.

'OK,' Chico said finally. 'We gotta block. We settle it the old way. Face for me, face for you. Bring me fortune cookies.'

The red-stick grinned. He disappeared down the ladder and came back five minutes later with two handfuls of the biscuits, each wrapped in a small wax-paper bag.

Chico pulled the Eurasian girl from behind the tall man where she'd been pouting, and stamping, and trying, unsuccessfully, to keep her mascara intact.

'You,' he yelled. 'Read 'em!'

The girl made a face, but she did what he asked, ripping the bags, breaking open the egg-glazed dough, extracting the thin predictions.

'See,' Chico yelled, 'good joss, we let pilot do a free run for us. Bad joss, we throw him in. More fun this way.'

' "You long to see the great pyramids of Egypt," ' the girl read.

Chico frowned. 'That no fuckin' good. Read more.'

The girl cracked another cookie.

' "There is no fool like an old fool." '

Chico waved this away in disgust. The tall man turned impatiently, a half-circle, turned back. The girl flicked her fingers to get rid of crumbs, which fell through the grating and were absorbed in the chow mein.

'"You love nature in all its forms."'

'What the fuck is this,' Chico shouted, 'who writes this shit? These cookies s'posed to have fortunes, joss, not what you like, what you don' like!'

'"The secret of happiness,"' the girl read, hesitantly, '"lies not in doing what you love, but in loving what you do."'

'When we stop writing fortunes?' Chico screamed. 'Get me head of writers' office!'

All of a sudden the tall man lost it. His tiny features seemed to go out of control, split from each other, widen, resolve in anger through the pungent fog. 'Fuck this!' he screamed at the pilot. 'You do a run for free or we throw you in now!' He signaled the goons. They jabbed their guns, wound their fists in the doctor's coat, hoisted him halfway over the railing so three-quarters of his weight hung unsupported over number 45. The pilot threw up his hands, in terror, in defeat. He could almost feel the slurping agony as the disgusting gray-green glue scarfed him, pulled him down, lifting puckered skin from boiling flesh. He could not be part of this crime perpetrated on the Cuban-Chinese food consumers of America. It was time for compromise.

'I'll do it,' he shouted, 'for expenses. Ten grand.'

'Five,' Chico said, automatically.

'Seven and a half,' the pilot countered.

At another signal, the goons dropped him back on the platform.

'Don't fuck up this time.' The tall man spoke at a regular pitch. It was hard to make out the words. His face was back to normal again. Not enough features for expression. It was almost as if he could turn the crazed anger on and off at will. It crossed the pilot's mind that he'd been had.

'I'll do what I can,' the pilot said. His hands were trembling and he jammed them in his pockets. 'Gimme a ride back?'

'What the subway for,' Fat Chico commented through a mouthful of chewing gum.

11

'Among those living constellations, how many
windows shut, how many stars burned out, how
many men asleep?'

Antoine de Saint-Exupéry
Terre des Hommes

When the pilot left the factory he found the sun was
up and the day had started without him.

He found no subway. People pointed the way to
the 'D' train but he got lost time and time again. His
body was cold, his stomach empty, his head con-
gested. His tired mind kept taking paths of its own.
He bought a hard-copy of the *News* and a bag of
Pepperidge Farm Double-Dark-Chocolate Milanos and
munched the cookies as he walked. The newspaper
headlines read 'PREZ SAYS, WE'LL HIT MEX!' leading a
story about a possible US incursion into Chihuahua
province to destroy cocaine depots and Paquito
Munoz bases. A Polish resistance group had blown up
a bus in EC-occupied Stettin, killing eight Saxon
soldiers. He dumped the paper in a trash can.
Eventually he ran into Prospect Park.

The trees made curious intricate shapes of the long

morning light. Joggers bounced and produced small feathers of steam from their mouths. A Neta courier on motorized rollerblades zipped, fast as ectoplasm, down a walk. A patrol of Safety Volunteers biked after the courier, waving summons forms for helmet violations.

Dogs traced frantic spirals around a leash radius while their owners held firm in the circle center. After the embrace of the White Angel and the locks of Bellevue and the serried vats of the Chinese food factory and the tight brick ranks of Brooklyn row houses, the feel of open space tugged at the pilot, the way magnets pull at iron filings.

He entered the park. His shadow stretched ahead and to the right. He followed it, around the confines of a lake, roughly south and west. Eventually he would hit the river this way.

Squirrels screeched and chased each other in committed fury. Mockingbirds simulated the sound of car alarms. 'Whoop, whoop, whoop,' they called. 'Ee-yah, ee-yah. Wahr, wahr.' Junkie raccoons tried to open crack vials discarded in the depths of the wild kudzu groves. They fumbled and experimented; the ones who succeeded grew more confident, more aggressive; their heirs, carefully coached, would get closer to tool-making. The pilot remembered the face of the Organizatsni man. It did not feel good to be threatened, and played around with, and fooled.

'You love nature in all its forms.'

A couple walked by arm in arm, the same long scarf wrapped around both their necks. 'God, I smell Chinese food!' the girl said, right after she'd passed him.

'You're right, so do I,' her companion replied. 'Egg foo yung, I think?'

'No, it's got meat.'

'Ginger duck?'

'Garlic chicken . . .'

Their voices faded. The pilot wiped his face with one hand, and smelled the hand.

Number 45.

But he would put off Chico's run. First he had to make another run, a real profit-maker, to go toward another plane and extra back-me-up for Carmelita. She had no health insurance, he knew, and even Bellevue cost bucks these days. Cost bucks to stay; cost even more to leave, what with the referrals, the therapists, the outpatient services, all the other guarantees they demanded.

His fault.

Carmelita's hair, sullen and lifeless as the ashes of suttee.

Roberto's face, what — shot up, torn, bloody? Or drowned, like that pier in the painting at Evangeline's, with his eyes full of small purple fish, and fiddler crabs walking in and out of the penny arcade of his mouth forever open in that involuntary smile he always had when his sister's boyfriend was teaching him how to fly . . .

There was a restaurant called Verdicchio's, somewhere in Bay Ridge, not too far from this cemetery, the pilot remembered.

They'd thrown Roberto a dinner there.

It was to celebrate getting his private pilot's license, only ten months after the first Halifax flight.

In a more roundabout way they were also

celebrating how the feeling between the pilot and Carmelita was starting to mellow, like grappa, gaining in strength what it lost in raw energy.

That night had been in a lot of ways the central light of his whole time with Carmelita, a sort of beacon to mark the little shipwrecks that occurred thereafter. It was a near-perfect event set amid plastic raffia-covered bottles of Chianti, in which Carmelita at last seemed to have grown clear of the spiderwebs guarding her brain.

He wanted to remember her as she was in that restaurant, equal parts spunk, and a jewel-like acceptance. Her hands, white as the hair was black, flew like nervous egrets as she talked fast to keep Roberto from cracking Italian Air Force jokes. She thought the waiters would get upset; in fact the waiters were all Macedonian. But there was contentment growing in her at the same time and it shone in pools from the vortex of her eyes when she looked at the pilot.

The nights of despair, when she'd lain in his arms, so cold that all the blankets in his lounge would not suffice to warm her – talking half English, half Spanish about the pre-dawn creatures that ate at her with mothers' teeth – that time seemed far away. Her capacity for utter hopelessness and total silence, the same capacity that sent her in untenanted flight for the cloying orange breath of Bellevue and Nurse Linda, seemed to have been sheathed forever in their huge appetite for the other's moves and feelings. In the restaurant she'd put a hand on his jeans and leaned closer, her mouth rich with garlic and oils. 'Skid,' she'd begun, in the middle of an untrue story about a Westbury air traffic controller who'd gone down mid-watch and begun flying the entire La

Guardia traffic pattern in strafing formation toward Fort Lee. 'For the first time, I think I really believe things don't *have* to go bad . . .' And he'd looked at her, and her brother, and felt all the displaced affection that had never been allowed to come out in his house, in his childhood, wheeling through the cathedrals of his chest till the candles of the room seemed to burn dim and fuzzy by comparison . . .

After that, of course, Roberto had gone the usual flyboy route, working two ground jobs, building up his time, getting a passenger license, picking up flying work when and where he could.

And eventually, whipsawed between starvation wages and skyhunger, he had lost the great energy required to stay straight against the odds. He did what the pilot had done, what a lot of young men with more skill than experience ended up doing.

He went to someone he knew in the Trade and asked for work as copilot, or even shotgun.

The pilot knew what Carmelita would say if he bought Roberto a ticket on that particular roller coaster, so he took the easy way out. Forget it, he told Roberto, not through me.

But Roberto did not have to go through him. By then he'd spent enough hours hanging around with the pilot to suss out who was straight and who was checking the state of the moon before forgetting to file a flight plan.

Roberto did his first run with Big Maxie in a Beech 18 to Abaco and back, just like the pilot before him.

Not the pilot's fault.

Except that it was the pilot's fault; because he was there, because the Trade was there, ready, available as

126

a woman with a past to anyone willing to take a chance or two.

The park ended. The cookies were all gone. He upended the package and shook the last broken chips into his open mouth. He kept following his shadow. He found an elevated subway line. Giant orange cranes hung over it and a sign announced that it was closed indefinitely for 'emergency' repairs. Another stretch of trees and fence loomed ahead, but this area was thick with gray right angles, the complex branching of icons, the crosses, and crosses recrossed, that drew out man's most ancient need to fill with Xs the zero he sensed lay at the heart of things. The granite crucifixes traced an atavistic tic-tac-toe, symbols of first fear.

The pilot walked into the cemetery, still fleeing the sun.

He was guilty in Roberto's destruction, to the same extent the Trade was guilty – to the extent kids got killed and people hurt and lives spun to nothing in BON detention camps or shot down in red flames over some lousy patch of coral no one had even bothered to name; all because men ran cargoes over borders for the likes of Fat Chico Fong.

Most of the tombs here were old. Large hunks of granite, polished and beveled. Lichen dusted the stones, like gray-green acne. The pilot wondered whether the weight of the stones was meant, in some complicated way, to keep these people pinned down so they would never pop back up and bug everyone with their dead worries. Son, the formaldehyde don't keep me warm. Sweetheart, it's lonely down there. Brother, don't piss away your life sitting in front of a VDT like I did.

The southern section of the cemetery was newer. Fresh flowers decorated some of the graves. Many of the tombstones had electricity outlets and black boxes, for the latest trend was to bury the deceased with a cable TV hookup so his or her corpse could watch reruns while it hung around, waiting for the last trump. The upscale models had timers and remote controls to program the buried television to favorite shows and channels. The truly expensive ones included a preprogrammed VCR linked to a second TV, this one mounted at ground level, sometimes with virtual reality capacity. In this way the deceased could, in a sense, talk back to the living, through the removes of time-lapse and VHS cassettes.

The dead dwelled as they always had lived, in neighborhoods defined by wealth.

The way out took him through the classier sections. The first remote clicked on two-thirds of the way down a row of comfortable Catholics.

'Kathleen,' a voice called from somewhere around his feet.

The pilot jerked around so hard he almost lost his footing. His lungs sucked air hard enough to hurt.

A terminal set into a pink sandstone vault flashed blue through a frieze of plastic flowers and rosary beads. The words under the screen read;

DUNCAN JAMES DONNELLY

Beloved Son of Mary and John
Husband of Kathleen
Father of Tracy, Kathleen, and Duncan Jr.

The dates of his birth and death were carved underneath.

On the screen, a forty-five-year-old man with skin as pink as his tombstone looked around in terminal frustration, holding a barbecue fork.

'Kathleen,' he repeated. 'Get the kids, the steaks are done, they're overdone.' The man spotted the camera and grinned. The camera swayed, panned unevenly to take in a couple of sullen girls and a dumpy woman in a plastic apron.

The pilot kept walking. His heart was pounding. Duncan James Donnelly had been dead seven years, the cookout had ended on some sunny summer evening over seven years ago, the steaks he was cooking had been long ago eaten, digested, excreted; his daughters gone to college on the life insurance.

The pilot's feet actioned a pressure switch. The next video came on only four tombs down.

'Hi! I'm Joe Catania!'

A jowly man in a white T-shirt appeared on a weatherproofed screen on a brown slab of marble to the pilot's left. Joe's T-shirt had a caption. It read, 'If life is a bowl of cherries, why am I always in the pits?'

'Let's all play volleyball, dammit,' Duncan James Donnelly yelled behind him. His voice was angry. 'Where's Duncan Junior?' Kathleen must have hated his guts, the pilot thought, to play that tape as a memorial.

A VR full face-sucker was locked in an armored box set in the marble. If your UCC-card matched the box's codes, you could put on the gear and see Joe Catania in 3-D, standing beside you large as life in his cherry T-shirt.

'I worked as chief financial officer at Burke Brothers for twenty-eight years,' Joe Catania said. 'My son is an engineer.' Joe was smiling big, but he looked like he was having a hard time thinking of things to say to people who would be living when he was dead.

'I am recording this at the studios of the William E. Hickworth and Sons Funeral Home,' Joe continued, desperately looking down at his notes, 'an' I just wanna tell my sister Elise . . .'

The pilot kept walking. Left and right and behind him more voices broke into electronic life. The voices spoke of family, uttering names, cracking jokes, sometimes singing, usually talking about God or angels or heaven. But always the voices invoked one word.

The word was 'love,' and in every case, without exception, it was pronounced as if this were the most magical word of all, the secret name that would smooth away the lines of exhaustion and pain, of loneliness and unhappiness in the corners of the faces on the video screens – a word of such power and weight it could balance out a lifetime of big compromises and small victories, and make everything fern-green and well again.

The southwestern end of the cemetery held a couple of relatively blue-collar neighborhoods. Here, though cable was hooked into every recent tomb, it was a one-way link and there were few above-ground screens, so the sounds of the park could reassert themselves somewhat. The bitching of crows, the calls of children, the whisper of branches, the far-off yelp of a coyote became audible again – yet even here, in the midst of the trees and kudzu that surrounded the boneyard, the primary input came on a register both deeper and higher than the tones of the living; a crackle of static, a fuzzed rattling of voices caught in the tweeter Bakelite, canned laughter, theme songs, machine guns, commercial jingles, the plastic pauses of soap operas; sound all mingled and stitched together; electronic underground tapestry that rose like vibration, muted yet deep, from beneath the clipped brown grass around the tombs, resonating with the five feet of loam that lay between the air and the TV screens bolted onto the coffin lid, the buzzing electronic images painted blue on the waxed and moldy cheeks, the dried yellow glaze of their sewn-open eyes reflecting dimly back on the TV screens that led to the wire that led to the cable that led to the junction box that marked where the dead watched TV.

The pilot walked faster. Sweat was pricking out on his forehead. The blue-collar graves already were over with, he was back in a ritzy section now, one of the ritziest, they were always more expensive at the gate, where you didn't have to walk or drive far to visit. He could see the skyline over the top of the iron fence marking the cemetery limits.

'—these words to my beloved son Dave—'

'I love you all so much—'

'Never could tell you I love you Rachel—'

'Never found someone else I could really love—'

Every cracked decibel of strain in the taut voices; every strung tendon in the video faces; every time the word 'love' was mentioned; every measure of silence turned in the pilot's ears, blew up into a vicarious despair, burst into a great twisting of minutes wasted, of wishes unfulfilled, of lives spent like two-dollar coupons at some cheap gypsy-trick carnival midway of the limbic system.

The pilot broke into a run, aiming for the cemetery gates. Images rose from the broken rhythm.

Carmelita's eyes, as one-way, as stopped-down as these tombs.

The huge blue revolving brushes of Krazy Karl's Kwik Kleen Wheels 5-Dollar Karwash where Roberto used to work.

Roberto's mother at the switchboard. Eighteen years of 'Operator 519, thank you for calling NYNEX.'

The strange burning glow of Orinoco emeralds.

The kid's eyes when he first climbed out of the Citation. The feel of flight between night and nothing.

The voices of the dead cried behind him. The pilot bolted through the gates of the cemetery and down 25th Street as if each one of them were personally chasing his ass.

12

'For many people smuggling is a way of life. The smuggler feels he is performing a service to his community rather than committing a crime. After all, he is supplying his friends, at a price they can afford, with goods that otherwise are either unobtainable or extremely expensive. The fact that he is breaking the law never enters his head. If he thinks about it at all, he feels that he is depriving politicians living far away of a portion of their income, and in so doing he is helping his neighbors. He may be right.'

Horace Beck
Folklore and the Sea

'The Trade, no matter how far-out or seditious some people think it—' this according to the Smuggler's Bible, Chapter One '—is only a mirror of the Square-up world. Since the Square-up world over the last fifty years has been taken over by those institutional mind-fuckers, the humungo, squiddy-tentacled commercial and political mega-organizations — it follows this should hold true in the smuggling 'hood as well.

'Well,' the Smuggler's Bible continues, answering its own hypothesis, 'si, and no. Sure, the horse and coke game has been entirely ripped off by the big Guyanan and Santa Martan cartels with their M-16s, their red-sticks, their pet judges. And yes, you've got more and more of the black trade in everything else being run by the fat-ass networks, like the Black Tuna gang, the DeLisi brothers, the Triad, the Spirit Knives-Organizatsni, the South Florida Sunshine Corporation.

'But no — no in a big way, because a majority of the real brothers; the skippers, the pilots, the coyotes, in other words, the border specialists — still work for themselves. They still run their own cargoes, make their own connects, in seedy Asian hotels, in small grimy bars in the Bahamas outer cays. In this respect, as in so many others, they are the last of the traditional bandidos . . .'

The pilot leaned over from the passenger seat of the old Crooked Island Airways Trislander to peer out the windscreen as Sandworm Cay appeared out of the hallucinating transparent X-ray of Bahamian sea.

Sandworm Cay was and is a mistake. It is too high to be a real sandbar, too low to be a proper island. During hurricanes it essentially disappears under surf and spray. It is four miles long by a quarter mile wide at its broadest point, a long thin turd, like the meager diarrhea of barracuda. It is the dried-up residue of two kinds of sea waste: coral, made of the skeletons of billions of miniature crustaceans; and basalt, formed of the solidified hemorrhage of the earth's melted blood, lava come oozing hot and tangerine-colored from the broken skin of the ocean floor, to congeal in the cool saltwater and build until it touches air, and is broken off by the Caribbean waves.

The creatures that live on Sandworm Cay are sea

waste too, sea waste feeding on sea waste: for all of them at some point in their evolution were thrown out of happier places until they finally found refuge on this oceanic accident, and either learned to live off the wrack that washed in after them, or died.

The web-footed gawpies are a good example. The gawpie is a seabird whose feet are too large and whose wings are too small for easy flight. It eats teredo worms off driftwood and broken ships and is too lazy and specialized to survive anywhere else. The iguanas who live here by eating gawpie eggs are the rejects of their own species. They would starve if the gawpies were not, incredibly, even stupider and slower than they.

As for the humans, they are the products of ten generations of marooned pirates, disoriented smugglers, lost fishermen, washed-up convicts, castaway slaves, shipwrecked mariners, sick and beaten Indians — a half-dozen races bred and interbred into one common denominator, namely, the utter geographic confusion, the spectacular absence of any directional sense, the zero spatial judgment required to get utterly, irretrievably lost, and wind up on the poorest, most godforsaken island in the entire Caribbean — and *stay* there.

And yet — Sandworm Cay has an airstrip. Its cracked and broken asphalt takes up about a fifth of the island's surface. The strip came courtesy of World War II, the island's east-west orientation into the prevailing tradewinds, and its location not far from the shipping lanes to South America and their U-boat predators. It is kept open and repaired largely because of the smuggling trade.

The Trislander jinked and putted over the island's

only village. Its shadow made fast, fickle angles on bleached pink sand, pastel shacks, hauled-up skiffs, scrub palms bent double, a scattering of garden plots picket-fenced against the single-minded wind and its eternal coriolis lick. The plane bounced over the heaps of teredo shells, the skeletons of surprised iguanas and gawpies who, in the wild and carefree rut of April, had mistaken incoming aircraft for big gawpies and initiated the dance of copulation, with lethal results.

The plane came to a stop by a sagging Quonset hut. The pilot climbed out. He was the only passenger. The Trislander's crew chucked out a sack of mail and assorted cargo and taxied away.

The pilot slung his ECM-pak and his chartcase, one on each shoulder, and walked down the runway, east-ward, into the warm iodine halitosis of the sea. As he walked he looked at the wrecks of planes that had come in too long, or too short, too close to a tropical storm, or too full of bullets from the guns of rival smugglers lying in wait behind the cascarillas. They were single- and twin-engine planes mostly; Aero-Commanders, Learjets, Canadairs, Dakotas, Beech 18s. Most had been modified for the Trade with STOL gear, radar-sensing domes, Dornier-Akai floats, RATO mounts, flare chutes. In all of them the rudders swung loose, the flaps sagged, doors hung agape. Eelgrass grew through shattered landing gear. The Trislander gunned its engines and took off, east into the trades, waggling its wings.

He walked faster through the boneyard till he came to the Connie.

The Connie was a Lockheed Super-Constellation, a four-propellor, dolphin-nosed, whale-backed, twin-tailed monster, the largest aircraft ever to attempt a landing at Sandworm Cay. She had come in on a March night, pregnant with fifteen tons of Antioquia blow, her pilots – true to Sandworm tradition – being under the impression that this was a much longer runway on an island thirty-five miles to the north-west.

Now she lay half buried in a dune, her nose over-hanging the concrete buttresses of the cay's only harbor. Someone had spray-painted a slogan on the radar cone: 'The Quest is the Quest.' Hawkley. Tattered awnings sheltered the raw aluminum from the sun. Small flowers sprouted scarlet-and-cream from the engine cowlings. The trades had blown sand against the wreck so it covered the fuselage up to the wings and carpeted the plane's interior. A sign read 'Super Constellation Tavern and Restaurant.' The pilot walked through the open First Class doorway.

The inside was gloomy, lit only by emergency lights and a couple of kerosene lanterns whose greasy smoke helped keep the mosquitoes at bay. A few air-line seats had been rearranged into booths under the ornate chrome fixtures and the faded blue fabric of an old passenger section. A bar built of silver sea-weathered wood took up most of the cargo area. There was a strong smell of ganja. A generator chugged in the background. From the cockpit, music thumped softly, heavy on the front beat.

Free yer mind, to the beat, to the rhythm, of yer ass . . .

Dr Funkenship.

A tall black man in jeans and T-shirt squinted at the pilot from behind the bar. He reached automatically for the Letuva bottle.

'Cree-azy Skid,' he said.

'Hello, Gershwin,' the pilot answered. He put

down his gear with a sigh of relief. The chartcase was heavy. The hidden compartment inside was full of VR-Portables. You could make a nice mark-up on VR-Portables on islands like these, so long as you did not inform Customs.

There was no Customs on Sandworm Cay. There was no Customs on Grand Bahama either – not when you folded a hundred-mark bill around your UCC-card.

'Been long time,' Gershwin said.

'Sure,' the pilot agreed. He looked around him, thinking it was probably a good thing. Once he had been fond of this place. Today there was something shabby – no, worse, there was something incredibly lonely about this wrecked plane, and all the other abandoned aircraft around the runway. Delicate systems of metal and electricity, gentle contours of lift and drag once meant to soar and swoop now rusted broken in the pink sand, all because of black money.

Shabby and lonely it was, this whole island of rejects, of men who fled other men by choice or necessity.

Shabby and lonely, like his apartment. Like the Trade itself. He shook his head, hard. He had to get over it.

'Been busy?'

'Busy!' Gershwin laughed. He had a good, rich laugh. 'Sure, mahn.'

Gershwin was in his fifties. His mouth was toothless and smiled easier than not. He had very calm eyes surrounded by deep ridges. The lines had been carved by long hours spent in open boats, looking for fish. Searching for the way back to harbor.

'No business anymore.' He leaned over the bar.

'Not for two months, now. Been no mahn comin' heah.'

A tall young islander with long plaited dreadlocks and a green plastic bag on his shoulder ambled through the doorway. He nodded at Gershwin, picked up a broom, and began sweeping the sand with slow, elegant strokes. After three strokes the broom handle poked out one of the cabin lights. Glass shattered. Gershwin sighed, and leaned closer, over the bar.

'Been no mahn comin' heah,' he repeated, jerking his head significantly toward the east, but he meant America. 'No mahn gettin' t'rough. Boats, aeroplane. No mahn getting t'rough six, seven week anyway.'

'Huh.' The pilot picked up his glass. It read 'British West Indian Airways.'

'Me nevah seen so dry a spell as this.'

Gershwin looked with calm eyes at his customer. He wanted something from him, either a question or an answer. The pilot looked through the vodka, at one of the kerosene lamps. The flame burned without movement, orange and black as Hallowe'en. Whatever Gershwin wanted, it would come clear with time.

You let da man steal yer beat? Dr Funkenship sang.

'Babeelon Emp-aye-yah,' a voice cried behind the pilot. A wiry man with sanpaku eyes jerked around himself in one of the booths. He wore a blue woolen cape. An Israeli knock-off of a Russian assault rifle hung from one shoulder. His hair was so matted and dirty it looked like a bad wig. A joint, thick as a cigar, drooped from one corner of his mouth. 'Fock wit righteous chalice of Jah Rastafar-aye.' He unslung his Galil, cocked it, and pointed it toward the south, still jerking, bouncing on his bench, pumping his feet to the beat of a tune only he could hear.

I-'n-I no listen, Babylon beat:
I-'n-I tee-ake out, Babylon heat

he sang. His features moved to the rhythm but his
pupils were still. He cocked the gun again, and a shell
bounced out the breach and fell without noise on the
sand floor.

The young islander picked up his broom and held
it like a gun to the wiry man's head.

'Leave it, Eltonjohn,' Gershwin yelled at the boy.
'Get out of heah, Presley,' he shouted at the wiry
man. 'No fock wit weapon my plee-ace.'

Black Tuna dead now, Babylon beat.
Boyd Brothers gone now, Babylon heat.

'Out, Presley.'

The wiry man looked menacingly at Eltonjohn's
broom. He got up, slung the gun back on his
shoulder. He jerked over to the wing emergency exit,
turned into a dark outline, and vanished. Ganja smoke
curled and faded in the rectangle of light.

'Babylon heat.' Gershwin grimaced sarcastically.
'Him know what he talkin' about, for sure. Presley
take BON money, half de time.'

The assistant put the broom down. He picked up
Presley's bottle of Red Stripe, threw it at the garbage
barrel, and missed. Glass shattered.

'F-f-fock,' the assistant said.

'Eltonjohn,' Gershwin said, with more resignation
than reproval. 'My wife cousin,' he added, by way of
explanation, or excuse.

140

The pilot nodded. He remembered how this island worked – the tangled knots of kinship, the way they named their babies for music stars, as if the buzz of high living that came over the transistor could be made truth by using names associated with it.

Outside the wind mumbled and the sea whispered back. Palmetto bugs made dry scraping noises as they copulated in the eelgrass. Gawpies uttered their strange choking call. The Dr Funkenship tape was cut off by a timer. Cheap speakers relayed the BBC World Service from a radio in Gershwin's office.

'The United States Justice Department, working from genetic samples, today verified that the man who came out of a New Jersey marsh last week proclaiming he was an American union leader thought to have died several generations ago is, in fact, Mr Jimmy Hoffa.

'Mr Hoffa, a former Teamsters Union president who disappeared from the parking lot of the Machus Red Fox restaurant in Bloomfield Township, Illinois on July thirtieth, 1973 – weeks before his scheduled testimony on charges of abetting corruption within that union – was believed to have been executed by organized crime bosses before he could testify against them. Mr Hoffa said at a press conference yesterday that he had been buried alive in a New Jersey marsh by killers from the Gambino crime family. The former union leader says he believes that he actually died during the ordeal, but was quote resurrected by the intervention of Jesus Christ to show the path of salvation to the people of America end quote. Followers of Mr Hoffa within the popular Johnsonist Evangelical Church, which believes in the necessity of paying bribes to powerful religious groups to ensure salvation, have announced a move to rename that church the "Hoffaist Church of the Resurrection."'

Gershwin shook his head as he polished glasses.

'What you t'ink of dat?' he asked the pilot.

The pilot shrugged. 'Can't say. Never heard of the guy.'

'Never heard of Jimmy Hoffa?' Gershwin looked at him carefully. 'Of course not. You weren't even bohn, then.'

'Whatever,' the pilot replied, draining his glass. 'Listen.' He jerked a thumb toward the wing exit. 'What was he talkin' about, Black Tuna, the Boyds?'

'Busted.' The bartender refilled the pilot's glass with the smooth measure and ergonomic movement of drink professionals the planet over. His eyes shone with the power of news. 'Week, ten dee-ays ago, maybe. You should listen to the airwaves, pilot.'

'I listen, Gershwin. I look too. There was the usual Trade traffic, on the Wildnets. Nothing different.'

'Same kinda talk?'

'Well, maybe not exactly.' Remembering those black spider patterns, the sense of traffic unbalanced. 'When there's a bust, though,' the pilot continued, 'the traffic usually goes way down.'

'Well, I tell truth.' Gershwin leaned over the counter. 'Dey go down same time. Boyds, Black Tuna. Bobby on Crooked Island tell me.'

'I run a couple of cargoes for the Boyds, once.'

'Most people done dat, once.' Gershwin wiped down his bar counter with a wet rag, shoving aside a dog-eared hard-copy of the *Smuggler's Gazette*.

The pilot leafed through the journal as he sipped his second vodka.

He liked the *Gazette* because it was ninety percent

142

classified ads. The editors claimed that a classified ad was the only honest form of journalism because it was the only info that went straight from people to people without a middleman.

No one knew who the editors of the *Gazette*, or the Smuggler's Bible for that matter, really were. The hard-copy version was printed in Nevada. The CD-ROMs were mailed from different places – usually seaports, the pilot had noticed – Rotterdam, Singapore, Corpus Christi.

The only article in this issue was titled 'Lead-plating and You: Foolproof Your Cargo Compartment Against Ultrasound.'

The *Gazette*'s classifieds sold everything from used freighters to satellite detectors to the services of privacy agents and beeper companies. The different Wildnets, and the pirate online services within those 'nets, competed by offering bonuses like VR sex with extinct mammals or anti-stochastic 'net-cyphers 'guaranteed to resist any BON code-breaker for three months or your credit back' – a safe promise, given that if the cypher didn't work, the customer would probably be dead, or in Oakdale Detention Center.

But the personals were the best, for the pilot's money. Nowhere else could you find queries from lesbian skateboarders seeking dildos with a two-hundred-megabyte capacity for contraband memory; or ethnologists asking for data on the Karayar smuggling caste and the hallucinogenic Venya fruit they used for their rites (samples gratefully accepted). A lot of the personals were obvious codes, and often quite funny, in their bizarre juxtaposition of random symbols.

In this issue was a two-inch ad that read: 'Spend

143

your summers in Halicarnassus! Mythomania field study project seeks short-order saucier with period Torricelli barometer reading to 163.22. Contact Box L.'

Gershwin finished wiping the bar and said, 'You wan' come fohwahd?'

The Connie's cockpit was Gershwin's office. The instruments were dead eyes set at crash settings – throttles zero, fuel shut off – everything flaked with salt and rust. Wires twisted loose, blue insulation hung from the ceiling. Only the radio – a large Japanese IC-M marine single-sideband set, with 1,136 channels including duplex frequencies – was maintained in serviceable order.

Gershwin kept the shortwave going twenty-four hours a day. It was his only reliable link to the world outside Sandworm Cay. He spent most nights at the set, Dr Funkenship thumping gently on his boombox, playing the tuning buttons with the sensitivity of a koto artist; jacked in via earphones to a universe of electronic waves that, since they were broadcast, needed no direction or azimuth but took him ungrudgingly across dark oceans and continents without his ever leaving the Connie's cockpit. He listened mostly to the amateur or marine bandwidths smugglers used.

Although the IC-M or any other modern transceiver, going through Iridium or InMarSat links, could handle datastreams with ease, Gershwin never jacked into the Wildnets or any other form of online network.

The obsessive nature of his listening schedule made up for this limitation. Gershwin knew more Trade scuttlebutt than anyone the pilot had ever met. The information Gershwin gleaned from the ether allowed him to work as an informational clearinghouse for independent smugglers, the kind who in any case tended toward more traditional methods, like ham radio or fast-boat operations. He often put together jobs and contractors, taking a cut each way.

'Cree-azy amount of scrambled traffic, last few weeks. 'Specially wit' DeLisis. Dey never use radio, before time. BON channels, ship-shore, aviation, you nee-ame it, dere been voices everywhere.'

'Too much radio,' the pilot stated in Hitchcockian tones, 'is dangerous.'

'Not so dangerous as Wildnet, mahn.'

'You can't use a direction finder, on Wildnet.'

'Othah t'ings.' Gershwin's tongue made a noise against his teeth. 'Othah t'ings.'

The pilot went back to the bar, fetched the ECM-pak, and opened it on the navigator's desk. Gershwin shook his head irritably as the pilot punched in commands for broad-spectrum, low-range jamming.

The shortwave reception broke up in a haze of white noise. Gershwin switched off power. He pointed at the ECM-pak.

'Good t'ing,' he commented, 'for wire – but dey findin' out anyway. Black Tuna, Boyd Brothers, dey use ECM too – Bokon catch dem anyway.'

'Bokon.' The pilot leaned forward, looking, not at Gershwin, but over the controls at the trade wind clouds, towering like a universe of piled-up peach-colored cotton balls against the setting sun. He could feel his heart thud. It was a never-ending source of surprise to him that it could keep on beating without his doing a damn thing about it. 'Who is this "Bokon"?'

145

Gershwin pulled out a pouch of tobacco from his jeans. 'Don' know. No one know. Mebbe not even a person. Mebbe him just 'nothah name for BON.' Gershwin shook his head. 'Somethin' cree-azy happenin' wit' BON. Somethin' hot an' mean.'

A frigate bird wheeled over the harbor. A couple of big-footed gawpies, figuring it was another, larger gawpie, tried to catch up to it and failed. Their wings flapped frantically.

'I'm lookin' for a plane, Gershwin. Or a boat, even. See, I need a cargo. I got to get some quick cash.'

The boombox timer clicked. Dr Funkenship rocked into 'Jungle Boogie.'

The islander rolled a cigarette between the first three fingers of his left hand. He lit the cigarette and blew smoke gently out the side window.

'Queek cash,' Gershwin said, and sighed. 'Queek runs. Queek life, mahn. Whole world goin' cree-azy for queekness.

'You know,' he continued at length, 'you nevah get best jobs before now. People say you too picky some-times, you no run certain cargo; mostly, people say you too cree-azy. Cree-azy Skid. Go too fast. How many boats you sink, pilot? How many planes you ditch? Goin' too fast for sea, for engines.'

'I din' lose that many,' the pilot began, his voice heated, loud, but Gershwin held up one hand flat, a peace gesture. He was laughing quietly.

'Don't harass yourself, mahn. Don't matter to me anyway. All I sayin' is now maybe people be lookin' for Crazy Skid Marak, same reason dey not seekin' you out before time. Because you go, fast as greased lightning. Because you no scared of weather. Mebbe BON no catchin' t'ief so fast as you.'

'I'm a good trader, Gershwin.'

'You elegant,' Gershwin corrected him. 'You not good, but you elegant. Pretty cargoes: yellow diamond, green jisi crystal, white gold, run 'em all fast, fast like cree-azy bahstahd. Come wit' me.'

They went outside, down the sand to the water. The harbor at Sandworm Cay consisted of a fissure in the coral protected by concrete pilings to keep the sand from filling it in. The Connie lay roughly halfway down the western side of it. A boatyard that once had specialized in repairing turtle schooners lay at the harbor's head. The turtles were gone now, the remaining schooners used to transport tourists. A French company had built a five-story cement hotel at the harbor mouth in hopes of attracting young singles to an isolated place where they could dive on staghorn coral and cavort naked in the fine, pink madrepore sand; unfortunately the same sand had betrayed the place, chewed at the concrete, duplicitously snuck out its underpinnings, eloped with the storm currents, so that now the beach was gone, and so were the singles, and the building lay canted at a fifteen-degree angle, foundations shattered, its dining room regularly scoured by surf.

None of the buildings on Sandworm Cay lay plumb and true, because of the sand. You had to drink to stay level, on the Cay, people said.

It was an old excuse.

'Plenty of boats.' Gershwin pointed at the marina, where a number of long, low, sharp-bowed hulls nuzzled the pilings. 'Coupla planes in de hangar, too, but dem slow, prop jobs. Plenty boats. Price of boats way down. Price of cargo way up, pilot.'

'Maybe I'll go sailin' this time,' the pilot said. He

147

picked up his bags from Gershwin's office and headed for the marina.

Plenty of boats.

There must have been thirty of them in the marina. An ancient Royal Air Force search-and-rescue launch, seventy feet of heavy engines and light plywood still painted in white-and-blue camouflage, rotted resignedly at one end of the dock area. A twin-hulled Scarab — both massive outboards burned — rubbed herself raw on a bulkhead opposite the SAR launch. Craft of every size and shape filled the space between, but all had two characteristics in common; all possessed the sharp, mean lines, the needle-nosed bow to poke into wind and waves with minimum resistance; all were built with hard chines at the side and flat, scooped-out sections underneath, so the thrust of horsepower at the stern would kick their light hulls out of the heavy drag of displacement, wedge them at an angle against the sluggish water, then smack them three-quarters out of the wet stuff altogether into a sweet fast plane that rode as much on air as on liquid.

Smugglers' boats. You could tell by the lines, and the horsepower, and the fact that most were painted in dark colors for night work. A few wore light skirts of Kevlar plating around the cabin, and had slits instead of windscreens in case BON or the Santa Martans were waiting with their heavy machine guns. Two had once borne active armor around the wheel-house, flat tiles of plastique designed to detonate armor-piercing shells before they had a chance to do their work. The tiles had all melted away or exploded in the sun's heat, leaving these craft with an oddly

148

chewed appearance, like puppy toys.

In all the boats, the cargo areas were large. They had too many antennas to be racing craft.

The pilot walked back and forth between the hunched-over worksheds and the crazy-angled docks, shooing away wild donkeys, looking for the right craft among the purple evening shadows. He noticed that Gershwin's wife's cousin had followed him from the Connie, but was too absorbed in his task to think anything of it.

The majority of the boats were useless, hulls cracked or rusted or gone soft with rot. Their engines were missing, or worn out, or burned. The few that looked half-serviceable were either too small or too slow. There were two exceptions; the first, a Deluxe Fountain, with triple Mercruiser powertrains, had a busted skeg and a crack down the port side. It was a little too stiff for ocean work.

The second was a big old Circuit vee-hull with a couple of big-block Fords that might do the trick. However, its hull was made of light fiberglass and looked brittle.

This brittleness was a definite drawback. The waves of the Caribbean, like those of the North Atlantic, had in the last ten years grown seven percent higher, and therefore more dangerous, for reasons no one fully understood but that people suspected had to do with the variations in temperature and wind direction spawned by the same factors that produced ozone showers.

The pilot walked behind one of the turtle schooners hauled up behind the SAR launch, and found more boats hauled between the schooner and the farthermost shed; in fact there were eight or nine of them. But from the huddle of beached craft one shape fanfared out of the evening, one set of dynamic surfaces came together in a pattern so familiar it drove all musings and ennui clean out of his consciousness, sucked the air from his lungs, and stopped him in his tracks under the schooner's scarred counter.

'Miss Benthol,' he muttered to himself, though he knew it could not be the Miss Benthol, the Miss Benthol had last raced fourteen years ago, it had to be one of her successors, the Miss Benthol II, III, all the way up to Six when the Benthol company had given up sponsoring giant unlimited ocean superboats; but they never changed the basics of the craft, for some reason to do with trademark recognition they always hung on to the same clean lozenge of transom, the incredible overhang of bow, the stubby wings on each side with the stabilizer flaps that made her, nearly, a flying machine.

The pilot was almost in a trance with the memory. He found a ladder and climbed till he was standing on the bow of the superboat, looking aft seventy-five feet to the cockpit.

He'd watched these boats when he was a boy. Never live; always on TV, or in the miniaturized fantasy of small plastic model kits. He'd bought the first Miss Benthol kit when he was ten, or eleven anyway – spent days laboring over the thing. He could almost see the tiny bits of engine, gray plastic in their unfinished state, still attached to those intricate plastic trees they were molded on, twenty or thirty different engine parts to a tree, they were so darn daunting when you first unwrapped the cellophane and opened the model box.

Flaking paint on both wings of the real thing confirmed the pilot's guess. Mi *s en ol* III, he read, the familiar red letters shining through a thin layer of camo.

The boat carried two F-16 canopies, port and starboard, one for throttleman, one for driver/navigator, but the controls all had been bunched under the starboard canopy, for single-handling.

The engines were Lycomings, twin T-99s. The port one looked like it might be OK. The starboard was half dismantled, and sand had seeped in through one of the inspection ports. It was getting too dark to see properly, and the pilot had to feel around inside with his hands, recognizing problems by their shape.

His father had not approved, of course. It was not the act of modeling he disapproved of, for he himself collected model trains and later on, when he got laid off from his last railroad, the Vermont Central, would go into the business of repairing and selling HO-scale sets. Rather, it was his own love for railroads, especially old railroads, that got in the way. He could not understand the attraction of superboats, or even the racing turboprops and jet fighters the pilot switched to later. To him they were toys: frivolous, unreliable, delicate aberrations, isolated from the heavy tread of real commerce. Speed meant nothing to Roman Marak; it was getting where you were going, on time, with useful import, that mattered.

He sometimes used to come into his son's room to look over his shoulder; and what was terrible then was not the reaction but the lack thereof, over and above his father's chronic spaciness. '*Miss Benthol*,' he'd say neutrally, glancing at the magnificent assemblage of cockpit and stern-drives and chromed heads, the product of hours of tongue-in-teeth effort. 'Very nice. Don't forget your homework.' And the pilot had got used to it, had even done his share of disappointing, the handful of times the old man tried to close the gap by trying to interest his son in this perfectly functioning BB 2000 electric locomotive, or that ten-wagon replica of the Brno Mail; had disappointed his father, not out of revenge, but simply because trains were slow, and predictable, and not what he wanted to do.

And his father would sigh, and say, 'Your brother liked them,' as if he, Joey, could remember anything his brother liked; as if that could cut any ice with him after seven years in any case . . .

The pilot squatted for a long time by the starboard engine, recognizing coils, intercoolers, injection nozzles, diagnosing how they were sick with the stubby pads of his fingers.

Below the splayed fiberglass wings of Miss Benthol, the tall boy in pleated locks stood, curiously still, gazing upward at the shade against shade that was the pilot.

By the time the pilot was finished the last glimmer of sun had soaked from the sky and the stars were very bright. He had a drink at the Connie, collected his gear, and went to find the owner of the boatyard.

13

'On waking up, before turning in, and any time
your ass feels disoriented, immediately fix your
position, using at least three bearings on known
reference points with righteous angles between
each. It does not matter if your space is psych-
logical or physical: it is good for the ass to know
where it is in space.'

Hawkley
Appendix 'F': 'Navigational Religion'
The Freetrader's Almanac and Cookbook

It took two days of negotiation and five bottles of
Pusser's Rum to get the boatyard owner, a notorious
horsetrader when it came to used boats, to agree on
a price. For twelve thousand Deutschmarks worth of
gold 'King Fook' wafers – the premium currency
of the Trade – as well as six VR-Portables, he agreed
to give the pilot the *Miss Benthol III* and her two
crippled engines. In exchange for another two
Walkmen he threw in use of one of the worksheds
plus tools and generator power for as long as it took
to make the craft serviceable.

It took Gershwin three days to find a cargo. This
was a farmed-out deal, through a DeLisi contact, from

a group in Guajira that talked revolution and Adorno but got rich, mostly, on cocaine and guns. The contract was not for cocaine but for heads, political heads in this case, eleven Chilean activists who wanted to emigrate to the States but had been refused entry because of subversive behavior in their pasts, stuff like opposing the extinction of harp seals, organizing rallies for international peace, supporting Node-communities in Patagonia, or joining rent strikes. A Chilean Adornista group was financing the run with Cumbia concerts and bank robberies. The pickup date was roughly three weeks away; a radio signal, at the last minute, would determine the final rendez-vous.

A courier flew over from Trinidad with the run-money, six thousand Deutschmarks a man, sixty-six thousand Deutschmarks, or forty-five thousand dollars, in thin 'biscuit' wafers of Bolivian silver. The pilot gave Gershwin ten percent. He made a round trip to New York, giving 'Brian Veitch' a rest, using a Canadian UCC-card this time, to deposit the balance in one of his safe-deposit boxes.

With 'head' runs, there were two rules. You always got cash up front, and you never brought it with you. People who forgot the first rule ended up broke; people who forgot the second often ended up face-down, *sans* cash, on whatever dock or airstrip they'd had the poor judgment to bring their cargo to.

With the business settled, the pilot got down to work.

Gershwin convinced him to hire the tall assistant, Eltonjohn, as go-fer and guard. The pilot figured Gershwin was trying to get the kid out of his bar without pissing off the wife. However he agreed, partly because he needed the help, mostly because he owed Gershwin for the contract.

The pilot made another round trip, to Lauderdale this time, to buy engine parts.

He got the port engine running within six hours but the starboard was another matter. Its turboblower was sealed and fairly clean but everything else was a mess. The electrics were frazzled, the Bravo drive rust-bound, the intercooler clogged. Valves and pistons needed retapping and grinding. He had forgotten just how clumsy Eltonjohn was. The kid kept dropping things, or slamming hard tools into soft metal. However, he was so full of enthusiasm, so heavy with sorrow when he screwed up, that the pilot did not have the heart to fire him.

So the pilot attacked the starboard engine like he was fighting a metallic wrestler; shirt off, thumbs in gouge position, using any purchase, any leverage, any mechanical advantage he could. He disconnected and hauled out the turboblower. He pulled out all the cowlings and baffles and jacked the engine up three feet so he could get to it from all angles. He lined up all his tools, then broke down the cooling jacket and the rest of the freshwater system. He bathed the drive gears in a solution of WD-40, Mystery Oil, and kerosene; then, using one-and-a-half-inch socket wrenches slotted into four-foot lengths of pipe, he broke the grip of rust and forced the different components apart. He jury-rigged a boiler from an old scuba tank and reamed out the intercoolers with high-pressure steam. Then he did the same with the fuel system.

The first few days were hard. The engine was a normal secondhand high-performance engine, which meant it was in far worse shape than seemed conceivable at the start. All the injectors needed to be taken apart and cleaned. Two of the alternators needed new bushings.

Pipes broke, bolts sheared, tools bent. Eltonjohn dropped a timing computer in the sand. By mid-morning the temperature climbed to over a hundred in the shed and the pilot had stripped down to shorts and still the sweat came off him, so he looked like he'd just gotten out of the shower.

The pilot's general doubts fed on specific problems. He cursed as he sweated, and strained his shoulders. He wondered why he was killing himself for work he no longer respected as once he had.

But as time passed he felt better. All the old skills were there. He took to diving off the dock every hour and a half, swimming hard underwater in the sapphire-colored sea, and that discipline helped keep him cool both emotionally and physically.

Four or five days into the job he got that odd transition feeling he used to get working for Cal Bigbee. It was the same mental shift he'd felt even earlier, when he started working on old Chevies, in the great hormonal stretch of thirteen when parents mutated, like in science fiction, from strangers to aliens, and girls became so ripe with power you could not look at them without running mortal peril, and a boy's only friends were the machines he worked on and a flatulent retriever mix named Herb. That was the first time he had felt the shift, and the feeling had not changed, it still had the same effect, as if he were one smooth trouble-killing process that started in his brainstem and flowed smoothly through his tools and into the engine he was touching. Sex became the perfect fit of the right socket wrench on a bolt, climax that first grudging ease as it started to loosen. Philosophy was the just understanding of lubrication; how WD-40 soaked into the heart of oxidation, and sweet-talked the molecules, convinced them to change valence, to give in; how oil bribed off friction like a City building clerk or a Johnsonist pastor. The fine erosion of grinding paste on high-tensile valve seatings was esthetic to the Nth degree. His hands — cut, scabbed, permanently black with oil — became high priests in a mystical cult whose chief aim, as in most mysticism, was the perpetual wearing down of tolerance, finer and finer, till you got as close to the primal emptiness as possible. Emptiness was zero friction; emptiness was perfect vacuum. In the space-out of intense work the pilot caught himself asking the same silly questions he used to worry about when he worked on Chevies, or on Cal Bigbee's boats; to whit, Why did man seek the absolute? (Where was the five-eighths socket?) Was it a nostalgia for the womb, for the beginnings of life, some deep yearning for that first shot of warm salty water that cradled the human embryo, and the fish it derived from, and the first amoeba that begat the fish, all the way down to the initial slam of lightning into a hundred primal soups, and the quickening of split and difference into life and, eventually, death (and where in hell was the pressure driver)?

One lunch hour he went looking for Eltonjohn and found the kid involved in a religion of his own. He was standing on the harbor bulkhead, measuring the sun's angle to the horizon with a yachtsman's cheap plastic sextant.

'What the fuck you doin'?' he asked the kid.

157

Eltonjohn did not reply. Slowly, methodically, he finished the sight. He repacked the instrument in its case. Then he took out an object so grimy and dog-eared it was barely recognizable as a book. Using tables in back he corrected the time, the sextant altitude, and looked up the sun's Greenwich Hour Angle. Finally he unfolded a chart of the area and measured a single line with parallel rulers he dug out from his plastic satchel. The line intersected a black rat's nest of lines already drawn, most of them within fifty or sixty nautical miles of Sandworm Cay.

'I'm lookin' for the hex wrenches,' the pilot said, trying hard not to sound annoyed.

'It m-my lunchtime.'

'I know – I just need – what are you doing, anyway? Think the island moved, overnight?'

The kid narrowed his eyes. He picked up the book and held it protectively in one dark hand. From this angle the pilot could make out the three linked squares surrounding a question mark that were the colophon of Charras Press.

'Oh.' The pilot nodded in understanding. 'Hawkley. *That* bullshit.'

The eyes darkened. 'It n-not bullshit.'

'Only for me. You think what you like.'

'It navigation religion.'

'I know.'

'No. No, you d-don't.' Eltonjohn scrambled to his feet. 'I take sun sight at d-dayclean, one at noon. Always grok where you are, always take t'ree bearing, Cap'n Hawkley say.'

'OK, kid. Where—'

'You *still* don't see.' Eltonjohn planted himself in front of the pilot. His expression was almost

158

desperate in its intensity. 'You know where you be, where you andalay. I – I can't. No one on Sandworm Cay knowin' direction. Everyone here stuck, on the island, in life, because of this. Fishermen who g-g-get lost, bartenders for lousy smugglers. Wit' dis religion, maybe I can leave the Cay!'

The pilot looked at Eltonjohn. He got a strong flashback of Roberto again. But he found the good feelings of machine work had bled off some of the shame, and the memory did not hurt as it would have ten days before.

'You don't want to learn how to fly, do you?' he asked suspiciously.

'No, mahn,' Eltonjohn said, and grinned. 'I want t-to learn how to pilot superboat; soon come you teachin' me, no?'

'Of course,' the pilot yelled at him, 'so you can become another smuggler and die like the rest of 'em, or end up in Oakdale, sure, and where's the fuckin' hex wrenches?'

As they walked back into the workshed the pilot noticed Presley, the wiry informer, sitting on the deck of the SAR launch, eating a star-apple.

Days melted into each other.

At some point the pilot took time off to go look for Presley. He found him at his mother's, smoking ganja, listening to shifta rap from a Montego Bay station pulled in by his tinny Walkman. Obeah bottles jingled in the open windows. Presley's mother, a tiny, Spanish-looking woman, fussed in the background, serving bush rum and candied tamarind. The pilot offered him a deal; in exchange for the last VR-Portable and three cheap Virtix serials, the informer would keep an eye on the airstrip and tell him who came in or went out. Presley jerked his machine-pistol slide suspiciously but his eyes never left the shiny black box, the lightweight face-sucker that came with it, lying on the lace covering a ganja crate that was their living room table.

The pilot had no illusions about Presley. He did not expect him to watch the airstrip, even less did he think the bribe would prevent him from telling BON exactly what the pilot was doing, if that indeed was his game – but he did hope the VR-Portable would dull the edges of his attention a little.

In this, it soon appeared, he was successful. The next time he saw Presley, the informer was lying in the shade of one of the boatyard Quonset huts, as quiet as if he were dead. Only his fingers moved, gingerly turning the miniature joystick that was built into the VR deck.

The pilot went back to work after that feeling both pleased with himself, and guilty. When all was said and done, he thought, he had suckered this man into trying something as dangerous in its own way as smack, or ice. Many studies indicated VR-TV trimmed the attention span to less than two minutes; it was suspected that, in the worst of cases, it increased vulnerability to TDF. This was what Presley was risking, all to enable the pilot to run a cargo with less interference.

The trade winds blew without a break. Although the ventilation was welcome, the winds remained hot and did little to cool the temperature in the hangar.

The sea pounded relentlessly on the harbor jetty. The generator thudded. Feral donkeys brayed.

Gawpies screamed at the slow and larcenous lizards.

Nights were long, and the stars accumulating under the pressure of trade winds made them lonely. The pilot slept in the second floor of the abandoned hotel, in a steeply canted room with no glass in the windows, on sand washed up at the lower end. Listening to the mosquitoes struggle to penetrate the netting he'd suspended from a chandelier hook. Feeling the hotel tremble as waves hissed in and out of the rooms below. He thought of Carmelita to ease the solitude. One night his want for her got so strong it spilled over into the physical, translated into internal pressure, the familiar keening tension. Seeking release, he made love to the soft coral sand underneath him, rubbing on his stomach until the repeated movement hollowed below him a female mold of himself. The forms were repeated in his brain, in sense impressions of Carmelita's near-perfect whiteness, in the cold gold memory of a saint's head around her neck, the soft curves between her breasts, between her thighs and belly. Mentally, the perfection of those curves melded to the ammonia-cleanness of feeling he'd once had for her. Her hoarse street laugh, her endless black nights, the slightly weighted pleasure she took in other men's admiration had all been minus-factors in that complex equation. Yet they had possessed value because they were part of the specific alchemy of infatuation and anything to do with that alchemy acquired a white-silver sheen of ultimate freedom, and anything not part of the alchemy was shit. In the tension of excitement he could hear her voice ring amid the soft chuckling of her own pleasure. 'Pilot, *corazon*. Oh, pilot.'

After his own release, however, the memories and

colors shifted into visions. Visions of the Trade; the kind of archetypal images that had kept him in the business after Poop-face; dreams of dark-hulled schooners waiting off night-bound coasts, and bull's-eye lanterns flashing in the dark; long lines of mules with swaddled hooves hauling hogsheads of brandy and boxes of China tea over mountain passes in unpronounceable places.

Slim cloaked women, with dark hair and green eyes, waiting at the inn over the border.

The tension of pursuit, the release of laughter once the cargo was safely through.

During the days they listened to the ECM-pak to kill the monotony. They heard shortwave news from the BBC, waltz music from Osterreichisches Rundfunk, the occasional burst-transmission of coded Federal traffic pulled in by the full-spectrum scanner.

Smuggling traffic on the ham frequencies was way down, as Gershwin said.

Once only, the pilot hooked into an Iridium satellite link to check the Wildnets.

He did this at noon, while Eltonjohn was taking his sun sight. He taped the half-sucker to his flying helmet, swiped his UCC-card, logged on, and let the surf-program pop him through the secure-servers then – just like catching the right wave – ride him through and down the riotous, infinite Web, back into the more spare circuits of the smugglers' Usegroups. Sniffing out, among the thousands of potential combinations, the Wildnets getting traffic that day; figuring, as he usually did, that he could sense, by the volume of illegal traffic, how much heat was being turned on in response.

The search took longer than usual, although that was probably the satellite 'plex. As he waited for the scan to gel he leafed through the only manual he had for *Miss Benthol III*'s engines, trying to make out, through the bottom half of his face-sucker and the mildew of the page, the specs chart for Bravo-drive gaskets.

When the top half of his face-sucker finally blossomed into the thin-lined, polarized world of a Wildnet scan, the patterns it made seemed thin, like flying over Wyoming, where before it had always looked like the Eastern Seaboard, as seen from the air.

He joysticked forward anyway. The feeling the 3-D gave was pleasant and familiar – it was like diving, he realized – like plunging into the transparent waters of the harbor beside him. Banked left, right, dove as the glowing boxes of secure 'servers flitted by, their Fedchip data blanked by security algorithms, which was illegal; but that was what made the Wildnets wild.

Pulling back the joystick, slowing his speed, turning again. Now it felt like he was suddenly much deeper, for there was far less light in this part of the 3-D world.

Most of the lines of communication connecting the various boxes were black, one-directional. It was like the last time he'd checked the 'nets, only more so. If he knew nothing about the Wildnets, the pilot thought, he would figure this was a dead area, a place where every living thing had either been killed, or escaped, or was so tightly protected it might as well be dead. But that last would be illusion; for while the SAPs, mostly, were secure, the lines between them were not, they were part of the overall Web and thus detectable by the Fedchip transponders that every Internet server, since the AGATE laws, was obliged to carry.

So the Fedchips were not all bad, the pilot reflected further as he followed one Usegroup from a cell-phone link in El Paso all the way to a SAP-satellite hookup in Fort Meyers; an old DeLisi hangout. It was the data from Fedchips, along with the pirated NSA software that parsed them, that made this scan possible, and allowed him to track.

Clicking onto the line he read messages written in typical DeLisi style, but with none of the incomprehensible bits of cypher and code that usually obscured their meaning.

Mole 16.

Get back to me, now.

Mole 16. Urgent.

Where the fuck are you?

Abort now.

Abort NOW.

Mole 16.

'Mole 16' was not responding. The pilot checked a couple of Neta hubs. They were on maintenance, carrier only.

Casually, he joysticked over to a South Florida SAP, clicking briefly on a black line; it was the only major datastream coming out of this one. The traffic here looked like a list of commands, all cyphered. He was about to go somewhere else when, in his far lefthand field of view, the Fort Meyers SAP blew up.

The box pulsed briefly; then the light inside it flared to an intensity that hurt the pilot's eyes so much he closed them.

When he looked again, the 'server was gone. The

black lines that had hooked it to the other SAPs in this route pulsed, shriveled like cat whiskers in a candle flame, and then – disappeared.

He glanced around him. The other 'servers were clicking off, the way tree-frogs stop peeping when something lands on a night pond. Within ten seconds every single one was offline. The Florida SAP sector was clear, like a dead sea – almost completely bare of Wild traffic. The only strong light came from a SAP in Homestead.

As the pilot watched, attracted despite himself to the strength of unchallenged light, a search engine came to life next to the 'server. It moved left, and stopped. The black circle holding its Fedchip ID was blacked out, which was normal for Wildnets.

Beside the ID-block, a single word glowed on its own, in sharp purple lines, as if written in neon.

'CONTROL,' the circle said.

The engine grew. From the size of a pinhead, inside a few seconds it had become the size of a quarter, a baseball. It looked like an eighteen-wheeler coming fast at you down a one-way street. Now 'CONTROL' was taking up a third of the 'sucker's world. CONTROL was coming after him—

The pilot ripped off the half-sucker. His fingers were trembling. Shutter fatigue made his eyes sting. He held down his own 'CONTROL,' the left-most key on his ECM, together with the 'ALT' and 'DELETE' keys.

On his lap, the half-sucker screen went blank.

From the helmet audio, he could hear a faint hiss, that gradually lost volume.

At length it was absorbed in the whisper of the trade winds and the sea around him.

* * *

The pilot kept a watch on the broadcast channels. He did not check the Wildnets again.

He did not know what had happened to that 'server — it could have been something simple, like a major power surge — but the sight of the explosion, and those channels shriveling up and disappearing, had left him deeply uneasy.

When he swam, the empty, clear sea reminded him of the silent Wildnet, and the memory cut his pleasure in the sport, so that now he did it strictly to cool his body down, and climbed out of the water almost immediately.

There was no time, anyway, for abstract searches, or sport-swimming for that matter. His spare days were dwindling as the first possible date for the rendezvous approached. Time now was part of the process of repair; it was a function of quality. You marked hours by the ground gained, in increments of fuel flowing, of vacuum achieved, of pressure built.

They got the starboard engine running again, and tuned, and were starting to fine-tune the port when one morning the pilot looked up thoughtfully and said to Eltonjohn, 'Let's see that Bible again — that's the sixth burst on the same frequency, and it's loud.'

The frequency was 4.4191 megahertz, on the single-sideband part of the scan. It was listed in the Smuggler's Bible as a BON Southern District operations channel based at Miami Command Center. The pilot listened for a while, then shut the ECM down. At lunchtime he asked the boatyard manager to travel-lift the superboat into the water before sunset.

He sent Eltonjohn home early that evening and left his pay, in Deutschmarks, at the Connie Bar. After dark he loaded *Miss Benthol III* with the remaining spare parts, storing these in the tight passenger sections he had built into the hull amidships. Then he hand-jerked fuel into two of the tanks, started up the port engine, and rumbled slowly out of the harbor, into the ocean swells, steering north and west for Saint Dominique island.

Almost the last sight he had of Sandworm was that of Presley, standing in the lee of a burnt-out hangar, his wiry body, turning, turning, graceful but with no relevance to the world immediately around him — turning to confront, or watch, or flee the tycoons and fashion models, the beautiful and largely white actors of *Pain in the Afternoon* or *Malibu Heat* or *Easthampton* as they danced and plotted, real as life, in full 3-D before him.

About two hours into the three-hour passage a thin black shape crawled out of the forward hatch and staggered aft against the boat's pounding. The pilot slowed the *Miss Benthol* down and opened the canopies.

Eltonjohn was shaking all over with cold and sea-sickness, but hope was blooming like small herbs in his voice. 'You t-t-take me now, pilot!' he yelled through castanet teeth.

'Get in, you loco islander,' the pilot shouted back, trying hard to press welcome out of his voice. But it was too dangerous now to go back to Sandworm Cay and anyway he had to admit he enjoyed the kid's company.

They got both engines all the way tuned two nights later in Saint Dominique. They filled the long-distance tanks with 103-octane from an airfield fuel truck.

That same night the radio code from the Colombians came in. This meant the rendezvous with the mothership would occur during the next satellite window, in four nights' time at a pre-arranged hour in a pre-arranged spot halfway between the Muertos and Double Headed Shot Cays.

The ECM-pak was still pulling in a lot of BON traffic so the pilot fueled up and left Saint Dominique twenty-four hours early. He anchored off the Muertos while he waited, watching Eltonjohn perform his navigational rites on the beach, in the crazed sun.

He'd not had the energy to maroon the kid on Saint Dominique. He did not know, or care to find out, what marooning would do in terms of psychic damage to a Sandworm islander.

He did not try to reach Gershwin on the ham band-widths.

Since Eltonjohn had stowed away on the boat – left Sandworm without his permission, or anyone else's – the pilot reasoned, a little lazily, that it no longer was his responsibility.

14

'When the Man set up the Anti-Gang and Terrorist
Environment Laws — usually known as "AGATE" —
he jived us like this was so he could waste
Chihuahuan Adornista bomb-throwers. Bullshit.
The bombers did him little harm in the pocket-
book. What hurt him in the wallet was freetraders.
When Congress passed AGATE every one of the
brothers knew it was so BON could off freetraders,
without reference to picayune shit like the Bill of
Rights, using maximum lethal force.'

> Hawkley
> Appendix 'C'
> *The Freetrader's Almanac and Cookbook*

Short-short-long; short-short-long; 'uniform' from a
red lamp.

The signal.

The *Miss Benthol III* groaned uncomfortably in the fat
swells. Her engines farted and popped. Warm rashers
of Gulf Stream water slopped around her narrow
deck. She was not made for idling, or going slow in
any form.

The mother-ship was a big charcoal shape in the
starlight. The twin islands of her silhouette revealed

her ancestry: an ancient, World War II-surplus T-2 tanker. The pilot wondered with the part of his brain that was not tensed for action, where the hell they'd found that rustbucket, when even Panama outlawed carrying oil in single-hulled ships.

The politicals came by rubber raft, outboard driven. In the escaped angles of flashlight the pilot saw with surprise that most of them were Indians. Auracanians, he thought, still on the lam from the heirs of Valdivia. Most of them were in their twenties or thirties, but a couple were very old. They'd all been limited to one bag. At least two of the men had chosen to carry a guitar instead, and one had a small harp. They looked at the superboat in wonder and dismay.

'Where is the sheep?' one of them said.

'Sorry?' the pilot asked, momentarily confused by the idea of woolly animals in the middle of the Caribbean. Automatically he thought of The Little Prince, where a flyer ran into a kid after a crash-landing in the deepest Sahara. The kid's first words were, 'Draw me a sheep.' He shook his head to dispell the association.

'The sheep,' the Chilean insisted.

'Dis is it,' Eltonjohn explained.

Ship.

One of the old men crossed himself twice.

'But, Señor, this sheep is a toy.'

'It's a fast toy,' the pilot answered. 'That's what's important.'

The Chileans looked wildly around them, but the inflatable had left and they resigned themselves to the inevitable with the grace of a civilization that had already weathered four hundred years of concentrated charity from the Catholic Church.

As he and Eltonjohn got the men belted down on the foam-rubber padding of the twin passenger sections, the pilot heard the distinctive held-breath scraping rhythm, the panting pipes of Andean music, and two of the men began to sing.

> Si no encuentro mi amor en la tierra,
> lo encontraré en la mar
> Si no hay justicia en la sierra,
> yo voy a caminar

he heard, before he dogged the hatches down.

He was halfway back to the starboard fighter canopy when the ECM alarm sounded. He sprinted the rest of the way, dangerously, because the hull-top was rounded fiberglass and wet from spray and therefore slippery as slush.

The green eye of the radar scanner display seemed to light up the cockpit. He strapped himself into the bolster-seat. 'Eltonjohn,' he yelled, 'get back here.' Fumbled on his audio helmet ('Attack radar, 306 degrees,' but he had no time for that now); pulling down the half-sucker, goosing the throttles—

But the islander is having trouble dogging down the starboard hatch and is still standing almost upright on the hull when the first lazy sulfur glide of tracers comes out of the horizon into the close confines of their realworld, spitting into the dark swells, snicking into the fiberglass for a second before feathering away.

Lucky shots. The pilot has no idea where they came from. The half-sucker screen is blank. Glancing fast at the ECM, he taps out the VR command. He is unsure why he does this. Seeing targets in 3-D will give him no more info than he has on the flat screen. He can barely spare the time to hook up the VR, he can spare no time to wonder why.

A second volley misses entirely, technicolor fireworks at someone else's party. 'Eltonjohn!' he yells, 'Get the fuck in here!'

There is no answer. No silhouette forward. It is not possible that those first tracers should have hit him. The odds against are too high, no fate so cruel.

A bubble of noise covers the boat. Turbine engines. A Viking takes over the world. It screams one hundred feet overhead like a giant bulbous-nosed bat, blocking the starlight. No rockets yet; the first Viking targets with laser, the second sends rockets down the laser beam. Sweat is greasing the space between his helmet and his scalp. 'Hang on!' he shouts again. 'Eltonjohn, you hear?' There is a round coaming beside that hatch, to protect the radar scanner. Eltonjohn will be fine if he just hunkers behind it.

The cockpit canopy whines down and locks. He shuts the port canopy too. Now the top of the half-sucker blooms with different lights. The pilot leans his head back so he can look through the clear half at the cockpit controls. He pushes the trim tabs to thirty degrees down, gooses the throttles to two-thirds, to attain planing speed. The old superboat drives up her bow, high on a swell, and crashes down so brutally she shakes. He spares a quick sympathy for the poor Indio bastards in the bow compartment, where the movement will be worst. Four, five more crashes, then the movement grows less violent. *Miss Benthol* is planing.

He pushes out the drive units halfway and alters the trim tabs to zero degrees, to keep the bow at a fifteen-degree angle. Checking the compass now, he pulls the boat around till the swells are more or less aft. These waves are definitely higher than the norm. Leans his head forward, making it easier to focus on the face-sucker's top half.

In the stage-set world of VR, four large radar contacts glow, bright lavender, so close it feels like he can almost touch their lighted space. Two are airborne. Vikings. The two other contacts have no readout yet; both are so low they must be ships.

'ADIZ radar.' The audio is on, which is not how it's supposed to work with the VR working but what the hell. 'Attempting lock. Two-nine-three, 186.'

The Vikings will have problems with ADIZ, not only because it works poorly but because it does not work at all on surface craft.

'Hey, fuckhead!' the audio butts in again. 'OTH radar. Seven point two four miles, 101. Weapons radar, 101.'

That's a sea contact, the pilot thinks. A cutter. No patrol boats carry the bulky over-the-horizon system. The presence of a cutter raises questions he has no time to ponder.

The presence of the OTH raises problems he would sooner live without.

A Viking passes through the night, to port, at low altitude, maybe one thousand yards away. Tiny pink dots zip around the swells as the Viking's weapons officer visually searches for his target with the laser.

'Weapons radar, seven-two, lock, one-nine-five. Lock, one-nine-five. Nine point zero one miles.'

The pilot twists the wheel. Raising his head once more, peering through the clear half of the face-sucker, he looks right and left at the ghostly foam. He

173

waits for the perfect combination, low swells that have collapsed on each other, then slows way down on the starboard engine, and speeds up on the port. He does the same with the trim tabs – down to starboard ten degrees, up to port, to keep the hull even – pulling her as abruptly as he can on a southerly course, parallel to the line of waves.

'Hang on, kid,' he thinks, trying mentally to send Eltonjohn his message through the spray drenching the outside darkness.

He goes to three-quarter speed, simultaneously evening the trim tabs, pushing out the drive-units all the way. A cream fountain bursts, far to the left. Shellfire, six-inch probably. Looking up at the 3-D he sees the Viking ranges changing even as he watches. Eleven hundred feet, 187 degrees . . . 185. Circling like vultures for another run.

But rockets, even shells, are no longer the primary danger. Now the turboblowers are winding up to a shriek. The speedo needle nudges eighty-five knots. His fists grip the small wheel hard enough to crush wood. He makes constant little adjustments to keep the superboat screaming just on the backs of the same swells, holding the point of bow on the faint shine of spume marking the crests. Snaking around when he runs out of one wave to find the line of another. The boat smacks right and left as she zips along the ridges, tabs and rudders tearing stiff fifty-foot roostertails from the water, skittering uneasily sideways on the hard edges of her hull. This superboat chinewalks worse than any other he has ever been on.

He is sweating like a squeezed sponge. The only reason his hands don't tremble is that he is holding the wheel so tight. One overcorrection, one tiny wrong nudge of the rudder and he will yaw too far from the ridge of wave. If this happens the boat will tip sideways off the line of swell. Her stabilizing wing will dip into the water, and the boat will cartwheel. Cartwheeling at eighty-five knots is not that different from cartwheeling at 125; she will simply disintegrate, come apart like a schoolboy's poem in a million bits and splashes, spread herself all over the Caribbean.

'You awake, fuckhead?' the audio rasps. 'Proximity alarm.'

Glancing upward, into the VR, to catch a sea contact glowing huge and just off his starboard bow. Shock shines white in the pilot's brain. Then he realizes the patrol boat is so close that Miss Benthol, paradoxically, is quite safe — their relative bearings change so fast at this speed and angle that rocket launchers will not track.

Looking back down, through the clearview screen, his eyes dart right and left like a cornered seabird from wave-top to wave-top. Anomaly rises without other warning from the broad back of a wave just to starboard of him — radar scanners, the long stealth hull, the phallic launchers of a patrol boat — without extra thought he pushes the throttles against their stops.

Spray rips from the maddened props. The Miss Benthol III and the patrol boat share a range of waves for a second, but the superboat's current speed is triple the patrol vessel's, and he loses her in the vicious wake.

The cream fountains are all around again. One hits close by forward and the saltwater cloud it throws rains down like hail on the canopy. The turboblowers scream so shrill he cannot hear the audio. A contact blossoms on the VR, astern, grows fast, as fast as that search engine in the Wildnet. The night glows as a rocket passes close overhead, dims, it feels just like the AMRAAM that missed his Citation over Long Island.

The missile glows a second time as it detonates against the shoulder of a swell.

Hard rain rattles, once again. Miss Benthol is much too low in the water to be a good missile target.

The boat bangs as if she is traveling over cement. The fast patrol craft is capable of speeds up to sixty knots but the Miss Benthol is hitting 110 and still accelerating. The wheel shakes like a fully active ouija board in his hands. His eyes strain through the clearview screen. He lifts the tabs, bringing the bow up a hair. He is going so fast now he does not have time to correct if the wave he is on should drastically change shape. His heart slams, fear scritches at his bowels, but his mind has come free of white light and seems as clear as it has ever been. Rarely, in fact, has he felt so fully alive.

He has no idea how much time has passed. No cream fountains have appeared in the last minute, of that he is certain. The ridge of a swell gives out beneath him; he pulls back on the throttles, to three-quarter speed, to a quarter, and gives her ten degrees downward trim. Momentum dies. Barely planing now, he slides the craft deep into the hollow between two swells, and keeps her there.

The audio mutters ranges. The VR shows three seagoing contacts now, one of them at 4.72 miles, which is too close. According to the readouts, the attack radars have lost their lock. The Vikings are well

176

to the south, flying a grid. The OTH picks him up at intervals.

He has no idea where he is.

He reduces speed even further and feels her settle into the water. He rips off his helmet, opens the canopy halfway and climbs out as quickly as he can on a spinal column that has been ground and twisted like a drill bit during the last few minutes. But there is no one behind the hatch coamings, no one behind the canopy.

Eltonjohn is gone.

His stomach takes the pain, familiarly, like a mother bear clasping her cub.

Back in the cockpit he jacks her sickly into planing mode till the speed reaches fifty-five. He flicks a chart diskette into the ECM.

The sat-nav gives him a fix that puts him only 2.48 miles west of the Double Headed Shot Cays. He is perilously close to their shoal water. He pulls the leather flying helmet back on, adjusts the half-sucker's faceplate. The Vikings are no longer on VR. One of the sea contacts is only two miles away, to the northeast. A voice comes in very loud through the scanner. '. . . this is the *Point Judith*. The *O'Grady*'s got a contact just a couple miles west of the Shots. He seems to have stopped. We're comin' up on him fast, over.'

'Roger, *Point Jude*, this is *Cape Fear*. *O'Grady* says we should circle in from the north, cut him off. We got him now, over.'

'*Nuke the motherfucker*,' another voice chimes in quietly.

Fury wells up inside his abdomen; it is unexpected in its intensity. The fury is mostly projected; he has never taken the government's enmity personally but

177

he will not let them disappear his Chileans the way
they disappeared Eltonjohn, he will not let them sink
Miss Benthol — not if he can help it. He knows his
chances are not so good at this stage but he flips the
all-channel toggle anyway, and presses his throat
mike.

'BON eats shit,' he says. It is not intelligent, far less
original, but it's the best he can think of at short
notice with the pain of Eltonjohn blocking his
synapses on top of it.

Again checking the chart on the ECM screen he
notices a detail he has not really picked up on before.
The channel between the Double Headed Shots is thin
and shallow but at its deepest it might just allow Miss
Benthol to pass. The drawback is that the superboat will
have to be planing at full tilt with her bow level when
she goes through the channel because that is
when she is highest out of the water. The channel is
too shallow to putter prudently through.

It is insane; also it is their only chance. Anyway,
the arrival of sadness has made him reckless.
Eltonjohn, Carmelita, Roberto — in all that damage he
bears a heavy load of responsibility. It makes no
logical sense, it makes perfect emotional sense, but
what he feels is this; if *he has caused damage he should be
prepared to risk it himself.*

Moving the cursor on the chart screen he measures
out a dogleg course, 016 degrees true, nor'nor'east at
sixty knots for three minutes and twenty-six seconds;
then through the gap between the Shots on 282
degrees, more or less in the same vector as the waves,
which will be curving around in the shallow water to
attack the coral of the cays directly at that point. He
punches in the way-points, almost forgets to convert

the true bearings to compass. It's the kind of detail that kills you.

Two hundred eighty-two degrees true, plus 2 degrees westerly variation; 284 degrees.

He checks his watch, switches the ECM to active radar, turns off the chartlight. Gunning the engines, he reaches sixty knots, heading for the first compass bearing indicated. 'Here we go, chiquita,' he tells the superboat. He sees Carmelita's face, pale and closed the way he last saw her. His lips tighten, his eyes narrow.

At 3.2 minutes the way-point alarm sounds. He lines her up to follow the scend of sea. He adjusts the course to 284 and kicks the throttles three-quarters of the way forward. Miss Benthol III rides up on her flat buttock-lines and starts skittering from wave to wave. She is listing a bit left, he notices. One of the bullets may have holed a port flotation tank. When she jumps a wave her port side starts to dip, lazily. It is a sign of extreme peril.

He adjusts the trim tabs, giving the starboard tab fifteen degrees downward angle and the port one close to twenty. The bow drops in response, the wheel stops pulling left so much.

A line of greater darkness seems to stretch right across the night. Somewhere in the middle of it there is a channel, quite thin in all dimensions. He risks another glance at the ECM's screen. The sat-nav cursor is right on target, heading for the break between the cays.

Tracers sear like hot wires above them, then, inexplicably, cease.

The waves are breaking now, losing their form, churning into amorphous fields of surf that actually smooth the superboat's passage. They are very close to the Double Headed Shots. He nudges the throttles forward again. Eighty-nine mph. The VR display is useless now, crammed full as an old attic with redundant radar echoes. The creaming surf spits into a curtain of spray before him. Tall black shapes of coconut palms rush out of the waves to his left – disappear. He has no way of knowing if he is really in the channel. All he can do is keep going. If he slows down, the keel will hit coral and the hull will turn into little crumbs of glass and metal and the flesh it carried. They are dead if they hit, they are dead if he slows. There is a curious freedom in this.

The dials look at him, sea-colored light with a message of systems still functional.

A long denture of coral grins to starboard and vanishes. He turns to port a hair. Checking downward, the cursor looks like it is stuck; it's too big for the channel displayed on the chart diskette.

And then, all of a sudden, the water is much calmer. They are to leeward of the islands. The VR display shows a solid chunk of land as far as the radar will reach behind him. The OTH radar, too, is screened by the Double Headed Shots.

The patrol boats are far too big to negotiate the channel. It will take them half an hour to go around. The Vikings are overhead at four thousand feet, but their own radar will not find him in the swells, and without surveillance craft to guide them they are blind.

He brings the tabs back to level, keeps the throttles on three-quarter setting, clicks the ECM display to small-scale.

15

'Oh, la soeur Anne n'a pas de jambes,
Maman est toujours sâoulée
Et moi je fais la contrebande,
Laisse le bon temps rouler.'

Barataria folk song

Fifty miles to the northwest of the Double Headed
Shots the pilot brought the *Miss Benthol* to idling speed
and went forward to see how his passengers were
doing.

They were not in good shape. A tracer round had
pierced one man through the fleshy part of the calf.
The phosphorus burned his flesh and he moaned and
sweated in pain. The rest without exception had been
violently seasick and the acrid stench of half-digested
frijoles permeated the passengers' sections. But none of
them asked to stop, or go back. They, too, were fresh
out of choices.

The pilot broke out the *Miss Benthol*'s first-aid kit. He
gave them five minutes to get some air and clean up.
As they washed themselves on deck he thought about
what he was going to do now. He was originally
heading for the Ten Thousand Islands but now he

181

figured the Florida swamps, as the only half-empty stretch of mainland close by, would be the first place BON would search.

On the ECM he called up the latest Smuggler's Bible update. The AWACS radar picket out of Homestead was down until 4:20 a.m.; anyway the synthetic aperture radar they used was calibrated for use against planes and though it could pick up surface traffic it was less than effective against small craft. The BON Vikings were behind him. The US Customs DC-3 ran a three-way pattern from Lauderdale to Key West to Sanibel but was on its way home.

The next satellite sweep was an hour and forty-eight minutes away.

He could head into the Gulf, then east to Sanibel. He looked at the chart again.

He had one further option. The Mississippi Delta lay some 550 sea miles to the northwest of here. The *Miss Benthol* was built for long-distance racing, and with her shallow draft could cut straight across the Gulf. Seven of her eight massive fuel tanks were still full. As long as the leak in the port compartment was not too serious, as long as he could maintain two-thirds speed, he could make bayou country by dawn. Once there he would have enough gas on tap to maybe find a village where he could hide the super-boat from the Feds, for use some other day. He knew of several such villages, from the *Smuggler's Gazette*, from Trade backfence, from talking to people like Gershwin.

He wanted to save this boat. Gershwin's words – 'How many boats you sink, pilot?' – still prickled. Well he wasn't gonna lose this one. He drove out of his mind the news he would have to tell

Gershwin next time he talked to him.

The pilot clambered out on deck again and opened the inspection hatches. The Number Two watertight compartment was half full of sea water. Number Four had a gallon or so sloshing in the bilge from a slow leak. Not too bad. He sucked out the water with a hand pump, then went forward to order his passengers below.

The short, shallow seas of the Gulf of Mexico seemed calm after the Caribbean. The pilot cruised at a steady eighty-six knots, cutting straight as a bandsaw through the New Orleans/Galveston shipping lanes, giving a wide berth to the barges and shrimp boats and oil rig supply vessels.

Maybe the traffic will confuse them, he thought, if they're watching up there.

The patrol boats were gone, though, and the Vikings had never picked him up after the first two passes. Perhaps they'd never understood the speed Miss Benthol was capable of.

The long run gave him plenty of time for thinking about Eltonjohn. He had come to care for the kid over the fortnight he'd worked with him. Eltonjohn had felt almost like Roberto had by the end, minus the time and miles of course. Still their friendship had some of that same kid-brother warmth, and the loss sat like a lead frog at the pit of his gut. It shaded all his thoughts and changed the colors of his small world of cockpit, and ECM, and sea.

But in some shape or form the therapy of mechanical work continued to act as long as the valves and pump systems Eltonjohn had helped repair whined and roared with the smoothly controlled hysteria of healthy machinery. Thus, when it turned inward, as it had to, to be digested, it did not shade into guilt or shame at the trade he plied. Instead, once again, it ripened into anger and a lust for confrontation.

Goddam them, he thought, 'Screw those sons-abitches,' he yelled at the plexiglass canopy. 'Fuck the BON, perpetrate them, rot their guts!' he screamed over the whine of turboblowers and the repetitive crunch of water. He smashed his fist repeatedly against the cushioned dashboard to bleed off the pressure.

It helped that he was not working for Chico Fong, this time. It helped that the cargo was not useless cold pale-green mineral, sluiced from the unhappy earth with the blood of innocents for people whose idea of value lay in the values others ascribed to things. The cargo he and Eltonjohn were carrying was the only precious cargo there was; it was humans, whom no one had any right to limit or proscribe; it was ideas, ideas on the hoof, darting delicate repetitions of infinitely small voltage lined up in complex equilibria in one mind; waiting only to be tested, in such honesty as he or she was capable of, against the balances and complexities outside. No one, least of all governments, had the right to stop such a miracle at borders.

Anger did not dilute or cheapen his sadness. It did not wear it out. It only directed it.

The leak in the port compartments got worse and he had to stop every two hours, then every hour and a half, to pump them out. The drag of the sodden hull cut his speed, both because of the extra weight and because of cavitation from the steeply canted trim tabs he used to even out the discrepancy. This, in turn, meant the passage took even longer.

184

When, nine hours later, he brought *Miss Benthol* burbling grouchily up Caillou Bay and through the Rivière Méchant Caillou, the pilot's body was tired and beaten. His eyes burned with shutter fatigue, and the effort of keeping constant lookout in four directions at once. But the mourning and anger still shone bright as an unknown-soldier's flame in the fathom of his mind.

The superboat moved viscously up the Bayou Noir, like a snake with a high-pitched whine. Once he got in the close waters of Caillou the pilot no longer had stopped to pump out, and the port waterline was a foot lower than the starboard, but her wake ran slick and straight through the green scum of duckweed into the trees.

The sun had risen an hour ago behind thick mauvish clouds. Upside-down perch heaved on the little waves. Sick alligators watched from cover. Tupelo and bald cypress bowed low on every side under the weight of kudzu, and Spanish moss. The kudzu was healthy but the moss was soggy and sick and hung in huge patches like bad, green toupees. The pilot, incongruously, was reminded of the White Angel's – the Yankee trees adorned with moss imported to remind Evangeline of home.

Where the bayou was not choked with duckweed, or water hyacinth, the water flowed around *Miss Benthol* in different colors; pink, lavender, pea-green, various shades in between. The colors came from the effluent of chemical plants and refineries up the Mississippi delta from Bayou Noir.

The village of Bayou Noir was exactly where the ECM said it should be. At the precise second the cursor touched the last corner on the liquid-crystal display, a thin pattern of wooden houses, painted white, interconnected by long porches and board-walks of locust, appeared from behind a stand of tupelo, around a bend in the rainbow river.

The docks of a boatyard loomed, overhung by swamp cedars, most of them brittle or dead.

The pilot dropped off his passengers at the town dock, right beside a payphone and a cement statue of Queen Ida. They walked with difficulty. The one with the leg wound did not walk at all. They did not kill themselves trying to thank the smuggler. He couldn't really blame them.

The pilot tied up at the boatyard. Although it was past nine in the morning, the yard manager's office was empty. He unhooked the ECM-pak, snapped it shut, slid the strap over one shoulder, hung his chart-case on the other. His back was full of kinks and his thighs ached from the compression-shocks of high ocean speed. Even on the motionless ground, his brain felt like it was still rocking.

He shuffled stiffly down the boardwalk. The locust planks groaned like women in pain. The sun beat down on dry dirt roads. Kudzu hung so thickly on the outside walls of houses that some of the windows were completely in shadow; they looked like eyes peering from under eyebrows of dark green. There was no sound – no cars, or people talking, or dishes being washed. No sign of life except for a couple of bald cats who hobbled off into the kudzu as he passed.

He kept walking, trying to put some distance between himself and his cargo. The village petered out behind him. In the thundering silence he could

186

almost hear Eltonjohn's voice.

A sound of big cylinders and bad mufflers floated around the first bend in the main road, followed shortly thereafter by a 1960s Ford, the kind with the sides that curled around like lettuce at the top, painted in Sherwin-Williams red. The truck stopped beside him. The cloud of dust it raised settled slowly. Three men in the front told him to climb in. When he hesitated, one of them poked a rusted shotgun barrel through the open window. When he asked where they were going, the men told him it was Sunday, as if that were explanation enough.

The people of Bayou Noir were assembled around a baseball diamond up the bayou from the village. A softball game was in progress. The men in the pickup brought him to one of the benches. The one with the shotgun stayed. The other two made him open his ECM-pak. They looked at each other, and carried it to one side, parking it beside a large and slobbery hound tied to a cedar post. Then they got back in the truck and headed down the road they had come on.

The pilot looked about him. He figured there had to be eighty or ninety people here. The men wore jeans and flannel shirts and chewed tobacco. The women had on cotton print dresses, and stirred pots full of food that smelled of garlic sausage. Everyone drank Rebel beer and ran the bases barefoot. No one spoke in English.

'Excuse me,' the pilot said, but the man with the shotgun told him to shut up and everyone else ignored him.

Shouts rose in Cajun French whenever someone scored a hit. It did not seem to matter to either side who scored. Between innings, people came and huddled around the near bench to talk animatedly with a trio of men. All three of the men were short and well into their seventies. Two of them wore long white beards. A group of younger men picked up accordions and guitars and sang.

> *C'est ça, Jeanne Marie, ouvre bien tes jambes;*
> *Oh way, oh way, c'est comme ça—*
> *Vois bien, Jeanne Marie, comme je bande;*
> *Viens me voir au Bayou Noir.*
> *Au Bayou Noir, l'eau est rose;*
> *Oh way, oh way, c'est comme ça—*
> *Dieu propose, Exxon dispose;*
> *Viens me voir au Bayou Noir.*

There were a lot of people with no hair around the bench, the pilot noticed, and a lot of wheelchairs.

At the next inning one of the short old men turned to the pilot and said, 'Tu joues short field.'

'What?'

All the little old men started yelling at once. For a brief, hallucinatory moment, the pilot fancied he had seen this exact scene before, and almost immediately he realized where; it was in The Wizard of Oz, and he was far from Kansas, and the old men were jumping and shouting at him to follow the Yellow Brick Road. But they all repeated the same term. 'Short field, short field,' they shouted in an accent that was half southern and half a contorted and ratcheted sound the pilot supposed was Creole.

'But I'm no good,' the pilot told them, holding up his hands.

It was true. All through school he had ducked gym

and softball to build models of racing machines, or hang around the Oswego Raceway.

'Short field! Short field!'

A girl with long, jet-black hair and huge eyes sat in one of the wheelchairs. She looked at him in contempt. The hot sun made spears of light against her stacked crutches. The pilot shook his head in confusion, picked up a mitt, and went to the position, wondering what in hell was going on. The Smuggler's Bible listed Bayou Noir as being fairly safe for the Trade, for three reasons. First, the people here were descendants of the privateer and smuggler Jean Lafitte, who had saved Andrew Jackson's ass in the battle of New Orleans, and they were proud of that role, and of its implications.

Second, the government did nothing to stop the refineries upriver from dumping their 'benign' wastes, mostly toluene and vinyl chloride, in the delta, causing miscarriages, birth defects, and levels of leukemia in Bayou Noir several times the national norm.

And third, ever since the cotton and rice fields were bought up by Bowlions. Westland and other agribusiness concerns, there was no work any closer than Lafayette. So most of the people here made their living handling cargoes of grass run from further south.

For all these reasons the inhabitants of Bayou Noir were supposed to help out when smugglers, even from a different sector of the Trade, showed up on their doorstep. But the way people looked at him as he twisted his mitt, and the way the adrenaline sang in his blood, told him something was off here; something was badly wrong.

189

The first batter struck out. The second slugged a line drive straight at the pilot as if he was aiming at his head. The pilot stopped it with his mitt, but the ball dropped and the batter made first with no problem.

The pitcher spat tobacco juice. An ancient woman in a straw hat stood up from the far bench and screamed in Creole, waving a rolled-up umbrella toward short field.

The third batter grounded, again in his direction. The pilot ran at the ball, picked it up successfully, winged it to first, which was the wrong play. The runner on first made it to second. The crowd murmured.

'*Vais t'apprendre à jouer, p'tit con!*' the old woman screeched. The pilot blushed; he knew what 'petit' meant. The crowd laughed. '*Bien dit, Madame Bergeron!*' someone yelled.

As the next batter came up, swinging four practice bats to loosen his shoulders, the pilot saw the pickup truck jouncing heavily up the road with ten illegal Chileans standing and one sitting in the back. He checked that the switchblade was still in his boot. He looked around the field, wondering how far he could make it if it came to running.

The fourth batter hit the ball skewy, bouncing it toward the pilot who fumbled it. The first runner made third. The pilot let the ball lie.

The old woman, Madame Bergeron, hopped out of the crowd and scampered on crooked legs at the pilot, screaming and flailing her umbrella. He dodged the old woman, picked up the ball and threw it out of play. 'What the fuck is going on here?' he shouted at the pitcher. Then he jumped backward a second time to avoid Madame Bergeron's umbrella.

The crowd fell silent.

A bird croaked in the mangrove outfield. There was a heavy scent of hyacinth, and the beginnings of a pattern. He always seemed to end up like this, the pilot thought; stuck up funny-colored rivers marking some kind of border; dealing, in a language he did not know, with cultures he did not understand, in matters that got people dead.

The old men on the bench waved him over. Madame Bergeron picked up a mitt and took over his position.

'*Calme-toi,*' one of the old men, the beardless one, said. 'Sit. Old Agathe, she always second-guess short field. Don't take it personal.'

Buttocks shifted on the rough wood. He sat.

'*Il est pas poulet. T'as vu son* catch?'

'Crazy, *mon vieux,*' one of the people in wheelchairs spoke up. 'Crazy, *mais pas flic.*'

'What they sayin'?' he asked the beardless old man.

'We thought you might be heat,' the old man said. 'We thought you might be BON. But the council—' he gestured around him '—we decided you prob'ly not.'

'You're the council?'

Nods.

'Because of how I play softball?'

'*C'est cela,*' the old man agreed. 'It's miraculous, what you learn, from how people play. That's how we suss this town; playin' softball. We got a bitch-up issue, *hein?* We call a game, to see which side will win. We get a stranger, we always make him play. That's how we make decisions – that's how we know who to trust. Also,' he added with a grin, 'we find your cargo.'

191

'You the first cargo to make it in two months,' the girl with the big eyes said, and there was a hint of curiosity in how she said it.

'Then you're not callin' BON?' the pilot asked, to make sure.

All three men shook their heads at the same time.

'We're like you, boy,' one of the white beards said. 'No friends of the government. But BON's net is tightening. Everybody knows that. They want to file-thirteen the Trade and everyone in it. We have to be real careful. Don't take it personal.'

'So I can andalay?'

The old men looked around. Some of the wheel-chairs moved closer. The girl threw a handful of something in her lap, looked at it, and closed her eyes. There were a few nods. 'On le laisse aller,' the girl agreed. A vote, of sorts, had been taken.

'Vas y, camarade,' the girl added. 'You can go when you like, and your cargo too.'

She gathered up what she had thrown in her lap. A dozen small white shells with pink openings lay amid the deeper pink of her palm.

One of the old men walked over to where the hound was tied up. He easily lifted the ECM-pak and the chartcase in one hand and dumped them at the pilot's feet. Then he reached in the pilot's right boot, and lifted the switchblade's handle clear of the top.

Looking up, he grinned.

He had very few teeth.

The pilot did not leave immediately. He drained and winterized the Miss Benthol's engines. He found the boatyard owner and asked him to patch the holes in the port compartments with West System epoxy. He arranged to send payment from New York, with an extra fee so the yard would move the boat up one of the rotten creeks and cover her with netting and moss to hide her from the cameras of Predator VIIs and the prying radar of manned BON aircraft.

He bought a 1983 Chevy Malibu Classic sedan and a boxful of tools from the big-eyed girl's father. The car was somewhat rusted, but its age was an advantage; auto manufacturers did not start putting antitheft transponders in passenger cars until the late Nineties. Without a transponder, the car could not be identified at a distance.

He tuned the engine, fitted a bigger exhaust port and tailpipe. He replaced the carb with two carburetors of the same size from a wrecked Olds, so it would really go. He had dinner at the girl's house.

Françoise's eyes held many levels, and each level contained a message. Winter was lonely on Bayou Noir, and that much lonelier if you could not walk.

Her eyes were the kind of black that, like a night sky, was full of deep lights made small by distance. They gave the pilot goosebumps when they made contact with his own.

But the death of Eltonjohn was too close to the surface of his brain to let her in. He ate the rice and garlic sausage without really tasting them. He gave Françoise the address of his forwarding service. After dinner he got in the car and headed north, up Routes 1, 90 and 10.

A day of driving took him to Interstate 95. Then it was a straight shot to New York City.

16

'. . . In the 1970s . . . the agency adopted the
trappings of bureaucratic accountability — control at
the top, superior-subservient relationships, orders,
close supervision, rules and regulations, and hier-
archical reporting relations began to dominate
NASA's technical culture. Many engineers, instead
of doing hands-on engineering work, were shifted
to supervisory oversight of contractors' work . . .'
                                    Diane Vaughan
                            The Challenger Launch Decision

Juanita Chavez visited Carmelita three days after the
pilot arrived back in the US via Bayou Noir. Twenty
minutes later, sobbing, she left her daughter, also in
tears, in front of the recreation room TV on the
twenty-ninth floor of the South Mental Health Tower
at Bellevue Hospital.

Billy Flagman saw her crying and went to fetch
Rocketman. This took a long time. Billy had to move
carefully because he realized how incredibly dangerous it was to put your faith in material things like
floor, or linoleum, or walls.

Billy had studied physics. He had once been an
artist in the East Village. His shtick, as a painter, was

194

to study the texts of Fermi and Heisenberg and Hawking, and reproduce in his canvases the relationships traced, at several removes, in particle accelerators.

Thus, he knew that what men thought of as the 'building blocks' of matter, like molecules, atoms – even quarks, strange particles, muons – was nothing more than vast lonely domains of empty space with a few minuscule bits of matter floating around, all by themselves – like croutons on a soup of great darkness – linked only by forces so vague physicists had to resort to poetry to name them.

So Billy took it slowly as he moved down the halls of the mental health unit, never relying on floor alone, but climbing from chair to couch to table, or at least keeping a hand on walls, and door jambs, and other fixtures whenever he could reach them.

He found Rocketman in his room, reading an article in the *Grassy Knoll Monthly* that explained how John Lennon, JFK, and Dag Hammarskjold, lured by a cousin of Jackie Bouvier who was also Lee Harvey Oswald's confidant, had all been assassinated by a cabal of Southwestern oil magnates known as the 'Sour Lake Roustabouts.'

Carmelita was still crying when Rocketman got there. A dozen other patients, men and women, sat around her. Their eyes reflected the TV's colors.

'Zero Cola,' the TV said. 'No calories, no nutrition, no diet problems. The only soft drink guaranteed to contain *absolutely nothing!*'

Carmelita sat stiffly. The tears rolled softly down her face, dripped off her nose and made gray splotches on the envelope she held in her lap.

She made no move to resist when Rocketman took

the letter. Rocketman, for his part, made no show of asking her permission. Like Billy, he was interested in the idea of solidity; unlike Billy, it was not the solidity of matter that interested him, but the weight and mass of pain.

In Rocketman's mind the concept of privacy had no weight against the reality of pain. Pain was something that carried substance everywhere, and above all in Bellevue. Here it was hard and concrete as the nurse's gaze, as the iron doors and screwed-down tables. The drugs the doctors tried out on you changed the shape and color of pain but never blocked its source. What it came down to was, you fought with pain hand-to-hand when you could and you shut it out like a horde of hyenas when it let you. It was the only way to function in this place.

Carmelita's letter was dated five days before. It was written in pencil on the back of a receipt for 'Personal Items Consigned during Long-Term Detention.' The receipt had the words 'Secure Corrections Corp.' printed on top. It was wrinkled and grimy. It was signed Roberto Chavez. 'Roberto,' Rocketman explained, 'look, it's from your brother, he's alive!' But Carmelita said nothing, and her gaze did not waver from the TV screen.

Dear sister,

(Rocketman read.)

I don't have much time to write this. If you get it you know I'm alive and Mama does too, I got rocketed and they blew off half my tailplane and I ditched. I hurt my leg bad and was picked up by a Coast Guard ship and they're going to send me to Oakdale.

'Damn,' Rocketman muttered, scraping a large hand nervously over his chin.

I'm with eight guys in a BON holding tank. They say it's at the El Paso computer center, but I haven't seen shit. One of the guys paid off a screw to send out letters and I hope to the Holy Mother he stays paid off and isn't a plant I don't know. So this is one bitch of a risk but if I'm going to Oakdale it don't matter so much.

Listen Carmie if you get this tell Skid to get the hell out quick because the BON have this new system that is a hundred percent surefire way to nail any even solid contraband operation and they are doing this system now. These guys here are from Black Tuna and the DeLisis and they got it and if they can get the big ones the small ones are cooked too. The only big guys left is a couple Santa Martans and a Tong system. Also the Hawkley people are still working. The guys say Hawkley knows how to get around this new system. If he does he better tell, otherwise it's bye bye to the Trade I guess, which is too bad cause like the man said it been berry good to me (joke). Also they could get to Skid through me. Tell him I say so, tell him to get out. Listen take care of our Ma and don't worry about me and do your go-go skating you're real good and I love to see you dance love

Roberto

197

'Damn,' Rocketman said again, when he'd finished the letter. 'Ah, *damn*.'

He looked at Carmelita, trying to push his sympathy into her with the pressure of eyes, with stomach tension, with sharp and concentrated thought, but the girl's position stayed exactly the same and her gaze did not change.

The TV babbled on. 'Ear Guard,' it yelled, 'Ear Guard. And you thought you'd never *heard of ear odor!*'

Rocketman thought about what Roberto had written. He tried to block from his imagination the press of fear and affection that had squeezed those words with hoarded ballpoint onto secret paper.

Affection for Roberto's sister; care also for the pilot, who Roberto said was in serious danger.

But it was up to Rocketman to warn the pilot. No one else was going to do it. And that meant—

He could not stay any longer in this place where the steel doors kept pain from coming in and agony from getting out so that a balance was achieved and policed by Nurse Linda and the various and ever-changing psychiatric interns with their plastic cups full of Stelazine and lithium carbonate.

This was it, Rocketman thought. This was what he'd been waiting for.

It was time to elope from Bellevue.

Rocketman got a light from the nurse's station. He sat beside Carmelita, smoking hard, for a few minutes. He held her hand, and plotted. As he plotted his back straightened slowly. His mouth pulled upward, gradually and surely, till he was grinning from ear to ear.

Billy Flagman and Lobo both wanted to go to the roof with Rocketman.

Billy was Rocketman's official assistant, but he had a serious drawback on roof trips. The trips always involved sneaking through a panel Rocketman had removed in one of the linen closets, and crawling on hands and knees through an elevator maintenance space and then up narrow service stairs. Billy found these new vistas of unfamiliar matter terrifying, and hung back, clutching the walls, taking five minutes to cover the simplest expanse of hospital tile, double that to get up the stairs, which could be a definite problem, to say the least, if guards came along.

Lobo, on the other hand, was an asset. He always carried spare hacksaw blades. He functioned as scout on these expeditions, loping up and down the forbidden passageways; sniffing the wind, dropping on all fours if he sensed something wrong, growling like a distempered dog if it came close.

This time, one way or another, they all made it. Around eight p.m. Rocketman unlocked the door to the elevator machinery housing with a set of skeleton keys the pilot had brought him. Lobo prowled the limits of the roof, and Billy Flagman hung on to a heat duct and suspiciously watched the snow drift down and the buildings blink lights and the black tide of the East River flow thirty-one stories below.

Inside the housing the rocket was ready. It was squat, only ten feet tall, and round. Its framework was constructed largely of aluminum pipes from the hands-on therapy workshop. Rocketman had been building it for three years. From top to bottom, it consisted of: a detachable nose-cone, with three USAF surplus parachutes folded neatly inside; an enclosed passenger nodule with padded seating and hydraulic controls; and two tanks of oxyalcohol hooked up through a Krauss turbopump to a Hermes hydraulic steering system, part of which the pilot had smuggled in on his last trip. The controls in the cabin led to the hydraulics solenoids, the tank valves and the parachute release. The letters OSTV were painted on the rocket's side in heat-resistant ceramic paint.

OSTV stood for 'Orbital Smuggling Test Vehicle.' It was the pilot's idea, of course.

Space smuggling, the pilot commented the first time Rocketman broached the idea of a Bellevue launch. It would be the ultimate contraband route. There were no borders in space.

Rocketman and Billy gazed at their creation in admiration and some wonder. Lobo looked at the stars outside and gave a plaintive and experimental howl.

'You really gonna do it, Dumont?' Billy asked. Dumont was Rocketman's real name. Only the doctors, and Billy, were allowed to use it. Rocketman was large enough to enforce his taste in monikers.

Rocketman did not answer. He was staring at the bearings of the thrust chamber and the valves of the fuel tanks above. He knew to within five degrees the heat they could withstand. He was familiar with their pressure limits, but he'd been familiar with the parameters at Thiokol and they'd still lost the ship and all the men and women in her.

His intestines tied in knots as they always did when he thought of how gases from the LOX squeezed through the seals on field joints connecting sections of the rocket booster. As always, the image of Judy Resnick projected itself on that memory. In his mind he could see her, doing her job right the way down, the capsule plummeting, shaking, nonetheless she had gone ahead and switched on emergency oxygen for the guy in front of her while G-forces stretched her slim body and the loveliness of her face was racked obscenely with the certainty of death.

He had seen Judy Resnick once on a visit to Canaveral, had lusted after her with the pure, ethereal lust one felt for stars, or people who seemed reserved for stars.

Rocketman's fists were balled and tight. His back was hunched, as if he were carrying a great weight.

But it was not his fault. The fifty-three-degree cut-off was his baby. They had asked him, during that famous caucus at Thiokol, why some tests showed good durometer on those seals at much lower temperatures, and he'd answered as best he could, arguing that you always got exceptions, that science was all about unknown variables, you had to take the safe approach. At first Lund agreed; but Lund was only a scientist, and he was fighting managers, a whole bureaucracy of them, and most of those managers were Air Force, or ex-Air Force, and they were not interested in uncertainty. 'Take off your scientist hat,' they told him, 'put on your manager hat'; and Lund changed his mind, though the temperature on the morning of launch was in the low 30s only.

So Rocketman was overruled. He bore no responsibility. The disaster, he since had realized, could be laid at the door of those who *wanted* the launch to fail; it was the fault of the clique at the Pentagon's top levels who wanted the Air Force to have its own 'independent spacelift capability,' in the jargon.

For the Air Force to have its own rockets, they had to scupper NASA's.

201

The Orion Group, the Orion conspiracy. They had sabotaged the NASA launch. The article he was working on for the *Grassy Knoll Monthly* would prove this beyond reasonable doubt. It all started with the Key West space-missile compact between the Navy and the Air Force; it ended with a deliberate decision to increase the level of risk in the shuttle program so a system eventually would fail, giving the Air Force Space Command an opening to take over the manned spaceflight brief that once was NASA's.

Evidence of that decision would clear him of blame, once and for all, and wipe the dark reproachful eyes of Judy Resnick forever from his mind.

It was very cold on the roof. The snow, light and dry, blew through cracks in the machinery housing. Rocketman shook his head free of the heavy touch of memory. The ghosts of the *Challenger*: the New Hampshire schoolteacher, the lovely Jewish engineer; stepped back into the shadows. He straightened his back and clapped his hands to warm them. He thought it was lucky there were no Morton Thiokol 'O'-rings on his makeshift missile to grow brittle tonight. He bent over to check carefully the Hermes solenoids, but nobody had tampered with them. No one ever came in this old vent housing anyway, because the equipment had been disconnected years ago so the hospital administration could buy new elevator motors from a firm owned by the brother of a man on the City Board of Estimate.

The three men easily rolled the light rocket, on gurney wheels affixed to its thrust skirt, to the middle of the roof.

'Let me do it, Dumont,' Billy burst out suddenly, as the Rocketman started doing a final systems check. 'Let me pilot it.'

'We been through this before, man,' Rocketman said. 'It's not going high enough.'

Weightlessness was Billy's great fantasy. He saw himself outside earth's orbit, floating free inside the tiny capsule, totally independent of floor, walls, and ceiling. He would take one of the hospital's portable oxygen units with him. For a few brief minutes he would not have to worry about outside matter. To all intents and purposes, there wouldn't be any.

'At six miles of altitude,' Rocketman explained patiently, 'you'd still be well in the gravity field when you ran out of fuel.'

Billy frowned. He thought his friend was hiding the truth. He thought this was because Rocketman wanted to fly the thing himself.

'But can't you take a passenger?' Lobo asked. 'I been losin' weight.'

'Not enough thrust, Lobo. You know that.'

Lobo nodded. He got up in a slow, graceful unfolding movement and padded over to the west side of the roof, to look longingly in the direction of the Central Park Zoo.

In the daytime, Lobo inhabited the normal, even staid psychic confines of a minor tax advisor in an H&R Block office, which was what he had been before coming to Bellevue.

At night, Lobo became aware of the greatness of that lie, for the darkness brought home a bigger and incontrovertible truth; that he was an Alaskan timberwolf trapped in the body of a man.

He knew of three other timberwolves in New York. They had been captured and caged against their will in a special 'Endangered Predators' exhibit in the

Central Park Zoo. He wanted very much to go and free them.

'When you leaving?' Billy asked Rocketman.

'What time's the nursing shift change tonight?'

'One a.m.,' Billy said – and all at once realized he was standing on an unsupported floor, without walls or ceiling to hang on to in case even a percentage of the earth's atoms suddenly called in their massive bluff and imploded. He took three long skids through the accumulating snow to the heat duct and clung to the steel like a koala on a eucalyptus tree. 'One a.m.,' he repeated in a whisper.

'So it's midnight,' Rocketman said, bending to check the turbopump wires. 'I guess that's a good time for an escape. Aah, I just hope I got my thrust curves right. I'm gonna look almighty silly, if I fart myself over the roof into the river, or shoot myself into Gracie Mansion, or just burn a hole in the roof and end up in the interns' station on the thirtieth floor . . .'

17

'If there's a war, it's got to be won, and there's
got to be three cheers for the Emperor. Nobody's
going to talk me out of that.'

Jaroslav Hasek
The Good Soldier Schweik

The pilot got back to the City at nine p.m. the
evening of Rocketman's escape; flurries of hard snow
crackling out of the sky like the scat of Antarctic birds.

The lights of the City winked through the white
scrim as he crossed the George Washington Bridge.

Manhattan. It always reminded him of a ship, the
pilot thought; the biggest, most intricate vessel ever
built. A ship laid out on a deep keel of metamorphic
rock, temporarily linked to the mainland by gossamer
gangplanks of light. A vessel of countless smokestacks,
wheelhouses, crow's nests, lockers, saloons, galleys,
holds, foc'sles, and cabins stacked precariously on top
of one another. A windjammer with mighty strutted
sails of glass and neon, steel and stone reaching high
as the cumulus. A steamship whose great black
engines spun, reciprocated, and thundered in the
ancient engine rooms deep below decks, filling vast

pipes with gas, steam, water, and high-voltage electricity to keep the great hull always humming and ready for sea; whose triactic antennas and radar scanners, ever alert, brought in from across the universe the data necessary for twenty-four-hour navigation.

The population of Manhattan reinforced his fantasy, for they invariably behaved as if their island were set to embark on a voyage as urgent as it was unique. They acted like watchkeeping officers, burdened with the responsibilities of navigation, speaking strange sea-tongues with relevance only to the commerce at hand. They were sworn to stay awake, eyes red through the deepest hours of the night, checking that the ten billion running-lights never went out. Nothing could stop or delay them. From the lowest bag-lady to the mayor himself, everyone stood ready to cast off at a moment's notice, to leave the Hudson, carrying cargoes they could not name, for a destination they would never divulge.

The pilot was exhausted yet wired from two days of almost-constant driving. He did not feel like going right back to the apartment. At one level this was because highway driving was like an addiction and always demanded more. At another level, driving was a half-conscious state, and the thoughts that bubbled up and hooked together into long and weird chains as you moved were the equivalent of dreams, linked by the epileptic rhythm of yellow stripes and the glow of cats' eyes. He needed time to let the rhythm die down, allow the thoughts to settle, so he could figure out which were real, and which were creatures of the Interstate that would die when deprived of mileage.

Most of all he needed a drink.

He thought of the Weather Café, and rejected it immediately. Too risky, if BON truly was heating things up. A lot of people were aware that freetraders hung out there.

He thought of Dan Lynch's, or the Hostage, but they would be crowded, and he needed quiet.

The Schweik Club, he thought. It was in Queens, but god was it quiet. He aimed the old sedan uptown, over the Triboro Bridge.

A friend of his father's who lived in Jackson Heights had introduced him to the Schweik Club. It was a glorified bierhall, a fifties ginmill decorated with cheap and varnished wood and pictures of Slotj Castle and the High Tatras. The neighborhood it stood in once was solid Middle European. It had been taken over by newer, more miserable waves of immigrants since the club was founded but the old men still came here every night to drink and tell lies to each other in Czech or Slovak or Sudeten German.

The pilot got to the club shortly before ten. He ordered a Budweiser – the original kind, from Bohemia – and listened to the hard 'r's of the first languages he had ever known. A white-haired man in a green trilby hat got up and announced that the secretary of the Masaryk Society had a report to make. Another codger stood up in his booth and stated that the society had conducted four more interviews of former Czech government officials since the last meeting, without coming any closer to verifying the identity of the mysterious individual with a broken nose who was spotted leaving the presidential palace around the time of the Czech president's alleged suicide in 1947.

'What do you mean, "alleged suicide"?' a chubby man with bubblegum-pink cheeks shouted from the bar. 'Surely our great and noble allies would never have stooped to anything so underhanded. The Russians are our friends!'

'So are the Germans,' someone said.

'The Germans love us!' another voice agreed.

'The World War is over.'

'So is the Cold War.'

A tall man got to his feet. He wore a thick wool cap. His eyebrows were very bushy and his nose was running.

'Truly we have much to be thankful for,' he said in a deep and measured voice. 'The European Union annexed Silesia to take pressure off our northern borders. Everyone knows what a threat the Polish tanks were to Prague.'

He cleared his throat, and wiped his nose with one sleeve.

'Nasty tongues among us would point out that the EC troops were in fact seventy percent German. For shame! The Germans have never had anything but the best interests of all Czechs at heart.'

'Same with the Russians,' the chubby man insisted, banging his stein on the table.

'And if they *did* deal with Masaryk,' another pointed out, 'surely they used only the most gentle persuasion, like a mother's touch?'

'In any case they did us a favor,' a third chimed in. 'Who needs trouble and strife? Masaryk would have ended up causing no end of problems; that much is obvious.'

'I knew Molotov personally,' the chubby man added. 'A charming fellow. He actually danced with the Pole, Berman, cheek to cheek they danced, while Stalin wound the gramophone. Molotov wanted to warn Berman what Stalin had in store for the Jews. Stalin grinning and grinding away at the handle while the men danced with each other. They played waltzes, I think.'

The fellow in the trilby ignored the chubby man. He would accept donations, he announced. The society needed more funds, he concluded, for search engines; some of the old NKVD files could be accessed through the 'nets, if you knew where to look. Money also was required to buy medication for interviewees, most of whom were old, and sick. That was the end of the report.

The pilot went back outside. Even the Schweik Club had too much going on tonight. He got in the Chevy, then changed his mind. He decided to walk, and took his chartcase and the boxful of tools back to the Schweik Club for safekeeping. The ECM-pak he kept on his shoulder. You did not leave anything in cars in this part of Queens. In fact, you did not even leave cars, unless they were as old and beat-up as his Chevy.

Everything seemed stark and frozen here after the highway, the bayou, the blue Gulf seas. The houses stood in right-angled ruins of black brick. The half inch of snow already fallen only hardened the edges of the black. Fire escapes looked like grids erected to measure soot and darkness. Flames roaring in metal trash cans consumed color faster than they created it. Shapes flickered in and out of the chiaroscuro; kids wearing motorized rollerblades with walkie-talkie headsets; men in threes, standing next to all-terrain jeeps. A tee-dee danced by himself, eyes closed on a street corner, the thirteen radios, Walkmen, and portable TVs strung around his neck all going at once.

A woman clad only in a cheap ski jacket lurched out of the shadows. Occasionally, the sharp ripping of automatic weapons sounded in the distance.

This was Fisk Avenue, aka 69th Street, locally known as Ice Alley. People in this neighb had not discovered or could not afford the laid-back delights of jisi yomo and still relied on cooked synthetic cocaine to snap their minds off where they lived. The 'hood was currently in the throes of a turf dispute between an Ecuadorian ice gang called the Putamadres and a general drugs-and-guns cartel run by Kurdish tribesmen. The pilot walked purposefully, without looking right or left, and the ice lookouts watched him, pulled their bulletproof baseball caps lower over their brows, mumbled in their headsets, and left him alone, because any white man who walked by himself in this area after midnight was either an undercover cop, or too crazy to mess with in any case.

After a mile or so of walking, the chemicals of risk and exercise brought him some kind of relaxation. The snow helped, filling in sidevision so you got the illusion of drunkenness, without the motor problems.

But the inchoate anger that had spawned his highway dreams continued to rage inside him. It still fed on grief; it still had nowhere to go; it still asked questions he could not answer.

Like, How had there been a cutter at the rendezvous at the Double Headed Shots?

He went into a Korean bodega and bought a bag of Sausalito cookies with milk chocolate and macadamia nuts. He opened the bag and stashed it in one of the secret pockets of his denim jacket for easy access.

He munched on the cookies as he walked.

His anger about Eltonjohn felt better than the guilt he used to feel over Roberto, however it brought a separate problem. Guilt always furnished a scapegoat. Anger was directed outward, but against what? The BON, a semi-covert arm of a secretive committee within the massive federal bureaucracy of Washington?

Or Bokon — Bokon Taylay — whom nobody really knew but who might, or might not, be one of the unknown people in the secret arm of the faceless committee?

The pilot kept walking. Fisk Avenue turned into Northern Boulevard which ran under the elevated subway line. The tracks towered high on cast-iron beams that once had been beautifully scrolled but were now encrusted with ropes of rust. Beside the tracks stood rows of what had been fancy nineteenth-century brick town houses. The French windows of the town houses, that long ago framed soft still lifes of silk and crystal and trays of fruit tarts, were all broken or blown out. Candles and lanterns moved in the dark doorways. Fires dimmed and glowed under sculpted mantelpieces that first were blocked when central heating was installed and until recently had not seen a real flame in seventy years. But the gas and electricity were shut off now, the fireplaces needed again for light, and heat.

As the pilot walked through the shadows of the El supports, he saw people standing in the doorways beside the stairs. They were dressed in layers to withstand the cold: head and shoulders cloaked in blankets, feet wrapped in plastic and rags. The scene seemed familiar, a square set-piece from his childhood.

He suddenly remembered where he'd seen it before – in black-and-white lithographs of London from an old leatherbound hard-copy of *David Copperfield* that lived in his parents' bookshelf. New York now, like London then, had spawned whole neighborhoods where everybody who was too poor or too sick – too fucked up or drugged out to slot into the chain reaction of 'normal' society – came to pass the winter. No UCC-card for these people, with the bar codes that held your bank and Visa account and office key code; no credit or reference for these men and women to bootstrap themselves into sudden productivity. The forms changed but the substance remained the same. Far from heralding a new world, the coming of the millennium had shipped large portions of the American population straight back to the 1800s.

A train crawled over the El from the Flushing end of the line. It was so covered with soot and the new Alstick graffiti-paint that it was black. Its two head-lights shone like jack-o'-lantern eyes. As it passed overhead, the ground shook and the rotten beams groaned. Flakes of rust rained onto the street. Because it was so cold every wheel of the subway cars, as it hit the bolted connections between lengths of track, bridged a gap of temperature and voltage, causing huge showers of sparks to explode from the joints like fireworks. People in the town houses moved to their second-floor windows to watch the free show. The sparks burst right at window level and beneath hooded blankets the people's faces shone yellow, pink, blue. The children were silent but some of their mothers laughed like kids. Others gestured wildly.

It looked like a scene from hell.

Perhaps — so the pilot fantasized as he watched the Number Seven train spark and clatter into the distance — perhaps that train did not run from Flushing, Queens, to lower Manhattan on a sort-of-regular schedule established by the Transit Authority. Perhaps this El — or at least certain trains, certain unlisted, unscheduled departures — formed a special line that hooked together not different streets but different centuries; something to take a ride on when you got fooled into thinking your own era, with its multi-plexed 'nets and space stations, had somehow managed to evade the hard realities of social physics. From the cold tread of the nomad hunt to Dachau, from the slave camps of Sparta to Mao's purges, from the Inquisition to Babi Yar, that train roared and rattled, late on a cold night, the hand of a skeleton on the deadman, the graffiti of hatred, of hunger, of despair spray-painted on every surface, the ancient engines humming and glowing and smoking on a third rail of genetic destiny, the rhythm of a curse in its wheels; showering the helpless, fascinated humans beneath with sparks that held no warmth, and light that held no fire, till its sound had faded, and the train was gone, and they stood once more alone and helpless — the reality, then, now, and forever.

The cookies were almost finished. He ate the last one as he walked down Hunter's Point Avenue toward Manhattan. Above the massed towers of the city he saw the spotlit spire of his building, the steel griffins and dragons, the great plated 'T' crossed by a golden lightning bolt that was the logo of TransCom.

He was still sucking fudge chips from between his teeth when he saw Rocketman's missile burn its way into the sky over the UN headquarters, pulling a

213

bright tail of fire behind it.

He stood and watched as it rose higher and higher, over the East River, over Brooklyn.

Snow fell and melted in his open mouth.

He stood, helpless, as at approximately three thousand feet the bright fire seemed to jerk, and expand, and shroud itself in a wide noiseless circular flash that stopped the rise — flared, faded, and dived in a thousand tiny bits, hope exploded, possibilities dead, dying embers trailed by white smoke that drifted down the grainy night and ended, right in line with the little glow where the Number Seven train rattled and sparked its way into the East River tunnel.

A light 'boom' rose out of the night, faded with the wind, was gone.

The pilot knew what it was, deep down in the pit of instinct where the ten million probabilities that formed the mathematics of his life were assessed.

He went to Bellevue anyway, catching the next train, to check.

By the time he got there the police had cordoned off the hospital entrances. Fire department helicopters were dropping foam onto a small blaze atop the South Mental Health Tower. TV eyewitness-news teams were already filing reports. Lights strobed, sirens yelped. The spectators rarely looked at what was going on at the tower's summit. Instead they watched, mesmerized, as three different reporters blew steam at the video lights and talked about mystery rockets and UFOs, excitement high in their cheeks and voices. This was top-of-the-line news; bizarre, exciting, sexy with exploding technology; devoid of the least hint of meaning or implication to dampen the entertainment; no pull-back or analysis to mar the moment's thrill.

The people clapped, and called out gaily to their favorite news-persons.

The pilot tried to get through the police lines, and was turned back. He ran full tilt toward the TransCom Building to fetch his surgeon's outfit. Adrenaline could suppress or bypass the general buildup of fatigue in his muscles but could not prevent its effects from surfacing in his brain in the form of chemical anguish and odd worries. As he ran, he found himself wondering wildly if he had become some sort of human jinx, spreading death or madness to anyone who cared for or followed him. Roberto, Carmelita, Eltonjohn, Rocketman. His lungs tore with the strain of breath, his chest seized up, his shirt was soaked, his throat knotted. His legs were still sore from Miss Benthol. The ECM-pak banged painfully at his left thigh and he had to steady it with both hands. The pain of accumulated losses ate like lye at the core of him.

He braked abruptly as he turned onto Lexington Avenue, a block away from the TransCom. The weight of the ECM pulled him in a half circle as he stopped.

Red and white, blue and orange lights flashed, just like Bellevue, near the entrance. Here, too, barricades blocked the doors.

A mobile command center was parked next to the marquee, its satellite dishes aimed at an AG-440 satellite beaming down pictures of the command center from two hundred miles up.

Looking overhead, the pilot spotted the tiny blinking lights of UAVs circling in tight formation around the spotlit griffins of his apartment.

Numbness spread around the pilot's hypothalamus. There was only so much emotion the brain could take. He pulled the collar of his travel jacket around

215

his ears. He wiped his face and tried to control his chest. He approached the building cautiously, though shock was making his ears ring.

Most of the lights came from City police cruisers, but there were a couple of carloads of Safety Volunteers as well. The Safety vigilantes pushed rubberneckers clear of the entrance and zapped tazers against the necks of anyone poor-looking. When the pilot, walking carefully behind the screen of crowd, checked some of the other double-parked vehicles, he found three unmarked brown vans with federal plates. All three tags began with the letters 'ZD.'

He did not have to consult the Smuggler's Bible to find out what those letters meant.

BON.

A thin line of spectators drifted around the barricades. An ambulance pulled up. A squad of men burst out of the corporate entrance, rolling a stretcher. A body lay on the stretcher. The men wore polyester suits and latex gloves. Short MP5K machine-pistols hung around their shoulders. The sheets over the body bore red stains. An intravenous bottle swung over its head. The clear fluid looked pink in the police lights. The pilot pulled back into the crowd.

A powerful hand grabbed his left arm, and twisted it behind his back.

The pilot gasped. He swung around on reflex, kicking and chopping to escape. Another hand clamped on his right arm.

'Cool it, baby,' Rocketman whispered. 'Cool it.'

'Dag!' the pilot shrieked. Rocketman jammed a fist over his mouth and looked around nervously. 'Shut up!' he hissed. 'What's the matter with you?' He pulled the pilot down the street, away from the

216

crowd, stopping between a truck and a rental van. 'Aaah,' he said, 'it's so weird, to be able to just walk down the street like this!'

Rocketman's voice was happy but, after four years of living in the South Mental Health Unit, his eyes struggled to hold the horizon.

'Jesus, shit, Rocketman.' The pilot had trouble getting his breath back again. The big man looked at his shoes. 'But I thought you were *dead*!' the pilot whispered, finally.

'I thought *you* were dead,' Rocketman replied, gesturing at the scene down the street.

'But the – that rocket,' the pilot stuttered. 'I mean, that's what it was, right? It *was* your capsule?'

'Aaah,' the big man said. 'I dunno. Lots of single-stage launchers takin' off from Bellevue these days. What do you think?'

'So you parachuted, before—'

Rocketman hesitated. He looked at the slush now.

'I don't know,' he said eventually. 'I had a hunch. You know? Something in my head wasn't resolved – even though I'd done the figures a hundred times. The valves, the rams, the thrust chamber. Aaah. Anyway, I chickened out.'

'You fired it off empty?'

'I guess.' The big man still would not look up. 'Billy was so disappointed.'

'Billy?'

'It's a long story. Anyway, yeah. I put on those doctor's clothes you snuck in for me. Lobo came too. You remember Lobo. Billy wouldn't come. Lobo an' me, we just walked out, down the emergency stairs. We used the skeleton keys. They were all confused, wondering how come their beautiful roof was on fire.

I'm really sorry, Skid, I know you worked so hard, for the orbital smugg—' His sentence was chopped short as the pilot threw his arms around Rocketman and hugged him tight.

'Who cares,' he said, 'man, I'm just happy you're alive.'

'Aaah,' Rocketman sighed. 'I guess.' He pulled out a pack of Kents. 'But I sure disappointed young Billy.'

A siren wound up. The ambulance pulled away, BON men clearly visible through the windows, bending over the wounded man. 'I guess I'm pretty happy too,' Rocketman went on. 'I was sure that was gonna be you.'

'Well, it wasn't.'

They both thought about this fact for a minute.

'But if it wasn't,' the pilot continued, 'who was it? Oh, *dag*,' he added, remembering the security schedules, 'Obregon. Dag, *Obregon!*'

The pilot stepped into the street, looking up at the TransCom spire. From 898 feet higher up, half obscured in the swirling snow, the Krupp steel griffins peered back at him. He started to walk backward, away from the main entrance.

'Where you going?' Rocketman hissed urgently. 'Hey!'

'I gotta go up.'

'You can't!'

'There's a way.'

'Wait,' the big man called after him. 'Those aren't ordinary cops, man! The Trilaterals are in this somehow. TransCom did deals with *Microsoft* – the multinationals . . .'

But the pilot had gone already, trotting up 29th Street, disappearing quickly in the snow.

There was a way into the TransCom Building no one but Obregon's people knew about. You slid your UCC through the turnstiles to get into the Lexington Avenue subway. Then, keeping an eye out for trains, and stepping well clear of the live rail, you walked along the downtown track to an emergency fire exit. The exit brought you straight to the third basement and a backup freight elevator in the north bank.

As a 'security guard,' the pilot had pass-cards to everything. He got off two floors below his own and climbed into the airco system through a maintenance hatch.

Travel through the lower airco was not easy. You had to scramble on hands and knees along the square horizontal ducts, and climb thin rungs of corrugated iron up vertical inspection chutes. The pilot choked on dust and soot, scraping knees and shoulders at every turn. The only light came through cracked welds and holes in the pipes. Luckily this part of the system was old and holey and the pilot could see enough to find his way.

At the junction with the airco pipe that led to his apartment he heard the voices of men. He followed another, even smaller conduit around the back of the kitchenette. He long ago had unfastened a panel in this duct to serve as an escape route. In the absence of urgency he'd used it to store extra supplies, in case the apartment got blocked for any reason. By opening the panel and easing open the cabinet door behind, he could see the refrigerator and part of the lounge through a vista of containers holding chicken noodle soup, Worcestershire sauce, baked beans.

Every light was switched on. The shoulder of a blue corduroy suit was visible through the kitchenette entrance. 'Brodin's not gonna look at it that way,' the blue suit was saying.

'Maybe he warned him off.'

Something fell and smashed. A door squeaked continuously.

'Well he had to be in on it,' the invisible voice continued, after a minute or two.

'Who?'

'The guard. Who d'you think?'

'I don't know . . .'

'It was him, who used the bogus service. No pro would do that.'

The blue suit's left hand held one of the pilot's fake UCC cards. The hand flipped the card, without pause, finger over finger and back again.

'What was he babbling about, on the stretcher?'

'He was hallucinating.'

'Yeah, but what about?' The card flipping, back and forth.

'Parking,' the invisible man said. 'Traffic. He said the Hutch was blocked all the way to the Merritt. Crap like that. Made no sense.'

The card stopped flipping.

'I thought it might be some kind of code,' the blue suit said, 'nonrandom substitution, but—'

'They'll find out at Oakdale.'

The pilot felt a cold spot develop on the base of his spine at the mention of Oakdale. Shit, piss, damn, blast, he said to himself, silently. Obregon, I'm sorry.

'Anything there?' the invisible man continued.

'Nothin'.'

'Control said he had good wire.'

'TA was negative. Maybe he was offline.'

More breakage. The suit put the card in its pocket.

220

The pilot eased backward into his duct, wondering what 'TA' was. The sound of squeaking doors was louder now but there were no doors in the ducts. There was no light either, and all his flashlights were in the apartment. He held his breath, crouched lower on the aluminum. Something quick and furry hopped around his legs and stuck a sharp nose between his fingers.

'God!' he whispered, and a spark of pleasure burned among the accumulated backlog of bad feelings. It blended with another ember lit from Rocketman's escape. Light wrestled dark for supremacy inside his duodenum.

'God,' he repeated softly. 'Well dag, old man. I think you an' I just been evicted.'

The rat was wriggling mightily in what the pilot chose to recognize as some type of rodent ecstasy. He picked up God and stuffed him in an inside pocket of his jacket.

Then, very carefully, he crawled back the way he had come.

18

'Never allow your own bodily secretions to enter
into contact with those of your partner.'
  Centers for Disease Control
  Atlanta
  *Guidelines on Countering the Spread of Sexually Transmitted
  Epidemics in America*

PC met the woman around the time the pilot and his
rat were being thrown out of their apartment.

He encountered her at a private party sponsored by
Orgasm Records at the Hostage Bar and Grill on Great
Jones Street.

The Hostage was named for the latest, and most
fashionable, crime since car-gassing. Because you
could use UCC-cards to buy everything from breath
mints to automobiles, people no longer carried real
cash and it no longer was possible to mug them and
make a profit; nevertheless men from North Newark
had worked out a way to make a living without going
back to fast-food jobs. Dressed in Versace monkey
jackets, carrying laptops and cellphones, they would
infiltrate Short Hills, take as hostages the family of,
say, a memory-derivatives VP, and then phone the

VP at his Beaver Street office and demand that he withdraw a weighty quantity of dead presidents on his card. At a prearranged time and place the family was bartered for the cash.

PC was in the upper bar of the Hostage when he first saw her. She stood with a gaggle of Safe People, all looking exactly alike. At first glance she looked like Safe People too. She had short blonde hair, streaked blue and bobbed in the popular neo-flapper style. She wore a black Israeli 'commando' jacket that had probably cost eight hundred bucks, and Northern Territory emu-skin boots. Her nose was flawless, her neck was like close-grained wood from the kind of tree you would cut to make cellos. Her hands were bare, her shirt cracked open to the waist, revealing an absence of stigs, and she looked easily away from the Virtix screens, demonstrating her immunity to TDF.

If she had the Plague, it was not visible. Her stance, too, was supple as a tree's, he thought; straightness in the curve, strength in the give. Perhaps it was something in that stance that set her apart from the exercise-club physiques around her.

PC was with Safe People himself; eighteen or twenty of his closer friends. They stood around their terminals, talking on cellphones or watching the 3-D videos the place was famous for. Five of them wore half-suckers with a radio link, and within their subgroup these people moved in rhythm with the action on the screen. An AGATE armored car approached a fortified ranch in El Sobrante while an Apache chopper, hovering behind the house, rocketed a jeep full of card-nappers. Flames bloomed, orange, brown.

On another set, Ned Reynolds showed dramatic footage of American F-25s blasting the shit out of an oil rig full of Mexicans. No one at the table was quite sure which Mexicans.

'Darkworld,' someone commented.

'Fry the slime,' Blake Nugent said, leaning forward with the Apache's weapons officer.

'Gad, Ted, like, what have you done to your hair?' Sue Levine commented. 'I saw it on ET.'

The girl with the blue-blonde hair turned toward their conversation. Her eyes met PC's. Their gazes locked. The look was like nuclear fission, pulling in the total normalcy of atoms and then releasing all the unbelievable energy it took to keep things so normal.

'You've got eyes like a supernova,' he told her.

She smiled, and turned back to her group.

PC grinned at her neck. It still worked, he thought. He'd only had two mimosas but one look at those pupils and he felt as drunk as he'd ever been in his life. His stomach was full of crickets and his heart rate way up. He no longer needed food, champagne, or oxygen to sustain life. All he needed was another look at her eyes; that long green, reminding him of the deepest, freshest spring on the planet, with little flecks of silver like the rare fish of Managordo Lake – that sense of purity and pain at the heart of it, as if she'd dived to the very nub of things, and seen the end.

He racked his brain for something else to spark her interest. All he could think of was the same things everyone else talked about. Adornista bombs, the El Sobrante card-napping, Brooke Denali's love life. Or, turning it on its head, the lack of interesting things to say . . .

God, he thought. Have I really become so unbelievably lobotomized that I can't think of anything original that does not concern this woman's foglamps? But the woman solved this problem for him by turning around and asking, 'So what do *you* think?'

'About what?'

'Brooke Denali. Is she, or isn't she?'

They talked easily. If the material was not particularly exciting, PC believed, it had more to do with the environment than with their inner natures.

She lived in NoCo – North of Columbia University. He owned a co-op in a big, prewar art deco building on Riverside and 100th. They shared a taxi north. He turned off both his cellphones; it was a message of commitment. She understood the codes, accepted the message but in the dark he could not read her eyes. She came to his apartment. Another major commitment, in this age of Plague, he thought.

He played Shift-shin, one of the latest bootlegs from Karachi, with five-power stochastics and real-time video capability that required both decks and a synthesizer as well as his PC to play. He offered her Doyen-Kruyff, which she declined, and jisi yomo, which she accepted. She used a 9-mm cartridge hung around her neck to dump a measure into the round glass bowl of the works. She heated the powder to exactly the right shade of turquoise, and sprayed in the nitrate at the perfect instant. The skunky smell of the cooked drug perfumed the air around them. He watched her ankles as she leaned forward to suck in the mixture. She had truly wonderful ankles. His father had been an orthopedic surgeon and an affinity for clean hocks had rubbed off on the son. Once the jisi was done they touched each other, delicately. On the Shift-shin mix they heard the harmonics of snowfields, strange gasps and cries of compacted crystal, just this side of avalanche. Next steps were reached, in feel, in talk.

Her name was Sara. She was afraid. Her mother (Sara said) had ignored her in favor of more entertaining hobbies. That was the source of one fear. The Plague, and stigs, were everywhere; that was another. The fears fed on each other. She was bound to contract a disease as she sought in men what she'd missed in her mother. It was no coincidence that both stigs and the Plague were transmitted through sexual contact. The diseases no longer were fatal, of course, but the treatments were so humiliating, and so expensive, that they might as well be. It was how the stars would pay her back for not being worthy of her mother's love.

'Horseshit,' PC told her, and kissed her forehead. Hope shouted hallelujahs in his chest.

But it wasn't horseshit — or at least, the fear was real. This became apparent as they went through the various angular progressions, from vertical to horizontal, of serious physical contact. At the armchair stage she would not touch his lips. At the couch stage she would not directly touch his cock, but he dismissed this in the wonder of seeing her breasts, which were milk-white, small, and perfectly conical, like volcanoes in Iceland; snow-covered, mathematically exact due to the laws of gravity and the consistency of lava flow. Only the tips glowed red, from the heat within.

On the floor she shucked off his pants and her skirt. The curve of her ass was so smooth and pure it made him want to sing. Like her breasts, her buttocks were very white. Her pubis had very little hair and he could follow the cleft in it from the small dimple at the top, through the deepening valley to the gorge that disappeared in the little space that nature had evolved between her thighs, to give her freedom for movement, and arousal. But when he followed the valley with a finger she stopped his hand.

'Wait,' she whispered, and took a pink plastic box from her handbag.

The box was a dispenser. She pressed a button and waited twenty seconds. A light flashed. With long, graceful fingers she pulled from it a sheet of thin, clear plastic, like cellophane, but very soft, for it sagged in the middle when she drew it to one side. When PC asked her what she was doing she put a finger to his lips. She pushed another button on the dispenser and the sheet was cut free. She held the plastic high and pushed him gently to the floor. 'Be still,' she said, 'you're going to like this.' She laid it gently on his mouth. The plastic was warm and gluey. It stuck to his lips almost as if it had melted there. She kissed him hard through the transparent film.

The film was very malleable and resilient. She put most of her tongue in his mouth without breaking it, and when she retracted her tongue the plastic snapped back. It was a good heat conductor. Jesus, PC thought, breathing through his nostrils; but he let her kiss him.

As she kissed him she put a large piece of plastic around her hand and caressed him with it. His cock was not fussy. Even through the barrier it did what it did best. But despite his own arousal a sense of deprivation grew in PC's chest, as if he had already come.

Sara unrolled a new sheet of film and pulled it between her legs. She straddled him and slowly lowered herself onto his mouth. The sight of the moisture

227

coating the inside of her thighs, smearing the transparent sheet, made him groan, but the feel of plastic on his tongue intruded between his nerve endings and the brain. The girl arched her back as he licked her. Her hands pressed hard on the plastic around his face. 'Sara,' he mumbled against his own saliva collecting on the glossy surface.

'Honey,' she answered. 'Honey.'

'I can't—'

She sat up in the half light. The Shift-shin sampled the sound of tectonic plates grinding forty miles under Hokkaido. A bagpipe keened, a Stratocaster whined. On the Virtix screen, huge tubeworms undulated around a hot gas vent 24,200 feet below the surface of the Pacific, in the lower Kermadec trench.

'You've never used LayWrap?' she asked. 'Don't you know what it's for?'

He ripped the plastic from his mouth and licked his lips to get the taste off.

'It's for the Plague,' he said tiredly, 'it's for stigs. I know what it's for.'

'You don't use latex?'

'Just condoms.'

'It only just came out,' she said diplomatically, 'it can take a while, to get used to. Let me help you—'

She took a tube from her handbag and smeared jelly over her stomach, her thighs, her buttocks. The jelly smelled of lilacs and shrimp. She squeezed jelly on her fingers and dabbed it inside her. She pulled out more film from the pink box and covered her stomach with it. The plastic skated on the jelly. She removed the old plastic from between her legs, pasted two fresh strips of it around her thighs and laid a rectangle carefully between the top of her buttocks

228

and her bellybutton. She even took a length of film and wound it around her neck like a scarf, so that PC began to suspect there was more than just fear or need at the bottom of this procedure, that she had grown used to plastic, and relied on it. Finally she lay on top of PC and guided him into her.

The film felt tight and smooth. Her skin was smooth but the plastic was much slicker. He did not get the same sensation of smoothness from the plastic as he did from her skin. The film crinkled in all the wrong places. It bunched up in the angles where her thighs folded. The world, the sexual night was filled with the sticky grip of plastic, the fake wetness of its sound, the artificial heat of its touch. She was pumping herself up and down on him. The film expanded with heat, so that with every pump he penetrated deeper inside her. He was feeling something, some kind of sensory input was getting through – this was not so different, after all, from using condoms – but condoms did not cover your face, or her hands, and what pleasure he did feel was meager and trickling and as nothing against the deepening sense of utter loss inside him. He put his hands on her thighs and stopped her movements.

'What is it,' she said. She was breathing hard. 'Fred, what's wrong?'

Her eyes were so sad, he thought.

'I can't do it,' he repeated. 'It doesn't feel good.'

He could see hurt flood the green, changing its color. 'It's not you,' he said, 'it really isn't. It's just – it's – it's—' The loss converted into frustration, and leaked.

'It's that goddamn plastic,' he burst out. 'It's like fucking garbage bags! It's like having sex with a

229

packaged lunch! It's like going to bed with mail-order! It's the lust of deli meat! Oh, *God*, Sara.' He pulled himself out from under her. 'I'm really sorry,' he said, more quietly.

The security buzzer rang. Someone was downstairs. He ignored it.

She looked at him steadily. He looked back at her. There was too much pain there, he realized suddenly, to allow anything out but fear, and its acolytes.

'If I could only fuck your eyes,' he said, 'without plastic,' and it came to him that these were the saddest words he had ever uttered, because this was either the 2,166th or the 2,167th attractive, eligible girl he had met since he got to New York, and he was no closer to losing his heart to Sara than he'd been with the first.

The buzzer rang again, insistently. As he got up to answer he realized, not for the first time, that he wanted to change his life completely, and he had not the slightest idea how to go about it.

19

'On the same day that LSD became a controlled substance, the *Oracle* hosted an outdoor gathering called the Love Pageant Rally . . . Rock bands played for free, and a master of ceremonies read a manifesto entitled "A Prophecy of a Declaration of Independence": "We hold these truths to be self-evident, that all is equal, that the creation endows us with certain inalienable rights, that among these are: The freedom of the body, the pursuit of joy, and the expansion of consciousness . . ."

At the appropriate moment hundreds of people placed a tab of acid on their outstretched tongues and swallowed in unison. The next year in the Haight would be quite a trip indeed.'

Martin A. Lee and Bruce Shlain
Acid Dreams: The CIA, LSD and the Sixties Rebellion

The pilot leaned on the bell for the sixth time, thinking this was undoubtedly a waste of energy. There was no way the guy was going to be in, it was only three a.m.

Still he kept ringing. It felt strange to realize that after four years in New York he had nowhere else to go.

He knew a couple of people downtown but they

were all in the Trade and to visit them now would be like going to a dance, knowing you were infected with stigs, and spitting into the brandy punch.

It was odd to realize that Rocketman, on exactly the same night, had ended up as homeless as he. It was the Curse again, he thought, fancifully, bitterly. The Curse of Marak.

He looked up and down the lobby, a little nervous. Since leaving the TransCom Building he had not been able to shake the idea that someone was watching, and taking notes, and following wherever they went. He had on a headset that looked like a Walkman's earphones, plugged discreetly into the ECM on his shoulder. It was tuned to the frequency scanner and the traffic, as far as he could tell, was normal; but his uneasiness would not pack its bags.

Rocketman, for his part, always felt as if someone was watching, following, and taking notes wherever he went — not just on him, but on every other innocent human who somehow had become aware of the sick skein of conspiracy spun by the world's military-industrial keiretsus over the last sixty years. He too looked around the lobby, but this time it had less to do with security than with his continuing awe of spaces bigger and longer than the shut-off corridors of Bellevue.

The lobby took up a quarter block. Long mirrors and fake Egyptian busts and couches filled its corners. Ranks of mailboxes stuffed with expensive journals hissed with the loony Muzak of buzzing microchips. The chips delivered seasonal tunes whenever you opened the journal to a certain advertisement and often when you didn't. Fifty or sixty electric versions of 'Old Hundred,' sandwiched in a whisky ad in the

232

New Yorker, played too fast, at different stages, at the same time. It sounded like an attack of killer June bugs. Other chips, triggered by the pressure of being stuffed in the same box with eight pounds of junk mail, released samples of perfume or played quick matchchip videos of Virtix productions. The cracks around the mailboxes flared with light and gave off different smells, with no recognizable pattern.

Security cameras covered the lobby's every angle. A Sikh doorman watched them intently from a cubbyhole full of monitors. Rocketman turned up the collar of his jumpsuit and the pilot, cued unconsciously by his friend, pulled his travel jacket collar higher around his neck.

Upstairs, PC clicked on a monitor and said, 'Jesus.'

'I've got guests,' he told the girl, back in the bedroom. She was pulling on her panty hose.

'Guests,' she said in a flat tone, 'at three a.m. Of course you do.'

She finished getting dressed so fast she took down the same elevator that brought up the pilot and Rocketman. She did not take the crinkled plastic with her.

'Hope we didn't interrupt anything important,' the pilot said as the elevator door hissed shut behind the woman.

'Nothing important,' PC said. He gestured them in. On the way through the entrance the pilot noticed a strip of clear plastic wrap hanging from the back of PC's pants.

'Dag, PC,' he said, 'you been wrappin' yourself up again?'

'Fuck off,' PC said sourly. He could feel himself blushing. He ripped a square of LayWrap the size of

233

a large napkin from his trousers, wadded it up, threw it in a corner of the hallway.

Despite the embarrassment he was quite happy he'd been able to get rid of the girl so easily. His 'guests' had allowed him to bail cold out of the confusion of feelings stemming from the dispenser incident. He led them into the kitchen. This was where he basically lived. The rest of the apartment was so big he got lost in it.

'So you guys really *are* in trouble,' PC said in wonder an hour later, after the pilot had told PC of the bust at TransCom, and Rocketman had told the pilot about Roberto.

'It's a well-planned plot,' Rocketman said darkly for the fourth or fifth time. 'The Sour Lake Roustabouts – they're *back*.'

'I don't know if busting smugglers qualifies as a plot,' the pilot objected. 'I mean, Black Tuna, the Boyd Brothers. Not exactly the Vienna Choirboys, ya know what I mean?'

He drained a bottle of PC's Oude Gansevoort, and got another from the ten-foot refrigerator in the middle of the kitchen. He was on his fourth or fifth beer and he still had not succeeded in laying the bitter aftertaste of Rocketman's news. Roberto was not dead, which was something – hell, it was a lot – but in his mind's eye the pilot kept seeing Oakdale; the four perimeters of mines and razorwire, the automatic machine-gun nests, the gleaming control tower, looming like an alien spacecraft two hundred feet high in the middle of the compound.

Frankly, Oakdale scared him. Like BON, it lived in a growing loophole in the Bill of Rights. Like BON, it had become what it was after the Manila raid, when

234

the AGATE laws were passed. It was supposed to be a gang war with walls. The only difference between Oakdale and South Chicago, people said, was you could leave South Chicago. People claimed the Oakdale goons never used harsh methods; they just fed you to the Kurds or the Chechens or the Santa Martans if you did not cooperate.

People said lots of things, but nobody outside knew for sure, because in the five years since BON, through its tame corrections corporation, took over the camp, no one had left Oakdale except to be buried.

'So what're you gonna do?' PC asked anxiously.

The pilot sighed. 'Hire lawyers, I guess,' he said. 'Give 'em what I know on Roberto, so they can tell me what they can't do, at four hundred bucks an hour.'

'Not much anyone can do,' Rocketman commented, 'against them.'

The big man twisted his bottle in his hands. He had chosen to sit in the corner nearest the butcherblock table. He kept looking around PC's kitchen, his eyes large.

The kitchen was big as an average living room. It was filled with every convenience known to City man. Super-Cuisinarts, tortellini-makers, automatic bread-bakers, paella-mixers. A Tibetan-food blender, microwave ovens, a VR satvid. Gigantic color posters of fruit covered the walls. Antiseptic blue formica covered everything else.

The screen of a Micronta Homeframe glowed in one corner. All the kitchen appliances, the airco and heat, the security cameras and proximity alarms and lights, were hooked into the Micronta. Its screen-saver featured Mai Tais flying toward each other, colliding, exploding in a gout of colorful juices.

The satvid showed an advertisement for a product that totally eliminated sweat.

The pilot threw his empty bottle at the recycler, and missed.

'Dag!' he exclaimed. 'I still can't believe it. Roberto, Obregon. And Eltonjohn's *dead*.'

Rocketman got unsteadily to his feet, paced a couple of yards up the kitchen and back again. PC opened the freezer and took out a small plastic bag full of jisi yomo. The jis' was fresh, probably Ecuadorian, so green it was almost phosphorescent. Rocketman paced quietly up and down. After twenty paces he said, 'We got to fight this. We got to stop things like this,' he continued, 'like what happened to my shuttle.'

'What's he talking about?' PC asked in the middle of measuring out perfect cones of jisi yomo on the butcherblock.

The B-Net news came on.

The lead story was about Jimmy Hoffa. The former Teamsters chief was announcing a spiritual crusade to spread the word of God. A view of Hoffa's bald head filled the four-foot satellite-TV screen. It was covered with fat pink scabs of skin cancer, and pucker marks, as if it had been underwater a long time.

'Heaven don't work no different from Washington, or Detroit, or Vegas,' Jimmy Hoffa yelled at the audience. Hoffa's face was as wrinkled as a piece of paper that had been scrunched up, then smoothed out, many times over. The skin under his eyes and cheeks drooped like warmed LayWrap. Cancer had worn away part of his left ear, and one of his eyes was completely bloodshot. He had large gold caps on his teeth that flashed in the spots as he spoke. 'Jesus had to deal with Pilate! You wanna save your soul, you gotta *pay off the Lord!* You wanna go to heaven, you gotta give some *kickbacks* to *Jesus!* That's what Jesus told me! He wants cash *up front!'*

Fierce approval from the crowd. Shots of chanting supporters – 'Haw – ffa! Haw – ffa!' A sleek man in an expensive suit clapped enthusiastically to one side of the podium, but his eyes were still and calculating. Hoffa pointed at the slick man.

'The good Pastor Johnson—' (another round of cheers) – 'Good Pastor Johnson has seen the way of Christ. He has passed on the word of our mission. So I say to you, brothers and sisters – go forth and get *rich!* Just *suck* them credits in! Then you come back to *me,* and ask me what kind of *protection* money you willing to *pay,* what kind of payoff *eternal salvation* is worth to *you,* and I will go *personally* to Jesus Christ almighty who saved me from the scum of the marsh and the wrath of the *Gambinos* and I will tell you what it costs to enter the kingdom of *heaven!* That's the way of Jesus Christ *almighty!* That's the *American* way!'

Hysteria in the crowd. Close-ups of people chucking UCC-cards in the air. Shots of people trying to storm the spotlit podium of Meadowlands Arena where Hoffa addressed a special convention of the Johnsonist Church of Jesus Christ Almighty Incorporated. The camera panned around Hoffa's bodyguards as they repelled boarders. The bodyguards were all deformed. They wore black robes and tall black rubber boots. They shoved off the religious with blows from the butts of sawn-off shotguns. One of the bodyguards had a withered arm, and a thigh with two joints. He swung his lupara like a shillelagh from the other arm, whirling it around his head by its rubber sling.

237

'Shit,' the pilot exclaimed, 'I know that guy!'

'Then you've got a shortcut to heaven,' PC commented, 'as well as some interesting friends.'

Rocketman had continued his pacing right through the revival meeting, mumbling quietly to himself, but at this point he stopped beside the table, jammed his fists in his jumpsuit and said, 'You know what?'

'What?' PC replied.

'We could go find Hawkley.'

PC had been cleaning out the jis' factory. He blasted it warm with a blow-dryer, spooned a cone of jisi into the pyrex globe. He played the lighter flame under the accumulated powder, waited till it turned turquoise, fitted the can of nitrous into the nozzle. Simultaneously, he blasted in the gas, and inhaled. 'Aah,' he sighed, when the toke was safely locked in his lungs.

'Seriously,' Rocketman said.

The pilot laughed. He could not help himself. The jisi yomo neutralized the globe's nitrous oxide, but the contact high from PC's hit made laughing easier.

'Some?' PC offered, passing the works along.

The stimulant made things appear green and brown, the color of jungle. It made you sense the pain of all living things. High on jisi, you could watch a vase full of tulips and feel the agony of the amputated stems, the dreadful parch as pistil and pedicel, losing chlorophyll, grew increasingly unable to draw water into their upper veins and filaments. You could stick your head through the window and above the noise of trucks and jets and wind hear the ten thousand different melodies of suffering, from disease, boredom, betrayal, anger, and solitude – above all, solitude – that suffused the city blocks immediately around.

238

And yet, in the eloquence of this new sense, the jisi also made you feel comfortable. If pain was every-where – this the drug whispered in the tunnels of your brain – so was the peace to be found in accept-ing that fact. High on jisi, you felt like you were sleeping in a hammock woven of soft vines, even when you were straphanging on the Seventh Avenue express at rush hour. It was an equivocal drug for an equivocal city.

'Hawkley's a myth,' the pilot observed, much later. He had found PC's vodka in one cabinet and was experimenting with Easter egg dyes he'd found in another. Three drops of deep blue turned a glass of superchilled vodka the color of kingfisher feathers. Add yellow. Add lemon. Add melon liqueur. 'Everybody knows his book was written by a whole buncha people. Like the Christian Bible.'

'What book?' PC asked, and walked to the other side of the kitchen.

'Hawkley's not a myth,' Rocketman said. 'You're too young to know the difference, but I saw him once.'

'Hawkley?' the pilot quit his alchemy in amaze-ment. 'You *saw* him?'

'For sure.' The soothing swells of jisi yomo had calmed Rocketman's nerves.

'It was in '67. I went to San Francisco that summer, like every other middle-class kid in the bourgeois state of California. Those were hippie days, man – sexist, egocentric-city – but Hawkley was making acid back then and his acid was the one thing that could make you forget all that.'

'And you *saw* him?' the pilot insisted.

'From far away. It was at the Love Pageant. You

239

know, the day they made LSD illegal in California.'

'Dag,' the pilot said. 'Really? Hawkley's real? No one ever tole me.'

'So anyway.' Rocketman brought down his hands and spread them wide, a symbol of simplicity and ease. 'To get back to what I was saying.

'My idea is, we find him. He tells us how BON manages to bust all the smugglers, what Roberto said. You come back and save the ass of all the freetraders left. You'll be a hero, man!'

'Not exactly,' PC pointed out. 'Not to most people.'

'Freetraders are cool, man,' Rocketman growled at PC. 'They slip 'n' slide, go anywhere, when they want.'

The pilot looked at his vodka glass, which was turning a disgusting swampy color. He shook his head.

'It's the craziest idea I ever heard.'

Rocketman flushed. 'Fuck you, man,' he said hotly. 'Don't tell me what's crazy, what's not crazy, I'm a fuckin' expert on that, I know the difference.'

'I'm sorry—' The pilot put his arm out toward Rocketman, but his friend jerked away.

'You just scared.'

'I'm not scared,' the pilot retorted. 'What's to be scared of, compared to everything else?'

'So what's stoppin' you?' Rocketman insisted. 'You got contacts. Anyway, what else you gonna do?'

The pilot opened his mouth to reply, and paused.

Thought it over for a minute.

He had no idea what else he was going to do. He certainly was not going to risk another run, not with the kind of heat they'd had waiting for him off the Continental Shelf.

He could not stay in New York, or anywhere he was known. If the Feds had found his apartment, they knew more about him than he'd ever thought possible. And those data would be online by now.

PC fed two pounds of barley flour, a gram of cilantro and a half-gallon of pre-soured yak milk into the automatic Tibetan tsampa-maker. He tapped out the right time and temperature on the Micronta but he had poured in twice too much sour milk, and tsampa started blooping out of the machine five minutes ahead of time and so fast that it had covered five square yards in as many seconds. 'Oh, shit,' PC said, and picked up a sponge to mop it. Tragically, the tsampa-maker was an industrial machine guaranteed to put out a minimum of thirty Imperial gallons every twenty minutes and the sponge was hopelessly inadequate to the task. 'Fuck!' he yelled, 'help!' He sprinted for the closet where the mop was stored. The grayish-white tide of sour gruel was invading the kitchen with the irresistible speed and momentum of Mongol hordes. It got under PC's feet as he ran. His legs vanished from under him and he hit the floor with a distinct 'Ooomph!' stomach-first in the advancing flood. 'Yaaagh,' he yelled, 'tsampa!' The pilot stepped carefully to the Micronta and clicked on the 'cancel' symbol.

Rocketman helped PC mop up the kitchen floor.

'To hell with tsampa,' PC said, 'I'm sick of it already. I'm sick of Vicious Vindaloo. I'm sick of the whole—'

'Shhh!' Rocketman interrupted him. His face was set and rigid. He pointed his mop at the Virtix screen.

The TV showed a night-perspective of Bellevue hospital. A reporter dressed in a thick sheepskin coat held the mike in a gloved hand. 'Authorities believe one of the inmates, a former aerospace engineer, put the rocket together in secret. His body has not been recovered—'

'Hey!' PC shouted. 'That's you!'

Rocketman did not reply. The sight of the South Mental Health Tower in the background had driven him back into his corner. God started licking the tsampa, taking up where Rocketman had left off.

'Jeess,' PC said, throwing his mop into the sink. 'You guys are really way out, you know. I mean you're on the news. You *do* things. It's – it's – it's interesting, goddammit!'

The pilot poured fresh vodka. He tried straight green dye this time.

'It's true, I don't want the Trade to die,' he said slowly to Rocketman. 'And if what Roberto says is accurate – and it must be, I mean, look at the facts – the Vikings were waiting for my jet; that cutter was right there where I picked up the Chileans. I mean, *right there!*'

The loss of Eltonjohn had not dissipated; it had simply gone underground, accumulating with other pain in pockets. With the heightened perception of jisi, he could see the pockets move, the pain spread inside him, in subtle color-lines that ran through his nerves, pooled, then overflowed the dams of ganglia, lighting his muscles in different hues. It looked like his new ECM program.

The pilot slammed the dye bottle down so hard it cracked right up its plastic seam. Livid jade spots appeared on the table and on his nose. He clasped one hand over the other to control his muscles. 'Those old Coast Guard cutters only go thirty-five, forty-five

242

knots. They had to know exactly where we were. I mean, that sort of information doesn't grow on trees.'

An ad for pest poison followed the Bellevue report. The ad used military terminology to describe how it would exterminate coyotes and rats, raccoons and cockroaches. The verb 'kill' was repeated eighteen times in the voice-over.

'You know,' PC said, peeling a package of frozen mussels and paella-flavoring and saffron-rice-mix and dumping them together in the paella-maker. 'Listening to you guys. It makes me think. I mean I criticize people for having nothing new to say. But tonight – I was trying to talk to this girl. The one you saw going out, her name was, her name – it'll come back to me. Anyway, I tried to think of something really new, really original to say. And I couldn't. Who wants paella?' he continued, keying commands into the Micronta. 'It'll be ready in 3.7 minutes.'

'Speaking theoretically,' the pilot asked Rocketman, 'how would you go looking for this guy?'

'Research,' Rocketman said promptly.

'Do you think my conversation is boring?' PC asked, four minutes later, serving bowls of mushy yellow rice.

'You ever listen to yourself?' Rocketman asked him. PC nodded.

'It's because,' he explained, 'all I really care about is meeting women, but I can hardly talk about that to a girl I'm trying to meet.'

'Shhh,' Rocketman said again, looking at the video screen where the anchorman had just switched live to Channel Five's reporter.

'This is Shaneesha Chaudhury,' the reporter said,

'coming at ya live from Central Park.'

Rocketman stared. The pilot thought Shaneesha looked even colder than her colleague at Bellevue. She wore a fluffy coat made of dead coyotes but her lips were purple and her eyes watered from the cold.

'I am talking to you live from the Bell Atlantic Endangered Predators Exhibit at the Central Park Zoo,' Shaneesha announced, 'where sometime between the hours of 2:00 and 2:30 a.m., a person or persons opened a number of cages and let loose some of the most dangerous animals known to man to, uh, roam the streets of Manhattan.

'With me now,' Shaneesha continued, glancing to her left as the camera panned, 'is Jim Burke of the City's Park Service. Mr Burke, how many animals were let out of their cages?'

Jim looked like he had been forcibly dragged from the nearest pub. His nose was the shape and color of a huge strawberry. He had trouble focusing against the TV lights.

'So we got, uh, three Alaskan timberwolves—' he counted fingers '—two cheetahs, one male polar bear, and a – a wolverine.'

'And do you have any idea where they are now?'

'Well, we do have one report.' Jim Burke looked dubious, but he continued anyway. 'The polar bear's s'posed to be at Wollmann Skating Rink. He scraped a hole in the ice and he's, he's just standin' over it.'

'I see.' Shaneesha Chaudhury looked dubious herself. 'And how much of a danger do these animals present to the people in the street?'

'Well now.' Jim thought about it. 'I mean don't get me wrong. These animals aren't dangerous in the wild, 'cept maybe the bear – but after three–four

244

years in a zoo they may not be feelin' too rosy about members of the human race, know what I mean?'

'Thank you, Mr Burke—'

'—still.' Jim had the spotlight now and did not want to relinquish it. The camera tried to pan away but he followed, keeping his red schnozz squarely in the center of the lens. 'I mean, compared to most of the humans in Central Park this time of night – I mean, if I were you, Shaneesha, I'd be a lot more concerned about the safety of the *wolves*. Hnngh! Hnngh! Hnngh!'

Jim Burke was laughing.

'Well, goddam,' Rocketman said happily, still staring at the TV. 'God-fuckin'-damn.'

'Lobo?' the pilot asked him.

'Goddam Lobo,' Rocketman agreed.

'Fuckin' ay,' the pilot commented, 'good fer him,' and slugged the rest of his vodka.

PC was on his second bowl of paella. 'I wish you guys wouldn't talk in codes,' he complained. 'Who's "Lobo"? And what about this guy you said – Hawkley.' He laid out the last of the jisi in three tall cones, and did the first two himself.

'I don't know,' the pilot said – and stopped in surprise. He hadn't taken Rocketman's suggestion seriously at first, hadn't even treated the issue as real. But there it was, shaped and fully-formed, like an infant abandoned on the doorstep of his mind with a note pinned to its diaper reading 'Please take care of this child.'

'You're thinking about it!' Rocketman sounded as surprised as he. For no reason that surprise annoyed the pilot. The jis' was wearing off – his emotions were skewed as a result, but there was nothing he could do about that.

'Of course I'm thinking about it,' the pilot said, crossly, 'like you said, where else is there to go?' And the guarantee of saying it out loud for the first time seemed to touch the raw hole in his gut that the loss of his friends had torn, and for the first time he had an idea why he might do this thing: because in the impossibility of truly helping his friends, he could do something for his memory of them. He could commit an act that meshed with Eltonjohn's thirst for direction, and with the dignity of Roberto's flight, and the logic in traffic that Obregon held so dear; and in so doing he would strike a blow for memory everywhere, for its role as the glue in patterns.

Of course this in itself would be a process of compensation, a mourning – eventually, perhaps, a cure – but that did not matter so much now.

An image of the silver-green cloud he had dived into off Long Island came unbidden into the pilot's mind. It faded as uncontrollably as it had come, as if whatever was behind it had resolved its own tension, dissipated, and drifted like fog into the night.

PC sniffed mightily, and licked the rest of the crystal off the table.

'Sara!' he said.

'What?'

'That was her name – Sara. I want to come with you.'

'You?' Rocketman laughed out loud. The pilot stared at PC. PC glared at Rocketman, and blushed, but he repeated, gamely, 'I said, I want to come with you.'

'Why?' the pilot asked, eventually.

'Why shouldn't I?'

'Well I don't know—' he looked for reasons. 'If we

246

go, it wouldn't be a joyride. It wouldn't be, exactly, romantic. There's not gonna be any chicks.'

'Doesn't matter.'

'We could end up dead. Or worse.'

'You don't understand, do you?' PC got up and left the kitchen.

God, suffering from acute tsampa overdose, made rodent barfing sounds in the corner.

PC came back a minute later with a wad of transparent sheet plastic the size of a small beach ball.

'Look at this,' he said grimly.

'What is it?' Rocketman asked.

'LayWrap,' the pilot said, and started to giggle. 'Safe sex. *Real* safe sex. Shit, I never seen so much safe sex in one place in my whole life!'

'But that's it,' PC burst out. 'That's exactly it. Safe. It's the safety! That's what's wrong. With my job. With the waltz-moshes. With the women here. They're all totally available, and totally protected, and totally *safe*. It's all so fucking boring it makes me want to *die*!'

PC stood in the middle of his kitchen, both hands buried in the sticky plastic. Tears formed in his eyes, rolled down his nose and cheeks, and fell audibly on the plastic.

'It can be just as boring, to be in Oakdale,' the pilot said softly.

'Maybe not for him,' Rocketman commented, and shrugged.

The pilot watched his friend sniffle. 'God, Rocketman,' he said softly. 'What's wrong with us? We got a civilization that throws good people like Roberto and Obregon into living hell on one hand. Then, on the other, we got perfectly normal, decent

247

people like Fred here who have everything anybody could want and they still bawl their eyes out 'cause they're so bored. What is wrong with us, man?'

'Aaah,' Rocketman said, looking at one of the six-foot tomatoes on the wall. 'We are failed spacemen. That's what's wrong.

'You see, they promised us freedom from this planet we'd poisoned. "Look," they said, "here is the moon. Tomorrow we'll give you Mars. Can the rest be far behind?" And we believed them, deep down where we make up the stories about our own lives. We believed in the films they made to convince us. *Star Wars, Outland, Silent Running,* 2001. In our minds we waltzed in space, aah, the "Blue Danube" rolling forever in all directions, man. We commanded starships. We sought out new life and new civilizations. We made friends with pointy-eared critters who somehow all spoke English. We boldly split infinitives where no infinitives had been split before . . .'

Rocketman put a cigarette in his mouth. He lit three matches. All three sputtered out in his shaking fingers. He took the cigarette out of his mouth.

'But it was all bullshit, brother. It was all so much pablum to keep our minds occupied. They weren't interested in space; what they wanted was our UCC accounts. And so our rockets blew up. Our rockets always blow up. The only ones that work are the ones with MIRVs, and kinetic-kill warheads, and high-resolution digital spy cameras. And now we're stuck in limbo. We've lost the earth, and we can't reach anything else.' He looked at the three dead matches in his right hand.

'Wouldn't you be unhappy?' he finished quietly.

20

'I dislike sedentaries of the heart. Those who trade
nothing become nothing.'

Antoine de Saint-Exupéry
Citadelle

So, with little fanfare and less planning, Rocketman,
the pilot, and to a lesser extent PC, began their search
for Hawkley.

The pilot started in a roundabout fashion from a
payphone on West End Avenue.

First he put in a call to Fat Chico Fong. When the
machine answered, he told it he was fixing up a
fourth-hand Learjet in New Mexico, and the repairs
were taking longer than planned, but he'd be ready
in three weeks' time.

There, he thought hopefully, depressing the cradle.
That should keep the tai-lo's red-sticks off his ass till
he made the free run he'd promised.

Then, swiping the UCC-card again, he called an
attorney to arrange for what help the law would allow
Roberto and Obregon.

The lawyer, Jack Botelho, was a Portuguese-
American from New Bedford. He made a living

249

defending smugglers. He spoke in guarded tones.

He told the pilot that under the provisions of the new Anti-Gang And Terrorist Environment amendments to the reenabled McCarran-Williams Act – popularly known as the AGATE law – he could do no more for anyone caught running illicit cargo than he could for a suspected terrorist. All were deprived of the right of habeas corpus by the Act; Obregon came under the AGATE purview by his mere association with the pilot as well as a tie-in through the ancient Racketeering, Influence, and Corrupt Organizations statute. Botelho's voice turned studiously casual. Did the pilot not want to retain a lawyer for himself, he asked, since he was being indicted in absentia by an AGATE grand jury?

'What for?' the pilot asked, taking off his aviator's glasses as if to see the question better.

'Illegal traffic in unlicensed and restricted equipment of significant value to national security,' Jack Botelho replied, 'aka running pirated organic microchips, which is always a bad idea, seeing how much dough TransCom's PACs put into the Christian-Republicans last election.'

The pilot switched to another booth to continue the call. He arranged to pay the lawyer, in King Fook wafers, by registered mail, for representing Roberto and Obregon.

And he asked Botelho if he had ever seen or talked to Hawkley, the author of the Smuggler's Bible, or knew anyone who had. But the lawyer just laughed.

'Does he even exist, that you know of?' the pilot insisted.

'Put it this way,' Botelho replied. 'There's a lot of smoke. Bound to be a flame somewhere. But the fire

I'd worry about is under your own ass. You *sure* you don't want to turn yourself in? I can maybe cut a deal, at this stage.'

After he hung up the pilot put his dark glasses back on. His scarf was wound over his chin and the collar of his denim jacket was pulled up to his ears. He opened the ECM-pak on the tipped shelf of the booth, pulled out the headphones, and switched the scanner to city range. He fitted the earphones, slung the ECM on one shoulder, and walked away from the pay-phone, listening to cop traffic, looking carefully down the avenue to see if he was being tailed.

The feeling of being chased was nothing new. The edge in every move, the tingle in every cell that came from playing rabbit in a game of foxes was something he had grown used to. Possibly he had even got addicted to it over the years. Always he'd associated that edge with voyage, the tension between foreign and domestic.

Yet for some reason it did not feel out of place on his home turf. Always he'd had the gut-awareness it would come to this someday, over and above the logic and probabilities. Always he'd known that the borders at a country's edges were only an expression of a border in its heart. He'd read the famous Smuggler's Bible chapters where Hawkley, or whoever wrote the book, described the way large organizations became actual life forms; he knew, in theory, this was expressed in bureaucratic terms by the hoarding, distorting, and cutting off of information. But the awareness the pilot had was less abstract and more personal. The Bible talked grandly about how organizations thought and behaved, ate and drank by closing and shutting and building borders around everything and anyone worth having, but he had *seen* how they worked firsthand, in the immigration officials who interviewed them in his childhood, with their endless forms and books of quotas and lists of demands they could not meet. He'd seen it in the state officials who tried to tell his father he could not live on the farm he had bought with his own money; he'd seen it in the regulations they slapped on superboat racers and fliers and people who only wanted to go fast and not deal with rules.

He had chosen to make a living hauling illegal cargo across international boundaries, but he knew that if he was committed to crossing the borders outside the country, sooner or later, one way or the other, he would cross the line inside as well, until he himself became the expression of the trade he plied – he himself became the controlled substance, the black market goods, the contraband, the 'unlicensed and restricted equipment.' And then it was himself he'd have to smuggle, in and out of his own country, his own city, his own life, simply in order to give that life expression.

Twice on the ECM the pilot heard his name mentioned on police channels. 'Marak, Mike Alpha Romeo Alpha Kilo, we got a suspect matches that description, stand by,' and then the stoic negatives as other evidence came in, as the faxed sheets failed to check out.

The pilot took the 7 train back to the Schweik Society to pick up the Chevy, and his chartcase. Hearing his name on the scanner made him feel kind of fluttery. In the yellow pages he found a magic store on Queens Boulevard, where he bought a kid's disguise kit from a fat Punjabi lady. In a Genovese drugstore he purchased a pair of large cheap sun-glasses. The moustache-glue itched, and overall the result made him look like an Atlantic City hustler, but at least it didn't resemble him much.

He fine-tuned the ECM, focusing on BON frequencies, and drove across the Queensboro to West 57th Street.

The tall white building with the car dealership on the ground floor looked exactly the same; not good, not evil. There was nothing to indicate the BON traffic center for the Northeast was set up on its eighteenth floor. The pilot drove around for a while, checking the vans parked nearby because one or more of them almost certainly was a BON surveillance or RDF vehicle. He noted the tags, the logos – 7 Brothers TV and Appliance, Summa Equipment Rental, Speedy Lock and Door, Orkin Pest Control. Scanner traffic was heavy. The BON dispatcher, a woman, had a light, pleasant voice but he could not tell what she was talking about because she spoke in code only. The code was a random polynomial generated by Fujitsu-Crays in a basement in Fort Meade and there was no known way to break it.

He hated being worried with nothing specific to do. He drove around the BON building, then got nervous about being spotted by security cameras or UAVs. He decided to look up Gene Gahagan. Getting onto the Trump-Venezia/Riverside Highway he segued onto 9-N, switched to 487, then the Hutchinson. Fairly certain he wasn't being tailed at this point, he got off the highway system in Rye, New York.

Going to see Gene Gahagan reminded him of how the Smuggler's Bible defined the different kinds of smugglers.

'There are three kinds of freetraders,' the Smuggler's Bible says. 'There are hardass dudes who do it strictly for long green. There are the romantics, the cats that do it for emotional, intellectual, or political kicks. In Darkworld – what used to be called the Third or Fourth Worlds – there are societies like the Pashtu, the Karayar, or the Hakka, whose members are freetraders in the most right-on sense because the tribes they belong to simply are not *down* with the idea of nation-states, let alone borders or Customs.

'Generally speaking,' the Smuggler's Bible continues, 'the Romantics are sloppy. They rap too much, they won't carry cargo they don't dig. They dress hip and get attached to their tool of transport, pay in gold because they like the feel of it, and drive fast wheels . . . The hardasses, on the other hand, treat smuggling like any other lunch-boxin', capitalist business. They look exactly like every other dude in straight society. In the US they use a UCC and go to Disney World with the kids. They live in suburban homes, pay taxes, punch clocks, drive a Saturn. They dress like lawyers and talk like accountants . . .'

Gene Gahagan, the pilot knew, was the very model of the Hardass. He lived in a modern three-bedroom ranch house off Rye Beach Road. He drove a leased Oldsmobile. He owned a small taco franchise and dressed in three-hundred-dollar suits. Once every ten weeks or so he traveled to Georgia under an assumed name, leased an anonymous single-engine plane, flew it to the Cockpit Country and ran back five hundred pounds of pressed Jamaican weed to one of a series of small strips in the South.

Gahagan ran the black side of his business like a CIA operation. He worked out of the office of his taco franchise. Like everyone else in the Trade he listened to Federal frequencies on his scanner.

But that was not all. Gahagan also polygraphed everyone who worked for him. He paid off someone in the USAF meteorological service to call him when they got weather data emanating from AWACS aircraft, which meant he had a backup warning for the deadliest surveillance system on the East Coast.

He had a blind front company in Liechtenstein. He always carried an open airline ticket for Tegucigalpa in his breast pocket. He was the only smuggler the pilot knew who had been in the Trade longer than he.

Gahagan was less than thrilled to see the pilot through the peephole of his office door.

'God, whaddya doing here, Marak,' he hissed, pulling the pilot into his office. He switched on a series of fans, radios, and full-spectrum jammers to shield their conversation.

'I just wanted—'

'You know you're hotter than nuclear waste? The scanner's full of you!'

'Here, too?'

'Here, everywhere.'

Gahagan nervously straightened his tie. The tie was silk, and decorated with little flamingoes. His nails were both manicured and chewed. His face twitched. It was swollen, of the same hue as the flamingoes. He looked every inch the successful junk-food franchise operator.

'I just wanted to ask—'

'God, I can't *believe* you came here!'

Gahagan opened a container of pills and a bottle of Wild Turkey. He swallowed some of the pills, drinking from the bottle's neck.

'I needed—'

'Just say what you have to say, and get outta here.'

'Okay, Gene, I—'

'Come on, come on!'

When he could break through Gahagan's exclamations, the pilot asked him about Hawkley. But Gahagan shook his head, repeatedly. Sure, he knew of Hawkley, everyone did, because of the Smuggler's Bible. He subscribed to the *Gazette*, the CD-ROM updates, through a private mailbox. He knew nothing specific, however. Not where Hawkley lived, or what his history was, nothing. Gahagan's fear was an unpleasant and expanding gas that blew the pilot out the door of the Taco Commander within ten minutes of getting there.

Outside, in the iced parking lot of the franchise, the smell of cheap enchiladas mingled in the pilot's nostrils with the trace stink of Gahagan's sweat as he thought about what to do next.

The pilot was very tired. His mind cracked with the clear vodka hangover and the dull fuzz from jisi yomo. The drugs themselves jazzed hard against the pop of adrenaline that came with added news of the chase. All of this slowed his nerve speed; it spread gloom and lethargy where energy was needed. He had to crank the thoughts open.

First of all, the best person to talk to would be Gershwin. But Gershwin did not hook onto the 'nets. Anyway, the Wildnets no longer felt safe. And physically, of course, Gershwin was on Sandworm Cay. The pilot would have to pass through at least three airports to reach the Cay, and the airports would all be crawling with BON goons. Judging by what was already on the scanner, the goons were all well versed in his vital statistics.

He could radio Gershwin. The ECM-pak had a single-sideband transmitter that was powerful enough, with outside juice and the right antenna. In his apartment he simply hooked it up to X-Corp's TV antenna and he could talk to Ghana, if he wanted. But the apartment was gone.

He fished in his chartcase and selected the US Coast and Geodetic Survey CD-ROM for the Cape May–Block Island region. The ECM screen showed the location of radio antennas, for use as landmarks to take visual or radio bearings, along with the call sign of the station that owned them, or the word 'ABAND' if they were not in operation. He found a series of six 'abandoned' antennas where an old Marconi station had once stood, on the outer beach of Sandy Hook, New Jersey.

He looked around the Taco Commander parking lot. The traffic seemed normal to him; no cars double-parked, no '7 Brothers' vans or late-model Crown Victorias, no double or triple whip-antennas, no ninety-degree arrays for direction-finding; mostly construction workers on lunch break, and overweight women with small kids, and compact cars helplessly spinning tires on the ridged and piled-up snow.

He looked up, and held his breath. Only a flier, used to spotting objects against a backdrop of sky, might have picked it out between the clouds and mall roofs, but there was a UAV, one of the rotary-winged types made for hovering over urban environments. It dipped and buzzed, for all the world like a fat dragonfly, above the seedier areas of Portchester. Almost certainly, the pilot reflected – breathing again – it was running surveillance on the Jamaican posses that still controlled that area. Still he didn't linger in the parking lot but filled up the Chevy at a self-service station in White Plains and headed south.

When he got to Sandy Hook he found only four of the antennas still standing. The others had been eaten through by the salt teeth of the Atlantic wind. The survivors stood forlorn amid the scrub pines, sandwiched between half-eroded dunes, eelgrass, and a transport dump for an oil distribution company. A row fifty yards long of yellow Sunoco signs, with the trademark blue arrow darting off to nowhere, followed a rusted chain-link fence into the graininess of snow-night.

On two of the four antennas, the ceramic insulators remained intact.

The pilot had to file away rust to make a good contact for the ECM-pak's alligator clips. For added power he hooked up the car battery to the ECM. Removing the half-sucker, he taped his headphones back in the leather flying helmet, jacked in the cord, switched to SSB and called for the Connie on 2078.5 and 2.153 megahertz, the call-up frequencies Gershwin monitored.

Snow drifted against the carryall. The sea sobbed in the embrace of an invisible shore. The wind stuck anesthetic needles all over his body. The leather helmet kept his ears fairly warm but he lost touch with his fingers as he typed back and forth between frequencies. He thought about Eltonjohn and Roberto to warm his resolve by the heat of his anger, to fight against the feeling that he was losing touch with the real world, stuck here between cold dun sand and gray winter sea, trying to radio for information about a man who might never have existed except in stories.

The tiredness grew in him. It turned everything black. The dead Marconi station looked like the end of the world, all communications finally cut, no one else to send, no one to receive. No other towers or buzzing transmitters smelling of hot insulation to blip the messages of hope and alliance – all true messages, in the final analysis, being of hope and alliance, or their destruction. The messages would never be written. Only one survivor, thin and disillusioned, squatting by the blasted husks of communication devices, whispering lost, useless queries to the seawind.

For seventy minutes he got nothing. However when he ran the overlap program, looking for a frequency directory, it automatically booted up the interface software he got with the last *Gazette* update. The software, working on schedules and X-ray feed-back from the Great Red Spot of Jupiter, asked him if he wanted to spike his transmissions to coincide with troughs in energy on Jupiter. The pilot, mumbling 'What the fuck,' clicked on the 'Yes' icon. Shortly thereafter he heard Gershwin's voice, tiny as a fly's, extrude the broad accent of the Bahamas across the ether.

'You get my cable?' he asked Gershwin. 'Over.'

'Roger,' came the reply. Neutral, even across that distance.

'I told him not to come.' He could not say Eltonjohn's name.

'Roger,' Gershwin said.

'I want to do something about it,' he shouted in the mike. 'To make up for it. Do you understand? People say Hawkley knows how to stop these ambushes. Do you copy? He knows how to fix Bokon. I want to find Hawkley. Over.'

'Hawkley,' Gershwin repeated. 'Over.'

'Can you tell me?'

'What you want to know?'

'Where he is.'

'Don't know nothin'.'

'Anything, man. Help me.'

Noise, white gray black noise scratched electric fingernails across the background wavelengths. Behind the noise, a front-end bass, a grunt, a phrase – 'Git da funk up off da floor! Yow! Come on!'

Dr Funkenship.

'Pilot, dis Connie Bar,' Gershwin said. 'Stand by.'

'Hurry up,' the pilot told him, conscious of the ever-watchful radiomen of BON, and their skill at triangulation.

Gershwin came back a few minutes later. 'Someone comin' Stateside, mebbe four–five days,' he said. 'Somethin' for you. Message wit Lee. Over.'

'What?' the pilot said. 'Who?'

There was no reply for a full thirty seconds, and then the transmission came again.

'Pilot,' the voice warned. 'Take heed. John Crow circlin', mahn.'

Four hundred and fifty million miles away, the Great Red Spot kicked into another storm. Static rose, and fell. In the hiatus, the pilot heard Gershwin's voice repeat, 'John Crow circlin' . . .'

The static rose once more.

That was no use at all, the pilot fumed as, trembling from the cold, he packed away the alligator clips and ECM and stowed them in the Chevy's trunk. John Crow, he knew, was the Bahamian term for buzzards. Easy enough to figure that one out. But he had no idea who Lee was.

He did not make the connection till he hit Newark, and saw the airport spreading its long light-sheathed legs before the tarry thrust of the eight-lane.

Lee was the waiter at the Weather Café. It made sense, in a bizarre sort of way, that in the worldwide fraternity of mixologists, Gershwin and Lee should know of one another.

21

'. . . the smugglers are dangerous enough. However
the committee must bear in mind the nihilistic
ideology underlying some of these groups – the
so-called Hawkley-ites. These people actually
believe they can establish communities – they call
them "nodes" – they create "market-lines" and
behave like sovereign states. They think they have a
right to trade freely with each other without any
regulation or permission from government. When
our special ops squads, with the permission of the
Philippines government, took out the Manila node,
one of our primary objectives was to demonstrate
the impotence of this ideology. Then we put a
media blackout on the strike, and we played up
the Mexican terrorists instead – we were not being
humble: no, we were trying to halt the spread of a
virus.'

—————(name blanked out)
Assistant Administrator, Special Operations, Bureau
of Nationalizations
quoted in *Nationalizations, Terrorism & Contraband: A
Report by the National Intelligence Committee*
William Gates, Chairman
Washington, DC.

While the pilot sent messages to Sandworm Cay,
Rocketman dug himself into the farthest corner of the

south reading room of the New York Public Library at 42nd Street. He felt safe there, protected by the stone lions outside, hidden from Department of Mental Health investigators by ramparts of stacked books. He wore a heavy disguise consisting of a huge Afro wig and yellow sunglasses, with a long brown chesterfield coat, somewhat too small, and tassel loafers borrowed from PC. He scrawled made-up names on his blue-white call slips as he ordered up every reference he could find on Hawkley.

He found a great deal of raw data, for Hawkley had (apparently) done a lot of things before he (supposedly) wrote the Smuggler's Bible. However most of the information was third- or fourth-hand; stories told by a buddy of a friend of the writer's, surfacing among several dozen volumes of dubious journalistic worth that all purported to describe the colorful rise and honky-tonk fall of the psychedelic movement in San Francisco.

A lot of the data were out-and-out myth, unlikely tales told in the vernacular of alchemy and magic without even a hint of substantiation. Invariably those tales grew more out of some need of the teller's than from the original taproot of fact.

Still, from the vast amount of chaff some grains of hard detail did emerge. The kernels of that information seemed so innocuous, yet so strange in their normalcy, that they killed the suspicion, sown in the back of Rocketman's mind by the pilot, that Hawkley might after all turn out to be as insubstantial as the stories told of him.

Forrest Hawkley Stanhope was born into the bourbon-and-branchwater aristocracy of Tennessee. His father was a surgeon and his grandfather a United

263

States senator. He was thrown out of a military academy in South Carolina for trying to brew hootch in a soapstone laundry vat in the basement. He left home at seventeen and drifted west. In San Francisco he shacked up with a chemistry major from Indiana named Martha Cahoon. Together they began manufacturing lysergic acid dyethylamide 25 – LSD – in the bathtub, and supplying the product to the burgeoning hippie population of the City by the Bay.

What started out as a hobby soon became a crusade. Hawkley and his girlfriend believed in their product. They wanted to make the purest LSD the world had ever known. They wanted to turn the world on to it in a chain reaction of hits that cost two bucks or even less and often were handed out free. They refined the chemical to the limits of the possible. Even the inventor of LSD, Dr Albert Hofmann of Sandoz AG in Basel, Switzerland, had only succeeded in precipitating it into a yellowish powder. Hawkley and Cahoon purified the basic ingredient, ergotamine tartrate. Then they refined the formula. They refined the refinements, again and again, till they ended up with a blue-green, crystalline substance that was so pure it had become piezo-electric – when shaken, or subjected to any other form of pressure, the crystals gave off sparks. They put this LSD into clear tablets and dyed it different colors. They made a liquid of it, tinted it blue, and called it 'mother's milk.' According to legend Hawkley believed that the feelings of the person making LSD at the time of precipitation shaped what kind of trip you got from the drug. Whatever the reason, Hawkley's acid – known as Orange Sunshine, White Lightning, or just plain 'purple,' after one type of colored tab – soon became known as the key of choice to a magic kingdom of rainbow colors and peaceful fantasies. This was a time when people truly believed that there existed another dimension to the mind which, once explored, would forever eliminate war, ugliness, and Ma Bell bills. At their peak, Hawkley and Cahoon were sought after by rock stars and philosophers, as well as by police and the phone company. They manufactured millions of hits, made hundreds of thousands of dollars, and gave away fortunes in free LSD tabs. They were never arrested.

But the trip started to turn bad in other ways. The great American marketing machine ate up and chewed down the hippie movement and barfed it out again in profitable, homogenized form. Every aspect of the counterculture was ripped off, packaged in glossy rainbows, and sold at a hefty markup. Pirates brewed low-grade acid and flogged it as Hawkley's. Magic kingdom or no, Nixon bombed Cambodia. Then Nixon himself was busted. Hawkley split up with Cahoon, who left California, taking their year-old daughter with her. The chief wizard of acid became a recluse. He became, frankly, weird. He lived on steaks because, he believed, Cointelpro was poisoning the vegetables. When he saw anyone, it was from the political fringe of what people once called 'The Revolution'; the Diggers, who wanted to change society by making fun of it; or the Motherfuckers, an East Coast splinter group of Students for a Democratic Society, who wanted to off the bourgeois pigs with Hawkley acid, free love, and bombs made from cleaning products. He also hung out with the Brothers of Carnal Bliss, a former Carmel motorcycle gang who had vowed to undermine US society by smuggling in as much cannabis as they possibly could.

Somewhere during this period Hawkley vanished from all records. During this period, too, the Brothers of Carnal Bliss developed into a major international ring that employed over seven hundred committed smugglers. At one stage they were shipping two tons of weed and hash into the United States every month, most of it from Afghanistan.

The Brothers were busted in '76. Although in smuggling circles Hawkley was rumored to have been a main man in their organization, he was not arrested, or indicted, or even located. He had, to all intents and purposes, ceased to exist – until, in 1987, the first edition of *The Freetrader's Almanac and Cookbook* came out, with the name 'Hawkley' on the cover. The book included a wealth of useful tips, dispensed in dated flower-power style cut with a few words of Lingua which (as gang talk) was just beginning to define itself in the backstreets. There was also a lot of flipped-out philosophizing and a do-it-yourself religion based on stellar navigation, and the adjustment of compasses.

Later on, as the Wildnets came into being, the Smuggler's Bible got wired. Its updates on various security arrangements were sent out in CD form, and subsequently downloaded through the 'nets.

But in all the books there was not one single clue as to where Hawkley was now, or what he was doing, or whether he was even alive.

When he had read through all the material he could find, Rocketman sat back in his seat and scratched his Afro.

He thought about the three weeks he had spent in

the Haight. He'd done Hawkley acid eight times, and slept with more girls than he could honestly remember. The craving for ballistic flight had started before; but the combination of Orange Sunshine and the sweet and repeated orgasms he experienced between the fresh tan thighs and soft lips of those self-styled love-children had for the first time opened wide his imagination to what rocket flight would be like. To Rocketman, Hawkley had become a symbol, over the years, of the power of the imagination, before it was contaminated by narcs, FBI informants, Pentagon spooks, and all the enemies of wing-ed man. He wanted to find Hawkley, he realized, not just to help out Skid, but to repossess the purity of imagination he once had known — the purity that had dissipated with age and vanished forever in a beautiful, white-clouded, deadly explosion over Cape Canaveral on January 12, 1986.

Gershwin's contact got in touch with Lee at the Weather Café three days after the pilot had radioed Sandworm Cay.

The pilot had already seen Lee, and given him the number of his new beeper service.

The beeper read out a number and a single name in matte LCD type; 'Francesca.'

When he called the number, from a payphone, and asked for Francesca, he got a pleasant female voice with a shade of Spanish to it which told him to go to a bar called 'La Ronda' in the Dominican section of Central Park North at nine p.m. that night.

La Ronda was very dark, with flashing colored circus lights on the sign outside and blue-tinted mirrors within. It was a guerrilla smoke bar, one of

267

scores of such places that flouted the Federal ban on public tobacco use. In the faint haze from Vantages and Camels two men played Santo Domingo love songs on over-amped guitars. No one spoke English. Everyone stared at the pilot. The sound of Spanish and guitars reminded him of his Chileans. He scratched his fake moustache and wondered what had happened to them.

A woman came up to the pilot and said, 'Skeed?'

Gershwin's contact turned out to be short, blonde, and cute in a well-fed tabby sort of way. She smoked cigarettes called 'Dillons' that were sponsored by a soap star and aimed at the younger female market. She smiled with one side of her mouth, and half closed her eyes when she talked. She had just smuggled fifteen grams of jisi yomo from Nassau through Kennedy Airport in three condoms up her vagina. She was mentally flying on Fundador and pur-loined jisi, and the high of just making it through. She put her arms around the pilot's neck and said, 'This is from Gershwin.' Her breath was warm, and sweet from the brandy. 'Aloysius van der Lubbe, Breslau, Western Silesia. The "Kneipe Spargnapani."' She spelled it out from memory. 'Also, Daftar Daud Khan, Chitral, Pakistan. All Hawkley people. Wha' choo need, Gershwin said.' She cocked her head, and kissed him. 'Creo que esta todo, babe. Choo wanna drink?'

The pilot bought a Fundador. The guitar players took a break halfway through his drink. In the silence of their rest, a long, low howling noise rose, and vibrated in the strings of the wind outside. The sound was so deep, so far past the modulation of electron-ics, so full of anguish it seemed to soak the world.

'*Coño de la Santa Vierga,*' the blonde girl said. Her eyes had gone from brown to black. 'What de fock was dat?'

'*Un lobo,*' the bartender told her. 'A wolf, from the zoo. They have shot all the others. That one has been singing all night. Last night too. He is all alone now, I think.'

The girl's eyes filled. She was tough, but the jisi had resensitized her.

'They killed them?' the pilot asked the bartender. 'Why'd they do that?'

'*Peligrosos.*' Dangerous. The bartender shrugged. It wasn't his problem. The pilot walked down Broadway, toward PC's, his mind dark from the howling. It was best that Lobo had given the wolves one last shot at running the way they liked to run – the wolves, the cheetahs, the bear and wolverine too – but it struck too close that they should be shot down so summarily. It made his stomach shrink into a little ball, with empathy, with loss, and extrapolated fear.

He felt disappointed, also, by Gershwin's message. There were a number of Hawkley groups around, smuggling 'nodes' that believed in the pseudo-religious and political newsprint in which Hawkley wrapped his fishy info; he could have dug up one or two himself, given time.

But, even if Hawkley really existed, the groups had no relations with him. They simply followed his rituals, as Eltonjohn had done. He was so deep in imagining what might make 'van der Lubbe, Kneipe Spargnapani' any different that he almost missed the croak coming faintly from the doorway of a tiny pet shop on the south-west corner of 104th and Broadway.

269

'Hegel, *mariCON!*'

The memory circuits woke first, and stuck an elbow into the side of his consciousness. He stopped short on the busy sidewalk. A young mother, snarling behind him, rammed him with her stroller. A pair of panhandlers saw him stop and lurched in his direction, holding out card-swipers, hoping conscience was giving him second thoughts concerning their urgent need for credit.

In the window of the pet shop, a parrot with a two-foot tail scratched its beak and muttered to itself. The greens and blues of its feathers were so brilliant that for the first time in all the long dying of fall the pilot felt that spring truly might be possible again.

'*Dialectico del diablo,*' the parrot commented.

'Goddam,' the pilot whispered to the window. 'You Hegel bird! You made it!'

The sign on the window said; 'Rare Macaw, $3,000.'

He went inside the pet shop, feeling for his UCC-card.

No one was at PC's when the pilot got back with the Hegel bird. There was a note in Rocketman's neat handwriting announcing news, and supplies.

He fed both the macaw and his rat with sesame seeds he'd bought at the pet shop. God sniffed at the macaw's cardboard cage, long but without comment.

PC and Rocketman came in just before midnight, arms full of plastic shopping bags.

'Did you find your friend?' PC asked. 'What happened?'

'Nothing much,' the pilot replied, tensing his face to keep from betraying the extent of his disappointment. 'A couple names, in Poland, or what used to be Poland. Asia, too. Not what I hoped.'

'Wooo-eet,' the Jesuit bird whistled from the corner. '*Chinga tu madre, carajo.*'

'What the hell is that?' PC exclaimed, dropping his bags.

'A parrot,' Rocketman said, in wonder, carefully setting down a case of beer.

'A macaw,' the pilot corrected him. 'A Spix's macaw. It's one of the birds I brought in, trip before last. I could tell, 'cause he speaks Portygee. And he doesn't like Hegel.'

'Who?' PC said.

'Pretty bird,' Rocketman cooed at the cage.

The parrot cocked his head at the big human.

'Go fuck yourself,' he said.

'He seems to have picked up some English,' the pilot added.

'Aaaah, well,' Rocketman said, turning back. Remembering the news he wanted to tell, he smacked one fist into the other. 'Listen, we gotta make a trip.'

'I took a sabbatical,' PC butted in, 'from my job. I'm free!' But PC did not look free, or even happy. He simply looked nervous.

Rocketman ignored PC. He stepped closer to the pilot, towering over him. 'I found her,' Rocketman insisted.

'Who?'

'Hawkley's daughter.' The grin came in, subtle as August sun. 'I figured she probably got married, seeing as she's in her mid-twenties by now. So I looked up the newspaper. They checked the wedding announcements for me. The Indianapolis *Online-Star.*'

'Indiana?' the pilot closed his mouth on the stupid

271

question. He felt he was playing straight man in a comedy everybody got but him.

'The girlfriend,' Rocketman explained, with the air of an amateur conjurer flipping over the third card. 'Martha Cahoon. She was from Lakewood. That's near Indianapolis. That's where she went, when they split up. Her daughter still lives there. We gotta go to Lakewood.'

'Well, dag,' the pilot said, in surprise, not displeasure.

'We could leave now,' Rocketman suggested, 'right this minute.'

'Wait a minute,' PC protested. 'I mean, what's the big rush?'

'You don't want to come,' Rocketman turned back in his direction, 'it's OK, nobody asked you anyway.'

'He can come if he wants,' the pilot said.

Rocketman looked at the pilot again. PC lifted his chin.

'I only meant,' he said. 'Why should we just drop everything like that?' He picked up his shopping protectively. 'I'd have to make arrangements. I got bills to pay. I need to e-mail my broker, and the bank. I have to talk to the super. There's a thousand things to do. I got to call a couple women—'

'Shit,' the pilot interrupted him. 'PC, man, you shouldn't leave now, this minute – you should leave about two years ago.'

'It's better fast.' Rocketman shone on PC the kind of stare he once used on junior metallurgists who wanted to pour flanges on only two sets of simulations. 'We find out fast, this way. Because if Hawkley's girl doesn't know where he is, no one does.

'Plus,' he added, 'the quicker we move, the harder it'll be for them to find us, when they come a-lookin.'

'Who?' PC said. His face was all frown.

'The Feds,' Rocketman told him, with grim satisfaction. 'You been harboring fleeing felons. You're an outlaw now, just like us. Isn't that what you wanted?'

PC just looked at him. The Hegel bird chuckled to itself.

The pilot went to pack.

22

'At first glance, everything looked the same . . .
it wasn't. Something evil had taken possession of
the town.'

Invasion of the Body Snatchers

PC, Rocketman, the pilot, God, and the Hegel bird
drove to Indianapolis in fifteen hours straight, motor-
vating linear down the interstate, doing exactly the
speed limit in the old Chevy the pilot had bought in
Bayou Noir.

PC wanted to take his Bavarian sports car, but
Rocketman insisted the Chevy would be more anonymous. The sports car, innocuous in the city, would
stand out in the Midwest, he said.

Also, like all late-model vehicles, the Bavarian car
had an anti-theft transponder that would send PC's
full name, UCC number, and a hundred other details
blooping onto the activator screens whenever they
passed through a tollbooth or got within a quarter
mile of a state police post. If BON had somehow
managed to link PC to the pilot, they would be picked
up within a hundred miles of New York.

The Malibu, on the other hand, could not be linked

with the pilot, since he'd kept the old tags, which were registered to a crippled woman in a godforsaken bayou in Louisiana. He'd bought the car under a false name in any case.

When, around eight o'clock the following night, they got to the area of Indianapolis indicated in the wedding announcement they found most of that suburb was taken up by a huge covered shopping mall.

The mall was a wall-mall — built in the new style, with three floors underground and five over, incorporating not only shops but clinics, an arboretum, a motel, a bus station; surrounded by razor wire, perimeter lights and interlocking-arc security cameras.

Behind the perimeter, the building itself controlled the suburban landscape. Built of brick and concrete, it resembled a gigantic two-dimensional slime mold that had grown and reproduced in right angles over a geological epoch. Its reptilian back was almost a mile long and covered with thousands of individual square growths, like scales. It excreted black asphalt — at any rate it was surrounded by three square miles of it — and was serviced by boxy metal creatures that drove in and out twenty-four hours a day to pick up nourishment in white plastic shopping bags or drop it off in large brown cardboard boxes.

Large neon signs flashed arrows whenever they approached. 'Parking available Level 7-G!' the signs insisted.

They drove around the mall, looking for someone from whom they could ask directions, but no humans were visible. Only two or three souped-up drag-jousting cars that periodically would scream out of the black depths of the asphalt and hurtle around the old Chevy. The drag-jousters were late-model Trans-Ams and Land Cruisers with truck engines and tractor shocks. They had multiple exhausts and twin or quad chromed carbs sticking out of their mirror-polished hoods. They sported silver wheels, and darkened windows.

Painted flames and dragons' teeth made snarls of their wheelguards and grilles. The long, hydraulic jousting booms were strapped down on support braces, for car-jousting was too deadly to practice at, and the booms were used only in official competition. Instead, arms gloved and clad in black imitation-leather twirled a heavy chromed chain from the passenger's side of each car. No other features were visible.

Once one of the drag-jousters came close enough to whang his chain on the hood of the Chevy, before tearing off again into the cold yellow light.

Yet someone must have been watching because at that point the wall-mall's anti-terrorist gates retracted and two cream sedans pootled out of the entrance to the underground parking lot, and gave chase. They flashed the pink lights of vigilantes and tore past the Chevy at forty or fifty miles an hour. Their drivers had white hair that streamed in the blast of the cars' heaters. The words 'Service Corps of Retired Executives — Security Div.' were stenciled on the doors. In the Midwest of today, with three-quarters of the population over sixty-five, old people queued up for any kind of work, and SCORE guards were as common as cops.

Behind the SCORE cars, a couple of Safety Volunteer Saabs pulled up in the sodium light, waiting for their crack at the dragsters.

'Fuck,' the Hegel bird screamed. 'Fuck Hegel!'

'Mebbe we better go inside,' PC suggested.

Inside they found a wasteland of a different order. The entire 280 acres of mall was flooded with neon and classic nineties music. There were hundreds of people in the main avenues, shopping or exercising or just riding the glassed-in escalators. The people wore earphones and some even had half-suckers strapped at eye level. These walked with the curious gait that showed they were moving mostly in a different environment from the one physically surrounding them. A few, showing the unmistakable first symptoms of TDF, wore three or four walkmen besides the usual brace of cellphones and beeper belts; they congregated by the screens of a VR arcade, a 3-D multiplex, a robot-sumo parlor, watching the screens that showed the virtual dramas, or mechanized mayhem in the arcade behind.

The pilot thought of Presley, the wiry informer on Sandworm Cay, and felt guilty, a little.

The shoppers would not talk to them. The mall-milers were too busy putting in their distance – up and down, up and down the warm bright tiled concourse in gaily-striped plastic shoes – to give them the time of day. The shop assistants offered little help once they realized the three men were not here to buy. Most of them seemed to have no idea of the geography of Indianapolis in any case. An ancient SCORE guard told them, 'You used to be able to get to North Lakewood down the Fairview 'pike that way, but now they built that Interstate, you can't get on or off of it, and you gotta go all the way to Greenfield, now.' He stroked the stock of his Tech-9, absently. 'That's five mile west of here, an' I dunno how to get there, then.'

They got back into the Chevy. Rocketman drove. The old man's directions were the only guide they had so they followed them. Half a mile from the wall-mall the four-lane was blocked at a much larger highway. A huge overpass rose into the confused night. Obviously it had been started ten or fifteen years before and never completed. Flashing signs guided them sideways around the detour. The concrete structure hung halfway over the interstate; its truncated end, bandaged in tarps and plywood, was a take-off ramp to nothing.

In Greenfield they found a sign reading 'North Lakewood; 2.5 miles.' They drove down streets that all appeared exactly identical; half-acre lots, dead clipped lawns, hardwood trees evenly trimmed every thirty feet. Ranch houses with vinyl siding. Many of the houses had a satellite-dish antenna or two, usually air-brushed with scenes of impossibly quiet lakes and mountains, in impossibly vivid colors. It was a comfortable suburb. Outside each dwelling, a telephone pole carried the yellow junction boxes of B-Net cable.

Two cars per house, on average. Kids' toys on the driveway. Dog barking out back. Sit-down mowers, remote-control garage doors, electric dog fences. Servo-mechanisms. The alien blue flicker of television behind each curtained window. Sometimes, the mirrored flash of a TV screen was visible, reflected against the goggles of a full face-sucker.

Every quarter-mile or so they passed a church. The only difference between the churches and the ranch houses was a short steeple, a bigger driveway, a larger dish antenna.

One of the churches was a Johnsonist chapel. A giant billboard, with Jimmy Hoffa's face raised toward

278

the light and his hands, filled with UCC-cards, raised higher, dominated the parking lot.

'Goddam,' the pilot said wonderingly. 'I feel like we've got lost, and ended up in another country. Or aliens have taken over. Or something. I mean, where is everybody?'

'It's weird,' PC said.

'We haven't seen a single person since the wall-mall, 'cept in cars.'

'But that's *exactly* what happened,' Rocketman said. 'The aliens *have* taken over. Don't you watch videos?'

'Oh, no,' PC groaned. 'Please, Rocketman, don't give us the pulpit.' But Rocketman ignored him.

'It's true,' Rocketman continued. 'It's been happening for fifty years. Slow but sure. Picture it. Every sci-fi movie since the early fifties.' He made a camera viewfinder with his hands, framing one of the ranch houses in palm and finger, steering with his knees.

'Quiet suburban town,' he began in a weighty tone. 'Dead center of America. Milk, apple pie, and defense electronics. Nothing happens, ever. But suddenly you feel something has gone wrong. You can't explain it. Maybe it's just you. But your neighbors seem – aaah, different. Unreadable. There's strange noises, odd lights, just beyond the range of normal perception. The kid looks at you like you've grown another head. The dog whines and hides under the porch.

'And one day, something does occur – something so horrible, so grisly, you will have to shut it up inside you forever. It's an event you can't even describe, yet it tells you, beyond the shadow of a doubt, what has happened. A force that is cold, and infinitely distant, and fundamentally *strange* has taken over, not just your suburb, not just your neighbors, but you. *They're here!'*

A Safety Patrol slowed down to look at the Chevy. The volunteers noticed the lack of car-helmets, and jotted down their license plate number. However this was not yet a stoppable offense in Indiana, so they continued on. Rocketman did not even notice the Safety Volunteers. He was getting into it; he was bouncing up and down on the driver's seat.

'The aliens are here,' he yelled. 'They're inside you, they're inside me. They have yukky scales and abdominal suckers. And you know what they are? Huh?' Rocketman with one hand grabbed the dashboard in front of him and squeezed so hard he tore the Naugahyde.

'This is what they are; they're a life that's so comfortable we don't need anything. If we don't need anything, we don't have to relate to our surroundings, we lose our relevance as a species. And how do these aliens work? Aaah, I'll tell you. Through a network of conglomerates that sell us, I don't know, *paella-makers* in exchange for our souls. A bureaucratic monster that gives us VR-sitcoms in exchange for power. That tells us our earwax smells, to make us buy ear deodorant, and all the while they pump growth hormones into our food, and transmit X rays through our VDTs, and, aaah, dump acid rain, and spray chemicals, and bury nuclear waste in our backyards, so our children end up with spines like jelly and little animals in the bloodstream. Making monsters on our own swing-sets. Turning our wives into fanged slimy creatures that crawl into the cesspool out back to breed. Body Snatchers. Aliens. Dawn of the fucking *Dead*. Shit, man, they're not coming, they're already here, they've taken over Washington, they kill whoever finds out, they—'

'Holly Drive,' PC interrupted. 'Didn't you say, Holly Drive?'

Rocketman stood on the brakes. He switched on the dome light. He took out a notebook. '14 Holly Drive, North Lakewood,' he said softly. He was out of breath. 'That's it. Mr and Mrs Roger Taylor.

'Eleuthera Hawkley Stanhope Taylor.'

But there was no one at number 14. A TV hummed and flashed at number 16 but no one came to the door. Number 12 was dark and shut down. They walked back to 14, sauntering casually around the house. From the back you could hear the hum of voices and music but it was all treble with the tweeter twist of synthesized stereo. The porch furniture was covered. A light blinked on in back of the house. Still no movement was visible. Very likely the house's security program was turning on different lights and appliances at preset hours to create the illusion someone was home. This was supposed to deter prowlers.

'There's a car in here,' PC said, peering through a porthole in the garage. 'Lexus. Nice.'

'They have two cars,' Rocketman told him. 'Everybody does, in towns like this. It's a psychological thing. One is for your day-to-day life, and one is for the alien that—'

'Shut the fuck up,' PC told him.

They returned to the Chevy. No one said anything for a long time. They were all tired of driving. The radio was tuned to KMAL, the '90s oldies station. It was the only station that came in clearly here. After forty-five minutes of cruising in no particular direction, listening to Alanis Morissette, they found a mini-mall with a Vicious Vindaloo franchise. They ate dinner, noses running from the spice, watching tough guys with leather jackets and car-jousting scars devour the Nero's Special (Triple-Hot) 18-Alarm Lamb Curry. The tough guys, adding red pepper sauce, laughed bravely. The tears coursed down their cheeks.

Then they got back in the car. The pilot fed the Hegel bird and cleaned up the mess he'd made in back and took God out for a scamper along the empty sidewalk of the mini-mall. When he returned, Rocketman and PC were asleep. Even the Hegel bird, perched on the back of the passenger seat, had his gaudy head tucked under one aquamarine wing.

The pilot got in his seat and looked out over the orange stain of street lighting and the gas station signs and the careful fringe of trees protecting the suburbs of Lakewood and the vast bulk of the Lakewood Wall-Mall squatting like the mothership behind. The atmosphere in the car was lightly tinged with tandoori and garlic.

He, too, fell asleep.

The next morning they ate breakfast at a Dairy Donut. The three men were stiff and irritable. They paid long visits to the bathroom and sat gingerly when they came back. The pilot said he would go alone to Holly Drive. It would look suspicious for three men who weren't Mormon missionaries to sit in a parked car in the streets of a town like this.

He found the street after only half an hour and parked twenty yards away from number 14. It was a nothing day – no rain, no sun, no wind; haze, cirrus, mid-range temperatures. It looked like a low was stalled overhead, the pilot thought. The Hegel bird made constant snoring and farting sounds, it was what he'd been listening to all night. The pilot found a college station that came in faint and scratchy but occasionally played a refreshing burst of Shift-shin and in any case covered the digestive noises made by the macaw.

Forty minutes after he had parked, the front door of number 14 opened. A medium-sized man in chinos and a sports jacket came out and slammed the door behind him. It made a noise like a rifle shot, but apparently that was not loud enough, for he unlocked the door, opened it wide, and slammed it once more, harder. The garage door opened by itself. The man went inside, the Lexus came out, the garage door came down, the Lexus took off down the street, squeaking its tires somewhat. After that, calm returned to Holly Drive.

The pilot waited twenty minutes, then got out and walked over to number 14 and rang the doorbell. He rang for ten minutes but no one answered and he heard no sound and saw no more movement than the night before.

That day passed the way nothing days pass. The pilot found an easy way back; if you did a quick dogleg out of the cluster development and got onto Willowbend Avenue, it was almost a straight shot to the mini-mall.

Avoiding the Vicious Vindaloo, they ate food that was nothing food and talked about nothing to avoid voicing the fear that they'd left everything behind and driven almost nine hundred miles for no reason.

PC obtained Roger and Eleuthera Taylor's phone number from information. He called and a machine answered. It said the owners of the house could not come to the phone right now.

Rocketman stood guard at the Taylor house for part of the afternoon. They all ate dinner at a QuikThai. Over shrimp in peanut satay they agreed that they would go back together to number 14 and if Roger Taylor was there, they would ring the bell till he answered. Then they'd ask him point-blank where Eleuthera was.

On their way back down Willowbend they passed an ambulance wailing in the opposite direction. A cop cruiser following behind the ambulance slowed and the cop stared at the Chevy, then sped up after the rescue vehicle. Number 14 looked exactly the same and they got no more response than before, but as they stood uncertainly on the brick walk an old woman called to them through the cracked and curtained window of number 12. The theme song from *Pain in the Afternoon* strained through the crack. 'She's at Fairview Hospital, the ambulance just picked 'em up,' the woman said, and quickly slammed the window and locked it shut again.

They got back in the Chevy. The pilot took the wheel. He turned left at the end of Holly Drive and opened her up. The twin carbs sucked air like a ramjet. At the junction of Willowbend and Bella Vista Drive a flatbed truck full of ten-foot fiberglass 'hamburgers' was backing into the parking lot of a new BAADBurger restaurant and the traffic was jammed up so solidly even the shrieks and lights of the ambulance could not dissolve it. The police car was gone, off on a tangent to guard the softer suburbs. The pilot ruthlessly cut around the jam, over the divider and back to slot himself into the emergency lane,

284

directly behind the waiting ambulance.

The burger-truck sneezed itself backward, into the parking lot. The ambulance, freed, picked up speed. The pilot kept the Chevy ten feet from its rear fender. As they followed the emergency vehicle, they could all see, through the left rear window, a woman strapped onto the gurney inside.

The gurney was set at an angle. The woman was very lean, almost too thin. She had a wide mouth and cheekbones. Her hair was light brown, and damp, and stuck to a large forehead. Her face was small, elf-like, and absolutely void of color. She lay in the square frame of the ambulance window, with the plastic straps and EKG screens and tubes and bottles above her, pinned to her helplessness by the cold blue lights. She looked like a sea creature long taken from water.

'God, is that her?' the pilot muttered wonderingly to PC, who was sitting beside him.

'She looks dead,' PC answered. 'Maybe she is dead,' he continued, 'but she sure is cute.'

It was as if she'd heard them. The woman opened her eyes and looked directly at the Chevy. Her eyes were very dark. She could not have seen much through the glare of headlights, but the pilot sensed, nonetheless, that their gazes touched, very briefly, and that she saw them, and wondered who they were.

The hospital looked like a wall-mall that sold health services. A sign read 'Fairview United Hospital: A Division of MicroDyne/Siemens Wellness Systems AG.' The ambulance pulled up at the emergency entrance. The gates closed behind. A guard pointed the Chevy to guest parking. The pilot got out, ran

Brian Veitch's UCC-card through the scanner, and trotted around color-coded corridors to ER reception. The paramedics were filling out forms on a MicroDyne workstation. He sat in the waiting area while Eleuthera's husband answered computer questions fed to him by a white-smocked Rwandan. Eleuthera Hawkley Taylor, maiden name Stanhope, had a pneumonial condition, complicated by asthma. Her condition had deteriorated drastically over the last couple of hours. Seen up close, Eleuthera's husband was fair, with a short nose and little cheek pockets, like a chipmunk. He wore chinos with a white belt, white shoes, and horn-rim glasses. He ran his fingers through his thinning hair as he worried. His age was thirty-four, his profession 'businessman,' his insurance comprehensive. He took out a wallet and swiped three different cards through the scanner to prove it.

An hour later they wheeled Eleuthera Taylor past the pilot on the way to a private room on the third floor. She was breathing through an oxygen mask. The pilot looked for doctors' gowns to steal but this hospital seemed much smaller and tighter than Bellevue. He would have to wait till the next day, for visiting hours, to make contact. He went back to tell the others.

They ate dinner at an all-night doughnut franchise. The place was filled with SCORE guards and overweight, incurious cops. The doughnuts bore names like 'Swizzle,' 'Cheree,' and 'Parfait.' Rocketman asked a trucker where to find a motel and he said there were none in this area but there was a truck stop on US 36 where they could get showers and a bunkroom. They found it in less than an hour and

286

cleaned up for five dollars apiece. The price included a small bar of soap and a thin towel. Another ten dollars in UCC credit bought them each a bunk with sheets that rasped like sandpaper.

The pilot wanted to see the Indianpolis Raceway. It took them an hour and a half to find it. They drove around its acres of parking lots, in slow-motion parody of the activity the place was famous for. They found no easy way inside. They went back to the truck stop.

Visiting hours at Fairview United started officially at one p.m. the next day. The pilot, whittled sharp by impatience, went back in at eight a.m., with PC but without Rocketman, who refused to go through the doors. He was finished with hospitals, the big man said.

Around eleven a.m. the pilot managed to slide into a men's staff room and rip off an intern's gown and a surgical cap. At 11:06 he found six or seven yards of hospital computer printout discarded in a waste trolley. By 11:15 he was on the third floor, pretending to look through the printout, asking nurses for Taylor, Eleuthera.

There were voices in her room. Roger Taylor's, a doctor's, another woman's.

The pilot found a wheelchair and sat down, still madly leafing through the printout for the benefit of the nursing staff, who looked in his direction and gossiped to each other, possibly about him, possibly not. In the haze of his own hoarded fatigue intuition was dull and could not decode their body language. Eventually Roger Taylor, the medic and a woman in her mid- or late forties came out of the room and

287

stood around the elevator bank, talking in sentences with long pauses on either end.

'There's no clinical reason she shouldn't be responding,' the doctor said. 'Her fever's down. Her vital signs are good, very good, considering. Fatigue is a factor, of course. Psychological stress, post-hyperthermic shock – I've seen it before.'

'But she won't even nod,' Roger Taylor complained. 'She doesn't even know I'm here. She doesn't do anything.'

'She ran very high fevers, as a child,' the woman said.

'Children do,' the doctor said.

The pilot looked curiously at the woman. She had light-brown hair, the same color as her daughter's but streaked and teased in a hollow perm. She wore clothes in very bright colors, cut like tubes to disguise a body that was losing the last of whatever tension youth once gave it. She wore big diamonds in gold and platinum settings on three fingers. Her perfume was *Lebensraum*, expensive, commanding. Her mouth was drawn in a tight hard line, to control and dominate the eyes, which were very big and gray and full of enthusiasms, every single one of them tied down and tightly muzzled.

'There won't be a problem, Mr Taylor, Mrs Crane,' the doctor said, flashing a smile like a traffic light. 'Trust me.'

The pilot went downstairs, taking off his gown in the staircase. He found PC eating fried chicken in the cafeteria.

'She's unconscious,' he told PC, 'they don't know why. But I think her mother's with her.'

'Maffa?' PC said, spitting batter.

'Martha Cahoon,' the pilot agreed. 'Hawkley's girl-friend.'

'Then why don't you ask *her*?'

The pilot shook his head. 'I didn't like her mouth.'

PC nodded. It was the kind of argument he understood perfectly.

The pilot went back to Eleuthera's ward twice during visiting hours, and three times overnight, between snatches of sleep caught in the waiting room. He snuck into her room, once, when her husband was in the cafeteria. He saw nothing but the unhappy hair, the oxygen mask, a slope of chinbone, a curve in the counterpane.

Rocketman grew unhappy. He was sick of sitting in the car. It was cold. The backseat smelled of parrot droppings. The Hegel bird was not happy either. Louder and louder, it imitated their flatulence, grumbled to itself in Portuguese, snapped its beak at their fingers.

God was bored. He too had bad gas, from a constant diet of curry and QuikThai and doughnuts. To relieve the pressure he ran around and around the backseat, farting. He drove everybody so crazy the pilot ended up taking him along on his hospital visits, lying doggo in the big pockets of his intern's gown.

PC had found a pediatric nurse to flirt with — casually, he claimed, just to keep in shape — but the pilot was growing despondent. Their journey was too tenuous, the results too uncertain to suffer a loss of momentum with any degree of grace. The brain-pictures of Roberto and Eltonjohn asked soundless questions to which he had no answers. His stomach was beginning to sour with the strain. And the hospital was getting to him: the plastic food; the

289

out-of-date magazines, like TV news printed on glossy paper; the chairs too long to sit and too short to lie on, the constant undertone of climate-controlled agony . . .

Late in the afternoon of the following day the pilot decided to force the issue. He waited till Roger Taylor and Martha Cahoon went to the cafeteria together, then snuck into Eleuthera Taylor's room.

She was in virtually the same position he had seen her in last. Her chest rose and subsided, very slow, very regular. An IV dripped. A half-sucker was propped on a tiny bump halfway down the thin ridge of her nose. The jack ran to a private Virtix set propped on the chipboard dresser. The set played a rerun of *Pain in the Afternoon*. Carrington MacBride told Amy Dillon that he was leaving her, again. Amy responded by telling him she was pregnant, by Carrington's brother. Their dark histrionics filled the room.

The room smelled of bedpans, and *Lebensraum*.

He sat in a chair, watching her face, reading her chart. The fever was down; it stood only one degree above normal. Her red-blood-cell count was low. A medic's note read 'Subject exhibits early classic dependencies of TDF, but none of the neurological symptoms are present.' He registered a sense of displacement, brought on by the confinement and smells. He felt that he was back with Carmelita, talking to another shut-down woman, locked down over mental pain as opposed to fever but shut down nonetheless. He thought of his own belief that despite the shock, mental or physical, Carmelita could still hear his voice and his message, carried on the low frequency of his concern and caring. There was a

290

level, he'd thought with Carmelita — maybe not conscious, but still active — where words spoken in affection and hope were never totally wasted. Not for fetuses, not for old people in comas. No matter what the doctors said.

'Eleuthera,' he said. He cleared his throat and tried again, louder. 'Eleuthera.

'You don't know me,' he continued. 'I'm a pilot. My name's Sk— my name's Joe. Joe Marak.'

No response. Not a flicker of skin reaction. Her breathing was unchanged.

'I'm here,' the pilot went on, 'because one of my friends was killed, and two others were thrown into Oakdale Penitentiary, which is an awful place where they might die, too. They're smugglers, or outlaws, but they were all good people and they never did anything really bad. But they got sent to Oakdale, and so did a lot of other people like them.

'I want to stop this from happening to these people, and the only person who knows how to stop this is Forrest Hawkley Stanhope. Your father. You see—' He knew he was going on too long, he knew that even if the girl heard anything she heard it from so deep, at so many removes, it would not do any of them any good, but as with Carmelita he needed to repeat this stuff if only to convince himself his motives were valid and this trip was worth it and he was not totally losing his mind. 'You see, I know you prob'ly haven't seen him in awhile, but maybe he writes to you, an'—'

He stopped. His lungs seized. The girl's head had moved. She swallowed. But these were the reactions of sleep.

'Anyway, I was hoping you might help me find—'

This time her head turned. All the way around, to look, with eyes that were open and blinking dark gray through the half-sucker at him. The pupils defended themselves against light, and focused. They took him in – the surgical cap, the gown, the contradiction of his face.

She fumbled at the half-sucker, pulled it off by its cord.

'Who—' she croaked, and licked her lips. 'Who – on earth, are you?'

'My name's Joe,' he repeated stupidly. She had very clear eyes, he thought. 'Joe—'

'Marak.'

His pulse rate went up. It was one thing to theorize she could hear. It was quite another to find she was listening.

'You heard,' he said. 'The whole—'

'Of course. You were practically talking in my ear.'

'But I thought—'

'I know.'

'But why?'

She scrunched up her mouth. 'Because,' she said. 'I din' feel like talking.'

'But the doctor,' he babbled on. 'Your mother. Your husband.'

She almost smiled.

'I don't get it,' he said.

'I know,' she said. 'It's weird.' She looked away.

'I din' say that.'

'I'm tired,' the girl said, turning to look at him again. 'I'm sooo, sooo tired. I needed a rest. They wouldn't understand. They're nice to me, they're so darn nice, everyone takes care of me, it's . . . exhausting. Roger is sweet. But all I need is some time

292

by myself. To get better. Just by myself . . .'

'But why don't you just go somewhere,' he said. 'They have places—'

'Funny farms?'

'I guess.'

'I'm not crazy. And I don't want not to feel. Those places, they make you not feel. Do you understand that?'

'That makes sense to me,' he told her, brightly.

'Does it?' She got up on one elbow. It took real effort. He kept his eyes away from where the hospital johnny hung wide, revealing the blinding soft whiteness of her lower breast. 'Does it, Joe Marak?'

'Of course,' he said. 'I don't like to feel, some of the time. When it hurts. But if I didn't feel, how would I know if I wanted to or not?'

She chewed that one over. There wasn't much to chew. Her shoulder got tired. Her eyes lost shine.

She flopped back on the pillows and said, 'You're one of them, aren't you? You're a smuggler, too.'

'Why do you say that?'

'Or a druggie. One of those kinds of things.'

'How do you know I'm not a policeman? Or a reporter? Or a doctor, for that matter?' He squirmed, trying to readjust his intern's gown. God had woken up and was trying to find a more comfortable sleeping position in the garment's pocket. His little claws dug through the thin green nylon.

'You need help from my father.' She knocked the word 'father' out of her mouth viciously, thwacking the consonants against her front teeth. 'Hawkley. *The Freetrader's Almanac and Cookbook.* You're no policeman.'

'I'm a freetrader,' he admitted. 'But I don't smuggle anything stronger than jisi yomo.'

'Yeah, right.'

'It's true.'

'Oh, that's just great,' she said, 'a moralist.'

'Look, I'm not—'

'I wouldn't even try.'

'It's not the point.'

'I should call the police.' The gray in her eyes was the gray of polar pack.

'Maybe you should.' He had a feeling she was testing him with that. Her eyes drifted down toward his lap. 'My God,' she burst out, 'what the heck is that?'

He didn't have to look.

'It's a rat,' he told her. 'Don't worry. He's just a pet.'

'My God,' she said again. The gray had warmed of a sudden, to the temperature of sun-heated rocks. 'Can I see him? Does he bite?'

He reassured her. He put God on the covers, near her waist. The rat sniffed the blankets, whiskers working like pulse radar. Her fingers moved, but she didn't touch him.

'Roger won't let me keep any pets,' she said. 'Not even a kitten.'

'He does tricks,' the pilot told her. 'Look.' He scratched God's belly. The rat rolled over and shook all four paws in the air, grinning in his sickly fashion.

The corners of her mouth lifted.

'What's his name?'

'God.'

'What?'

The rat farted, audibly.

'God. That's his name.'

The girl's cheeks blew out. She started to laugh. She didn't want to, she tried to hold the laugh in, actually holding on to her chest with her fingers, but it was too strong for her. The laugh grew in proportion to the barriers erected against it till it racked her lungs with its spasms and moistened the corners of her eyes and echoed like April down the antiseptic corridors.

'God,' she gasped, 'I can't believe it. I have to – tell you,' she said. 'Haven't heard from him – fifteen years. 'Cept Christmas card.'

'Hawkley?' he asked, not wanting to believe.

She nodded. The effort of trying to control her laughter made her hiccough and utter noises that sounded like agony. 'Eeee – eee.'

'He's abroad—' she gasped, ''s all I know. Last Christmas.'

Footsteps rang down the hall.

Roger Taylor burst into the room, and recoiled, both hands spread tense, partly at the sight of his wife, awake and laughing her guts out, mostly because of the rat on her bed.

'Ela!' he shouted, 'God!'

'God,' she gasped. 'Oh! Roger. God! Eeee!'

'Ela.' He started to approach her, but the pilot was in the way. He stared at the rat in utter disbelief. 'Stop it, Ela,' he said, and 'Who is this?'

Martha Cahoon Crane hustled in behind him. She saw the rat and muttered, 'Shit.' She looked at her daughter and said, 'You're awake!'

The pilot grabbed God by the scruff of the neck and stuffed him in his pocket.

'You aren't a doctor,' Roger Taylor said, running his fingers through his comb-over. 'Who are you? What are you doing in my wife's room?'

'I'm a – uh, therapist,' the pilot said. 'I'm a, uh, mammal therapist. I use animals as tools. Very few people are aware that rats are one of our more intelligent mammals. Sensitive, too. They, uh, work wonders on this type of case. It really works. See?' He pointed at the girl.

'Are you okay, honey?' Martha Cahoon Crane asked, bending over the bed to touch her daughter, but keeping her eyes on the pilot.

'Honey' was unable to talk. The initial displacement of humor, the world-out-of-joint, banana-peel kick that first jolted her into laughing had created a second displacement, and a third. She was laughing even harder, only now it was because she probably shouldn't, and because of the disapproval in her mother's mouth, and most of all because of Roger, and the expression on his face, which looked somewhere between a possum launched unexpectedly into earth orbit, and a cow who had just swallowed a ten-pound bag of pop rocks.

'Control yourself, honey,' Ela's mother said.

'Eeee,' Honey said. But she quieted down eventually.

'He wants to – find my father,' Ela whispered, between giggles.

'I don't understand this,' Roger repeated, taking off his glasses and polishing them as if this would allow him to see things in better perspective.

Ela's mother was looking hard at the pilot. Her eyes were like airframe aluminum. If her mouth had been tight before, it was taut as a cable on the Golden Gate Bridge now. 'I think I do,' she said. 'I do. He's one of them. He's one of Forrest's goddam freaks, and I'm calling the police!'

'Don't do that,' the pilot shouted, 'don't do that!' But Martha had already pulled out a cellphone and was punching the buttons.

'Nice meeting you, Ela,' the pilot told her. 'Nice family you got here. Real nice. Real happy you're better, an' everything. Nice to meet you too, Mrs Crane, or should I say – Cahoon.' He moved backward out the door and into a nurse who was coming to see what all the hoopla was about. He could hear Ela's laughter winding up again. It rang most of the way down the staircase. Then it stopped, all of a sudden.

Luckily PC is in the waiting room. They move fast, out the door, to the Chevy. Rocketman is at the drooling stage of sleep and does not budge as they get in and start off, but the parrot yelps.

'Fuck this hospital shit,' he screeches, in faithful mimicry of what he's been hearing from Rocketman over the last twelve hours.

A security guard pops out of the front entrance and looks around bemused just as they slip behind the emergency-room wing, headed for the exit. A figure in a pus-green hospital johnny comes hurtling through the ER doors, arcs of lily ass flashing out the loose garment. The figure brakes to a halt in the middle of the circuit road, arms and legs and sandy brown hair seeming to catch up independently, she's been moving so headlong. The girl looks around, bewildered by the cool sun.

'Stop!' the pilot yells – PC is driving. 'It's her!'

'What do you mean, "stop"?' PC hits the brakes anyway.

The pilot jumps out. He is looking back at the girl. For her part, she takes one look at him and runs toward the car. Comes to a halt one foot away from the open sedan door.

297

'Take me with you?' she says.

'What are you talking about?' he asks her.

'Please. Just let me come.'

'Why?'

'Because,' she says, 'I have – to get – out of here.' Coughing lightly between every two words.

She looks behind her, anxiously. She is sweating and unsteady. She puts a hand on the car roof for support. The other hand clutches a tiny vaporizer, and a bottle of pills.

'It don't make sense,' he tells her.

'I can help you find him. My father,' she adds, unnecessarily.

He looks around the parking lot.

'But you're sick,' he says.

She glares at him. Her eyes, like a deep well, summon echoes.

'No, I'm *not*,' she tells him in exactly the tone of a ten-year-old child proclaiming the opposite on a school Monday. 'I was mostly pretending.'

The pilot thinks about it, then stops thinking about it. If you think about things too much, he decides, nothing makes sense anymore.

'What the fuck,' he says, and stands away from the door. 'Get in.'

'Missiles closing,' the parrot intones. 'Evade, evade. Coño!'

They move away at speed.

23
'It's not where you go. It's how you get there.'
Hawkley-ite slogan

They drove east and north toward upstate New York where the pilot knew he could get them across the border into Canada with no more effort than it took to cross his parents' living room.

BON would likely have checked out his parents, but he doubted they would keep surveillance teams active for more than a few days.

Anyway, there was something at home he needed.

They stopped at an Army and Navy store to buy clothes for Ela; blue jeans, army jacket, flannel shirts, WAVE underwear, paratroopers' boots. While Ela was shopping the pilot went into a police equipment store to purchase electronic antisurveillance gear, not because he needed any – the ECM-pak was more than sufficient for his purposes – but because it was the perfect cargo to run into EC-occupied Poland, where such gear was illegal and therefore expensive.

The men had become suddenly conscious of personal hygiene, now there was a woman in the car. They stopped at a truck stop in western Ohio to buy gas and deodorant and take showers. Once Ela asked to stop at a post office. She had to tell Roger what had happened to her, she said. No specifics, Rocketman warned, nobody should know where they were. No specifics, she agreed. Rocketman followed her in anyway, watching her as she bought credit and stood in line for the e-mail terminal; watched the screen as she typed.

After that they kept going, holding to the anonymity of the second- and third-rank interstates.

The girl slept most of the time. She slept with dedication and enthusiasm, as if she hadn't rested for months. She cried out a lot when she slept, and coughed, and threw her hands about. Sometimes she would say things to Roger. A lot of the time, she would simply say 'No,' in tones of pleading or great finality. She slept so hard that when she woke up there were always one or two minutes of wild-eyed disorientation as her dream-soaked mind struggled to take in the highway, the car, the strangers riding beside her. Then, what had happened would filter through, and she would take a hit from the vaporizer to soothe her scoured lungs, shift around in the long Naugahyde indulgence of the Chevy's front seat till she found a good position, and doze off again, coughing softly.

So it was easy to get used to her presence. PC, stunned by her physical appearance, by the details of how she brushed her hair back or shifted her hips in the seat, tried to talk to her at first, rashly expending his reserves of interesting conversation, but she shut him off with monosyllables – and went to sleep.

Rocketman observed her with great suspicion. When she was unconscious, he made fell comments about coincidence, police plants, and the Trilateral Commission. But it was difficult, even for Rocketman, to remain paranoid for long about a girl who slept as hard and seriously as she did.

As for the pilot, he figured that this whole expedition was so strange, the extra bit of strangeness involved in bringing Ela aboard would not matter. It might even help, he reasoned. If you were going to cast off from the normal rules of logic and probability and set off on a wild expedition that based itself on other laws, you might as well do so as thoroughly as possible.

What those other laws were he had not a clue. Maybe some sense that cause and effect were not the only realities, that the universe sometimes worked by affinity, like-patterns attracting like, circles pulling in circles, squares, squares. You could call it sympathetic magic, or the separate existence of form; whatever you called it, to associate Hawkley's daughter, and Gershwin's rumors, and some kind of arcane secret that in mysterious fashion would enable square-up smugglers to evade the clutches of BON had more to do with high gambling than logical positivism, and if Ela was one of the expressions of that gamble, then they should take her along and see how the dice rolled.

On a more intuitive level he suspected that they were all adrift at this particular point in their sad adulthood, even, or especially, Ela — and that the most vital thing in such circumstances was to set yourself a geographic goal and head for it, and never, ever stop. It was the movement that counted, as the Smuggler's Bible said somewhere, not the destination. The movement would create its own rationale.

Highway driving was perfect for this kind of mind-set. The art of the American road; the parameters of sex and submission packed into traffic rules and the play of brakes, wheel, accelerator; the impulse to go, go, go without stopping, go without thinking, go; the idea that movement was salvation; that when the Sarin winds had come and gone, the Eisenhower Interstate System would remain to lead the survivors to safety, roads just like this one, broken, crazed, weeds growing in the cracks, dangerous with pot-holes and pitfalls and rust-weakened bridges, lined with pillaged cars and prewar steamrollers, but still basically in one piece. The esthetics of the highway tranq-ed their minds in a clash of Pepto-Bismol sunsets, a sense of horizons parsed by telephone poles, a game of license-plate numbers – one long unending moving violation. The wipers snapped at ozone flurries; they polished arcs on the windshield that let in sparkle after the tiny storms had raged away. The V-8 rumbled quietly, raising a taste of power and purpose. The heater warmed them, the defroster blew the windscreen clear.

They never got out of the car except for pit stops, and once, in Lima, Ohio, to buy sandpaper, brushes, and two gallons of navy housepaint. Down a dirt road, well outside town, they sanded the Chevy down and painted it blue. He did not think anyone in Indiana had linked the car with Ela, the pilot said, but it didn't hurt to take precautions.

They scored food from drive-in pizza franchises. They bought beer from drive-in liquor stores, and maintained the brews at a perfect temperature in a cooler full of ice.

The pilot kept the ECM on spectrum-scan,

absorbing the buzz of cop chatter through the headset in his flying helmet. The others listened to pop tunes, country music, talk shows, and all-night religious fund-raising gospel electronic hallelujah hoedowns on the big AM Motorola. The call signs changed, as did the addresses in the ads, but otherwise the shows were all the same. Even the 'Jimmy Hoffa Resurrection Gospel Hour,' newly syndicated to just about every country music station in every state they crossed, used the same dynamics, the same in-group out-group techniques as the other evangelists.

Huge agribusiness grainfields alternated with former factories in which small automated security-electronics firms had taken root. In between stood suburbs where dwelled the people who served the machines that cranked out the electronic equipment – churches, zoned developments, satellite-TV dishes, and wall-malls blurring into one whole, a satellite-TV-mall-development-church where salvation could be obtained like Ginzu knives, direct from Mobile or Newark or Burbank, only nay-unh-teen ninety-nay-uhn, UCC-cards only accepted, thirty days trial, satisfaction guaranteed or your credit back.

There were a lot of penitentiaries on this stretch of road, and asylums for the criminally insane. Most were brand new, built of concrete and alloy, ringed with barbizons and ditches. All were farmed out to corrections corporations, outfits with names like American Remedials Inc., High Security, ProCon. One of the prisons sported a huge billboard with a picture of an IV and the boast 'OHIO PUTS AN END TO CRIME' and 'Next Execution Nov 18' and 'Get Your Tickets NOW.' At night their searchlights feathered the horizon, and during the day the sun glinted on their razor-ribbon perimeters. Whenever they appeared Rocketman would grow thoughtful and withdrawn.

'I feel like we've completely lost track,' Rocketman said at one point when there were no jails in sight. They were, in fact, somewhere between Cuyahoga Falls, Ohio, and Canton. 'That we've become some kind of American road-critter, that eats dust and no-lead and shits miles out the back. Some kind of expression of the American psyche. I don't know.'

'Like hobos,' PC said helpfully. 'You know. King of the Road. Emperor of the North.'

'Or performance art,' the pilot put in, vaguely, pushing his flying helmet back. 'The all-American art form. Something to do with the consumption of space. Just raw space. Eat it up on six-lane highways. Roads that never end. Cars so huge you could fit the average Asian engine in one of our fuckin' *carburetors*. Leave behind a trail of styrofoam and, and poly-ethylene containers. America's great hope for immortality; styrofoam permanence. Like this we mark our passing; in this we praise the vastness of the land we've consumed. Dag,' he added, listening to his own words, surprised at his own eloquence, pleased Ela had heard it.

'Our unhappiness lies in small spaces,' Rocketman put in, thinking of Bellevue.

'Maybe that's why Nixon,' PC said.

'Who?' Ela said.

'Richard Nixon.'

'Oh,' Ela nodded. 'The president, in history.' PC looked at her. He wasn't sure if she was kidding or not. 'Any-hoo,' he continued, 'when Nixon needed to relax. The only way he could do it was to get in a limo with a secret service man and, like, drive for hours up and down the freeways.'

'That's interesting, PC,' the pilot said.

'Your conversation's looking up,' Rocketman told him.

'Oh, thanks,' PC said, 'cool,' in a hurt tone of voice.

Early snow bleached the hills. The landscape changed imperceptibly. The people moving beside them in cars and vans and trucks remained the same. So did the bumper stickers. 'How's my Driving? Dial 1-800-EAT SHIT.' 'My Son and My Money Goes to Tulane.' 'Let me tell you about my grandchildren.' 'Pay off the LORD.'

Once they were overtaken by a speeding convoy of Jumpers in three late-model RVs. The vehicles were plastered with labels that read BIOHAZARD and POISON and RADIATION DANGER or carried the little black-and-yellow propellor logo of nuclear waste. What they could see of the faces that glanced at them through the shaded windows was off-balance, mis-shapen. Radiation suits swung on hooks in the back. The pilot was driving; he braked hard, so the Jumpers would pass them quicker.

Otherwise it was salesmen, restaurant workers, computer repair people in Burmese-made Japanese cars two years old. Families in vans, retirees in Dodges. To kill the visual monotony they sometimes picked up a hitchhiker. Two of the hitchers were older men who both had seen their luck chipped away, like a brittle cliff on an angry seashore, each slide of rock starting larger cracks, till they had nothing left but the bitter freedom to move at the mercy of the highways.

The third hitchhiker was a dark young man with a goatee and slick hair. Raw anger filled his eyes and a violin case his hand. His movements were tight, almost miniature, and very fast. He was traveling to a fiddling contest in Dubois, Pennsylvania, he said. There he would compete for a prize called the Golden Bow, and prove to everyone he was the best fiddler in the USA. He would prove it to them, as they drove. He pulled out his violin, tuned it, tightened his bow. Sawing at precise angles in the confined area he reeled off the Faustus overture, all seven movements, in forty seconds, modulations included – fitting the rhythm of the tune to the percussion of potholes. The parrot whistled. The girl woke up, and let out a chain of low coughs.

'I've got a feeling we're not in Kansas anymore,' she told the bird. Her right thumb rubbed her left wrist, where the IV needle had rested.

She curled up in a little ball and went back to sleep.

The fiddler got out in Oil City. As he pulled out his violin case he leaned toward Ela and said, 'You have three wishes. That's my gift to you.'

'I don't believe in that crap,' Ela told him. The fiddler left behind a half-empty pack of Merits, and a cake of rosin, and a smell of bad eggs that didn't dissipate for another twenty miles.

In Roulette, Pennsylvania, they purchased cheap car-helmets because New York State required them and they didn't want to get picked up for something that stupid.

Toward the end of the trip the girl spent more time awake, or at least three-quarters conscious. She was very hungry and ate two or three slices of pizza at a sitting. She drank lots of beer with the result that they had to stop beside a significant percentage of the kudzu groves between the Pennsylvania border and Gouverneur. They got good at this, however. They got so they could do a combined male-female pit stop in under two minutes. All the art lay in holding the bladder till you found the perfect combination of a steep embankment falling off the highway in a sparsely populated area, with lots of kudzu for added privacy. The men did not care so much, but Ela needed the protection. The dropoff shielded her from passing cars. It helped if the embankment faced south, since there was less snow on these slopes, and none farther down among the mutated weeds and the rusted bedsprings, the faded Zero Cola cans and the junked Uniroyals. The woman could squat in her own private shelter of matted kudzu, bladder output increased by the fantasies of lily-ripe bodies – stool pigeons, carjacked moms, child victims of the Buck Knife perversions of a small-town hardware store owner, lost kids come face-to-face with the sudden vacuum in the nub of the American dream and dumped by the side of the great American highway – flesh gone sweet and hollow as the badgers and maggots chewed it out from inside the duck tape bonds in the bottom of yonder culvert. She would race back up the slope when she was finished, still dripping a bit, buttoning her jeans, wondering if her nightmares were as visible as her underwear.

The Chevy, which had been running a little ragged since Pittsburgh, broke down south of DeKalb Junction, New York, on a hilly stretch of four-lane where the wind rushed like a midnight freight. It took the pilot fifteen minutes to figure out the fuel filter was blocked with sludge from the gas tank. It cost him another half-hour to disconnect the filter, blow out the fuel line, and improvise a new filter using shredded fiberglass from Rocketman's cigarettes and wire mesh from the throat of a plastic funnel PC found under the backseat.

Everybody got out, gratefully unstrapping car helmets, to stamp around in the cold wind, and piss. PC tried to draw Ela into making a fire in the woods by the side of the highway. She was not interested. He made the fire himself, a little Boy Scout pyramid of gray smoke, litter, and hope. Blowing fastidiously on the meager glow. A pair of coywolves stopped to observe him, fifty yards down the shoulder. They sat like a married couple, two feet apart, their ears pricked and alert.

The girl came over to watch the pilot work, her arms stiff as she tried to stretch the pockets of her army jacket to deeper proportions. The pilot didn't see her but he knew she was there. Maybe he could tell from her breathing by now, the slightly shorter breath of her smaller and constricted lungs; or perhaps their great proximity in the car, in this half-chase half-flight toward an unknown destination, had altered the consciousness of them all, the way jisi did; made them highly aware of the vector and intensity and color of the other person's presence.

In any event, the force of her being there distracted him. He skinned his knuckles on a recalcitrant bolt. He'd been more conscious of her generally for some time, as a matter of fact; sometimes of the curve on each side of her mouth. Sometimes it was how dark shone the gray of her eyes. Sometimes he focused on the delicate bow in her lips, the tiny wrinkles beside the eyes when she smiled. Often it was the china frailty of her cheekbones, or the little bump in the ridge of her nose; he had a special fascination with that bump, it was a tiny flaw in an otherwise pleasant proboscis that set off by contrast the condensed delicacy of her features. How she curled herself in sleep.

He could not get out of his mind the brief glimpses of ass he had caught in the Fairview Hospital parking lot. It was hard to concentrate when you were so conscious of something else. He tried talking, to bring the awareness into the open. 'I love old cars,' he said, only half ironic. 'I love the way they break down in odd places. That way, you get to become real intimately acquainted with a place. A place you'd never in a million years hang around in by choice. You drive an old car, see, you put random variables in your life. Should be compulsory for people whose lives are too stable for their own good. Put it in the law books; anyone who pays their income taxes, oh, over two weeks before April 15th. Anyone with two 401 (K) accounts or more. Anyone whose vacations are planned and booked a year ahead. They are not allowed to drive anything except an American car built after 1983.'

'Why 1983?' Ela asked.

'Because that was ten years after the big oil crisis,' the pilot said.

'I don't get it.'

'Well.' The pilot put back a ⅜ socket wrench, and opted for a quarter-inch. 'If it's built before '83, it's old, so parts wear out, and the car breaks down. But we're lookin' at the positive side, too. It took Detroit ten years to retool after the oil crisis. Detroit wheels before '83 were built heavy, bad for fuel, but with good solid Indiana steel. Engines you could practically crawl inside to work on, and lots of space for feet. It's sort of what we were talking about, yesterday, in Ohio? The idea of space. That's the other part of my law. You have to fix your own car. Brings in the other random variable in your life; how many different ways your engine tends toward entropy. See, you have to figure out what goes wrong when it breaks down. Suss out how to solve the problem. Keeps your mind alive. Keeps you from getting bored . . .'

He noticed a drop of condensation collecting at the end of the carburetor intake valve, which he thought he'd sucked dry. He put it in his mouth and sucked it again, cautiously, but not cautiously enough, because gas had collected in the angle of the pipe and he got a thimbleful in his mouth. The gas seared his mucous membranes and flooded his head with dead vapors. He pulled back from the engine as if he'd been shot, whanging his head on the open hood. He spat out the gas, gagged, spat again, hopping in pain, clutching his head all the while. He grabbed a beer from the cooler, ripped off the top and rinsed out his mouth four or five times, but his membranes continued to burn.

He noticed the girl walking up the road, away from the car. Her shoulders were shaking. When she turned around he could see she was laughing, and trying to hide the fact. Her face was pink with the strain of it, and the cold. She looked a thousand times healthier than the first time he'd seen her, through the ambulance window.

'What's so fuckin' funny?' he demanded, hoarsely.

'Nothing,' she said. 'I'm sorry. I don't mean – are you okay?' The laughter turned into a coughing fit, and subsided.

He took another sip of beer, and spat it out.

'It's poison,' he said, trying not to feel hurt by her response.

She bit down on the cough. Her hair whipped in the wind. 'Can I do anything to help?'

'It's okay.' He rubbed his head, where it had hit the hood.

'It's just – you seemed to go crazy there, for a minute. I shouldn't have laughed.'

'I'll give you a shot of unleaded ten percent ethyl someday, see how you like it,' he told her.

'It feels so good to laugh,' she said. 'I feel like I haven't done that in years, till I saw you.' She was still smiling, but she put her hand on his arm and said, 'Please forgive me'; and his bad mood and pain seemed to be sucked up into the warmth of her fingerpads, and was gone.

Back in the car, PC, who was annoyed with Ela for ignoring his campfire, vented his frustration on everyone.

'This is getting crazy,' he said. 'This crummy broken-down car. Like, this trip makes less and less sense. We don't know what we're doing.'

'Sure we do,' Rocketman said, glancing at the pilot. 'We're going to Poland. Right?'

'It's a lead,' the pilot agreed, with more confidence than he felt. 'And Ela can help us, there. Right, Ela?'

The girl was humming to herself in the front passenger seat, Cole Porter; 'You're the Nile, you're the Tower of Pisa; you're the smile, on the Mona Lisa . . .'

311

'Ela?'

'Of course,' the girl said. 'I heard you.'

The pilot glanced at her sharply.

'You *do* know something, right? I mean, you said you got Christmas cards.'

She nodded. 'Someplace in Switzerland. Some kind of service. I can't remember the name.'

'He wrote you. He must have mentioned something?'

She shook her head.

'He didn't write?'

'I *told* you he did!'

'So, what did he say?'

She looked out the window. An ozone flurry was scudding, parallel to their course, to the south, sprinkling snow like confectioners' sugar on a wall-mall with outriders of service strip running alongside it for several miles in each direction.

'Ela?' the pilot prompted.

'No,' she burst out, 'not really. Just a few lines. "Thinking of you. Hope you have a happy holiday season."' The bow of Ela's mouth flattened out. 'It was like one of Roger's Christmas cards, from the company. "Thank you so much for your patronage. We look forward to doing business with you in the coming year." But there was one thing.'

They were all looking at her now.

'The pictures.'

'What pictures?'

'On the postcards. They were all going east.'

'Sorry?'

'I noticed that,' she said. 'I thought it meant something. My mother says he's crazy, but I thought it might. Mean something, I mean.' She took in their

312

expressions, and her chin stuck out in defiance. 'The scenes. They were always sunrise. And the paintings, they were always of places further east. "Greece on the Ruins of Missolonghi," by Eugène Delacroix. "The Golden Horn at Daybreak," by Fritz Thalow. "Sunrise on Alexander's Camp at Persepolis," by Jean-Auguste Ingres.'

'Phew,' Rocketman said. 'That's all you know?'

'Like the addresses,' the pilot murmured, watching the ozone flurry depart.

She did not answer.

'I been wondering.' Rocketman looked at the trees that their speed turned into ribbon candy on the side of the road. 'I mean. Why are you doing this? It's — strange. I don't mean to offend you, Miss. But you could be a BON plant.'

Still the girl said nothing. She was looking at her lap now. Her mouth had regained its curves, and they were all strapped down. The pilot felt a rush of sympathy for her, an instinct to protect something complex and pure.

'That's bullshit,' he yelled angrily. 'Bullshit. What's the matter fuh you, Rocketman? We just busted into her life, man. We went to her house. We snuck into her hospital room. No one knew we were coming here. You tellin' me that's some kind of BON setup? Once they start using that kind of subtlety, it's all over.'

'I just wanted to find my dad,' the girl said, softly, still watching her lap. 'And I wanted to get out of that place. I was gonna die, in that hospital. I knew it. I could feel it.' Her voice shook, almost imperceptibly.

'God.' Rocketman's breath went out of him, at the sadness in her tone. 'I din' mean. You know.' He waved his hand awkwardly.

'Anyway.' The girl's chin lifted again. 'None of us know each other. For all I know, you guys are the cops!'

'I guess we'll just have to take each other on trust, to some extent,' the pilot said. 'All of us are runnin'. None of us can be too fussy, since we're on the run. That's something about running. It's kinda like highway driving. You gotta narrow your perspectives, till all you see is the road ahead. The sideview only slows you down.'

He leaned on the accelerator, to underline his words. The V-8 growled, and pushed them back in their seats. A sign read, 'MOOER, NEW YORK, 27 MILES.'

It came to the pilot, he had no idea how much BON wanted to bust him, and therefore he did not know, and had never known, how long they might pay for surveillance on his folks' house. But the momentum of this journey was considerable. It had built with every mile spent going in this direction, and he wasn't sure he had the energy to change destinations now he was forty-three miles from home.

24

'And once again he was overwhelmed by the
vague and mysterious idea of border.'
Milan Kundera
The Book of Laughter and Forgetting

The pilot drove up Shoot Flying Hill. He used the
binoculars from his chartcase, carefully checking
the two roads leading to, and around, his parents'.
The stunted trees of the old orchards, like an encamp-
ment of dwarves, occupied the fields around. The
hills humped each other comfortably into Quebec,
into Vermont. The green of pines, the metal fuzz of
birch and maple. Rust of old wire fences, granite
of far older walls.

No parked vans, no UAVs.

Finally, with a feeling of dice already thrown, he
rolled the Chevy down Apple Farm Road, and into the
frozen-dirt driveway of the house he'd grown up in.

Home. Two-storied, frame-and-shingled. Eaves
crooked, dormers snaggled, the house looked like a
bunch of yellow wooden boxes all crashed into one
another. The Canadian border ran invisible under
the woodshed, the porch and the kitchen, and out the

315

other side. The oldest part of the house – the kitchen, front parlor and root cellar – was built when George the Third still called this land his own.

The pilot carefully opened the gate by the wood-shed and drove the Chevy and its passengers into Canada before going inside and telling his folks he was back.

When he walked through the kitchen door his father was standing at the parlor entrance. The light was behind the pilot, and the old man was not wearing his glasses.

'Hello, Papi,' the pilot said.

The man just stood there. He still had a lot of hair but now all of it was white. His moustache was gray. His eyes were a little pink. The lines in his face stood out strong and grim. He wore the same green cotton workclothes he'd always worn. He gripped a pair of needle-nose pliers in a hand whose tendons were drawn taut.

'Eduard?' he said softly. 'Is that you, Eduard?'

The pilot's grin faded, a little. He walked into the room and said, 'It's Joey, Papi. Joey.' Side to the light so his father could see him better.

'Of course, Joey. It's you. I meant you.' The old man made sure there was lots of welcome in his voice. 'I didn't know you vas coming, son.' He shifted around slowly to peer down the cellar stairs. 'Mama,' he yelled, 'come look who's here!

'Your ma's in Canada,' he added. It was the oldest joke in the house.

Maria Marak came slowly up the stairs from the cellar, carrying a basket full of raw turnips on a bed of hay. The pilot's mother was quite short but did not look it because she was so thin and angular. Her eyes were very blue. Her face, like channels of a complex delta, was webbed with wrinkles. 'Joey!' she said, and hugged him. 'What a surprise. Joey!'

The old dog, Herb, bumbled up after her. She was half blind and all deaf but she wagged her tail like a propellor when she smelled him. Stanislaus the cat gave him a resentful look and went back to sleep on the shelf over the stove.

'I brought some friends, Mami,' the pilot said. 'We'll just spend the night. We're going to Montreal in the morning. And I got a parrot for you to take care of.'

He brought the others in. His father was very polite; he did his little Germanic bow for the girl's benefit. His mother looked at Ela with the female-chips all firing at once. Rocketman, PC, and Ela checked out the kitchen curiously, taking in the big enamel stove, the red-checkered curtains, the dried lavender. Most of all they looked at the framed pictures of old locomotives and train stations, and the long bed of HO-scale track that rested on angle brackets against the wall, leading all the way around the kitchen at eye level and out again through a square hole cut in the double doors of the parlor.

'My dad fixes model trains,' the pilot explained. 'It's his test track.'

He went out to get the parrot. Roman Marak looked at it carefully, sucking on his empty pipe. 'That's not a parrot,' he announced. 'That is a macaw.' Maria Marak clapped her hands in overplayed delight. 'Roman. You must make a cage for it.'

The parrot turned its head this way and that, and made little chirruping noises. The pilot relaxed; he had worried the bird would let fly with some of the

317

Anglo-Saxon invective he had recently learned. Then he caught himself relaxing, amazed at the persistence of training, that he should still worry about offending his parents with the bad language of a bird.

'Always he does this to us,' the pilot's mother told PC. 'Always he brings in stray animals. Like Stanislaus here.' She pointed at the cat.

'I haf to get to work.' Roman Marak tamped tobacco in his pipe. He lit it with a long splinter from the vents of the hot stove. He nodded at Ela, and disappeared, like a locomotive, following his own line, smoke fading in his wake. A wooden sign hung on the door he closed behind him. 'Dominion of Canada,' it read. On the other side of the door hung another, similar sign, with 'United States of America' carved in tall, burnt-in letters.

Ela asked for a bath.

'You should haf told me, Joey,' his mother said, after she had shown Ela the bathroom. 'I vould have bought more food.'

They both knew this was a lie. The pilot's mother might make excuses for her table, but she was never short of food. Her root-cellar was filled with potatoes and turnips, onions and carrots, parsnips and apples, all carefully insulated in dry hay. Her basement shelves hung heavy with pickled cabbage and beets, beans and corn. Roman had bought her an industrial freezer fifteen years before and this was kept filled with beef, pork, and sausages. The kitchen cupboards were crammed with tinned goods. Cans were stashed in the barn and buried under the woodshed. Maria Marak had spent the war years and a few after either starving or on the verge and she was resolved, somewhere deeper than her stomach, never to let that happen again.

318

And so supper was plentiful. It consisted of a stew with cabbage, potatoes, and pork, followed by apple dumplings with fresh cream. Maria Marak had broken through the shock of country dwellers who suddenly find city people thrust upon them, with all their strange rhythms and sharp reactions. Now she seemed happy to have guests to serve. The old man did not say much but tried hard to ensure everyone ate more than they really wanted.

The pilot watched the dynamics with amusement. Rocketman appeared to get along almost instinctively with his father. PC seemed fascinated with Maria. He had never met a woman who could garden and can and cook as easily as a city woman popped around the corner to the Korean. He showed off his knowledge of Central European food for Ela, pronouncing slivovitz and goulash correctly.

Ela didn't say much, but she and Maria Marak moved carefully for each other's benefit. I have nothing to do with him, the girl said, with wrists and neck movements. You are young and pretty, and with my son, the pilot's mother answered, in the way she handed over a bowl of pickled cabbage — a touch quicker, with a shade less care, than how she handed it to the men.

As for the pilot, he felt like he had strayed into a no-man's-land in his own life. In the cabinet on the wall all his speed-skiing trophies were displayed. Over the mantelpiece, in a frame too big, hung a black-and-white enlargement of his brother Eduard, aged sixteen. In frames along the railroad tracks were articles Eduard had written for the Prague Young Pioneer Youth Journal.

In the table below his plate was a scar the pilot had

created when he repaired his Flexible Flyer on the living-room table. It had cost him a spanking and no sledding for a week. It was odd how familiar objects, like props in an old play, could suspend the animation of your life and take you back, mentally speaking, to whatever period of time they were associated with. The smell of cabbage, pipe tobacco, and 3-In-One Oil; the whisper of trees outside, his father's phlegm; all brought back a feeling of childhood that was specific as a strand of DNA.

He still treated her like a servant. She still fought him with silence, and good timing.

Roman Marak offered to show PC and Rocketman his workshop after dinner. Ela helped Maria Marak clean up. The pilot went upstairs to his room, the ECM over his shoulder. He was sitting on the bed with the light out, listening, on audio only, to the scanner, looking through the window, when the door opened behind him.

'They came. Four days ago. The secret police,' his mother said.

He nodded. She meant BON, but for Maria Marak, who grew up under the GSP, the SS, the SD, the NKVD and finally the SSP, secret police were secret police. Only the initials changed; the men were always the same.

'Computer things,' his mother said, without hope or judgment. The secret police never needed reasons, so what did the words on paper matter?

'Yes.'

'Do you need money?'

'No, Mami. Thanks.'

A silence. The ECM was silent, too. BON had come and gone. The danger was big. The stillness of the scanner meant little. They could have set up silent surveillance — watch-posts, wiretaps. The excitement buzzed in him, but there was nowhere for it to go, no job for it to do. If BON was still around, it was already too late.

He took off his flying helmet. She walked around the room, absently checking the chest of drawers for dust.

'You know, Josef,' she said, in Czech. 'He needs you. Eduard is only — only his obsession. Like an icon, for him. Don't forget.'

'I won't forget.'

'He is making you a present. A travel-box. For your rat.'

The pilot said nothing. She sighed, hopelessly, and left as quietly as she had come.

He stroked the old stuffed dog that lay as it always had by his pillow. He kept looking out the window. How could the scene look so exactly the same? he wondered. He'd taken down the chicken shack, was all. The apple trees were trimmed like they'd always been. The snow shone against the darker woods, the hills, the sky. The moon hung bashful behind the same dip in Shoot Flying Hill. The axe was slammed into the chopping block at the same angle it was always slammed into the chopping block. Same block, same axe. He supposed the handle was new. Someone knocked at the door. 'Yeah,' he said.

He thought it was his mother again, by how lightly the boards squeaked; but the voice belonged to Ela.

'This is your room?' she asked. 'The one you grew up in.'

He said nothing. The answer was obvious. His models were everywhere. *Miss Benthol* I and IV, P-47s,

F-15 Tomcats all still dangling from the light fixtures. Posters of bobsled and speed-skiing heroes. He felt a slight edge form on his metabolism, it always happened when she was near, nothing unpleasant, like that first hit of jisi, or the rush of acceleration from a 545 Pratt and Whitney. It almost cut the effect of his mother's words.

'I'm not disturbing you, am I?'

'No,' he said, 'it's all right. I'm just – thinking, I guess. It's weird to be back here.'

'But you're not all right,' she said. She had come around the bed and could see his face from the doorway shine. 'It's hard for you.' She stepped back. 'I'm sorry. I shouldn't—'

'Don't go.'

He did not want to be alone. More – he wanted to tell her.

She stopped, by the foot of the bed.

'I feel I should explain,' he said. 'If you got a minute? About my parents.'

She sat on the bed, by way of answer.

'They're from Prague,' he began. 'Anyway, my dad is. My mother's from a village outside Prague. I lived in Prague too, in Stare Mesto, till I was seven.'

'The accent,' she said, encouraging him with her voice, 'the way your father bows.'

'Yes,' he said. 'My dad was an engine driver,' he went on. 'For the state railroad. That's why he's so crazy about trains.'

'They're beautiful,' she said. 'His trains.'

'Uh-huh. That's not where I meant to start. I don't know where to start. My mom had a horrible time in the war. Half the people in her village were deported and killed by the Germans. She met my dad in the

322

black market, she was buying vegetables. I was the second son. My brother, Eduard, he was nine years older than me. I think she had trouble bearing kids, somehow, because of the war.'

'Where is he now?' she asked. 'Your brother.'

'I'm getting to that.' He had a story to tell. For some reason it was important to him that she get it whole; the logic, the balance of a story were killed if you shortened or broke it.

'I don't remember Eduard that much. That gives you a clue, huh? But I do know I idolized him. He was big and funny and strong. He was good at soccer, and swimming. He liked me, too. He used to grab my hands and whirl me around, centrifugal, like one of those rides at the county fair, the Zipper or the Octopus, so fast everything was a round blur and I couldn't stand up afterward. This was in the years between the Prague Spring and the 'velvet revolution' – before the Russians left. The regime was getting softer, but it was still pretty hard, especially when Solidarity happened in Poland, they got downright paranoid. Anyway, right around then, Eduard started writing essays for a youth journal. They were pretty funny, I guess. They made fun of the old regime. My mother was nervous about them, but she was proud of him too . . .'

The girl ambled around the room as he talked. The new moon had made it over Shoot Flying Hill and its light shimmered through the window. He saw her move among the small air force suspended from his ceiling, touching the planes with one finger so they twirled gently, or swung. The light favored edges; it silvered her nose and cheeks and the leading edge of her wrists; it flashed on the aircrafts' wings as they rolled.

'It turned out he had joined a secret society at that time. "Free Prague Youth," or something. They would go and hand out leaflets at army posts. A couple weeks after the Jaruzelski crackdown in Poland, real late at night, there was a knock on the door. It was a man with a beard, someone from Eduard's school. He stayed for a long time. I could see them through the door. My parents were weeping and yelling. Eduard was smoking. I didn't know he smoked till then. When the man left, my parents immediately started to pack. I was scared. Cigarette smoke, and flashlights, and my parents were so frightened you could almost touch it. Only Eduard was calm. He made sure I brought my stuffed dog.' He touched the smooth-worn toy, reflexively.

The trip came back to the pilot in little details. They'd left the following night, late – the feel of cobblestones, cold and unfriendly as steel on sleepy feet, and night air – he'd never been up so late before. He sat in the cab of the coal truck, behind the seat, with two other kids. There was a crowd of people in the back, covered with canvas. No one said anything except the men. They only said 'Go,' or 'Turn left.' They drove to the marshaling yards and boarded a freight train.

The cars usually carried livestock. They smelled foul. The wind ran through their car like a banshee as they traveled south. It stirred up the dried cow dung and made them sneeze.

'The train stopped by some fields,' the pilot continued. 'They made us walk very carefully, in a straight line, across a field. We came to a river, the Moldava. There were men in little boats, waiting near some trees. They rowed us across. Everything was so dark, the river seemed like ink. We were almost across when a motorboat came down the river. It caught us with searchlights. There was lots of shouting, the men were rowing like crazy. Then the motorboat began to shoot. Some of the people in our boat panicked; some of them tried to jump overboard, other people tried to stop them, and the boat tipped over. Eduard grabbed me, and swam me to shore. You could hear this rustling overhead, I never realized it was bullets. Then Eduard cried out. He pushed me up on the bank. I don't know what happened to him. My mother came up and started screaming. I remember her running up and down the bank calling for Eduard, while the boat was still shooting. But he was gone.'

The girl was watching the planes. Made restless by the memory, the pilot got up and went to the window.

'We spent two and a half years in DP camps, then we came here. But my parents might as well have stayed. They never got over that night. They never got over losing him. They're still lost in that time. I think they still believe he might be alive, even though the GrenzPolizei searched and searched. I don't know why. I never understood it—'

Her arms were quick and strong. They laced around his middle, comfortable as a girth on an old saddle. She was only planning a quick hug but the comfort was so good he grabbed her arms and kept them there and she had the grace not to resist.

Through the surplus value of her touch he felt Eduard's face form in his brain. But the face had brown eyes and a 'come-on-I-dare-you' grin and its features were those of Roberto. He tried to recall the face of his natural brother, but all he got was Roberto's. It bothered him that he could not visualize Eduard's features. He supposed the love he'd felt for Roberto had been some kind of twisted compensation for losing his own sibling.

'You don't have to make excuses for them,' she said. Her voice was low, almost a whisper. 'It happens all the time. It becomes easier to live with it. With losing people. Easier than to take care of the living, anyway. Though the living are the ones who suffer.'

'There was nothing easy about it, for them.' He winced a little, without knowing he did so. 'You saw their eyes.'

'I know their eyes,' the girl replied. 'I saw them every darn day in my mother.' She pulled her arms away from him, gently but firmly. 'Why do you think I'm doing this?' she said. 'It's not just because I was bored crazy. It's not just 'cause me and Roger weren't working out. It wasn't just Lakewood. What it is, it's I've lived with her losing my father every day of my life. I've lived with her being so desperate to reject him and everything he stood for she turned herself and me into people just like everyone else in Lakewood. Junior League. Girl Scouts. Cheerleading. *Jeess!*' She walked over to the bed and kicked it, hard. '*Ow!*' she yelled. '*Dang* it!' She rubbed her toes, and gnashed out words she was not supposed to say in company. 'Shoot! Fudge! Dang!'

'Ela,' he began.

'Don't "Ela" me.' She turned her pain on him. 'I've been "Ela"'d ever since I was three years old. I'm sick and tired of being "Ela"'d. I'm sick and tired of being good. I'm sick and tired of never having anything important in my life! Everything is in two dimensions

326

– the only things in three dimensions are the people in *Pain in the Afternoon*. The only thing urgent and important in my life, is, is the *absence* of anything important. And I'm sick and tired of living with the knowledge of loss, that love can be lost, forever.' She swung around on herself. 'I want to find him, darn it! I want to find what went wrong, and prevent it from happening to me.'

She faced him at the window. Her eyes were full of moon. He put his arms round her neck and rested his cheek against hers. She smelled of his mother's cream and lavender soap – odd Oedipal concoction, strange check and balance. He remembered the bath she'd taken here. He wanted to kiss her so much he trembled from it. But she said 'Don't,' and added 'Roger,' in a tone full of confusion at her own new losses, and they ended up going downstairs instead.

In the living room, Roman Marak had taken out his best plum brandy. Maria sat beside him, falling asleep from the liquor. The room was thick with tobacco smoke. A ⅟₉₆ model of the 1938 Balt-Orient Express – a couple of 4.8.2 locomotives, Compagnie des Wagons-Lits sleeping coaches, restaurant, mail, and luggage cars – clicked and chirred around the walls of the dining room, emitting little clouds of graphite dust. The passenger cars glowed with lights, as if ⅟₉₆-scale humans sat inside discussing this fellow Chamberlain, and what the conference in Munich might bring. The tiny train disappeared into the kitchen.

'They stood for all the best things in our country,' Roman Marak said, a little vaguely. 'Nezval, Hasek. We had a great tradition. Rabbi Loew. He created the first golem, a mechanical man. Eduard loved Franz

327

Kafka the most. He attended a special meeting in Bohemia, in Langberg Castle, with the best literature students in all the schools of Prague. It was to bring back Kafka as a writer. It was one of the most serious charges, when the police came . . .'

Beside him, Ela touched the pilot's hand, and squeezed. PC looked up at them, and the shadows made on his face by the table lamp seemed to darken. The pilot slipped into the kitchen, and went outside to the woodshed, where he pried up a plank and dug out the wooden box full of Maria Teresa gold coins he kept next to his mother's stash of canned kidney beans, for emergencies.

25

'The heart has the best eyesight.'
Antoine de Saint-Exupéry
Le Petit Prince

The next week was filled with the housekeeping of flight.

Portuguese rooming houses smelling of coffee and disinfectant in the Saint Louis section of Montreal. The pilot used up much of his Canadian UCC-card on payphone calls to arrange for long plastic, and new UCC-cards with embedded passports for Ela and Rocketman.

This was a complicated business, based on personal knowledge of forwarding services. He bought a throwaway digital camera and snapped pictures of their faces, then downloaded them, via the ECM, onto floppies. He Fedexed a boxful of the salvaged Maria Teresas with the floppies to the forwarding service in New York. Tony at the forwarding service, recognizing the pilot's voice and password, would transfer the floppies and twenty-eight thousand dollars to the forwarding service and through that to a couple of Sabras who specialized in international UCCs.

While they waited, the pilot went to a node market in Saint Denis. Using more of his Maria Teresas he bought 140 megabytes' worth of hot Fujitsu-Cray encryption chips — enough to fill a baby's sock, or a condom — from a pair of hackers who were so nervous about Mountie surveillance they kept looking, quite literally, over their shoulders as they made the deal.

Four days later, a messenger delivered two UCC-cards with State Department validations, and a letter, via Tony, to a mailbox service in Saint Denis.

The plastic was legal in all but the names embossed on the face. The cards carried the coded magnetic strips that would swipe them back to the State Department computer bank for verification of identity. The identities were clean and credit chips held seven thousand dollars each.

Both cards were guaranteed for a month.

The letter was from Françoise, the crippled girl in Bayou Noir. His boat was safe and under cover, she told him. She would like to see him when he picked it up, if he had time. But her words did not affect the pilot as they might once have done. All the free receptors in the parts of his brain that dealt with women increasingly were taken up with Ela.

As soon as they got the fake plastic they went to the airport and took the next 777 to Berlin.

Humming isolation of transatlantic travel. Servo-control. Total life support. Four massive Rolls Royce/GE jet engines gulping down the refined and flammable shit of swamp creatures that had been dead so long their oozy homes had turned into deserts; all in order to warm and oxygenate and maintain 368 humans at forty-five thousand feet of altitude and a speed of 525 knots.

Inside, the generic luxury of German champagne and French cologne. The hiss of air-conditioning, the distant thunder of those engines. The four of them, belted and blanketed, cushioned and fed. Ela straining against the seat belt in her dreams and saying, 'It's all the condor thing. That's what.' The thrown-clutches of sleep, and time zones. A crying infant.

Outside, minus-sixty degrees Centigrade. So far north the stars looked unfamiliar. Landscapes so blue cold and icebound no one ever saw them except from this high up.

The airline rented disposable face-suckers. The film was cheap VR, a laser Western. A hundred travelers swinging their heads in unison, dodging 3-D fists over Cape Farewell.

As they swung south and flew over Ostend, the pilot went into a rest room. He poured the encryption chips from their envelope into a lubricated condom. He dropped his pants then, sitting half on the toilet, very slowly squeezed the condom up his rectum. It was uncomfortable work but he did not think twice about doing it. This was a Trade imperative, part of the discipline, for high-grade encryption was risky cargo. If he was caught by the Kriminal Polizei they would hand him straight over to BON and even if no one connected him with his real identity he would get the standard fifteen-to-life in Oakdale as a matter of course. When he was finished his asshole was sore but he could sit with no more than a slight pressure in his colon and it would take an X-ray scan, or a body-cavity search, to reveal the hot memory.

They landed at Tempelhof around noon and caught a feeder flight that landed them at Breslau/Strachowice Airport an hour later. The airport was

331

busy with Bavarian businessmen in double-breasted jackets and EU troops with Bundeswehr shoulder patches carrying H&K carbines. They took a cab to a hotel the airline recommended, a modern place on the Ringstrasse, south of the city center.

The Hotel Silesia felt exactly like the jet. It was high, altitude-wise. It was pressurized and air-conditioned and structurally strengthened. Its perimeters were guarded by soldiers and barricades. It hummed with distant servomotors. Announcements came faint in several languages over loudspeakers. Large TV screens showed canned movies. The decor was molded plastic. Even the soap and toilet covers were like the plane's, and the toilet water was bright blue.

Jet lag affected them all. The German plainclothesmen in the lobby were looking out for Polish irredentists, not smugglers, but their hard cop gazes felt threatening just the same. Rocketman made comments from old war movies about 'Krauts' and the Gestapo. He looked around carefully for ODESSA agents. He put on dark glasses, extracted a Deutschmark credit chip from a terminal. The information VDT told him there was a flea market in Solny Square. He slunk out immediately to buy local clothing.

The jet lag hit Ela with the force and effect of a welterweight punch. She lay down to rest on the couch in her room and was asleep within two minutes.

PC opened the door connecting his room to the pilot's. He leaned on the jamb while the pilot took out the traveling cage Roman Marak had made for God.

This was a carved applewood box, about ten inches by seven, with a trough for nuts, a water bottle, and a latch on the outside.

'She's the most desirable woman I've met in at least a year,' PC said.

The pilot opened the door. The rat raced in circles around the hotel carpeting.

'I've been trying to get through to her all week.'

The pilot unlocked his ECM-pak and started setting it up.

'She's beautiful,' PC continued, 'not in the usual ways, but subtle. I mean it's bone prettiness, not skin beauty. Way down in her mouth, and in how straight her nose is, except for that bump of course. Deep in her eyes. You expect whole Latin American revolutions to come charging out of those eyes on horseback, waving wide hats, firing pistols in the air and yelling "*Arriba!*" You know? Like, that's how deep they are. And her laugh,' PC went on. 'She doesn't laugh easily, but when she does – well, that's the core of her. It's like a million birds being released from cages all at once.'

The pilot still said nothing. He wore on his face the nauseated half-smile of a man with broken loyalties.

'But all she does is *sleep*,' PC went on, unhappily. 'And when she talks, she mostly talks to you.'

PC looked carefully at the pilot, who devoted equal care to dusting off the half-sucker's jack and plugging it precisely into its com-port.

'You're not sleeping with her, are you?' he asked anxiously.

'Hell, no,' the pilot replied. But he said it too loud, and PC looked away, his eyes full of doubt and questions.

As soon as PC had left the pilot put on the half-sucker, swiped in a SAP account number, and did a scan of the surroundings. He was getting hooked on VR scanning – he could sense a small lust in him for this. It was the same impulse he'd felt switching on the VR at the Double Headed Shot Cays. Part of it, he figured, was just the itch for sexy medium, the almost physical ease of turning symbols back into things – objects you could move around, touch, play with.

But some of it was real. In the short time he had owned the VR program he found that his 3-D 'swim' through the structures and lines of information offered a visceral body-knowledge of the changes in traffic that you didn't get from watching a flat screen. And these changes might warn of danger, a focusing of security forces.

But today the subtlety was lost on him because he was not familiar with the patterns of info flow here, on the border between EU-occupied Silesia, or Schlesien as the Germans called it, and what remained of independent Poland only a couple of miles across the Oder River.

A red, pulsing glow in the corner of his vision indicated abnormal current in the suite's workstation, probably a voice-activated passive device, which was to be expected. In any case he never said anything worth saying in hotel rooms. The ECM would give him scrambled communications, should he need it.

There were a lot of scarlet-coded hotspots that the scan program tagged as Bundeswehr radio. The dark-red lines of other security frequencies were heavy, bright, and evenly distributed; if anything, the south-ern Ringstrasse area, where the Hotel Silesia stood, had (with the exception of the railroad station) less traffic than the rest.

Red dots tagged as EU drones flew up and down the Oder frontier, sending home realtime video. The pilot switched to Wildnet scan.

The feeling of swimming grew stronger; only this time it was in a sea far lonelier than the one he'd dived in before. Under the great throbbing ceiling of the Web, the points of light indicating Secure Access Providers were so few they stood out like beacons and he had to joystick forward at full speed for five or six seconds to get close without getting bored. Most of the datalines were thin and, as far as he could tell, innocuous. One of the rare thick lines was a graphics download, probably softporn video, from a server-link in Srinagar to one in San Diego. The tampered Fedchips of these SAPs glowed with the energy of traffic. A 'server mostly dedicated to Cybermilitia Usegroups was pretty active, and so was one small FBI ferret – blue light blinking steadily – trying to follow that scan.

He dove to escape the ferret's attention.

The same Neta maintenance, in Florida, he had seen from Sandworm Cay.

Apart from that, nothing but vacuum; dark space in which swimming, or flying or joysticking, became an act of loneliness, like solitaire, or masturbation.

Although the vacuum was not all empty.

He became aware of datalines so dark they were all but dead. Only housekeeping blips, like the EEG of a stroke victim, marked their difference from the night.

He pushed the joystick forward, diving deeper, longer. He found himself holding his breath, and forced his lungs full again. The darkness increased.

The charcoal lines passed overhead, to the side, like tree limbs in a thick jungle. Following one to its source, he found a box so black he would have missed it altogether had it not been for the line and its thirty-second blip of carrier-beam activity.

Even the site acronym was erased.

Beside it, in script that looked like an absence of light — stark Futura font etched in velvet vacuum against the dark — you could read the single word: CONTROL.

He did not wait, this time. He hit the reset immediately and watched his liquid VR world blackhole into a dark circle. Waited for it to negative into a dot of light, and die.

And it did.

But just before that happened, an image appeared on the face-sucker screen before him. A landscape stretching endlessly to a bruised horizon. It was a country so flat, so dark, so devoid of life that it looked almost abstract. Each grain of detail was a variation on ebony and onyx, and the gradations of shadow. Every square foot of terrain was pocked with shell craters and chunks of exploded wood. The sky coiled in banks of smoke. Where evidence of something animate existed — a burnt-out battle tank, a shattered oak — it had been twisted until it looked different, as if a force that was not human had altered it to suit its own concept of form.

The image lasted only a second — came and went so fast the pilot was not sure he'd seen it right. He winced, and shut his eyes.

When he opened them again he saw only the blank sheen of the top half of his face-sucker, and the screensaver icon of his Wildnet program, three squares hooked up by bars of green, turning on and off as they crossed and recrossed his line of sight.

When he had locked up the ECM-pak again the pilot went into the bathroom and extracted the condom full of memory. He emptied the chips into a Hotel Silesia envelope, washed up, and put the envelope in the hidden pocket of his travel jacket. Then he went to look for the 'Kneipe Spargnapani.'

It was not easy to find. The info-terminal said 'WE HAVE NO DATAS CORRESPONDING TO YOUR INPUT.' The concierge said basically the same thing. An overweight German woman next to him at the concierge's desk explained, in excellent English, that a 'kneipe' was some kind of bastard mix of bar, café, and restaurant. There were thousands in Berlin, she said wistfully, glancing at her husband, a tubby man in a Borsalino hat. A few dozen kneipes had cropped up here, her husband continued smoothly; they were the kind of couple who looked at each other when talking to strangers. Many of the kneipes were unlicensed and illegal. They were located mostly in the red light districts, to serve EC troops.

'Spargnapani' was not listed in the Breslau telephone book. With the couple's help he finally found it mentioned, next to the listing 'Rosenbaum Allee,' under 'experimental performances' in an alternative music guide.

The pilot hailed a cab, a creaky Skoda, from the rank out front. The driver, who knew no English, had to look up Rosenbaum Allee in a taximan's index. He drove west down Pilsudski Strasse, then across a park marking the old fortifications of the city, past grim domino-rows of Stalinist-era housing. The car plunged suddenly into a warren of narrow, older streets. The predominant gray colors turned charcoal, umber. Women in tight leather stood in doorways. Soldiers strolled down the cobblestones.

The Spargnapani occupied the lower basement of a building one block from the old Breslau synagogue. The building was new, Gierek-modern, reinforced concrete; but it had been built, perhaps wisely, on foundations that had withstood the Russian shellings of World War II, and numerous contretemps before. The lower basement was very old. It had a stone floor and vaulted ceilings built of massive chunks of lime-stone. The light was bad and black shadows filled the arches. It reminded the pilot, uncomfortably, of the place he'd just glimpsed in the deeper regions of the Wildnet.

Smoking was not yet illegal in occupied Poland and cigarette smoke fully dominated the upper atmos-phere in the kneipe's three rooms. A couple of tables were solid with French soldiers, but the majority of the customers were civilians. Thin Poles with bristly haircuts and shaded Jaruzelski-style glasses sipped shots of bimber acquavit, their backs carefully to the wall. Intense and angular Germans hunched over small round tables, showing each other notebooks whose contents were obscured by the flaps of leather jackets; huddling for clarity and survival beneath the fug even as they lit up and puffed on long black cig-arettes to generate yet more smoke.

The faces were generally thinner and starker than in America, and few people smoked like this at home anymore, even in the illegal places where you could light up, but the feel of this bar was familiar to the pilot.

It was a Trade hangout. You could almost smell the pervasive suspicion, the burnt odor, not of cigarettes but of deals set up, or discarded.

Everyone wore leather jackets. Almost everyone was playing, or pretending to play, Akmba, an African version of chess newly popular among those who kept up with what was newly popular. A handful of immigrant workers, Turks and Pakistanis and Filipinos, was mixed in with the soldiers and Poles and Germans. A bar of wood and brass supported mountains of shiny steel espresso gear, *latte* bowls, and pastry displays in one corner. A small stage in another corner featured a trio of thin transvestites playing, with feigned boredom, electric violins and talking-drums; syncopating their beat to a George Collins riff meshed in turn with a sample of honey-bee buzz-harmonics on the kneipe's sound system.

Shift-shin. The sign on their drum set read 'Central Dada Sex Office.' The sign above the stage read *Willkommen Zum Bunker*. Everyone turned to peer at the pilot when he came down the stairs, wondering if he was KriPo.

The bartender cleaned the espresso steam nozzles. He was large and bearded and spoke bartenders' English and was more forthcoming than your typical bartender in this kind of joint. Yes, he'd heard of Alois van der Lubbe. Tall guy, with glasses and a moustache, no? He'd not seen him for a few days. He'd be around. All you had to do was sit here, and sooner or later everybody showed up. Even actors from the Jerzy Grotowski Experimental Theatre. The bartender seemed very impressed by the fact that Grotowski actors came to his kneipe.

The pilot hung around for a couple of hours. The

Spargnapani offered newspapers wound on little varnished sticks for the benefit of patrons. Among the Frankfurter *Allgemeins* and *Herald* Tribunes and Neue *Breslauer Zeitungs* the pilot found a hard-copy of Hawkley's *Gazette*, dated 4:33.72 p.m., Sept. 7. The *Gazette* was the only paper he knew of that published its actual time of printing. It had something to do with the navigational religion thing. Flipping through the paper he found an ad that read: 'Don't be a prisoner of your own thalamus: learn neurosurgery in your spare time! Glia-sculpture, emotional tuning using 122.03-series cryolasers. Contact Box L.'

The *Gazette* also featured the annual rating of US airports according to how hard they were to smuggle through (Fort Lauderdale, the pilot noted, was voted 'most risky' for the second year running) as well as a half-page photo of a row of thin brown corpses lined up under a veranda roof. Three white men wearing camo gear and night-vision goggles, but with no insignia of unit or rank visible, looked down at them impassively. The headline read 'WHY DID LITE-WORLD NOT SEE THIS? *Smuggled Photos Show BON Eliminated Manila Node.*'

It was interesting, the pilot thought, it was even hopeful that the Spargnapani should subscribe to the *Gazette*.

Out of some sense of obligation to the greater geopolitics of this planet he tried to read the *Trib*. Dire headlines announced a worsening of the Mexican crisis. The daily feature on the back page described the discovery a group of University of Rhode Island scientists had made in a salt marsh in Narragansett Bay. 'The scientists claim a form of organic life, with a DNA whose structure closely replicates the logic system of a factory-built microchip, is invading the marshes beside this former Navy yard,' the *New York Times* reporter wrote. 'These cold-water algae not only incorporate the digital on-off switches of a computer inside their tiny leaves and branches, but duplicate this structure fractally, on a larger scale, so that the various algae colonies are multiplying in exactly the same way that microchips are lined up in a computer.'

'Dag,' the pilot muttered.

The photo accompanying showed a man holding a piece of complex moss in his tweezers. A stretch of cattails, with the dark arch of the New Davisville Bridge, lay behind.

'What is even more bizarre than this marsh becoming the world's largest living computer,' the article continued, 'is that no one has the slightest idea where the algae came from. But computer buffs from as far away as California are flocking to Rhode Island to dig up the weed and put it in anything – test tubes, thermos flasks, even discarded Zero Cola cans – with the idea of growing memory circuits in their own basement.'

The sight of the Davisville marshes made the pilot nervous. The warmth and smoke of the kneipe, the backlog of exhaustion were stronger than his nerves. Five minutes after he put down the *Trib* his eyelids started to feel heavy as Polish cooking so eventually he left a message for van der Lubbe with the bartender and went back to the hotel and bed.

Pressure sought its own release, and the following day Rocketman, PC, Ela, and the pilot all went separate ways, each cozy in the belief the others were still

341

sleeping off jet lag: the pilot to buy rat food; Ela to visit a hairdresser, and mail postcards home; Rocketman to walk the streets, picking up tips on how to look German, or Polish; PC to sit in a café on the south side of the square called Rynek and watch the girls flit by in leather skirts.

It was a pretty day, a fast-boots-and-apples day, with a low, cool wind that felt like high octane fuel in the lungs. After buying pet food the pilot walked to the river, noting the dozens of Polish flags flying defiantly across the river in Lvov-Dwa, the dug-in anti-tank units on both banks.

Signs announced that the tomb of the Blessed Czezlaw, patron saint of the town, had been closed by EU military authorities until further notice.

When the pilot got back to the Silesia he knocked on Ela's door and asked her if she wanted to go to the kneipe with him.

She opened the door and he said 'Christmas!' involuntarily.

She'd got her hair cut and frazzled in long waves like fusilli. There were streaks of white-and-purple dye on one side. She had put on makeup, and lipstick the shade of dark cherries.

'Whaddya think?' she asked, cocking her head.

'I think,' he said, with deep conviction, 'I think you're more beautiful than ever,' though he also thought those streaks were not going to make it any easier to cross borders unnoticed. But there was such uncertainty in her eyes that he would sooner have chewed glass than tell her so.

PC was sitting in the restaurant drinking hot chocolate with whipped cream when he saw Ela and the pilot go by the window together. The suspicion he'd

342

kept glowing gently in one corner of his mind grew hot and caught fire. He ran his UCC through the counter swiper and hurried after them, brushing by a large, deeply suntanned German in lederhosen, hiking boots, loden hat, and cape, as he rushed out the revolving doors of the hotel.

Rocketman adjusted his loden cape and watched PC hurry through the insect crowds after the pilot and Ela. His face was set in anger. He had suspected something like this for some time. They'd had way too easy a time escaping North America for his liking, Rocketman thought. The pilot was under indictment for AGATE offenses under the McCarren-Williams Act, he himself was wanted for evading protective custody, and maybe criminal arson, and probably contravening FAA regulations concerning the firing of ballistic missiles from a City hospital roof without proper authorization.

The Feds by all rights should have pulled them in long ago, the pilot's precautions notwithstanding. If they had not, Rocketman reasoned, it followed that *maybe BON knew where they were the whole time.* Maybe they were trying to trap the pilot into revealing his illegal contacts. Maybe the Feds were still after Hawkley, and hoped to follow Ela to his lair. Maybe – Rocketman pulled the cape tight around his face as the logic of it all completed its cycle, locking solid onto one single, inescapable fact – maybe the Feds had let them go because they *already* had an informer close to the pilot and Rocketman. A police plant. A BON agent.

Not Ela, as Rocketman had previously suspected.
PC!

Rocketman fired up a cigarette. He adjusted his sunglasses and left the hotel. Walking as he had seen

343

Germans do, in a fashion conducive to group hikes, he carefully shadowed PC as PC followed the pilot and Ela down Pilsudski toward the Kneipe Spargnapani.

The pilot and Ela stayed so long at a corner table in Spargnapani that the regulars stopped glancing at them.

They talked easily – had done from the first, actually. Something clicked, something deeper and more important than mere verbalization. Rhythm, perhaps; the use of pauses.

The way he sat on one side of his ass, as if impatient to get on with the next project. How she hunched over her drink and let her hair drift over her face when she thought.

His freckles. Her nose-bump.

Most of all they had in common a respect for lebensraum – not the perfume, but of the mental kind. Both instinctively believed in the potential for change in any issue. Both allowed a DMZ around every word spoken or body-talked to preserve that ability to alter, to deny the lie of permanence. Indiana had temporarily pressured that DMZ in Ela, buried and crushed it under the well-meaning and brutal mass of couple intimacy, but the instinct went too deep for the roots to have died, and in the sudden absence of Roger Taylor it sprouted back like weeds between paving-stones. Therefore, as they talked, they both let the issues change shapes and colors even as they framed them with words and syntax. In the final analysis it was a gloss of childhood, something left over from being solitary with odd grownups, and it was symbolized for them by a single image:

'Look at that *hat*,' Ela said. A woman, coming in to

tack up posters for a Node demonstration, was wearing an outrageously battered fedora of the type worn by Edward G. Robinson in movies about SD agents.

'That's not a hat,' the pilot replied, 'that's a boa constrictor digesting an elephant.'

She glanced at him. Her pupils dilated, a couple of microns, no more.

'Draw me a sheep,' she challenged him.

He looked at her for a long moment.

'Nothing in the universe is the same,' the pilot said finally, 'if, anywhere, a sheep we do not know does, or does not, eat a rose?'

'*The Little Prince*,' she agreed. 'You know it.'

He nodded.

'I don't know,' she said, after a beat or two. 'Somehow it figures you'd have read Saint-Exupéry. There's something in you – something not satisfied.' Her voice trailed off. 'He was a pilot, too, wasn't he . . . ?'

Then her eyes clouded, as if the memory of the children's book dragged in other images that were not so pleasing.

Her eyes grew wary often, and sometimes her voice would take on caution. An obvious connection emerged; the caution had to do with America, Lakewood, Roger. When they got going on something else she talked easier and easier as the conversation progressed, like a freight train picking up momentum downhill. When she was involved in banter her laugh often sprang loose before she could control it. Her face would go pink with the effort of suppressing it. But often her speech centers were constipated by the thought of home. Then, she didn't stop talking, or even laughing, not entirely; but there was a smoke around the way she said things.

'You've taken to this like you were born to it,' he insisted. 'Fake UCC-cards. False names. Living on the run.'

'I've been living like that for years,' she told him. 'One way or another. Like I'm two people; one of me is normal, and legal, and goes to the wall-mall for groceries, and buys tube socks for Roger. And the other is this, like, total outlaw who doesn't even know who Roger is.'

'Poor Roger,' the pilot said.

'Roger's okay,' she said, 'he knows what I'm doing.' The caution was out in the open now, red lamps waving in circles.

He looked up at her sharply.

She shook her head.

'Nothing specific,' she said. 'But I told him, in my e-mail. I've been sick for months. I've been feeling bad for months. I think it's because I just wasn't happy, down deep. He'll understand.'

'And your mother?'

The girl made a face.

'She'll understand better than Roger. And she'll like it even less. She thinks I'm doing what she did, when she was my age. Rebelling or something. Which is crazy.'

'You don't think you're rebelling?'

'Against what?' she said, and smiled. 'There was nothing to rebel against in Lakewood. That's the whole point. There was nothing *wrong* with Lakewood. No one abused me. Nobody held me back. Nobody tried to make me do anything I didn't want to do . . .

'On the other hand, I never really wanted to do anything. And I always had the feeling that if I ever

346

did, it would be so, like, different from Lakewood that, even though it wasn't really wrong, they would try to bring in zoning to ban it, 'cause, 'cause it brought down their *property* values or something.'

'I don't understand,' he said. 'You sounded so upset, at my parents' house. You said, nothing good ever happened.'

She picked up her glass, and put it down in exactly the same circle of condensation.

'I didn't say "nothing good." I said, "nothing important."'

'OK.' He opened his hands as if to ask 'What's the difference?'

'Well, that's true,' she continued, staring at his hands. 'It used to drive me crazy. I used to feel like I was dead; like when I died I wouldn't be able to tell the difference. That's what really scared me about that hospital, if you want to know the truth. If I didn't know when I was dead, how could they? The lines on their machines would read the same. After a while they could just roll me down to the morgue, and nobody would stop them . . . But there was nothing wrong,' she insisted. 'I mean, if there was, it wasn't planned, it was without malice aforethought.' She did not look up. This created an absence.

'You just seem to shed it so easily,' the pilot said, 'your whole life up to now. You don't seem to think about it, even.'

'Jeezz,' she said, whooshing the word out with her breath. Her eyes, looking straight at him now, cut light into bright and angry angles. 'You ever heard of not being sure about how you feel? Ever heard of being in two minds about something? Not everybody has everything figured out in black and white like you.'

'OK—' the pilot raised his hands. He did not want to fight the point. 'OK.'

'OK,' she agreed, but looked away. After twenty or thirty seconds had passed she said, 'You know, I had two dreams when I was younger. Well, three, if you count the best one, which was to be Ella Fitzgerald, or at least have her voice and, like, sing Cole Porter the way she did, but I always knew that was impossible. So if I couldn't have that, I wanted to be a majorette.' She looked down at her glass and twisted it on the table. 'It seemed like the peak of everything. To be out marching, maybe even leading the squad. Those crazy hats, with the big pompoms, the white boots, those sexy short skirts. And all the boys and everyone in town looking on as you marched down the football field.'

Again she twisted her drink on the table, pushing down on it so hard the glass squeaked.

'The other dream,' she said, 'was to die. In a big flaming car wreck. I know it sounds weird. But I used to imagine it, almost every night. Always with whatever boy I had a crush on at the time. We'd do it because we were different, we'd do it because our parents disapproved. We'd drive real fast down the Fairview 'pike and not stop at the Forest Lane lights, we'd go right through the barrier and onto the overpass they never finished and over the edge and die with our arms around each other and that's how they'd find us.'

She sighed.

'It was just a fantasy. But it went kinda deep. When the space shuttle blew up – we were all watching it live, in class – I felt terrible, of course, about that teacher and her family, but another part of me was

348

saying, "God that's beautiful, to die like that, way up in the sky, trying to get away from earth." I watched it over and over, on the news, every chance I got. It was so pure, that explosion. Just a clean white line going up into deeper-and-deeper blue; then the blast, the white cloud, starting at the base of the rocket and quickly going up till it covered the whole thing; and then, like, nothing. The end of the white line. No downlink. Just peace and utter quiet and a few chunks of wreckage, falling into the sea . . .'

'Do me a favor,' the pilot said.

'What?' She did not look up at him; she still watched her glass as if she could see the *Challenger* again in its reflections.

'Don't ever mention that to Rocketman.'

'Why not?'

'Just − don't. It would bother him a lot.'

'It's OK,' she said. 'I'm not about to go mentioning it around. You're the first person I've ever said that to, as a matter of fact, since high school anyway.'

Ela and the pilot spent the evening and most of the next two days at the Spargnapani. Van der Lubbe was nowhere to be found but the pilot used the waiting time to trade his American surveillance equipment through the bartender for a deal on Deutschmarks plus six compact, high-powered Czech night-vision goggles.

The encryption chips he was more careful with. Eventually one of the Akmba players introduced him to a friend of his who worked the Wildnets. Hacking into a Motorola-system satellite from a laptop in his Wolfburg, the friend set up an auction that brought in eighty thousand Deutschmarks for the chips from an ID-screened buyer in Luxembourg. The cash came by Purolator, the next day; delivered, minus ten percent, via the hacker.

PC gave up following Ela and the pilot. There was no point, they never went anywhere else, they never seemed to do anything. In the great bruise of his pride he decided the pilot had gone back on an implied agreement, and stopped using words any longer than 'any' when speaking to either of them.

'I should leave,' he would say vaguely, whenever anyone was around to listen. 'What good am I here? What good is any of this?' But he never left. Instead he went to cabarets and discos, mostly on the Rynek or in the University quarter – restless, drinking beer out of glass boots, scoring jisi – semiconsciously looking for trouble to signal Ela that he was destroying himself, probably because of her.

Ela did not notice. But Rocketman did. He tracked every move PC made. He shadowed him in taxis, on foot, on city trams. When PC signed on with a tour group visiting the 'historic' town hall of Breslau, Rocketman was in the next group, hunched almost double, hiding behind a gaggle of Japanese in Day-Glo hats. When PC crossed the Oder to Lvov-Dwa, Rocketman followed him, negotiating the Wyspa Piasek checkpoints six or seven people behind his compatriot.

He took notes. He changed disguises in alleyways. He enjoyed himself thoroughly in the process.

26

'Not the Cargo, but the run.'
Hawkley-ite slogan

At 2:16 a.m. on their fifth night in Breslau someone
knocked softly on the pilot's door.

A stooped thin man stood in the putrid neon. He
had a pronounced chin, glasses. He was clean shaven,
and wore a leather jacket and jeans. The pilot recognized him, vaguely, as one of the Akmba players in
the Kneipe Spargnapani.

'I am Alois van der Lubbe,' he said. 'I think we
both have a friend. In the Connie Bar. Yes?'

'But,' the pilot said. 'I mean, you don't have a
moustache.'

Van der Lubbe smiled. 'Vladislav, the bartender, he
is a friend,' he explained. His accent was thick and
Rheinlander-ish. 'He does not say who I am, when
people ask. I have to check up on you. I need time. I
have been very busy this week. Get your girlfriend,'
he continued. 'Do not get your other friends. Two is
enough. I must show you something.'

'She's not my girlfriend,' the pilot began, but the

thin man just shook his head impatiently.

'I don't know where Hawkley is,' van der Lubbe told them later as he drove his rattling old Citroën down Europa Avenue then left, toward the river. 'He has been here, several years before. I have met him. But he has gone east, I think. His gay-hatch-ahs are declining.'

'What?' Ela said.

'Gay hatches,' the pilot said: 'Homosexual trapdoors.' He looked at van der Lubbe, expecting an explanation, but the German only smiled. He had bad breath, and his smile was full of gaps. He stopped the car in the lee of some oaks that were part of a large park stretching to the east and south. A sign said 'Panorama von Raclowice,' over an arrow pointing left. A long glare of white light and steel towers behind the trees marked where the Oder River cut through the city. Police dogs barked insanely in the distance. A sign to the south flashed out the message; 'Zero Cola: Frisch mit Nix!' An ozone shower sprayed cold spittle at them, and gave up. To the north and west the pilot made out a stretch of black river and a bridge, covered in checkpoint boxes, tank barriers, leading to the stone bulk of what looked like a monastery.

Van der Lubbe noticed his glance. 'University Library,' he said, simply.

'Aha,' the pilot said, remembering the tourist info-terminal in the Silesia. 'Gestapo headquarters, right? Last stop for Jews and gypsies.'

'It wasn't only the Nazis,' van der Lubbe replied, seriously. 'You know the first two things the Poles did after the war?'

'I give up.'

352

'The first was, they restored the Chopin Museum, in Warsaw.'

'And the second?'

'They killed the Jews that were left. Pogrom.'

'Charming,' the pilot commented, thinking of his mother and her stories of Lidice.

'Yes,' van der Lubbe replied. 'But it is not the Poles who waste the Manila node. Or the Germans.'

A thin group of people walked down the sidewalk, under the trees, muttering among themselves. They had the bald heads and scabbed faces of hibakusha, from the region around Ignalina, in Latvia, where an RBMK-type reactor core had melted down three years previously. They turned off the sidewalk, behind a stand of cedars, and disappeared. Van der Lubbe waited till they were gone. Then he stepped into a small copse of oaks and rhododendrons and began fiddling in the bushes. He gave a deep grunt and pulled up a filthy, moss-ridden hunk of concrete, revealing a brick-lined hole that seemed to lead to China, it was so black.

'Follow me,' van der Lubbe instructed. 'Pull the stone back over you when you come down.'

'Down' consisted of a dozen rusted rungs to a thin tunnel that smelled violently of subaquatic life. The tunnel ran north and south. Van der Lubbe pulled out a flashlight and they started walking. The walls were fuzzy with moss. You could tell water had once occupied this tunnel and was infiltrating again. Water dripped and streamed from the arched brick roof. It sloshed underfoot. It soaked their fingers when they touched the walls. The pilot shivered in distaste. He pulled his jacket high over his neck and put his arm around Ela's waist to haul her over the deeper pools.

She put her arm around his. Perhaps in response to the darkness, they both used pressures uncalled for by the simple mechanics of lift and carry.

The tunnel ended after a couple of hundred yards. Hanging his flashlight on a nail, van der Lubbe felt around a rusted support beam in the end wall. He stuck his hands in a puddle, picked out a crowbar and levered the support beam from the bricks. It moved easily; the beam was a fake, it supported nothing. Weak light shone from the long rectangle where the beam had been. A much larger tunnel ran at right angles to the one they were in. They heard the chug-chug of a pump. A smell of coal tar slid into their nostrils.

'Lvov Dwa,' van der Lubbe whispered, pointing toward the opening. His sibilants resonated in the circled space.

'Free Poland,' Ela whispered back, in awe, like an echo.

The pilot tightened his arm around her waist. His heart was beating hard, from exertion, from excitement, but all the adrenaline highs were as nothing compared to the feeling of her softness and warmth, the privilege of touched skin, the gentle burning under and above his stomach. The stink of moss and stale water smelled to him at this moment like the glorious funk of first life.

Ela's arm tightened in response.

'We are under the Oder, here,' van der Lubbe continued. 'Right under the frontier, where it follows the river.' He looked at his watch. 'Now I explain.

'This is my tunnel,' he pointed at the rectangle. 'I am an architecture student, I find it in the *archiv* – the history plans, yes? It is part of an old tram repair adit, before the war, but everybody thinks the SS troops dynamited it, when the Red Army came in 1945. They think it is drowned, flooded with water from the river. Well, it is.

'But I find it. I make excuse to pump it out. I say this is an architecture project. Everybody says, he is crazy, let him do what he likes. There is only a small hole, and I put a caisson in. Old trams were in the dry part of the tunnel when they dynamite it; I put in engines I buy from junkyard. With two friends only I do this. Then, one night, I open the tunnel on both sides. For nine-and-a-half months I run cargo and people between Free Poland and EU-Schlesien. Every month.'

Van der Lubbe cocked his ear to the next-door tunnel but apparently heard nothing, for he continued, 'This is how we do not get caught. The BND – the German secret service – they have machines for listening underground. The Milicza too, yes? But the tram bridge is four hundred meters to the west from here. What we have done, we have waited for the heavy tram repair train, 0317 hours to Ostrow Tumski station. Every run, we have moved our train at the same time exactly. They think we are repair train, too. It is pretty, no?'

'Why are you telling us this?' the pilot whispered. 'I thought Hawkley groups were three people. And you never tell anyone else.'

'That is right.' Van der Lubbe nodded hard. 'That is exactly right. Three people in group. Maximum three groups, nine people. Gruppe Elefant, Gruppe Löwe, Gruppe Wolf. Always word-of-mouth communications.

'But one of the groups was not good. Gruppe

Löwe. They were greedy. They wanted more cargo, more money – they wanted to distribute, in Lvov Dwa. They let in eight new people last month. I think they have let in BND. But that is life, no? I wanted to show you, so you can tell Hawkley, if you find him. Tonight, the Gruppe Löwe is bringing back the tram. Tonight we will know, for sure.

'Wait here,' van der Lubbe continued. 'I am back in ten minutes.' He unhooked his flashlight and went through the opening into the larger tunnel, slotting the beam carefully back in place behind him.

Ela and the pilot stood in utter darkness with a fear they tried to ignore and arms around each other's waist and the water of the Oder invading everywhere around them. Darkness hid more than the details of matter; it screened all but the messages of touch and taste. When they could not pull closer without causing serious internal bleeding they folded in on each other, each part of one body crying out for, and finding, sympathetic vibrations from the same part of the other: lips touching lips, hands hands, groin groin.

'I want to make love with you,' Ela said. 'I want to make love with you so much. I want to make love with you under the river.' She pulled at his belt. He leaned against the support beam, so they'd have warning if van der Lubbe came back too soon.

Lifeless objects tried to kill the clear thrust in their brains – belts snagged, zippers jammed, hooks would not unhook – but nothing could stop them. The struggle only added to the tensions of warmth and muscle. The absence of all other input magnified what input there was. The touch of human epidermis was multiplied by contrast with all the lifelessness around. Her lips were ten times more soft, her hair a thousand

356

times richer. The consistency of her breasts made ragged imbalance of the most perfect theorem. She was so hot his fingers burned on her skin.

As for Ela, she wound her fingers through the hair on the pilot's chest, and the smooth wiry strength of it seemed to reach into the depths of her. The strength in the tendons at the root of his thighs was a truth she could do handstands on. The warnings of Plague, of stigs, drummed into them as they were into all other members of their generation, carried no weight against the cold mass of the river above them and the limitless potential created when they touched each other. The made love like flamingoes, keeping their clothes out of the dead water with one bent knee. The water inside her was as pure and warm as the river water was cold and filthy around and under them. 'Come into me,' she whispered. 'Oh come, Joe,' and he did, making silly choking sounds, seeing birds spread out in V-formations from some golden marshland in his mind. 'Oh,' she yelped. 'Oh jeezz'; her fingers felt the sweat pour out of him the instant before coming and she locked her ankles around his ass in response.

'Take that, *Bundesnachrichtendienst*,' he thought as they swayed against each other in the aftermath. He felt as if somehow by fucking each other, by touching in ways that allowed no borders or defenses, they had made the river and razor ribbon and anti-tank barriers above them vanish in some basic way, sabotaged by laws of particle more elemental than the molecular adhesion of concrete or steel wire or water even, and clear angry joy leaped in him at the victory. The soft hot curve of her bare ass under his palms seemed powerful enough to cancel out the frontier, not just

357

the Oder but all the Silesian border's 150 miles of barbed wire, fixed machine-gun arcs, Todeszonen, minefields, and searchlights. The revenge of the half-zero, he thought, still giddy from the Mazurka of sperm and egg.

She started coughing again, even after they had their pants and shirts rucked back around them. He rubbed her shoulder blades, outside anger gone now, cursing himself for not realizing how bad this place was for her. It had been so long since he'd made love with anyone. He'd forgotten how his thoughts floated, afterward.

She took a quick hit from her vaporizer.

'What are you thinking about?' she asked, when her cough had died down.

'I was thinking about borders,' he replied, 'how much I hate them.'

'Why?'

'I'm not sure. Prob'ly from when I was a kid.'

She waited.

He listened, but there were no extraneous sounds.

'We went to so many camps after we left Prague. Austria, the Netherlands, Germany. Every time I got used to one place, some men with uniforms and papers would come and send us to another town, another country. Once I even got lost – separated from my parents.'

She put her forehead against his chest and butted him, lightly, repeatedly. He put a finger on her nose and stroked the bump there gently.

'We never really believed in any of it, after Eduard,' he said. 'Home, homeland, national boundaries. It was all just a lot of barbed wire to us. Wire, and ghosts. The ghost of Eduard, the ghost of borders. It became something bigger than us. I don't know. The hopelessness of war. The Phantom of Checkpoint Charlie . . .'

A rumbling grew through the tunnel. The beam scraped as it was pushed out of the wall. The sound increased by a factor of five.

Van der Lubbe slipped through the hole the beam left. His flashlight was switched off. He shoved them aside, missing their wide eyes, chopped breaths, untucked shirts. He squatted by the fake beam, leaving it open only a half inch. The sound was very loud now; the puddles beneath them, the braced wall beside them trembled with the power of whatever was coming.

The pilot put his eye to the crack above van der Lubbe's back.

The ties and support beams of the old Ostrow Tumski-North Park tram branch made black Xs in the 'O' of tunnel. The tracks leaped with silver. An ancient trolley car tottered out of Poland in the reddish light. It was shaped like an amusement-park ride. Cinderella's carriage with Edwardian coachlights. It was black from rot and run-off. Someone had sprayed a slogan on the front panel; '*Nicht die Ladung, aber die Bewegung.*' Paint flaked from every surface. The trolley's windows were blown out. It glowed from inside with a dull scarlet sheen. Sparks jumped blue and flew from a huge copper engine made of batteries and bushings and coiled wires at the rear. The pilot had a sudden flash of recognition, and his spine prickled in response. The Death Train, he thought, inbound from Flushing, inbound from Lwów Dwa, under the Chingado, under the East River, under the Oder, under the black desire at the heart of every mythic watercourse.

359

'Next stop, Hell,' he muttered to himself.

'What?' Ela whispered, and slid her lean hand down his pants.

The train trundled into Silesia.

Nothing for a minute. Then van der Lubbe tensed beside him.

Dark shapes were following the tram, like the shades of dead commuters.

In the red glow from the tram's windows the pilot made out the helmets of the Polish paramilitary. They wore dark tunics. Some carried machine guns, some oddly shaped metal tubes. The latter had canisters strapped to their backs.

Behind them came men in different uniforms. They held short ugly machine-pistols and wore night-vision goggles not unlike those the pilot had purchased in the Spargnapani. He recognized their caps; the traditional high peaks of the German Bundesgrenzpolizei. In the backwash of rail noise the assault team moved silent and solemn as mourners in some strange funeral for forgotten rail links, for people not yet dead.

She brought her hand up to his waist, feeling the strain.

'What is it,' Ela whispered. 'What's going on?'

'Shhh. Milicza. It's a bust,' the pilot told her.

Van der Lubbe pulled back. The rumble of iron wheels slowed and stopped.

Nothing happened for a couple of minutes. Then someone shouted, clear and far away. Shots echoed down the tunnel in pairs and threes. The thin rectangle van der Lubbe looked through turned bright orange. The color died, flared, and died again. A dim hissing took up all space. It sounded like the breath of dragons. Van der Lubbe pushed the support beam all the way back into the bricks and lit his flashlight. The small light dug caves all over his face. His eyes were hollow as well.

'*Flamenwerfer,*' he whispered. 'How do you say it? Flamethrowing. I should have thought of this.'

'Flamethrowing?'

'Yes. They burn the tram.'

'I saw Grenzpolizei. Behind the *Milicza.*'

Van der Lubbe nodded.

'It is no surprise. They are working together now. They work with BON too. No one wants trouble, *ja?*'

'But your group,' the pilot said. 'Your men. What's happened to them?'

'He escapes, I think,' van der Lubbe said. 'I have told Konrad this is big *Gefahr*, big danger tonight. I do not think he has sold to the BND. He has stopped the tram by his escape place, I think.'

'But your route is finished,' Ela said, watching the tiny edge of red define where the beam slotted into the bricks.

'Every run must finish sometimes,' van der Lubbe said. 'In the Smuggler's Bible Hawkley says, the perfect run is one that includes its own end in every segment. It is born, it grows; when it grows old it must die. Then you start again. Hawkley says, you must run your life like this too; like a smuggling operation.'

'He should know,' Ela said, a little bitterly. 'He was always very good, at ending things.'

'*Flamenwerfer,*' van der Lubbe said again. 'I should have thought of that. Europeans like fire. Fire and Freikorps. We try and try. We can never get rid of them.'

An explosion shook the tunnel behind them. Black dust filled the air. The dust made dark lines on van der Lubbe's cheeks. The smuggler was crying.

'If you find him,' he went on, 'if you find Hawkley, you must tell him. He is right. The six-six-seven. The ratio. Remember this. It is *essential*.'

'The six-six-seven,' Ela repeated. 'What the fuck?'

'How do we find him, then?' the pilot whispered.

'Go east,' the German said. 'You have another contact that way. Go east.' He pointed down the tunnel, in the direction from which the Milicza had come.

'That is where it always comes from,' he said. 'The East.'

'What comes?' Ela asked him.

'History,' van der Lubbe replied, simply.

The woman giggled. 'What a lot of baloney,' Ela said.

27

12-Mile-Limit Cocktail

2 oz. bush rum
2 oz. fresh OJ
2 oz. tamarind juice
juice of two limes
3 No-Doz, crushed, or juice of three cola nuts
3 tbs. brown sugar (5 if you use cola nuts)

Blend contents with ice at high speed. Drink up.
This will keep you high, alert, and on top of
things when you cross the line.

Hawkley
The Freetrader's Almanac and Cookbook

What happened in the tunnel under the Oder
unhooked some catch in Ela.

The combination of secrecy, escape, and the threat
of being caught bypassed blocks in her own brain,
and allowed nerve impulses she had never felt before
to touch and light her in places she had not known
existed.

One of those places was a tightness in her chest that
used to hinder her ability to laugh. The tightness had
started to dissipate the moment she met the pilot but

the incident under the Oder had vanished it. When she laughed now it was without control, as if before the impulse stemmed from a mere chemical reaction and now it came from a shift in nature. She saw absurdities everywhere, and they made the change happen, and she came to terms with it in deep, gasping, almost masculine brays of mirth.

Another symptom of sea-change lay in her ability to touch. Where before she had been held in from touching the pilot the way she knew she wanted to, she now found it easier to touch him than not. Nothing drastic was called for; a finger laid on his hand at the breakfast table, a calf against his leg; even letting the Herald Tribune she was reading brush his frayed denim jacket was enough. She preferred light contact, pulled strokes at this stage. There were no shackles in such a caress, no vows she could not keep.

As for lovemaking, the memory of it was sufficient to sustain her. She did not need to sleep with the pilot; in the halls of her imagination she carved a niche for the feeling that had touched her in the tunnel.

And when timing and space fell right – like dice on neural felt – she would come to him as quickly and naturally as she had under the river between Free Poland and Silesia.

Somehow timing and space fell right more and more often as they traveled east, following, on van der Lubbe's advice, the last clue they possessed as to Hawkley's whereabouts.

The day after the incident under the Oder they took a plane to Frankfurt and changed to the daily Airbus bound for Karachi.

Ela got the window seat this time. This time she

was not sleeping; that need, too, seemed to have slackened, been released. She rode glued sideways against the plexiglass porthole as the jet rose to forty thousand feet. They flew over the pinched blue-white-greens of the Austrian Alps, folded and whipped in their own shadows. Down the length of the Balkans, her mind buzzing with echoes from largely exaggerated TV myths of what these places were like: vampires and sniper-fire, virgins and brigands; Turks, mass graves, and dying archdukes. As they flew south and east the greens below them became more olive, took on an infinite complexity of umbers and yellows. They crossed the Aegean north of Thessalonica, and blue reached its maximum development, a sort of robin's-egg to the Nth power – and evaporated.

Ela watched all this like a thriller movie, acutely aware she had never seen colors like these in Indiana.

After the Aegean, all softness faded slowly from the earth. They flew over the massed gray cruelties of the Anatolian plateau, then southeast across Syria into the Arabian desert. Circular patches of irrigation by the coast only emphasized the featureless wastes inland. The sky took on the same ochre hue as the Rub 'al Khali and all the other empty quarters below.

Ela's body reacted violently to the dying of gentleness underneath her. She felt herself go soft and wet as if in one personal mind/Barthelin reflex she could reverse the desertification process; the overpopulation, the goats too thirsty to bleat, the corn dying in the ear, the children born to starve, the whole vicious cycle of dryness, overcultivation, erosion, and drought again.

Night was falling. The plane entertained its humans

with a 2-D movie about a forty-year-old lawyer from Bel Air who through some strange biological trick turned into a thirteen-year-old girl. The first symptom of this was a sudden addiction to Safety Volunteer Barbies, and motorized skateboarding in judges' chambers. While everyone was watching and listening on headphones Ela pulled at the pilot's sleeve and led him aft into one of the restrooms in the plane's tailsection. This time they fucked braced against a tiny stainless-steel sink and dispensers of little flat soaps, surrounded by the great metallic roar of backwash from the jets. The 'no smoking' signs blinked in their eyes.

He made love to her happily, his eyes hot, immediately turned on by her turn-on, and the mystery of how men managed that melded for her into the mystery of how a planet could hold so many new colors that blended into the question of why she had taken so god-darned long to find this out. When she came it was in swirled shades, like a sheen of bunker fuel on water; different hues with different meanings; a color for the pilot, and a color for what she felt for him, something silver/lavender, unresolved, potential; a color for the great confusion behind her (yellow), and strong burning orange for what she had set herself to do. The swirl, on aggregate, was a warm one, a great striped love for the planet starting inexorably to die under her, and she cried out 'Shit!' when the orgasm multiplied inside her, and 'Fuck!'; words she'd never used, never thought it proper to use, never needed to use except now, to express her endless frustration at not being able to express herself better; telling also of her wonder and confusion that she was coming at all, only two days after she had last had an orgasm, but a good seventeen or eighteen months since she'd been able to achieve one with Roger.

They made love again in the Thai Air baggage room in Karachi Airport, and again on the 737 to Islamabad. The pilot heard the loud noises of breaking chains in her lovemaking as well as her choice of places to make love, and did nothing to discourage her, though he knew they were moving deeper into Islam with every segment of trip accomplished. Karachi was OK – the more relaxed codes of the Industrial Qu'ran held sway there, as they might also in Lahore and Rawalpindi; but the farther away they got from the cities the farther they got from the subtleties of distinction, and attenuated canons.

Every segment of flight now brought a smaller plane, and a rattier airport, a shorter hop, and more metal barriers slamming shut in the eyes of men, with attendant dangers for those who transgressed such barriers. In the deeper provinces of Pakistan, as in much of Central Asia, the crypto-fundamentalist diktats of the nineties remained largely unchallenged. Ela was married and he was not, so what they did, in the eyes of the Old Koran, was sin of a most technicolor degree.

They bought Ela long dresses, scarves, and silks in the old bazaar of Peshawar, because in the stressed language of fundamentalism Ela's jeans and paratrooper boots and above all her post-punk haircut translated directly into concepts like 'prostitute' and 'adulteress.'

And still she brought him out to make love bare-assed under the stars among the rotting bougainvillea'ed splendor of the Dean's Hotel

367

gardens, in great danger of being spotted by the patrols of Frontier Police and tribal levies.

There were lots of such patrols, for the new Russian State Committee in Moscow was attempting to turn the local tribes against the Pakistanis, just as the Tzars had tried to do with the British before them, and thus the situation was tense in the entire Northwest Frontier Province.

Ela's excitement appeared immune to the danger of discovery, but the pilot grew more nervous, checking around them constantly as they made love, assuming the role of jigger-man, jumping at shadows as they sweated and ground against each other. However, despite the dangers he was still excited by her excitement, and so the net effect was the same. The lovemaking brought down emotional defenses between them at the same time as it demolished physical barriers, to reveal the final balance of her; proportions of face, counterweight of movement, stasis, and change in the harmonics of vocal chords; the rushing asymmetry of her new curiosity.

This was the secret to the new side of her, he believed — a curiosity that had been buried alive for all of her bare quarter-century. The curiosity seemed to have blossomed outward, in response to geography, the way a stunted shrub responded to repotting. Her eyes were never still anymore, and now she seemed to need less sleep than any of them. She asked questions none of them could answer.

Flights to Chitral were canceled because of bad weather in the mountains. In their dingy room in what had once been barracks for Bengal Lancer officers at Dean's, the ceiling fan slowly redistributed the same dun shadows around the peeling walls. The pilot set up the ECM-pak, put on the half-sucker and did a careful security scan of the radio environment. He was surprised, and rendered somewhat thoughtful, by what he found: a lot of encrypted radio traffic between the Air Force base, and transmitters in the direction of the Khyber Pass, running codes used by Inter-Services Intelligence, the Pakistani secret police; a source in University Town the program labeled as an American Defense Intelligence Agency cypher; and far more radar than he would have expected coming from small tactical posts as well as a theatre-surveillance aircraft over Quetta.

The traffic made sense, he thought. After all, this segment of the Great Silk Road was one of the oldest smuggling routes in the world. Also, the Pashtun tribesmen living in the NWFP supplied a third of the smack going into the US and it would be odd if American agencies did not have a presence here. But the hiss of security traffic amplified the buzz of adrenaline in his gut. All of a sudden, standing still felt wrong, and dangerous.

He checked them out of Dean's the next morning. They hired a couple of motorized rickshaws to get them to the bus station, where they boarded an ancient, crowded, intricately painted British Bedford, heading north.

He watched Ela's face as they rode, seeing her once again absorb the changes in scenery, the different trees, flat crocodile-dry plain lined with bazaars and colonial roads, the endless convoys of artillery and surface-to-surface missiles. The sudden rise into hills. He knew he was infatuated with her, because of the warmth in his chest, because he was beginning to need the specifics of her, actually *need* the way she led

369

him on in hopes of a joke. Within that he needed to watch her lift one corner of her mouth in the start of a smile, and within that the first hint of lightness in stance or voice. All were necessary to life, like clear water on a hot day.

And all the time, underneath that need, he saw the shadow that still hung behind her eyes, and the pullback that lay behind the light touch of her fingers, soft though it was, strong though the forward movement had become in her.

'It's a boa constrictor,' he murmured, 'digesting an elephant,' only half-meaning for her to hear – though the code would be obvious, if she did.

'No, it's a hat,' she replied, quoting *The Little Prince* in turn, smiling gently but not looking at him from behind the lavender shimmer of her shawl.

The awareness of barriers in her scared him. There had been barriers in Carmelita, too. Thus behind the warmth of his affection lay a gentle but constant colic, as of indigestion, or impending loss.

In Dir they learned the pass into Chitral Valley was closed to all traffic but jeeps. They hired a jeep and driver. The driver was a young Pashtun tribesman named Jamal. He smiled a lot to make up for his lack of English. He drove like a repressed fighter jock. In common with all the other Pashtun he carried an AK-47 assault rifle the way a Wall Street commuter would carry a laptop computer, like a Tenth Avenue prostitute would carry her pack of Trojans, or an artist his sketch pad. To complete the martial effect he wore on his belt a curved, ivory-handled dagger.

The shadows were packed with eyes as they moved out of Dir. Shots rang out; somewhere a bomb went off. They were stopped at a roadblock. A militiaman warned them to keep their heads down. The Oraksai clan were warring with the Yusufsai this week, an old enmity based on women, or the split of profits from opium traffic, or water rights, or something else. No one seemed to be sure, or care. Blood feuds, fought with mountain howitzers and rocket-propelled grenades, were common as weeds in this region, Jamal told them as they pulled away from the road-block. They must watch out as well for ambushes set by Afghan agents for Nooristani separatists. Dacoits, or highwaymen, also thrived on the road to Chitral. He touched his rifle as he said all this, and smiled with honest pleasure.

The trail climbed swiftly north of town. Snow began to fall, lightly. It grew arctic cold. For this stage of the trip PC sat with Ela in the cab of the old Willys. Twisted sideways, shivering, he watched the snowflakes fan and swoop hypnotically in the arc of slipstream over the jeep's hood. He looked at Ela beside him. Even under the shawl, the sweater, the army jacket, and red silks draped over her body, even sitting in the front seat of a jeep, she managed to convey a feeling of slimness and grace.

PC was silent. He seldom talked now. In itself this was a form of communication, a flag flown upside down. It was no longer because of Ela. The rush of infatuation had passed, as it always did, blown out partly by the fact that she obviously had fallen for the pilot instead of him, and partly because his own infatuation had waned. What shut him up now was a cliché, a truism, something he'd always known but like everyone else had never really believed; namely, that he could not escape the iron parameters of his old life simply by jettisoning the outer shell. Travel might erase the signs others drew on you, but it only etched deeper what was written inside. He had canned his job, and opted out of the party circuit; but love remained, for him, something that faded, even in places where no one spoke English; and indifference came back, unconquerable as time, omnipotent in gray, deadly and cold as cancer, even among mountains as strange and bare as these.

He had come to feel the cold touch of that indifference was poisoning the rest of his life. The indifference – and its symptoms, the gaps in his conversation – were only the sign of a far deeper rot that had gnawed at the green pith of his undramatic childhood outside Philly. The rot, he believed, was contentment, and a certain deficiency in drama. His father had been gentle and supportive, his mother had loved him without excess. He had the largest collection of baseball cards in grammar school. He broke his arm at twelve years of age, lost his virginity at seventeen, and went seamlessly from high school to Williams to Wharton to a position in Webware sales that netted him 280 grand a year. He had often wondered as he clicked off the required mileage if you had to be unhappy and fucked up to become interesting, and if so, was it worth the pain?

What was so unacceptable now, of course, was that even the lack of pain had begun to hurt. His dearth of interests had finally created an indifference in his life that was so huge it bored even himself, so that now he had nothing left but his own disgust, and a certain cynical humor that was basically as funny as a hand sticking out of a frozen lake.

So he stared glumly through the windshield as the jeep ground fast as Jamal could push it up the washed-out trail, wheels regularly slamming from bump to bump, the left-hand side bumps often a lousy two inches maximum from three-hundred-foot drops as they climbed the approach road to Lohairi Pass. Barely responding when Ela chattered beside him.

'I keep thinking,' she said once, 'this is so like *The Wizard of Oz*. I must have seen that film a hundred times when I was a kid, and it all seems so familiar, in some ways. I mean, like, I get sick, you know? And I get a fever, and all of a sudden it's like a whirlwind – here I am with the Tin Man, and the Scarecrow, and the Lion.'

'Humph,' PC grunted.

'No lion,' Jamal said cheerfully, grinning, holding the wheel with one finger as the jeep skidded around a switchback turn, pointing with the other hand toward a glacier cutting high above them. 'No lion – snow leopard.'

'It's a story, Jamal,' Ela told him. 'See,' she continued, to PC, 'the Tin Man is Rocketman. He's worried 'cause he thinks he doesn't have a heart. He's never told me what it is, but I think something happened once, to, like, make him feel he doesn't deserve to love, or be loved anymore. And the Lion – that's the pilot. He's constantly looking for the guts to face what his parents did to him, after his brother died. Only he doesn't realize that he's had the guts, all his life, just by surviving; he doesn't realize that his parents can't do any more to him than they've already done.

'And you, PC; you're the Scarecrow. You've lost your brain. You've got a good brain, obviously, but you've never had to really use it. You've never really

373

had to do anything, and since you're basically lazy, like me, like most people, you've never made the effort to really think.'

'This is what I think,' PC growled, 'I think *The Wizard of Oz* is just, you know, a symbol for America being basically immature—' knowing he was talking about himself, nevertheless, he gritted his teeth and continued '—always looking for a Hoffa, or a Pastor Johnson, or a Hawkley to save us from our responsibilities. Always wanting to click our heels three times and go home to Auntie Em and her big soft cozy hermeneutic titties and, and to *hell* with the Munchkins and their problems.'

Ela stared at him.

'I don't understand you,' Ela said. 'I don't understand why you're here.'

'I don't understand either,' PC said. 'I thought it was because I was in love with you. I was wrong. But I'm glad you brought up Oz. Because that's what this is – fantasy. An escape. For me, you, all of us. It's bullshit.'

'You're wrong,' Ela told him. 'Not all of us are escaping. Some of us are looking for something . . .'

PC ignored her.

'I mean, I knew you couldn't change yourself,' he said, 'just by going somewhere new, but I thought I could find new info, you know? Just data. But it doesn't make any difference.'

'There's such a thing as ruts,' Ela said, watching the track, which was full of them.

'I've made up my mind,' PC told her. 'I'm going back. I don't know what I'm doing in this crazy place, in these crazy mountains, you know, with machine guns and bandits and snow leopards and no one takes universal credit cards. I'm going to turn around tomorrow. I'm going back to New York.'

'I don't know why that makes me sad,' Ela told him, 'but it does.'

They stopped at a chai house on the near side of the pass. It was a dark wooden structure built around a large adobe fireplace. Guests could stay for tea or the night on woven rope beds grouped around the central hearth. They drank strong sweet tea in tiny Chinese cups, and ate potato stew on an unleavened Afghan bread called *nan*.

Rocketman observed PC and Ela. He would have given a lot to know what PC had been saying to the girl in the jeep. He hoped he was not trying to turn Ela against him. He liked Ela, but he did not trust her, no matter where she came from. There was no purity in her – no purity to any woman, he had to admit to himself, compared to those whose obsession led them past the stratosphere, past the Van Allen belt, into the cold darkness of space. Compared to Judy Resnick.

Jamal had loaned them wool blankets to keep warm in the back of his jeep. Rocketman drew the blanket around his shoulders. In the bazaar where Ela got her silks he had bought Pakistani clothes, the ubiquitous *shalwar kameez*, the baggy pyjamas and long shirt, but they were of light cotton and not as warm as his American gear. It was cold and getting colder. He looked at the pilot, who was shivering as close to the earthen hearth of the chai hut as he could get without knocking over the cook. The pilot held his hands in such a way that Rocketman knew he was giving his rat warmth. Rocketman felt a sudden rush of protective feeling for the pilot. Here was a guy who in his own way was so naive he should not be let out alone without little clips on his mittens, so he wouldn't lose them.

Rocketman looked down the valley they had climbed. The pilot had not noticed, for example, the pair of headlights that stayed with them, never coming too close, never dropping too far back, as someone shadowed their jeep the entire way from Dir.

Bulldozers from a Scottish engineering firm had swept away most of the snow toward the crest of the pass. The pilot's eyes lingered on a massive grader parked by the roadside, and he searched the machine for what had caught his attention, finding at last, on the side of the diesel housing, a silver 'T' crossed with a golden lightning bolt that was as familiar to him as the roof of his own apartment. 'MacAndrew's Ltd' was printed above the logo, and 'a subsidiary of TransCom International.'

The pilot shook his head. It was not so strange to find that logo here, he told himself. TransCom was bigger than a lot of independent nations, and it had interests in every corner of the planet.

The grader had done its job well; the road was even at this point, and clear of potholes . . .

They crossed the saddle just before dusk. Snow was banked so high under the glaciers they could not see above the roadside as the jeep plunged into the valley.

Dark contorted pines brought darkness early. In the gloom the valley's rocks looked like trolls frozen in a position of winter larceny.

28

'We don't need visas, or whatever they are . . .
We just walk over the border.'

Alan Jan, quoted in Peter Mayne
Journey to the Pathans

Chitral was a long valley in the mountains where
northern Pakistan touched Afghanistan and China.
Chitral was also a town of silver and dark flame. Black
settlements throbbed with campfires on a silver river.
Starlight made silver of the shale lining the water.
Shining white peaks rose like distant gods on both
sides and on the spurred shadows that marked the
valley's continuation north and south. A Russian
Federation gunship slunk between two of the peaks
and chopped into the valley, drawing fire from troop
emplacements at the snow-stoppered airport, then
drifted, lazily, north.

As they drove up the town's only road they saw the
river embankments were covered with tents erected
on walls of shale. Light reflected off the snow and
onto the canvas walls, most of which bore the names
of relief organizations that had donated the tents:
'UNHCR' or 'Saudi Red Crescent.' Kerosene lamps
blossomed in the depths of market stalls. Eyes hooded

in blankets gazed at their passing, withholding judgment.

The pilot remembered the tenements beside the El, in Brooklyn, and shivered.

Jamal drove them straight to the District Commissioner's office. This was a whitewashed house in a courtyard, protected by two brass cannon and a squad of militiamen armed with antique Lee Enfield .303s. Large snow-shrouded trees loomed by the greenhouse; under their shelter the sole representative of the King-Emperor had once heard the petitions of local tribes. A varnished board hung in the office, inlaid with the names of the district commissioners who had gone before. 'Capt. A.E.B. Parsons, OBE, 1920–1921. Capt. C.E.U. Bremner, MC, 1924–1925.' Men with moustaches as long as their sense of mission was deep, who believed an island that built palaces of crystal and twenty-thousand-ton Dreadnoughts must enjoy the favor of a deity who himself was white, and spoke English, and could probably play a fair round of snooker, if he chose.

The current district commissioner was very lean and dark and taut. His name was Zayid Shah. He wore an old white silk scarf under a faded tweed suit and spoke English with an Oxbridge accent that Captains Parsons and Bremner might not have sneered at. He looked long and hard at their pass-cards and did not believe them for a minute when they said they were tourists.

'We are having a bit of bother in Chitral, at the moment,' he told them. 'We have fifty thousand refugees from the trouble over the mountains—' he gestured toward the west '—living here. We do not have enough food, we have almost no firewood left.

378

The airport is open only sporadically, and the road will close with the next snow. The Russians, as usual, are setting bombs in the bazaar, in order that the Chitralis will turn against the refugees. Men paid by the Afghan government and men from the Nooristani Liberation Front shoot each other every day. On top of everything, I have just heard a report of a new fever that is sweeping the camps.'

Zayid Shah picked up a dagger from a foot-high stack of triplicates on his desk. The weapon was richer than the one Jamal wore. It had a handle of yellowed ivory and masses of silver inlay. He patted the sheath idly on the palm of one hand. An orange fire spirit groaned and strained to get out of the potbellied stove. An orderly typed out visitors' permits on a 1930 Underwood. The DC's eyes were dark and taut as the rest of him. He looked at each of them individually.

'You will be my guests,' he told them abruptly. 'Your driver will bring you to the fort.' When the pilot started to protest, on the pretext of not imposing on Zayid Shah's hospitality, but above all not wanting to place them under constant scrutiny from the authorities, the DC interrupted him. 'All farangi — all foreigners — are required to stay with me until further notice.'

He did not stop looking at them. He unsheathed the dagger and drove the point violently into the teak top of his desk. The metal sprang and quivered. Zayid Shah smiled pleasantly.

'Dinner will be at eight,' he said. 'I don't suppose,' he added, 'any of you play the game of Gō?'

Chitral Fort was a massive affair of timber-reinforced earthen walls with stone towers at every corner and one overhanging the river. The only way in was through a postern beside a giant wooden gate. The battlements were patrolled by militiamen. Under tall aspens outside the wall, next to the single dirt track leading to the gate, a Saracen armored car was dug in, its 7.62-mm machine gun pointing toward town.

Inside, the fort was cut up into a maze of dark offices and living quarters. The power was out – the power was out more often than not in Chitral, from sabotage, or malfunctions, or simply snow – and the rooms and hallways were illuminated by Chinese-made kerosene lamps spaced at strategic intervals. They were shown to different rooms and water was poured in their washstands but by the time they washed up and their bags arrived it was already 7:50 and a steward was walking up and down the hallway ringing a gong for dinner.

At eight o'clock precisely servants brought into the dining hall a dozen heavy silver tureens still scrolled with the serifed heraldry of the Indian Civil Service, and laid them down the length of the DC's table.

The table was thirty feet long, massively carved in mahogany so old and polished it was virtually black.

Carved silver lamps extruded thick yellow light in diamond shapes. A fire crackled in an enormous fireplace.

The walls of the dining hall were built of umber brick. In the deep-set windows, through leaded panes, you could see a newly risen moon pour sparkling light on the snowy top of Tirich Mir. The moonlight seemed to splash downward like a fountain, cascading over the icy crags, onto the scraped, deforested slopes next to the town, on the reflecting canvas of the refugee camps; on stark aspens, the

380

ghostly ivory minarets of a nearby mosque, and the river's white water.

Four American engineers, a Pakistani hotel owner, and a British anthropologist as well as the pilot and his party sat at the long table. A half-dozen servants dressed in grimy wool waistcoats and turbans served potato, lamb, and lentil stews. These were sopped up with the *nan*, the unleavened bread. No alcohol. Alcohol was prohibited by the Koran, and the colonels who ran things from Islamabad, though they personally enjoyed their whisky, deferred to the crypto-fundamentalists in these obvious tests of faith.

When no one was looking, the pilot filled a water glass with clear vodka from his pocket flask.

Zayid Shah came in late. He sat at the head of the table, drinking liquid salted yoghurt, staring at the fire. Everyone seemed used to his silence. The engineers talked among themselves. One of them, who wore a beard to conceal the fact that he had no chin at all, said 'We have to get in touch with Islamabad, and it's up to them to get in touch with Washington.'

The anthropologist told Ela about the pagan tribes who lived down the valley in Kafiristan. Some said they were descendants of soldiers of Alexander the Great, who once had bivouacked near Peshawar. They wore black and made rough wine and worshiped the moon. Until recently the pagans had enjoyed special dispensation as a sort of ethnological sideshow but now the regime was cracking down on their use of wine and their stubborn refusal to convert. It was hard, the anthropologist added with a sort of post-imperial relish, to tell these mountain people what to do.

The Pakistani hotel owner competed for Ela's

attention from the other side of the table. He was in his thirties, bored, a chain-smoker. He was also a big fan of what he believed was true American music. He had a stereo system in his jeep. He would play 'Enegada Davida' for Ela, he would play it for all of them.

A woman came out of curtained shadows in one corner of the long room. She was wrapped in voluminous silk robes and a heavily embroidered wool jacket. A silk shawl covered two-thirds of her face. Her fingers were thick with rubies. She nodded politely to the table, then sat down to the right of Zayid Shah, who ignored her.

'I don't understand,' a younger engineer said, 'why do we have to do an EIS, if Washington's gonna fund it anyway?'

'The stars are very beautiful tonight,' the woman told Zayid Shah in English. 'I have seldom seen them so close.'

The woman had a very low, almost husky voice. It sounded the way brown enamel finish looked. Her accent was an attractive braid of Indian and upper-caste British.

Rocketman shifted his gaze from the door, where he'd been checking for eavesdroppers.

The woman picked up a piece of bread, pulled down her shawl to eat it. Her cheeks were very strong but they would have to lie down and surrender if you compared them to her eyes. These were enormous, a little almond-shaped, dark and soft as two ponds of night. The lamps reflected in them like twin moons. Rocketman suddenly felt as if he'd been released into zero gravity, floating in a spacesuit above earth like Billy's dream, or Major Tom; his umbilical cord full of oxygen and pressure and radio communications with the rest of humanity suddenly cut.

She looked back at him steadily. Seconds ticked by. Half-glances sprouted in the dead air. Zayid Shah pulled his eyes from the fire and watched the woman and Rocketman stare at each other.

'Noor,' Zayid Shah said sharply.

She dropped her gaze to the table.

'Yes, Zayid,' she said.

'This is my wife,' Zayid Shah told his newest guests.

Silence fell. In the mosque outside, a muezzin climbed stiffly in long robes to the shining tower and began to chant into a loudspeaker. 'There is no god but Allah, and Mohammed is his prophet.' From the hills all around, the jackals howled in response.

'There is no more medicine,' Zayid Shah's wife said suddenly. 'Why can't they bring us more medicine?'

'They have done all they can.'

'But all they can do is very little—'

'They have a budget—'

'—after they have bought their Chinese missiles—'

'Be quiet.'

'I cannot,' the woman said. Her voice was still soft but determination had reinforced its timbre. 'People are dying. They have not enough food to resist, and this fever is killing them like fleas.'

Rocketman watched her. His hands were sweating so hard they left marks on the wood. His heart beat like a kettledrum. He had no idea why a few words from this woman's mouth, a simple glimpse of her eyes, should do this to him. Or why the concordance of voice and grace and eyes should affect him so

383

strongly. All he knew was that the room had disappeared for him, with all its eavesdroppers, informants, and government spies, and nothing existed but the quick darts of glance she still sent in his direction, once in a while, in resonance, in response.

'What kind of fever,' he said hoarsely, 'Mrs Shah?'

She looked at him directly now. Her face was full of light. His breath stopped. The woman's words came quick and intense.

'We think it is a variation of the flu. Only much stronger. It strikes very quickly. There is much diarrhea and vomiting and dehydration. The body temperature goes to thirty-eight, thirty-nine degrees almost immediately.'

Zayid Shah clapped his hands. The dinner trays were replaced with bowls of sweet nut candies, small cups, and a samovar full of thick tan tea, already mixed with condensed milk and sugar. He clapped his hands again and one servant placed a clunky laptop computer before him, with a rechargeable battery pack hooked up. Another, to one side, set a game board on the table beside a wooden bowl containing hundreds of shiny polished stones.

'Central Asia,' Zayid Shah announced, spilling the 361 little pebbles on the table before him. 'Nexus between the great civilizations of Persia and China, India and Europe. The land road between Europe and the East. A thousand languages, a hundred races. We are sitting in the middle of the world's greatest Gō board, gentlemen. Who wishes to play on the little screen with me?'

'We need doctors. We need nurses. We need people just to help give water,' his wife said, talking to the

384

mahogany again. 'There is only one aide there now, and he is old—'

'The Chinese invented the original Gō,' Zayid Shah stated loudly, 'to practice dealing with threats from this area.'

'The tribesmen believe the flu is a curse – they will not come near the hospital until they are so sick they have no choice.' Noor's voice was rising slowly. Her cheeks were very dark. Her eyes stayed cast down.

'Civilizations in conflict.' Zayid Shah said the words with a sigh. He tapped out a command on the laptop. 'For three thousand years empires have clashed over this earth we stand on. In this very fort, British officers and Indian troops held off a Chitrali mutiny for forty-seven days. History is like a living animal here. It scraps and snarls on our doorstep in this valley. And my wife worries about the flu.' Zayid Shah smiled broadly at his guests, but his eyes did not change.

'Do you know the Beatles song "I am the Walrus"?' the hotel manager asked. 'If you play it backwards at 78 RPM it says "Paul is dead." And the Viking symbol for death was, the walrus!'

Rocketman had no idea what to do next. He only knew that, in this limited segment of time, of space, the woman was all that existed for him; that contact with her was the only contact that mattered. *Can you hear me, Major Tom?*

He played with his teacup – it was so delicate it practically vanished inside the palm of his hand. The words came from the pit of him, almost against his will.

'We could help.' He cleared his throat. 'I, uh,

385

worked in a hospital for many years. I could help. PC, here, too.'

The woman looked at PC, to avoid looking at Rocketman.

'We need help desperately,' she said. 'We need hands.'

The pilot watched her avoiding Rocketman's eyes.

'Don't go there alone,' one of the engineers said, 'the Dacoits come in, after dark.'

'And what of history?' Zayid Shah asked, taking the long dagger from a fold in his woollen coat and laying it quietly on the Gō board. He looked at Rocketman as he said this. 'Are you such men, that you must go with the women to treat the dying, and leave me with my strategies, alone?'

'History,' Rocketman said, 'is in the details.'

'Balls,' Ela said softly, and giggled at her own remark.

Noor looked at PC and the engineers.

'I can show you how much they need help. I can show you,' she said, and spread her hands, at a loss for words.

'This is what happens,' Zayid Shah commented in a tone of great disgust as he laid out the Gō stones carefully on the crossed lines, checking the laptop screen to remember where he was in this part of the game.

'This is what happens, when you take a woman of the East, and send her to Girton College for an education.'

386

29

'Badal (retaliation) must be exacted for personal
insults, damage to property, or blood feud.
The most fruitful sources of feuds are;
(a) Intrigues with women . . .'

> Maj. R.T.I. Ridgeway, 40th Pathans
> *Pathans*

In the end they all went — that is, Rocketman, PC, Ela,
the pilot, and the British anthropologist went down
the bazaar road, past the stalls selling vodka and gems
and refrigerators, all smuggled on the backs of
donkeys over the Suleiman Range from Afghanistan.
Men pulled machine-gun parts from small ruby-
glowing forges and filed intently at the hot metal.
Others scrambled goat brains in broad woks full of
clarified butter and spices. Coals glowed satanic from
braziers in the teeming dark.

The hospital proved to be a small wooden two-
story building built around a courtyard. It was quiet
enough from the outside, unremarkable save for a
line of men and women, many too sick to stand,
waiting to get in the courtyard gate.

Once you crossed the threshhold the place was so
full of the sounds and smells of human misery it

387

seemed about to burst at every joint. Wood smoke, lamplight, and filthy linens textured each surface. The operating areas were lined with ancient enameled tin. Cracked tiles and faucets stuck out of the walls. People lay on any available space, on cots or pallets on the bare floor, excreting wastes and pain. This variety of fever, Noor said, produced both in abundance and colors – the pain gave the victims a sensation of purple, and the wastes were typically liquid and yellow.

Only a few of the ill had blankets, and these were old and in many cases dirty. There was a high percentage of infants. The hospital's only doctor, a thirty-year-old Afghan medical student named Nassir, was so tired he barely noticed them when they came in, but carried on diagnosing the walk-ins, murmuring to them in the flat brittle tone of utter exhaustion.

The British anthropologist took one sniff at the stench and departed, leaving them with a handful of pills. 'Novogrippe,' she explained. 'You're not immune, you know.'

PC hung by the entrance to the ward. He had lost color, and kept shaking his head as if trying to refuse something his five senses were telling him.

'This is crazy,' he whispered to the pilot. 'Who knows what kind of virus they have here? This is Darkworld, man – selenium-deficient areas, where *plagues* come from. We *get* this shit, we could be dead in a week.'

The pilot shrugged. What PC said was probably true, but somehow hard statistics seemed less important in mountains like these. The knowledge of high granite, and the clarity of the constellations above the Hindu Kush, and the sense of human history piling up with the snows over millennia to isolate this valley, made risk less singular here, life's imperatives more abstract.

Zayid Shah's wife turned and saw them hesitating. 'Are you coming?'

The pilot looked at PC. Noor followed his gaze.

PC was going to tell her he was leaving, now, but once he looked at her eyes he could not pull his own away. Her pupils had all the tones of expensive wood and precious metals mixed at night. They were dark as smoke and clear as the moon above this place. He took a breath to refuse, to deny what those eyes were asking, and could not speak.

All of a sudden, to deny what Noor wanted of them seemed tantamount to denying the part of him that made him worthy of loving, and being loved by, Noor or someone like her.

PC was not falling in love with Noor. She was not the type he sought. He had coined a term once for the infatuation of an instant – an *affaire de* fruit-fly, he called it, after the short life span of drosophilae – and in that short instant he had an *affaire de* fruit-fly with Noor's eyes; and he cleared his throat and found himself grunting, 'I guess we could, uh, do something, as long as there's no fluids—'

'Good,' Noor interrupted. She turned, took off her shawl, put on a white coat, and started working without further delay. She got Ela and PC to boil water and take temperatures. She asked the pilot to clean up the men who were too sick to take care of themselves, while she took care of the women. The pilot, suddenly paying more attention to PC's warnings, touched the men gingerly at first, keeping towels between himself and their hot bodies. After a while,

389

though, the olfactory centers grew numb to the stench, and despite his efforts his hands were soon splattered with human secretions. After half an hour he had to remind himself to wash off between patients.

Two babies and one old man died in the first hour they were there. PC and the pilot wrapped the dead in some of the dirtier linens and laid them in the courtyard to freeze. Ela – already tired from the trip and dizzy from the fumes of ether, the only medicine the hospital seemed to possess in quantity – tried to take a six-year-old's temperature and found the child had stopped breathing so long ago he was cold. She went into an empty supply closet and hyperventilated to keep down the sudden rush of nausea.

PC was not immune to the initial stomach-level block that came from dealing with the deaths and excretions of others. His stomach too reeled from the effects of these implications of common weakness.

Despite his earlier reluctance, however, and in a surprisingly short space of time, he began to get the hang of taking care of sick people whose language he could not understand. There was no time to wonder why he was doing this; the urgency was such that he completed each task and went on to the next without questioning. Maybe this was the downstream effect of being a doctor's son. He communicated with hand signs and a firm sense that this had to be done. Within twenty minutes he felt as if he'd been mopping mucus from nostrils and cleaning the bottoms of sick babies for months. His hands absorbed the lesson faster than the mind could keep up with them.

Ela, peering out of her closet as the spasms of revulsion died away, focused on PC's hands as they gestured and moved and swabbed.

The embarrassment and shame of her own inability to help got lost in fascination. For the first time she noticed how strong and sure his gestures could be, how long and expressive his fingers, how sensuous the hairs on the back of his hands. She felt the re-action come, soaking, violent, totally unanticipated. She found she wanted to make love with PC the way kids stuck in a gray classroom wanted to go out that window among those bursting maples and roll in the sunshine on the first warm day of spring.

She saw the pilot pull a stretcher through the cacophony of noises and smells. He came through again, looking for her, and in the confluence of desire and emotion she could read her body like a therm-ometer and know, by the extent and frequency of loosenings, exactly how much of this new and powerful current of emotion came from knowing the pilot, and how much came from the changes that being with the pilot entailed.

Jeeps ground through the entrance gates, full of blood-soaked clothes with limbs angled anyhow inside. A bomb had gone off in the market of Garam Chasma, twenty miles up the valley.

Nassir took five of the most critical and lined them up on the tin counters. The hospital, which had seemed crowded to the utmost with the sick and dying, with their noises and smells, somehow swelled to accept the added inflow.

In her closet, Ela felt her stomach rebel again. She went to find the pilot and asked him to take her back to the fort. He hesitated, then, remembering the Dacoits, agreed — telling himself, and believing it mostly, that he would return later.

* * *

In the madness after the bomb victims came, Rocketman and Noor Zayid Shah emptied pans of blood, changed linens, moved cots and blankets from room to room. They said little to each other, just touched gazes when they could. It seemed to Rocketman that among all the entropy of pain they had each found a basic proposition of trust. The proposition was so simple, so flagrant even, that it offered no angle to attack it from, or texture to grip onto. They simply looked at each other, and that was sufficient for each passing moment.

At four that morning he helped her back to the fort. No bandits were visible, but the road was slippery and she was drained of strength. He held her around the waist to support her.

She almost fell a couple of times, and he lifted her easily. She felt as light as a tiny bird to him, and to carry all her weight gave him an overwhelming sense of joy and value. If someone had come up to him in that instant and made him emperor of all China he would not have felt more important. The second time she slipped he did not put her down. She let herself be carried, let her head fall back so she could see the sky.

'Look,' she said. 'The stars are bright again, now the moon is down.'

'I think I care for you very much,' he told her.

'Even if you do,' she said, 'it is no use. In this country, I belong to my husband. And in this valley, to belong to Zayid Shah is to belong to God.'

'Maybe I'll get religion,' Rocketman said.

'Religion isn't enough,' she replied. 'That is one thing you learn, in Chitral, in the winter. Religion isn't enough.'

But with Noor in his arms, Rocketman was ruler of

the most valuable place in the world, and he did not allow himself to be damped down. Nor did he pay as much attention to the road behind as he usually did. So he did not notice the dark shape that hugged the black shop stalls on the street that led to the fort, keeping pace exactly with the tall man and his burden.

The pilot woke up with the dawn, and the muezzin howling outside his window, and the jackals, ever responsive, barking back from the hills.

Through his window he saw clouds with saffron tops curdling around the peaks of Tirich Mir. Vultures rode the updrafts by the hospital. It was cold in the room, and Ela had stolen most of the rough blankets. He dressed quickly and went outside.

It was not hard to find the Daftar Daud Khan. The pilot went into a chai house on the main drag and drank sweet brown tea with the ritual *nan*. Men gathered around the open shop to watch the westerner. They all wore turbans and sandals, long shirts and baggy pants. They were wrapped in earth-colored blankets for warmth. All wore beards, and carried Chinese-made AK-47s, and most of them had one or two sidearms buckled around waist and chest for added comfort.

This was the purest form of smuggler, the pilot remembered, from the Smuggler's Bible – the ones who smuggled because they simply did not recognize borders, or nation-states.

When he asked them how to find the Daftar Daud Khan, all started talking at once. A couple of men were merchants and knew a little English. 'Daftar' meant place of business, an office. Daud Khan's daftar

393

was outside town, across the river, they said. They dragged a seven-year-old boy out of nowhere and volunteered him as a guide.

The boy led the pilot through refugee camps, and dead cornfields, and across a beautifully engineered, stone-anchored suspension bridge built by the British Army in 1920. Snow rattled sporadically, driven from various quadrants by a mountain-crazed wind.

They marched for an hour and a half. Toward the end the pilot was dragging. The road here was paved in stone, ancient worn cobbles of a type no one had made in five hundred years, but they were mostly covered in slush and his boots did not grip, and anyway he had not got enough sleep, what with the late night at the hospital, and Ela. She had left the hospital with some great need in her eyes, and had come into his room at one in the morning to slake it on his body. Her orgasm had been powerful, shuddering, silent. She had not looked at him as she came. He had lain confused and awake till well past three.

Eventually the pilot and his guide reached a long low building built of stone and wood, with watch-towers set on the corners. Armed men squatted at the gates. Horses and mules stood tethered on every side. To the north, men on horseback were charging each other across a field, yelling wildly. One of the riders tackled another rider, clawing at a round object held underneath the first rider's elbow. His horse fell, he fell, the round thing fell and rolled on the packed mud-snow. The round thing had hair, a short nose, and brown frazzled twine where the neck once had been. The pilot looked away. The kid laughed, and pointed at the head.

'Dushman,' he said happily. 'Tshuravi.'

394

A Russian.

The courtyard of the daftar was filled with crates of ammunition and truck tires. Cases of vodka and pieces of ore sewn in canvas lay on the sides, half shrouded behind burlap screens. In an office under the tower, two large men with very long beards sat at a desk writing up columns of figures with cheap Chinese fountain pens. The man with the longest beard was Daud Khan.

Daud Khan was very serious. He sat quite still and let his companion do the communicating.

Daud Khan's colleague was called Abd el Haq. He had a good laugh. It shook his large belly and made his cheeks quiver. He used it frequently because he knew no English and laughter seemed to him the only sensible means of communication. His eyes were very dark and liquid. They gave off sparkles whenever the pilot mentioned the name 'Hawkley.'

'Hawkley, *acha*, Hawkley,' Abd el Haq would reply, nodding wisely, shrugging, pointing up in the air, all at the same time. Then he'd go off in a gale of laughter again. '*Achaaa*, Hawkley,' and Daud Khan would nod, seriously, and add another figure to the column.

After thirty minutes of this they found a Kabuli who spoke a few words of Lingua.

'Hawkley, long before time,' he told the pilot, making flying gestures. 'Him come, him andalay, summertime, *acha*.'

A Pashtun came in with pots of tea and bowls of goat stew that you ate by scooping it up with *nan*. Abd el Haq and Daud Khan squatted on the mounded Shiraz in the room's center and slurped at the food. An ozone shower passed overhead, whipping snowflakes through the wooden shutters. The stew was good but too greasy. The pilot finished his bowl because that was what courtesy demanded among tribes such as these.

His spirits hung around his ankles as he trudged back into town. His stomach was still a little smarmy as a result of the gore in the hospital, and from watching the Russian soldier's head being used as a polo ball, and on top of that, the goat grease. The ozone shower had disappeared; standard cumulus piled up heavily against the peaks. A cold wind had steadied out of the south, and it numbed his face. The hotel owner bounced down the track in his jeep and gave him a lift back. Sam the Sham and the Pharaohs sang 'Woolly Boolly' on the cassette player.

So this was the end of the trail, the pilot thought. Defeat washed over his brain in a tide of mental pus, and gray chemicals. The quest had seemed so pure while movement gave it meaning. Now it had petered out to nothing, and its basic uselessness was revealed, like a broken monument on a stone plain, all worshippers dead. The men who guarded the borders had won, would always win in the end; as inertia overcame movement, as fossils outlived the quick worm that once squirmed in their shell, as death waited out life.

Some small rebellion must have still been alive in the pilot's gut, however, for once back in town he found a gems trader who was happy to swap a kilo of the purest blue Panjshiri lapis lazuli for the six high-power Czech night-vision binoculars the pilot had smuggled in from Breslau.

When he got back to the fort the pilot found Rocketman lurking in the blue snow between stripped aspens and battlements. He beckoned the pilot to one side, pulled him into the shadow of an earthen barbican, out of sight of the guard posts.

Rocketman looked sick, the pilot thought. His mouth hung open in a Punch-and-Judy mask of despair. His hands clasped and unclasped repeatedly. He lit a cigarette from the butt of the last.

'She's gone,' he told the pilot without preamble.

'Who?'

'Noor. Zayid Shah's wife.'

'What do you mean, she's gone? I don't understand.'

'I can't find her. She's not at the hospital. She wasn't here for breakfast, or lunch. And Zayid Shah just smiles. Aaaaah – that man is a monster. He's done something with her, I know.'

'It doesn't make sense,' the pilot told him, though a small flutter of nerves contradicted the words inside himself. 'Have you asked him?'

'I told you – he just smiles! I asked him maybe three – four times already.'

'Calm down,' the pilot said. 'She's bound to be somewhere.'

'It's a military dictatorship,' Rocketman moaned. 'It's an Islamic military junta. They can do what they want with her.'

'Why would they want to do anything with her?'

'Because,' Rocketman said, torturing his fingers into positions they were not meant to assume. 'Because we have this thing. Her and me. I don't know. I can't say. We didn't sleep together, ya know, we didn't even kiss or anything! Aaaah – but we have this thing, when I look at her; when we change bedpans together. I can't explain what it is, but it's there.

397

We know it – and Zayid Shah knows it, too. Christ, Joe,' Rocketman continued desperately, 'why did I ever leave Bellevue?'

'Don't think like that,' the pilot reassured him, 'we'll find her.'

But they did not find Noor Zayid Shah.

Dinner that night was very quiet, in terms of voice and volume; but the room shrieked with tied-down tensions. The emptiness of Noor's habitual seat was as loud in their minds as a bass drum. A huge fire roared and snapped to itself at one end of the hall. Zayid Shah sat like a column of carved stone, tapping brittlely at the laptop, shifting pieces on his Gō board to match the new moves his program prompted, eating nothing.

Even the engineers said little. The chinless one played with a rupee piece, flipping it constantly from knuckle to knuckle. Rocketman sat rigid in his place, and did not eat anything either – just sucked on cigarettes and looked at the district commissioner with an expression that could cut oak.

The wind, clawing its way through leaky casements, whistled among them in drafts and currents, persistently blowing out the oil lamps so they sat half the time in smoke and darkness, and the other half in a flickering kind of yellow gloom.

Ela was silent and calm.

PC was at the hospital.

He walked in halfway through the lamb stew, in clothes that stank of ether. He had worked with Dr Nassir all afternoon. He sat down next to Ela and the pilot, and talked quietly as they ate.

'I've changed my mind,' he said. 'I'm not gonna

leave. I'm gonna stay here for a while. I'll sleep at the hospital.'

PC so far had slept two hours total, and there were magenta half-moons under his eyes, but the eyes themselves were bright, and his movements quick, and he spoke with more spring in his words than any of them.

'You better clear it with Zayid Shah.'

'I already did.' He glanced at the head of the table where the district commissioner sat alone with his war game.

'You could be here a long time,' the pilot warned. 'You remember what Jamal said; the snows'll cut off the pass any day now.'

'I'm so sick of *nan*,' one of the American engineers commented quietly, 'I could scream.'

'And you could die from too much *nan*,' the pilot finished, looking at the engineer.

'I don't care.' PC leaned forward. 'I'm just getting this amazing feeling. From working at the hospital. I mean, it just makes me feel so awesome! I'm totally into it.' He tore off a chunk of bread from Ela's plate and chewed it quickly.

'Emptying bedpans,' Ela said neutrally, watching PC's hands. 'Sticking thermometers up people's ass-holes.'

'But it matters,' PC said, 'don't you see? What I do matters. I save lives! Maybe not directly, but what I do helps. Like, I'm useful. I'm needed.' He took another bite of bread and repeated in a quieter tone, 'I'm needed. I've never really been needed, before.'

'It always affects 'em this way. I've seen it other places.' The pilot turned to Ela. He pulled the dark glasses from his jacket pocket, put them on like bifocals. Affecting a Marin County sort of accent he said; 'Classic capitalist bourgeois individualist complex, man. Based on guilt, nicht wahr? The guilt of America, for being so rich, for living off the sweat and blood of the world's oppressed.'

'It's not like that,' PC interrupted.

'Please, no more monologues,' Ela pleaded. 'Between you and Rocketman—'

The pilot ignored them both. Because of the fire it was very hot in the dining hall and somehow the heat had sapped his tolerance.

'You work in the Peace Corps for eighteen months, you get your hands dirty, you get dysentery from the water – then you come home, and figure you've paid your dues, and you can tell your exotic tales for—'

'What's the matter with you?' PC hissed at him. His eyes were so narrow they seemed to hiss as well. His mouth was still full of bread. He spat crumbs as he talked. 'Sure, maybe all of that's true. But what difference does it make?'

'PC's right,' Ela said.

The pilot leaned back in his seat and observed PC through the sunglasses, as if meeting him for the first time. He picked up a napkin and wiped his brow. He shouldn't give PC a hard time, he thought. It wasn't PC that had got him upset.

'I know,' the pilot agreed, finally. 'I just wanted to make sure he knows; because two weeks from now, when the novelty's worn off and all the passes are blocked – well, PC, you just better have your motivations straight, 'cause by then it'll be too late to change your mind.'

'It's cool,' PC said. He picked up a piece of nan and got to his feet. 'Anyway, there's always the plane.'

'The plane only runs when the clouds are higher than the pass. Anyhow, the plane's not the point.'

'I know.'

'Good.'

'You know,' PC added, 'I've never been here before – but when I think of Manhattan, it's the City that seems totally foreign to me. And it's this valley that seems real.' He slapped the pilot on the shoulder, gave Ela a quick kiss, and disappeared through the curtained doors.

'I think we just lost the Scarecrow,' Ela muttered.

The pilot looked at her. He was about to respond when Zayid Shah tapped one final time at the laptop's keys, stared at the screen, removed three pebbles from his board, and said, 'That is the end. I have completely surrounded myself.'

Everyone looked at him.

'Sometimes I think that is all we do here,' Zayid Shah continued. He rattled the Gō pebbles in the palm of his hand, gauging their tiny weight. 'Centuries after centuries. The Pakistanis, the British, the Sikhs, the Russians, the Han, the Mughals. Surround ourselves.' He looked at his wooden board for a full minute. The polished granite glinted in the flicker of lamps. Then in one brutal movement he swept all the little rounded pebbles off the board. They rattled and bounced, a hard cold hail on the stone slabs of the dining hall floor. The wind, knowing good stage management when it saw it, gusted hard. The lamps flickered out.

In the shadow play of light from the fireplace Zayid Shah spoke.

'It is the Great Game,' he said. 'Bluff and counter-bluff. Tribes and empires. Feint and withdraw. The

401

center holds or folds. But if it folds, does it cave in on rot, or is the emptiness at the center a trap, till the sides fall in on the pursuers, and they drown? It is not unlike the questions we ask about ourselves.

'I have not found a rule,' Zayid Shah continued, 'that can explain both the Hindu Kush mountains, and the suffering of children. Kipling said it best: "For the North, guns; quietly, but always guns." But the British did not understand. Not really. The Russians do not see it either. The tribesmen react without comprehending, and the mountains are silent.'

Zayid Shah fell silent himself.

No servants ran around relighting lamps. Doors swung shut and shadows moved in the back of the large room, but no one noticed, so intense was the district commissioner's performance.

Rocketman rose into the vacuum, as if his legs were impelled by a force far stronger than he. His voice cut through the rush of wind in the chimney. It came deep and angry, as if the mountains had found voice to answer Zayid Shah.

'*Where is Noor?*' he roared.

Zayid Shah did nothing. The shadows fooled with the fire. Rocketman shoved his chair out of the way and moved next to the district commissioner's seat. His fists were wound tight as roots. He repeated the question.

'You do not understand, either,' Zayid Shah said at length, in a voice like velvet glued onto tank armor.

'I understand one thing real clear,' Rocketman told him. 'You've done something with her.' He started closer to Zayid Shah's chair. Zayid Shah raised his hand, almost languidly. From all along the wall in back, like a drumroll in metal, came the ratcheting sound of rifles being cocked.

A line of Chitral Levy militiamen moved out of the room's far shadows. Their Lee Enfields pointed up and down the long table. Most were aimed at the big dark-colored man who hung over the district commissioner like a storm cloud. Three of the militiamen surrounded Rocketman, the barrels of their carbines only centimeters from his skin.

'You do not understand,' Zayid Shah insisted. 'You have never understood. It is not just Islam. It is a basic division of labor — a survival trick, in a region so harsh, in human terms, that any change in the division here, you see, could spell death for our way of life.'

'But you don't love her,' Rocketman said, in a voice as low as it was desperate. 'That's a crime.'

'She is an adulteress.'

'What are you talking about? I don't understand you.'

Zayid Shah smiled.

'You have been with her,' he said, 'alone. It has been witnessed. In our society, that is enough to bring shame on my entire family. In our society, adultery is punished by stoning. Stoning to death. If she is lucky. However,' Zayid Shah sighed, 'times are changing. The Industrial Islam has softened our customs. She may only get life in prison. I would not wish that for her.'

Rocketman stared at him. Then he appeared to topple forward, like a tree, in slow motion, and the pace and import of his action froze the passage of seconds and his hand goes for Zayid Shah's throat.

Four militiamen jump on Rocketman's back. His grunts and curses overcome the wind. Someone swings a rifle butt into his stomach and the fight goes out of him.

Anger is injected quick and violent into the pilot's brain. He reacts without thinking, leaping at the militiamen who have hit Rocketman, and gets much the same treatment. A rifle jabs his chest, a couple of solid soldiers pull him down. 'You sonsabitches,' the pilot yells, and someone smacks him in the face, backhanded. Another militiaman frisks him, expertly. He finds the switchblade in the pilot's boot, presses the button, and grins as the shiny blade lashes out of the handle.

Ela screams, prettily.

'It has no meaning,' Zayid Shah says vaguely.

A sergeant leaned over the district commissioner's chair. They whispered at length. Zayid Shah pointed at Ela. Militiamen pried her from her seat with rifle butts, like digging out an oyster.

The engineers watched with stony faces. The British anthropologist looked uncomfortable. 'I hope you have grounds,' she said to the district commissioners. 'You must have grounds.' She played with a necklace of cowrie shells given her by the pagans she studied.

Now servants came in with candles and relit the guttered lamps. The militiamen lined up their three prisoners by the door.

The pilot tried to move his smarting mouth. He was trembling from rage, short of breath, and sweating like a racehorse to boot.

'What're you doing to us?' he hissed, 'Zayid Shah!'

The DC did not look at him. Instead he watched the fire. The flames leaped and swirled like dancers.

'I have decided you are a terrorist,' Zayid Shah said after several moments had passed.

'You're not too bright,' the pilot told him, 'but you ain't that stupid.'

'My intelligence is not the issue.'

'I'd say it is. I'd say that is exactly what is the issue.'

'There is something about you,' Zayid Shah countered, 'that smacks of defiance. In Chitral, defiance and terrorism equate, they are one and the same.'

'In Chitral,' the pilot started to say, 'you think you can get away with equating any fucking thing you want,' when the militiamen dragged them toward the door.

'But,' Ela protested.

'Noor!' Rocketman yelled suddenly, arching his back away from the soldiers holding him up, anguish stretching from his bruised guts, '*Noooor!*'

But no answer came. No one else in the dining hall uttered a word. The militiamen made canine comments as they hustled their prisoners along the stone passage. The wind moaned in a pain much older and more general but no sharper than that of Rocketman, as the postern door opened and the group passed into the night.

30

'Five and twenty ponies
Trotting through the dark—
Brandy for the Parson,
'baccy for the clerk;
Laces for a lady, letters for a spy,
Watch the wall, my darling,
while the Gentlemen go by!'

Rudyard Kipling
The Smuggler's Song

The militiamen fastened iron shackles around their wrists. The shackles were of the real Dracula's-dungeon variety; screw-set, forge-wrought, black with age, and very heavy. The shackles were hooked to a single black chain. A Bedford truck, intricately pastiched like all the other antiquated Bedfords in this part of the world, ground up the track and stopped before the fort. The militiamen loaded their prisoners in the open back and threw in gear collected from their rooms. They giggled at God's box, and poked their fingers through the airholes at him, then chucked him in with the bags and the ECM-pak.

Two guards, not militiamen, climbed in with the prisoners. The truck moved off, rumbling across the

British bridge, onto the stone road past Daud Khan's daftar, then north, as the track turned back to dirt, up Chitral valley towards Tirich Mir.

The cold had fangs of ice and claws of wind. The guards let them dig jackets from their gear and put on as many layers as would fit around the shackles. The pilot checked God was OK in his box. He needed to make sure the ECM-pak was securely shut but when he reached for it one of the guards leaned forward, placed the Kalashnikov muzzle in the angle of the pilot's jaw, and said, very firmly, 'Sit.' He sat back down, next to Ela, trying to cover her with as much of his body as he could, but he had little warmth to give her and she continued to shiver violently beside him.

Rocketman collapsed on the floor of the truck and wound himself into a large curl around a spare tire, holding his knotted stomach. He moaned repeatedly, from pain or anguish or both, they'd asked him several times and he'd not responded. The name of Noor was usually part of his groans. The guards stepped on Rocketman whenever he spoke but this did nothing to deter him.

The guards both wore the usual turbans, blankets, and pistols besides their AK-47s. One of them looked like a goat, with yellow eyes and big brown teeth. The other had jug ears and laughed repeatedly in a high-pitched voice. The pilot tagged them silently; Goat and Yuk-yuk. Goat knew one word of English. The word was 'sit,' and he used it for all purposes, whenever he had information to impart to his prisoners.

The trail narrowed, climbed more steeply. Clouds unveiled the rising moon, like a magician pulling the scarf off a dove newly appeared in his hand. The customary death-drops and chamois crags loomed and plummeted on either side of their bald and spinning tires. Ela stopped looking. The snow got deeper on the precipice tops. The pilot peered up into the indigo light, into the silver-blue ice of the peak country they were low-gearing into. The desperation in his mind took on color, the way pain did in the minds of the flu victims of Chitral hospital. The despair was of gray hue, with lots of green and scarlet, pushing mauve.

When he looked down, and sought Ela's face, she was the same pale gray, and he realized his desperation stemmed from her; beyond the kisses, despite the private smiles, over and above their midnight intimacies, she was drawing further and further away from him for no reason he could fathom; the pull-back he had first begun to sense right after Peshawar was growing, imperceptibly but remorselessly, the way a big ship came unstuck from the quay. Mooring warps were being tossed in the water and hauled up the fairleads; the paper streamers grew taut and broke. Her face was fading away from him, down a long ringed tunnel of the same insipid lavender-gray, and there was no way of calling her back.

Despair caused the usual reaction, and the pilot felt a brutal physical longing for cookies. Slightly warm Pepperidge Farm Nantucket cookies with chocolate chips and pecan chunks would be great, but any kind of cookie would be good at this stage, the sweeter and crunchier the better. He tried to unbutton his jacket. All of a sudden he felt very warm – hot, even. Goat looked at him incredulously in the back haze of headlights.

'Sit!' he yelled.

When the pilot tried to unbutton his shirt Goat pulled out blankets and angrily threw them over both Ela and the pilot.

The wind rose and fell. The truck whined and roared. Ela sang softly to herself. '. . . you're Inferno's Dante; you're the schnozz, on the great Durante.' Two hours into the trip Rocketman rolled with no warning toward the back – dragging the chain, the pilot, and Ela – and tried to buck himself over the tailgate. Yuk-yuk and Goat hauled him back into the truck bed. Yuk-yuk giggled hysterically. Goat screamed 'Sit! Sit! Sit!' as he pounded Rocketman's back with his rifle butt. In a red fury the pilot tried to kick at Goat and missed. Ela put her arms around the pilot and kept the blanket tight around his shoulders. She could feel the fever radiating in waves from his face. 'You're sick,' she said. 'Go easy.' She fetched three Novogrippe pills from her bag and forced them into the pilot's mouth.

'Not sick,' the pilot gurgled. He was truly convinced this was depression striking. He thought he knew the cause. 'You won't let me love you.'

'Sick,' Ela repeated, as firmly as she could through chattering teeth. 'You've got the Chitrali flu.'

'Don't understand why,' the pilot said, feeling the pain in him swell like a tumor. 'This happens to people who don't wan' it. PC's the one wanted to fall in love. Not Rocketman. Not me.'

'PC was never interested in women,' Ela replied. 'Any fool could see that. Like Rocketman was never really interested in rockets—' but at that point Goat stuck his AK-47 practically in their faces and yelled 'Sit!' to shut them up, and the rest of what she said got lost in their slipstream.

409

The trail swung left, seemingly pierced a cliff, wanted to go through a mountain, but at the last minute turned up a tiny, winding valley. Big gloomy trees, of the sort Ichabod Crane rode under on his way through Sleepy Hollow, stooped under fresh snow. Fields appeared. Stone walls framed crowds of dead cornstalks. Intricate waterworks of carved wood brought long ice from invisible springs to equally invisible cultivations sandwiched onto hillside terraces. Occasionally the glow of lamps would appear, as living structures loomed out of the snow. The villages too were built into the hill; cubed heaps of tiny dwellings, stacked on top of each other, built of black wood and mountain stone, channeled with water conduits. Every spare inch of the dwellings was stacked with goats and firewood.

Women stood at the entrances of chai houses. They wore black dresses and their faces were unveiled.

Twice, behind the women, they spotted the pink shiny intrusion of European ethnologists, madly taking notes.

'Kaffir,' Yuk-yuk said, and chuckled. Pagans. It was not clear to whom he was referring.

'Noooor,' Rocketman wailed from the bed of the truck.

At Rocketman's cry the pilot woke sweating from a dream of flying. 'There's Vikings all over the fucking place,' he said. 'I'm never landing in Rockefeller Center again.'

'We have to stop,' Ela told Goat. 'This man has a bad fever.'

'Sit!' Yuk-yuk shouted.

'But,' Ela said, and gave the guards her most evil look; however this was a country where men did as

410

they chose no matter what faces women made and it had no effect.

Just before dawn they reached a village at the valley's head. A frozen torrent of ice split the village in two. Every space with a slope of less than fifty degrees was occupied by tents and supply dumps. And horses — there must have been two thousand horses and mules, packed in corrals, hobbled in fields, tethered in corners, chomping on hay, being loaded, unloaded, and watered.

In one of the corrals boys kicked and yelled at a herd of chopped-mane Mexican mules, imported by the CIA from Texas to supply Nooristani rebels on the border. The mules, who were used to Tejano accents and commands, seemed confused. They milled in ten different directions, braying pitifully.

Bearded Muslim tribesmen wearing robes, machine guns, and impassive looks watched the truck grind up the main drag and into a mud-walled courtyard.

A gate closed behind them. A door opened in the courtyard. In the light of a kerosene lamp the pilot saw very clearly the broad frame, the large white beard, the distinctive smile of Abd el Haq. Beside him stood a small man with red hair. He was robed and bearded but there was something in his posture and the way he held his hands that seemed distinctly Anglo-Saxon.

The door slammed abruptly shut. The prisoners were hustled into a long room with wooden beams and an earthen floor. Their gear, with the signal exception of the ECM-pak, was tossed in after them. That door too was shut and barred. Through chinks in the daub-and-wattle roof they saw the rising sun pick selected mountaintops and paint them in broad strokes of apricot.

The pilot's fever ebbed and flowed. The day was filled with fantasies of Ela. Always she was a distant figure. Once she stood on a station platform. The station smelled of coal and stale urine. Dim figures stood at every corner of the gray platform. The figures wore cloaks and carried rifles. Armies were marching, war was imminent. He and Ela were waiting for the last train to leave this doom-sodden country, but the train never came. Fog blew in from the open fens, like the long breath of skeletons.

At midday a kid brought in plates of potato stew, hot nan wrapped in burlap, a pot of sweet tan tea.

God had been eating too much nan, and his digestive tract was acting up again. He skittered around the walls of the room, sniffing in dank corners, squeaking his discomfort.

Throughout the day Rocketman refused to talk. Wrapped in his blanket, hunched in a corner, he continued to groan at intervals. The pilot shivered. Ela was the only one besides God who took an interest in her surroundings, and she explored their jail, to the extent of the possible, to the limits of their common chain.

'Where do you think they're taking us?' she kept asking the pilot. And once, 'Why do you think they're doing this?'

She tucked the blanket closer around his shoulders. He shrugged the blanket off. He tried to assemble the straws of lucidity in his brain, and arrange them in some kind of order.

'Who knows,' he muttered. 'I just think it has to do with you.'

'What, me?'

'You know. You and me. You an' me an' fate.'

She snorted. 'You're feverish, Joe.'

'We could do it,' he insisted.

'Oh—' Comprehension dawned. 'You mean.' She jerked a thumb at Rocketman. 'But he's awake.'

'I don't mean *that*.' The pilot wiped sweat. 'I mean down the road. But I don't think you want to.'

'Oh Lord,' Ela said. '*That*, again.' She cocked her head at him, and used her fingers to wipe sweat from places he had not reached. 'Love, etcetera. You're rushing it.'

The pilot winced.

'No,' the pilot said, 'I'm not.'

'With me you are,' she told him. 'You know,' she continued, 'this trip's been good for me. It's like I'm really six, seven different people. Till now I only knew two or three of 'em.'

'But I'm the same way,' the pilot countered, a little wildly. 'Me, Joe, Skid, pilot, Marak! All same-same.'

'Everyone's like that.' Ela spat on a corner of blanket and used it to wipe dirt off his forehead. 'With men, most of the people are all booked up. Work, power, sports. For Roger, designing security systems. Selling LSD, for my dad.'

'But you *know* we've got something together,' the pilot insisted, feeling his chest constrict from the effort of talking, feeling his throat contract from the hurt generally. Now the pain was purple, just as Noor had said. He wondered, with a pang, what had happened to her. She had pretty eyes, he thought, though not as pretty as Ela's.

Ela nodded thoughtfully. 'I cared for you,' she said, 'right from the start. But there's something in you that frightens the hell out of me. I haven't figured it out yet.'

413

'Me?' the pilot pointed at his chest. 'But I'm just a little pussycat. I'm a young pussycat, my eyes are barely open, blue, harmless.'

'You're a tomcat,' she told him, 'a teenage tomcat. Never mind all the high philosophy about borders; you just wanna roam around, knocking down garbage cans. Yowling when the moon's up.'

'Don't forget the she-pussies,' he said, and pretended to yowl, though he felt more like making the sounds Rocketman was making.

Ela had the gift of switching subjects back and forth when it suited.

'Also,' she continued, 'there's something in me that says the world is so full of new and interesting things – why focus in on one man? Why try to see all those mountains and rivers and valleys and oceans just through the filter of his little blue eyes?'

They came for the prisoners that evening, hustling them up and out of the courtyard with the sharp light of stars and the smell of cold wood smoke in their noses.

When they got outside the courtyard they found a whole caravan had assembled in the village's main street. Mules and horses stood lined up and decked out in ribbons and tassels of such bright colors you could distinguish them in the dark. Metal cases full of AK-47 ammunition and BM-40 mortars rode piled high on each side of the animals' backs. A dozen long black fibreglass cases with no insignia at all were being wrapped in rugs and tied on top of the lead mules.

Yuk-yuk and Goat hooked one end of the chain to a dapple-gray mule. After twenty minutes of men shouting and running around in random directions, the caravan began to move.

They marched all night, steadily upwards.

The moon rose, full or close to it. The landscape, forbidding enough to begin with, grew downright scary. The valley narrowed to a gorge whose walls somehow seemed to rise two steps with every step forward. Frozen streams made lovely organic forms in the silver darkness. Footing was perilous. Snow piled high on the mountaintops, occasionally exploded into the gorge, pushed by the wind, drenching them every time with pounds of freezing crystals.

The pilot was very weak, but his weakness ebbed and flowed. At first each step was difficult and he was convinced he was going to die – he could not possibly survive even an hour of this, and the gorge showed every sign of going on right up to the clouds. Then he would get a burst of hot strength and walk more easily for forty minutes or so, until the exhaustion caught up and he sagged back against the chain.

To make matters worse, the pilot had entered the diarrhea part of the flu cycle. He had to stop at hourly intervals, which meant the whole back of the caravan piled up behind as he squatted ignominiously in the snow, chained between the horse and Ela, blowing his insides out in smelly liquid bursts. He was too exhausted and fever-ridden to give a hoot about embarrassment, and the girl was good, ignoring the smells and noises, holding his forehead for him as if he were a kid vomiting, unconsciously mimicking what her mother had once done for her. But the tribesmen had no such solicitude. '*Dushman*,' they screamed, pointing at the cliffs above. They aimed their machine guns at the sky, made firing noises and shouted 'Tshuravi!' They pulled at the prisoners' chain until the pilot was finished and, wearily, could stand up with the help of Ela and Rocketman – Rocketman functioning wordlessly, pulling at the pilot's arm, as Ela told him what to do – and plod upward behind the spotted gray rump that seemed to have become the only horizon they had to look forward to.

But every time was harder for the pilot. Each hour brought levels of exhaustion he had not thought possible the hour before. The wet snow melted on his clothes, multiplying his discomfort, making it harder to lift his feet. Finally he came to a point where he no longer had the energy to stand up from his latest squat. Goat and Yuk-yuk gave up screaming to confer. Then they unhooked him from the chain that tied him to his friends, hoisted him like a sack of meal over the dappled-gray mule, tied him lengthwise across bundles of mortar ammo, and set the caravan in motion once again.

They reached a pass in the early morning. A couple of tall conifers marked a traditional campsite. The wind blew vigorously from the north. The snow was very deep here but the caravan halted anyway, to make tea and pray.

Ela helped the pilot down from his mule. She huddled next to him and fed him tea a sip at a time. He watched her eyes as she did this. It seemed to him that her pupils had changed color, into a blue-gray marbling that had its own combustion tightly locked and dampered down at the center.

In the first fingerpaints of dawn they both watched a mollah stand on a high rock next to the conifers and take something out of a varnished wooden box, with hieratic gestures. It was an old brass sextant with a bubble-level for land observations. The mollah aimed the instrument at a morning star, carefully checking his wristwatch and then a pocket altimeter after each sight. He drew a line in the snow. The line pointed toward Mecca more accurately than any line outside of the big religious centers of Herat and Bokhara. Every man in the caravan came up to the line and laid out a prayer rug parallel to it.

The mollah wrapped and packed away his instrument. Then he took out a battery-operated loudspeaker and began to chant the morning prayer.

The mountains rang with his clear voice. There were no jackals this high to hear or bark back. In the pure light of dawn, in the crystalline ecstasy of coming winter, the robes of the tribal smugglers seemed to radiate, perfectly white.

'It's so new,' Ela whispered.

'That mollah's read Hawkley,' the pilot answered. 'I don't know what's going on here, but it's more than meets the eye.'

Ela looked at him. She saw the red spots on his cheeks and decided not to answer. She fed him some more flu pills instead.

The downhill route was easier. There was much less snow on this side of the pass, and the valley opening before them showed flanks of reddish brown earth that grew broader and more frequent as the day progressed. '*Al hamd* '*ul illah*,' Goat said, taking a pinch of that earth and rubbing it between thumb and forefinger, 'Nooristan!' His yellow teeth flashed.

Their path switchbacked through a rare and fragrant forest of pines. The pilot, tied once again to the back of the packhorse, had somehow got used to

417

the violent rhythm of the mule's saunter, the sharp corner of the wooden ammo boxes. He dozed, opened his eyes, dozed some more.

Farther on the caravan rattled down a dry riverbed, coming out eventually in a deep valley that lay, like a conch muscle in the smooth folds of its shell, among the huge and snowy mountains. The valley was checkered with fields of corn and hemp, and dotted with forts known as 'khors'. All the khors had thick earthen walls and tall adobe towers studded with pill-boxes and embrasures.

In the valley the mules could go at a faster pace and the men hustled them along with wooden switches and cries of 'Tchak-tchak!' Rocketman and Ela limped from blisters. The pilot, tied on his back to the ammo boxes, felt like he was being disassembled from the mule's quicker motion. Sometimes, when he opened his eyes between bouts of fever dreams, he saw women dressed in gaily colored silks traversing the valley in single file with huge airy mounds of hay on their heads. The silks billowed behind the women, like sails of burgundy, saffron, and royal blue. They never came near the caravan and in the refraction of sun they seemed to float like spirits, upside down over the backdrop of mountains, of sky. The pilot dismissed them as dreams; it was only later, in comparing notes with the others, that he discovered the women were real.

Around five in the afternoon the caravan drew near to one side of the valley. Here a khor big as a town guarded a deep-cut arroyo. The towers of the fort were tall and dangerous-looking, yet they were nowhere near as tall and menacing as the huge orange cliff set in the mountain beside the dried river. As they got closer the prisoners saw that the lower third of the cliff had been carved into the likeness of a human form. By the time the caravan reached the gates of the khor they could recognize in the rock the calm pose, the portly shape of a Buddha figure. The Buddha dominated the fort like a real god. It had to be two hundred feet high.

The odd thing about this sculpture, apart from the size, was this: the features of the Buddha were pure European. In fact, the face, with its very straight nose, horizontal eyes, and thin lips, looked exactly like the idealized features of Achilles, or some other hero in a Greek myth.

Inside, the khor was so big it took in the whole caravan without seeming crowded. The general feeling was of a city. People stared from thin windows in the three-story walls. Square adobe buildings were tacked every which way to walls and towers, separated by thin alleys, till it was hard to distinguish defenses from living quarters. There were squares, markets, a mosque, even fields full of living hemp and dead squash vines. There were sounds of goats, water buffalo, and women; but no women were visible, then or at any other time.

The only reminder that this was a country in the throes of war were the pockmarks of bullet holes in many of the walls, and a trio of Chinese-made Ziqriat anti-aircraft cannon, clumped together in a nest of sandbags in the main square.

The leaders of the caravan retreated into a porch-like enclosure under one of the towers. Yuk-yuk and Goat shepherded the three prisoners into a small room containing a number of rope-woven beds. Their gear already had been dumped on the floor. God was safe in his box but again the ECM-pak was missing; and in all the disconnection of fever, the pilot felt even more alone, knowing that his instruments were gone.

A tiny fire burned in the earthen hearth, its meager smoke escaping through a hole in the roof. 'Sit,' Yuk-yuk commanded, and made a sketchy wave. '*Khodafis*,' Goat said, smiling with his big teeth. The door shut behind them.

Thick woollen quilts covered the beds. The pilot ambled wearily over and lay down on one. It jerked – hard moving shapes roiled the cloth forms. A thin, very pale face over a scraggly black beard and very pale naked shoulders popped out of the covers and shrieked '*Lasciate mi dormire! C'e giá stato abbastanza di, ma chi siete?*'

The pilot fell off the bed in fever-enhanced panic. Rocketman came out of his depression long enough to stare. Ela said, 'Who the fuck are you?' and 'Do you speak English?'

'Marco,' the face said, 'I am Marco. I am Italian.'

'Are you a prisoner too?' Ela asked him.

'No,' Marco replied. His chin lifted. 'I come here, two weeks before for business, *a costruire un* – *ció é*, to build a shee-lift.'

'A what?' Ela replied, surprised out of her fatigue.

'A ski lift,' Rocketman said neutrally, before succumbing to depression again.

'Yes. A cable car.'

'Here?' the pilot gasped from the floor where he'd slumped.

'Of course.' Marco pulled the quilt around him and hopped off the bed to the room's single window. '*Guardi*,' he said. 'Look these mountains. They are

420

perfetti. Long alps under this *cime*, how do you say? Peaks? Friable rocks, like the Dolomite, but long *alture*, *si*? Good snow, on the east side.'

'A cable car.' Ela sat down on one of the beds and began laughing, helplessly. 'Ski Afghanistan.'

'Nooristan,' Marco contradicted. 'Is separate now. They even have a minister of foreign affairs. Abdul Rahman. He will give me a contract, one day, for *turismo, tutto quello.*'

'You came here on your own?' Ela said.

'I am freelance,' the Italian replied, with great dignity. 'I am entrepreneur. I am here to see. I will be number one to develop *turismo* here, when the war is finish, *ció é.*' He scratched his ass under the quilt unselfconsciously, and looked at Ela.

'You have beautiful ankles,' he told her, 'beautiful face. It is so fantastic to see a woman again. I hope you will stay here very long.' He got back into bed.

'Thank you,' Ela said, 'I think,' and moved over, automatically dragging her chain, to feed the small fire and stop her shivering. There were chips of very resinous wood next to the hearth, and shreds of newspaper. Kneeling, she threw in some of both, then arrested her efforts, staring at a torn page she was about to crumple in one fist.

'Joe,' she said, 'look at this.'

She stood up and brought the paper to the pilot. He looked at it through half-closed eyelids. '. . . zette,' he read, and his eyes opened all the way as he recognized the typeface. 'The *Gazette*,' he said in astonishment. 'What's it doing here?'

'Yeah,' the girl said, 'I thought you'd be interested. It's the same one we saw in Breslau.'

'This one's later,' the pilot contradicted her. He

421

took the torn paper and tried to read it. It was hard to focus with the purple burn behind his eyes. He held the paper closer to the fire. There was a bunch of the usual classifieds taking up the back two-thirds of the paper. He even found the latest installment from the weird classified writer. 'Sapphic historian seeks SDM Bantu-speaker (non-smoker) with SS# ending 113.20 for comprehensive oral history on influence of Sir Clowdisley Shovell's ring finger on modern concept of time,' the ad read.

He tried to think about connections, and why the district commissioner of Chitral valley should work with Daud Khan and why Daud should bring them here, but he had to void his bowels once more. He banged on the door. An armed man opened, and led him to an outhouse and, when he had finished, back again. He picked up the *Gazette* once more but was too tired to read and fell asleep sprawled on the earth floor against one of the beds with the torn paper still crumpled in one fist.

Roughly an hour before sunset a boy brought them a large pot of tan tea.

They all sat around the floor and drank solemnly while the little fire did the best it could against the gathering chill. Even Rocketman drank. The exertions of the past twelve hours had dried their bodies like wrung sponges.

'You come back to here one day,' Marco said, after the tea was finished. 'You take a gondola to the peak of Khatinza.' He pointed at the mountains, through the window. 'There is a restaurant, serving hot chocolate and Tiramisú. You put on skis outside this restaurant, no? You push off weet your poles.'

Marco made airy gestures in the air with his fingers.

'The snow will be — *come si dice*? Light. Your skis, they feel like you ski on — what is on cake?'

'Icing,' Ela suggested. 'Whipped cream?'

'Cream, *ecco*. Your skis are so smooth, is easier to make turns than not make turns. You will go like a bird. The snow will become flowers. Red, yellow, green flowers.'

'Flowers?' Ela said.

'Purple flowers, with yellow dots.'

The pilot noticed Marco's voice was getting very hollow, as if it were coming from that long gray tunnel into which Ela already had receded. He leaned forward to check Marco was OK. The Italian did not seem farther away in terms of distance, but he was growing blurry because of a blue mist that had clustered around his face and hands, like a cloud of microscopic blue hummingbirds.

'*Saronno bestie*,' Marco continued, 'in the pretty flower snow, will be tiny animals, yes? Lions, only three centimeters tall; they roar like mice.'

'Something's ha-happening,' Ela said in a silly voice, like a rabbit's. She stretched out her hand toward Marco, but her hand would not move. She concentrated on lifting a finger. It came, very slowly, upward; then fifteen or twenty lovely yellow butterflies settled on it and began to sing. 'I'm always true to you, darling, in my fashion,' they warbled. 'I'm always true to you, darling, in my way.' Her fingers sank under their weight.

The valley, which until then had been entirely free of any mechanical noise, filled with the tearing roar of internal combustion. The pilot tried to get up to look out the window, and found that every molecule he owned was tied by yards of nylon kite string to the floor.

Roman Marak, the pilot's father, came into the room and began collecting his gear. He picked up the cage he'd made for God. Inside, the rat stretched, and yawned. Bright ivory-handled daggers sparkled where his teeth had been. His paws were tied to large gossamer wings stretched over struts of light bone.

'Noor,' Rocketman called out in a voice so full of childlike wonder it made everyone in the room burst into black tears, 'they let you come!'

The tiny blue hummingbirds kept congregating. Soon they filled the room. Their song was so high and pure it was the expression of movement itself. It sounded like Schumann, played on two million arpeggioni the size of thumbtacks. The song sliced every kite string tying the pilot to earth, wafting him easily into the breeze, out of the khor, into the air; high above the huge red Buddha, so close to the cathedral walls, the blasted russet rock, he could see every vein of quartz and lime; past the flash-frozen waterfalls of suspended glaciers; up, skimming the scalloped snowfields of the high passes; spinning him, without weight, without substance, without matter, pure form, perfect song, impossible to detain or stop at checkpoints, free of hurt, clear of pain, into the warm golden benediction of the sun.

31

'Spaceflights are merely an escape, a fleeing away from oneself, because it is easier to go to Mars or to the moon than it is to penetrate one's own self.'

Carl Jung

A faithful thunder filled all spectra between hearing and touch.

The world trembled – not constantly, not even hard, in fact with the softest of hiccoughs and corrections – but it trembled enough to remind you the planet was no static thing, that even daisies had an energy budget, and a need to blow it off at times.

The pilot's eyes snapped open and encountered:

A narrow aluminum bunk bed above his head, its robin's-egg blue paint chipped and scarred;

Blankets tumbled over his body, the edges of a thin mattress visible to one side;

A torn curtain to his right, with a bent aluminum ladder showing through the rip;

A chrome air vent, hanging by one screw;

A blue canvas screen, zippered shut in the curved, scratched aluminum wall by his left arm.

God's box lay at the foot of his bunk. A very soft, thin rumbling rose out of the box as the rodent snored.

The pilot rolled over to open the screen and found a small brass padlock holding the zipper shut. Bright sun dappled the canvas from behind.

He rolled out of the bunk in panic. He had absolutely no idea where he was. No horizon; no points of reference. No knowledge of altitude. Flotsam and jetsam of flying dreams (thud of landing, stench of avgas). The fever had broken — he had that strange tinted clarity of vision he'd gotten after he licked the Chingado infection, as if he were looking through a pair of expensive spectacles only lightly colored with rosewater. Someone had taken off his clothes, his handcuffs, everything but his underpants. He rubbed the pink band on his wrists where the cuffs had been.

Outside the curtain lay a corridor, maybe two feet wide and not much longer; closed door to his left, sound of running water. Three steps led to a door that was more like the hatch of a boat. He stumbled down the stairs, motion centers still vague, steadying himself against both walls. He became aware of a pain behind his eyes.

He found a cabin maybe ten feet by twelve, with a row of four square windows on both sides. All of the windows were screened and padlocked. The room had wooden paneling on the walls, and small fruitwood coffee tables. The wood had once been varnished, but years of neglect had left it streaked and gray. Kilim rugs, stained and bald-looking, underlay miniature Bauhaus couches with sprung stuffing. A tight spiral staircase, a miniature white upright piano, a small bar occupied the far corners.

Behind the bar, the bulkhead was hung thick with nightmare — huge wooden masks whose tongues stuck out. Their eyes were rimmed in red fury. A row of human skulls, cobbled and fashioned into mugs, lurked behind mahogany fiddles.

Rocketman sat hunched on one of the couches. He wore a faded jumpsuit two sizes too small for him. His left arm was chained and padlocked to a thin steel column.

The trembling was more pronounced here, the thunder stronger.

The pilot put a short rein on his panic. He drew a very long, deep breath and went over to Rocketman's side. He tested the handcuffs, but they were of Chitrali design and only a vampire could have undone the things without a key.

Rocketman looked up at him. Rocketman looked awful. His face was blurred and mottled, his beard heavy, his eyes red from crying. The fingers of his right hand shook as he lifted a cigarette to his mouth. The pilot felt his own chin; he, too, had enough beard to pull with fingernails.

The date on his watch said it was a full day after he'd lost consciousness in the khor.

The thunder altered slightly. Thin cracks of light escaping the shuttered portholes moved slowly, in a ten-degree arc, across the cabin's opposite wall.

A sudden, heavy wash of hopelessness flooded his brain. The pilot had no idea where it came from. Maybe it was a residue from whatever drug cocktail they'd been slipped in the khor beneath the great Buddha. Whatever the cause, it was more than simply disorientation. It rushed in like a tide, inward diastole, chasing broken driftwood and dead dreams out on the undertow. Pushing out even the horizon-fear.

'I killed her.' Rocketman spoke very distinctly, to make himself heard over the thunder.

The pilot sat on the couch beside him and put an arm around his shoulders. A little hole in the bum-out; Rocketman was talking, at least.

'Why you still cuffed, Rocketman?'

'I tried to get out of here. I wanted to go back. I tried to break through a door.'

This is an *airplane*, man!'

'I know that − now.'

The pilot had known it in his gut since before he woke up, but he had never before been in a mood that the magic of flight and the knowledge of speed could not attenuate, and so had suppressed the fact.

'You didn't kill her,' he went on, trying to bypass the dread of his realization.

'She was so beautiful.'

'I bet Zayid Shah was bluffing.'

'That *bastard*! No. He wasn't bluffing. I could tell.'

'You didn't sleep with her. He wouldn't do any-thing.'

'He would.'

'He would not.'

The pilot rose and walked around, testing all the window screens. Their canvas was thick and tough and reinforced by aluminum battens; he would need his switchblade to get through them. But his switch-blade was in Chitral.

'You have any idea where we are?'

Rocketman shook his head.

'Who cuffed you?'

'Coupla guys.' He shrugged.

Ela came down the steps from the sleeping area. Her hair was wet; it splayed around the back of her neck like a lavender-blonde paintbrush. She wore an old jumpsuit, patched and oil-stained like Rocketman's, only hers was so big she'd had to roll up the cuffs and pantlegs. She was toweling her face. Her cheeks were pink, her eyes calm. She looked like someone who knew exactly what she was doing and where she was headed.

'That's the cutest shower,' she told the pilot. 'You should try it, you stink.' She wrinkled her nose at his shorts.

'Do you know where we are?' the pilot asked her.

'Not a clue,' she answered, 'but I don't think it matters much.' And hearing her voice the pilot's guts flopped around like a caught flounder giving a last defiant slap of its tail on the sun-baked deck. She was separate from him already, leaving the warmth in him to flow by itself, brave and foolish in the dark.

Marco appeared, climbing the spiral staircase, prodded by a short man in blue jeans and a T-shirt. The short man's face was black – not American black, not café-au-lait like Rocketman, but black as no-light, dark as four-a.m. dreams. He had about three teeth, all filed down to sharp yellow points, and a huge afro. His eyes were intense, his nose very straight. He was maybe eighteen years old.

The T-shirt read, 'John Frum Is Coming.' A large Army issue Colt pistol distended the back pocket of his jeans.

Marco turned to glare at his escort. '*Ma che succede,*' he yelled, 'what is going on, where is this house, what happens to me?'

'Drugs,' Ela said succinctly. 'LSD, probably.'

The short man clapped his hands together. 'Conference,' he announced in good American English. 'Everybody's coming to a palaver! You,' he pointed at the pilot, 'you should put on some duds. There's a groovy jumpsuit in your cabin. Dig?'

'No, I don't dig,' the pilot told him. 'I'm not putting on clothes. Not till somebody tells us where we are, and what altitude we're at, and opens some portholes for the love of Mike!'

'Suit yourself,' the short man said. He pulled out his .45 with one hand. 'This isn't one of your fancy-ass high-altitude Boeings. I could plug you, and the bullet would go right through the fuselage, and all that would happen is, you eighty-six, and the rest of us, we'd get a little cold.' He unlocked Rocketman's cuff with his other hand and sheepdogged them all down the staircase.

The lower-deck saloon was the same compact size as the smoking saloon, only narrower at the staircase end. Its walls were of cherrywood veneer inlaid with art deco designs. A large table of the same wood took up half the space. As they reached table level an elderly bald man in jeans and a flying jacket came through a door at the narrow end, followed by a broad white-bearded figure in *shalwar kameez* and a Chitrali cap.

The pilot had never seen the bald man before.

The second man was Abd el Haq.

The pilot caught a glimpse of a long cavernous cargo bay behind the door; in the dim emergency lighting he saw stacks of metal ammunition boxes with cyrillic stencils and BM-40 mortars and the long black fiberglass boxes he'd noticed on the caravan, all tightly lashed down with cargo netting. He could also make out the distinctive housing and hydraulic lines of Dornier-Akai amphibious landing gear, the same kind he'd had in his Citation. He felt a stab of homesickness, for his plane, for clearer times.

Abd el Haq laughed in lieu of speaking. Then he caught sight of Ela, and his eyes darkened and briefly took on an odd tint, as of madness, or indigestion.

Ela looked at him defiantly, well aware of her nakedness from the perspective of an older Islam.

'He din wanna wear duds, Cap'n Hubbard,' the short man said.

'He can wear what he likes,' the bald codger replied.

'I'm not wearing anything,' the pilot said, ''till someone tells me what's going on here.'

'That's what the conference is about,' the bald man said.

'What you wanna drink?' the short man asked.

'It's obvious,' Ela told the pilot. The calmness lay like spread butter over her voice. 'Drugs. Sextants. It's my father behind this. Why are you looking at me,' she said to Abd el Haq. 'If he doesn't want to wear clothes' – pointing at the pilot – 'I don't have to wear a veil.'

'What do you want to drink!' the short man yelled at the pilot.

'Are you flying this crate?' the pilot asked the bald man. 'What kind of plane is this? And where are we going?'

'I'd tell him what you want to drink,' the bald codger advised, pointing at the short man. 'He learned English driving cabs in New York, but his father hunted human heads.'

431

'Good training,' the pilot remarked, 'for driving cabs in New York.'

'English?'

'No. Headhunting. I'll have a vodka,' the pilot continued, 'double.' The short man nodded, and trotted up the spiral steps to the bar.

'The answers to your questions,' the bald man continued, 'are, yes, a Shorts Empire-Class 26-G Flying Boat, and it doesn't matter, respectively.'

The pilot stared at the bald man.

'A Flying Boat? Empire Class? The one with the Hercules IVs, 1380 rated horsepower?'

The bald man nodded.

'That's crazy. They don't exist anymore.'

'This one does.'

'I don't believe you.'

'We found it on Nui, in the Ellice Islands.' The bald man smiled. 'The headmen were renting it as a floating bordello. But someone had kept the engines greased.'

'I want to see the person who ees in charge,' Marco insisted. 'I am friend with the minister.'

Everyone ignored him.

A round Chinese man came out of the paneling with a platter full of cocktail dumplings. The short headhunter came over with a tray of drinks and peanuts. The liquor was served in the skulls, which had their tops sawn off and a tin lining fitted inside. But the pilot was not interested. He picked up his plate of dumplings and dashed them violently to the deck.

'Where are we *going*?' he shouted furiously.

'It doesn't matter,' the bald man said.

'Dee voyage,' Abd el Haq intoned in a

432

horrendously thick accent 'ees dee des-tee-nation.' He laughed uproariously at his own accent.

'I tole you,' Ela said, looking dubiously at her dumplings. 'We're going to see Hawkley. Are these full of Orange Sunshine,' she asked brightly, 'or is it safe to eat 'em?'

The bald man told them not to smoke in the head. He asked them to be patient, and offered to take away Rocketman's handcuffs permanently if he promised to behave. Rocketman promised.

Then the bald man disappeared.

The conference was over.

'*Porco Madonna*,' Marco commented, sadly.

Everyone else including Abd el Haq went up to the smoking saloon. The pilot made a side trip to his cabin to fetch a blanket. The fever was not that far gone and, clad in nothing but underpants, he was getting cold. The blankets were thick and embroidered with the legend 'Imperial Airways'. He took from his skivvies the butter knife he had filched from the tray of appetizers, and hid it under the mattress. He gave God a dumpling, then brought him back to the smoking cabin to let him run.

He stretched out on one of the couches and asked the short headhunter for another vodka.

'Make it two,' Rocketman called from the opposite couch. 'Make it doubles. I don't care.' The booze he'd had during the 'conference' was making him morose.

'It's just the last in a long series,' he said to the pilot. He felt automatically under the couch for listening devices. 'Beautiful things that I fuck up. Ya know, my dad used to tell me, right from the start. "You're going to mess up," he said. "You're aiming too high," he said.'

433

The headhunter brought the skulls and dumped them roughly on the coffee table.

'He wanted me to be a teacher, like him,' Rocketman continued, gloomily sipping the chilled liquor. 'He was a full professor of history at UCLA – the first brother who held that position. He thought the social sciences were the only thing that would improve mankind – by mankind, he meant Negro people, mostly. He used to say, after the Industrial Revolution it would be the Social Science Revolution. He meant, we could improve humans the way we improve machines. But I wanted to work on rockets . . .

'You know,' Rocketman continued, 'once, I almost had him convinced. I was working at White Sands on the Orion Project. You ever heard of that?'

Ela had found the little piano. She plunked out tunes on the keyboard. Marco stood behind her, pretending to follow the tune, mesmerized by her neck.

'Don't get no kick from a plane,' Ela sang. Her voice was sweet, but it was unable to stick to one key. 'Flyin' so high, with some guy, in the sky is my idea of – nothin', to do.'

'The Orion Project,' Rocketman said. He looked around him, almost dreamily. 'It was a fantastic plan. To send payloads into orbit with normal boosters, and build a really big ship out there. We were gonna use a series of fusion bombs as propellant. Ten, fifteen astronauts. Go as far as Mars, maybe beyond. Even my dad said it was a project worth doing. For the good of humanity, I guess.'

Rocketman shook his head. He tapped out a cigarette and lit it, thoughtfully.

'What happened?'

434

'They scratched it. The military people wanted something they could use to kill people closer to home. No Mars, no real space flight. Just the moon. We never even left Earth's orbit! It's like a curse; everything we touch, dies. And now the curse rubbed off on me.' He buried his face in his hands. 'Aaah, I should never have looked at her!'

'I get a kick, every time, I see, you standing there, before me,' Ela sang.

'Listen, Rocketman.' The pilot's voice was urgent. 'You gotta stop thinking—'

'If it hadn't been for me—'

'You're the best thing ever happened to her.'

'I killed her.' Rocketman looked up in total misery. 'How can you say that?'

'I get a kick – though it's plain to see, that you obviously, don't adore me.' Ela and Marco tried it out together.

The pilot glanced in their direction and continued, 'Because you guys had a feeling together. And that feeling's one of the best things that can happen. PC wasn't wrong, to look so hard for it. I mean, it doesn't always work, and sometimes it can get downright destructive. But the feeling itself – I mean, it's pure communication. All frequencies. No blocks. It's like secret cargo. It's like you were a smuggler just then, Rocketman – a love-smuggler. Contraband of the heart.' He downed his drink, slamming the skull on the table so hard its jaws clacked. The piano music had stopped.

'Or look at it from the other side,' he went on, still watching Ela. 'Power. It's the great enemy of the love-smuggler. Power means hoarding, right? Dollars, gold, information, whatever – it's how you accumulate

435

power. By getting it yourself. By *blocking* access by others. So power means blocking. So if you want to be a free-trader – no matter what the cargo, Swiss watches, or diamonds or guns, or even a feeling for someone – you're always gonna run foul of people like Zayid Shah. People who try to hoard the love of others.'

'And never mind who gets hurt in the process,' Ela said in a voice that was low but so full of torque it seemed to rival the rumble of the Hercules engines. 'Never mind that Noor Zayid Shah gets stoned to—'

'Shut up,' the pilot whispered to her fiercely.

She ignored him. '—death. Never mind my mother, spending the rest of her life in a place she hates, with a man she never respected.' Ela got up from the piano bench and padded over catlike and kneeled on the faded carpet.

'I think I loved you, Joe,' she told the pilot. 'For a while. Maybe I still do, in a funny way. But there was always something wrong. And I just figgered out what it is.

'You're *dangerous*,' she continued. 'You're all big talk, and no staying power. All breakthrough, and no building. Tons of moonlight walks, but no one to change diapers with. And no one to hold your hand twenty years down the road, when the stretchmarks have covered even your face and the kids are gone. All trips, and cops and robbers,' she added; 'but when the excitement's over, you won't be around to take care of the people who get hurt. There's a level missing, somewhere.' She coughed, winded by her speech.

The pilot looked at her. He looked at Rocketman. He looked back at Ela. He noticed her cheeks were very red. There were shiny highlights under her eyelids, a quick sniff in her nostrils. His throat grew tight in response.

'Your cough's back, Ela,' he said gently. 'I hope you're not getting the flu.'

'Don't patronize me! Don't you have anything else to say?'

'Well, I think maybe—'

'Do you know,' she interrupted him, 'the last time I saw my daddy? I was nine years old,' she went on, 'I was walkin' home from school, and he pulls up in a dirty, beat-up ole car and calls to me. I knew it was him, 'cause he called me by – by a name he used to call me. Then he got out of the car. He was dressed in dark glasses, and a dirty raincoat, and a grimy porkpie hat; he even had Mars Bars in his pockets.'

She looked away.

'I mean, he was, like, nice an' everything. We talked. But years later, I understood. He had dressed up like a pervert! A dirty ole man! He could never do anything without making it a joke, or a game. Or some kind of weird adventure. And if the joke was on him, so much the better!'

She rocked back on her haunches. Her streaked hair looked sad against the shine of tears.

'You know the worst of it?' she added, very low. Still not looking directly at the pilot. 'I never even made that marching squad—' A hand touched her shoulder, and Ela swung around in surprise.

Abd el Haq had noticed her tears. He pulled his hand back from Ela's shoulder like it had been burned. Digging into his shalwar, he fished out a square of brown handkerchief which Ela, after a second's hesitation, accepted.

'You know,' Rocketman said to no one in particular, drawing on a Pakistani cigarette as if it were his last drag on earth, 'I'm actually starting to miss Bellevue?'

When night fell – you could tell because the lines around the porthole screens went dark – the pilot returned to his cabin. He took a shower, stood in the steaming water for a long time, soaping himself luxuriously.

Afterward, wrapped in an Imperial Airways towel, he fed God bits of steak from dinner and let him hop around the sleeping quarters. Then he lay back on his mattress.

The pilot had done nothing all day, yet still he felt as if he'd been wrestling large Kodiak bears for hours on end.

Some of it was exhaustion, molecules screaming implosion from mule saddles, and drugs, and flu.

Most of it was structural breakdown. If he saw his mind as an internal moral framework, some micro-electric jungle gym that balanced losses on one side with positive gains on the other, then he was suffering stresses three times past shear point, alarm lights flashing, sirens whooping, collapse imminent.

Every time he looked at Ela he felt as if the framework gave another wounded shriek, and another stanchion broke, and the structure lurched another couple of feet off-balance, as in the final fifteen minutes of a disaster flick.

Even flying was no help. A month ago being in a plane, any kind of plane, even if he was not doing the flying, would have given his mood a positive spin.

Now, all of a sudden, the rumble of engines, the

occasional bank or shudder as they flew through turbulence had no perceptible effect on his mood. Flying no longer could save him. The awareness of speed no longer had the power to heal.

'I don't believe it,' he mumbled to his reflection, vague in the scratched aluminum of the bunk above. 'I can't believe it.'

The reflection mocked, threw his questions back at him.

She had called him dangerous.

Why 'dangerous'?

It was the word Carmelita had used.

And yet he was sure it was the danger — by that he assumed Carmelita meant the drive in him, to fly at night, under radar and over borders — that had attracted her to him in the first place.

It was Carmelita who had phoned him, after all. Only two weeks after he sat at her table in the South Carolina bar.

They had set up a date in Alphabet City, not far from her fifth floor walk-up, a part of town where people habitually wore mourning and made 'art' out of garbage and bought smack from holes in the walls of condemned buildings.

A dangerous place to live.

And it was truly the risk-taking in her that had excited him, the first defiant John-Paul-Jones flaunt of her hair, the privateer determination to be the best in the world at one thing. It all came out when she roller-danced. It was what drove the fat, beer-guzzling, sad-eyed men in the barroom wild; a sense that she herself had no borders, no restraints, in this one thing at least.

The men believed she lacked it in all respects.

439

He could not believe Carmelita did not see a mirror of herself in his compulsion to smuggle. And he was sure that side of him had sparked on some hint of flint in the puzzling conglomerate that was Eleuthera Hawkley Taylor.

His mind flew circles in its bewilderment. The circles grew tighter and more repetitious. Finally some damage-control mechanism in his brain shut down the major circuits, the circular pain. In the silence of switches thrown the small emergency power section of his mind took up a discipline to scale. He got out the butter knife and began unscrewing the screen covering the porthole beside his bunk.

It was tough work. The heads of the aluminum studs on the sliders kept stripping or breaking off; however he finally got a left-hand corner of the screen loose. He put his face to the resulting wedge.

The perfect night of high altitudes touched him as if it could pierce his skin like Van Allen radiation. A moon shining from behind the plane poured indigo over the world. Stars burned their distant fire through the blue. An even canopy of clouds stretched to the horizon. The cloud-scrim allowed occasional glimpses of a wrinkled darkness that looked like sea. Some deep spirit level inside the pilot shifted closer to even again.

He was still mostly naked in protest at not being told position or destination, but, now he could see horizon, his geographical anxiety was attenuated.

Now he felt almost peaceful not to know where they were. It reinforced the feeling that this Flying Boat was its own world, a microcosm of humans to whom origin was a fable and destination a myth; seven people lost between the stars and the earth with twenty hours of fuel endurance, telling each other stories to fight the unbearable and beautiful loneliness of belonging to something so cold and distant, so totally without beginning or end.

The pilot stared out the porthole for a long time. He picked out constellations and planets. By their position in the sky he figured they were heading roughly southeast. He spotted Venus, Regulus – Mars, blearily orange to the east.

In his mind's eye he saw a ship with titanium castings on her ass end, jerking toward the red planet in fiery atomic bursts.

In the bunk above him Ela shifted and coughed. Through the worn foam he could trace the soft contours of her back and thighs. Something curved in the pilot's gut, as if in symmetry. He went back to the porthole and measured Mars' height over the horizon in finger-widths, and checked the time. Twenty-two hours, forty-two minutes, eighteen seconds; one day after they had slipped under the effects of that strange tea in the khor. If they were still in the same time zone, that made it 17:42:18 GMT. Useless info, for the cloud horizon was not the mathematical one, and you needed the mathematical horizon to find the true altitude of a star. You needed to compensate for the plane's altitude, and you needed an Air Almanac to find the Greenwich Hour Angle, or GHA. This was the only way to establish your longitude and fix your position with certainty.

He wished he had the ECM-pak. It had a stellar navigation sub-program where you just plugged in the corrected observation and three seconds later out popped your Lat. and Long. He wondered what had happened to the ECM. Daud Khan's men had conscientiously shipped their bags across the mountains, but it was too much to expect they would not steal something that valuable and useful.

He dug the Smuggler's Bible out of his gear. As well as microcharts of the world's major air routes, the Bible contained an index of GHAs, five-digit numbers that, once corrected for parallax, height-of-eye, and time, would give him an approximation of longitude.

GHAs.

Somebody had mentioned them, he thought, not long ago.

Now he thought of it, he'd seen five-digit numbers recently as well.

It all came together in completely-stretched-out fashion, the memories lighting off first, then sparking common denominators till the whole made a pattern that was too cohesive to ignore.

Alois van der Lubbe.

He'd mentioned something about 'Gay Hatch-ahs,' a nonsense word unless you looked at it as initials. 'Gay,' 'hatch' and 'ah' were the German pronunciation for the letters G, H and A. He knew this from his father, who had learned German during the war, and still used it for his trains.

'His GHAs are declining;' he remembered van der Lubbe saying that.

The postcards from Hawkley. Always going east, Ela had said. East, in terms of stellar navigation, meant 'declining' GHAs.

And those nonsense classifieds he'd been noticing, even looking forward to, in the *Gazette.* He couldn't remember if the numbers had been declining or not. He got his jeans out of the chartcase and checked his pockets on the off chance. Luck was with him; he'd automatically stowed the ripped section of the October edition in his back pocket when he woke up in the Buddha khor.

Sapphic historian seeks SDM Bantu-speaker (Non-smoker) with SS# ending 113.20 for comprehensive oral history on influence of Sir Clowdisley Shovell's ring finger on modern concept of time. Contact Box L.

Was this how van der Lubbe knew Hawkley's GHAs?

For a GHA of 113.20 to mean anything, it had to have a time.

But the Gazette was the only newspaper in the world to print its precise time of publication.

The pilot sighed.

It was one hell of a complicated way to tell your cronies where you were, even if you were in hiding, even if you claimed to lead a 'religion' founded on arcana such as these.

The pilot checked his rough measurement of Mars with the almanac at the back of the Bible and crossed it with the course he'd figured, southeast from Nooristan.

By his calculations, they were somewhere in the middle of Cambodia.

He looked at the glimpses of sea below him in utter disgust.

He converted the numbers in the *Gazette* to longitude. It turned out to be 121 degrees, 13 minutes, 44 seconds east. If you took a chart and drew out the Flying Boat's course, well ahead of his calculated position till it crossed longitude 121, you found yourself in Borneo.

The pilot threw away his pencil and closed the

book. He was pissed off at the whole exercise. When you hit bottom, he thought a little melodramatically as he went to sleep, all directions were up, and all speeds too slow. They would find out where they were headed in due course.

32

'People claimed to have *seen* the Cargo ships unloading.
Planes were coming; the ancestors were returning; and
docks were built for the Cargo vessels . . . The secret of
the Cargo, so long hidden by the whites, was now
revealed . . .
In the initial stages, rifles were included amongst the
expected goods.'

> Peter Worsley
> *The Trumpet Shall Sound*

A change in the Flying Boat's rhythm woke them at
around 2:30 that morning by the pilot's watch. The
characteristic whine of Dornier-Akai hydraulics
started, stopped. The engine's r.p.m.'s diminished, the
plane banked left, right, left again and began to
tremble as flaps thickened the flow of air under the
wings. The hull boomed, bounced, boomed as they
left the air; the roar of engines was replaced by a
rushing of water; within twenty seconds the Flying
Boat had settled into the water and was taxiing, rocking
a little in this more solid element.

The propellors changed pitch, got louder, died
away to nothing.

The pilot peered out his wedge of porthole. He saw

445

the greasy black teeth of low waves reflecting lights from the cockpit forward and above his head. A line of what looked like bonfires ringed the dark, and was answered beneath him by the portholes of the Flying Boat, mirrored in the black water.

A black craft slid silently through the splits and saucers of the plane's reflection. It had a single narrow hull, a thin outrigger on the starboard side, and was powered by a claw-shaped sail, very tall. It disappeared like a prehistoric bird into the night behind the aircraft's tail.

'Door's locked,' Rocketman reported from the entrance to the sleeping quarters, and sat on the pilot's bunk.

Waves tapped and played the S-26's hull like an aluminum xylophone. The Flying Boat shifted around its bow. They had anchored, the pilot thought. In the distance he could hear shouts, and the bang of hatches.

The relative silence, after hours of engine noise, was awesome, huge; an indistinct monster of something-gone.

On the bunk above, Ela started to cough.

'You OK?' the pilot asked.

She ignored his question.

'Where do you think we are?' she said.

'I thought it didn't matter.'

'Don't get technical.'

'I don't know. I just saw a boat. It looked like a prau — Indonesian.'

'Where's that?'

'South of China.'

'Wow,' Ela commented. Her voice was hoarse, and a little tense. 'I didn't know there was anything south of China.'

446

At a quarter to three the short headhunter came in with a wooden-stocked Chinese AK-47 in one arm. He pointed the machine-pistol in their direction and said, 'We're here, dudes. Get dressed. You can put your pants on,' he added, pointing at the pilot. 'Cap'n Hubbard says he gonna tell you where your ass is at.'

The headhunter led them through the deserted plane to the cargo area. He stopped at an open hatch under the huge wing, under the hot bulk of engines. Through the hatch they could see a large dugout catamaran, twice the size of the prau the pilot had spotted earlier, snubbed between the plane's side and its left float.

Smells blew in the hatchway: salt, rotten vegetation, dead fish. The air was moist and very warm. A haze blocked the sea horizon, dimming an ambient moon. It reminded the pilot of the Rio Chingado.

He had sworn never to fly to places like this, and now here he was again.

Darkworld.

The dugout, like the prau, consisted of one long hull and an outrigger made of carved tree trunk. The outrigger was connected to the main hull by bamboo struts. Planks had been tied across the struts and a tiny palm-leafed cabin raised across the planks. A small fire glowed in a little clay hearth inside the cabin.

The prisoners were told to sit on the planks. A couple of men of the same ebony color as the headhunter unloaded crates from the Flying Boat and lashed them next to the cabin with sisal rope. Then they pushed off from the huge plane and hauled up a sail. The dugout picked up speed, heading for the distant line of lights. Salt spray tainted their lips.

447

The mist covered them like a moist blanket.

Behind them, in the mist, the seaplane looked like a magic ship, with its three rows of portholes, and the meaty, endless wings with the great props frozen in four different directions, and its great silver tail rising like a mizzen from the sea. A name was painted on the tail, *Silubloan*, in black, old-fashioned letters.

Sleek glimmering shapes shot underwater across the catamaran's path, leaving shadows of green light behind them. For an amazed instant the pilot thought they must be torpedoes – then one of the shapes surfaced and he recognized the sloping back, the black, curved fin, and heard the dolphin's explosive breath.

The ring of bonfires grew larger. Ten minutes after leaving the plane a huge structure rose from the black water. It looked like a bizarre and giant crab, or a wooden oil rig perched on scores of very long, spindly legs. They sailed into the shadow of pilings. The pilings were laced with bamboo cross beams, steps, ladders, catwalks. It did not look very strong. They could hear the structure groan in the minimal wind. The crew brought the dugout into the breeze and snugged the craft easily into a bamboo dock. A murmur of voices rose from above their heads.

The headhunter slung the AK-47 over his shoulder and pointed up a ladder leading from water level. As they climbed, carefully checking their purchase on the moist bamboo rungs, the bonfires resolved into torches of pitch and brush, stuck up and down a coral beach under a brow of tall and thick-leafed palms.

They reached a sort of wooden landing. The headhunter, who'd been following behind, led the way now, across a catwalk, up another ladder, and finally over a short deck into a long, wooden, palm-thatched house. The longhouse was set on stilts that blended into the deep structure of the wharf's underpinnings.

Inside, the space was brightly lit with hurricane lamps. Their glow painted strong shadows on fifty or sixty men and women as black as the headhunter, or the prau's crew. The men were dressed in cheap jeans; the women wore only plain cotton skirts, and their breasts were bare.

Most of the people were engaged in unpacking the goods that had come in on the Flying Boat.

A few sat, nervously active, at makeshift desks.

The place smelled of wood smoke and gum grease, of moldy leaves and roasted meat.

The headhunter pointed under a loft of palm fronds halfway up the length of the only room. The bald codger in the flying jacket was squatting on an empty crate by an open fire, drinking from a gourd.

Beside him sat a white man in a trim white beard. He wore John Lennon glasses, headphones, a denim jacket, and a faded Pan Am pilot's cap. His cheeks were wrinkled with age, though his way of looking was interested and young. A portable sat-nav lay beside him, and a Walkman. The Walkman's 'play' button was lit. He wore a paisley bandanna, knotted around his neck.

Both men watched a couple of young women stick twigs in a pig roasting over the coals. The women's breasts were very long and pointed and hung perilously close to the fire. They giggled in astonishment at Ela's two-tone hair as her group drew near.

When he saw them arrive the bald man pulled out another gourd and slopped it full of brown-colored liquid from a large earthenware bowl at his feet.

'Oho, our sleeping beauties,' he said. 'Want some kava?'

The pilot took the gourd, partly because no one else would. The kava tasted bitter and strong. It was heavily flavored with ginger, and fizzed on the tongue like soda. The codger looked like he'd already had his share. His face glowed pink, and he was sweating.

'Long flight,' the bald man commented, by way of excuse or explanation, and refilled his own container.

From over the rim of the kava gourd, the pilot looked at the other man. There was something curiously familiar about his eyes. He was still trying to place the connection when Ela bent forward from the waist and peered hard at the bearded man's face. She stuck her finger out and said, 'Abd el Haq. Son of a gun. You're Abd el Haq!' Her voice pulled so hard it was close to breaking.

The pilot leaned forward as well. Now he could see it. The man looked thinner without robes and turban and the beard had been so drastically cut back it looked almost like he was clean shaven. The skin was fairer and, even in places that had been visible before, there seemed to be more wrinkles – this version of the man was a good ten years older than Daud Khan's crony. But the dark eyes were the same, and the wide curve of mouth, now stretching over an embarrassed chuckle.

The bald man said, 'Forgive me. Terribly rude, I know. Ladies and gen'mun.' He stuck his gourd in the bearded man's direction – 'meet Forrest Hawkley Stanhope.'

The pilot choked. He blew his mouthful of kava all over Ela.

Hawkley took off the Walkman headphones. A funk beat pounded brass. A voice yelled, 'Shit! Goddamn! Dance till yer *ass* falls off!'

Dr Funkenship.

'Hello, Pookie,' Hawkley said shyly to his daughter.

The girl went rigid. Then she started to tremble. It wasn't just the fever, though the pilot had already noticed the steadily increasing glassiness of her eyes, and heard her cough, and was certain now the Chitrali flu had found another victim.

She looked like a thin branch, covered by a jump-suit, shaken by a strong wind. Her face went from white to pink and back again as she stared at her father. Her eyes had heated up to a temperature that would melt asbestos.

When she spoke, her voice was at a low, vibrating pitch that the pilot had never heard before.

'I knew it,' she said. 'I didn't realize I knew. You've lost a lot of weight. That beard looks horrible on you. But I knew it. You son of a bitch! You *bastard*! You never could resist it, could you? Dressing up, joking around. Why did you call me that name in public? I – I – oh *fuck*, I don't even wanna *talk* to you!'

And she swiveled, and stomped in her heavy jump boots down the length of the longhouse, pushing aside men, and porters with mortar rounds balanced on their heads, and women with pots of kava. She disappeared down the ladder at the structure's end.

Hawkley – Abd el Haq – the mythic acid guru, author of the legendary Smuggler's Bible, head hiero-phant of his own navigational religion, spiritual leader of the world's indie smugglers, self-styled nemesis of every national police and customs force on the planet – shrugged, and winced, and bit his lip.

'I always miss, man,' he muttered. 'Like, I can never get it *right*.'

There was an uncomfortable silence. Finally the pilot said, 'So, where the fuck are we? Headhunter said you'd tell us.'

'Pulau Karang,' Hubbard informed him agreeably. 'It's an island in the Halmahera Sea.'

'Thanks a lot.'

'Off New Guinea,' Hubbard added, taking a piece of crackling from a palm leaf one of the women was stacking dinner on. 'North of the Cerams.'

Hawkley took off his glasses and polished them on the sleeve of his jungle shirt. 'We gotta split this scene by day-clean,' he said. 'Before the Indonesians start flying patrols on our ass.' He pointed the spectacles' earpieces at the pilot. 'I wonder if I could rap with you,' he said, 'if that's cool?'

'Does that mean you're leaving us here,' the pilot said, 'here among eaters of human flesh, and quaffers of human blood?' The kava was already getting to him.

Hawkley laughed. It was still a good laugh though the volume was trimmed and diminished to a couple of notches short of the uninhibited, rolling belly-rumble of 'Abd el Haq.' The quality of it was also changed; it had gone a little stretched, as if its owner's heart were no longer in it, as if he were really think-ing of something else.

'Don't worry, man,' Hawkley said. He got to his feet, still chuckling. 'I'll explain everything soon, come.'

They sat on a sort of split-rail bamboo porch built on a side entrance to the longhouse, above the deep lap-ping waters of the lagoon. Lamps hung on the pilings sent shrapnel of light shooting around their faces and hands.

Hawkley looked past the wharf to the lights that marked where his giant seaplane lay anchored.

'Manley told me about you,' Hawkley began.

'So he does know how to find you! He never let on.'

'He's the only one with the cross-references, man. And he knows how to keep his mouth shut.'

'He gets longitude from the *Gazette* classifieds?'

'Dig it — you sussed it out!'

'So did your pal. Alois van der Lubbe.'

'Alois knows only the longitude.'

'And the latitude?'

Hawkley smiled. 'There's a different — medium — for that.'

'Which gives Manley your address.'

'No. It only gives him a town he can snail-mail to. Poste restante, man.'

Hawkley took a deep swig of kava. 'You know,' he continued, a little apologetically. 'I had to make it hard — give me time to check you guys out.' He noticed the pilot had left his gourd inside, and passed over his own. 'Manley said you want to find this BON dude?'

The pilot, instinctively, looked for the horizon, couldn't find it. The moon, in setting, turned the mist a dangerous hue, like boysenberries mixed with black ink.

'Bokon,' Hawkley continued. 'Bokon Taylay.'

'I heard you could help,' the pilot said, neutrally.

'That's how you hooked up with Eleuthera?'

'Yup. Can you? Help, I mean?' The pilot's tone was still uncommitted, but he couldn't keep a leash on the curiosity. He'd come a long way to find the answer to this question.

'I don't know,' Hawkley said, looking at the Flying Boat again.

'You must know something. The Feds been goin' crazy, last couple of months. They say your groups are the only ones don't get busted.'

'They're just well-organized.'

'But it's how they're well-organized – it cancels out whatever BON does – whatever this Bokon guy does.'

The clamor of voices inside the longhouse died down, briefly. In the lull you could hear the croak of fowl, the grunting of pigs, the lap of confined water.

'Van der Lubbe mentioned a ".667," a ratio?' the pilot continued.

'Yeah,' Hawkley said. 'The .667. I guess that's part of it.'

He took out some rolling papers and a pouch. He rolled a joint fast and expertly, his fingers avoiding the slightest wasted effort, his tongue moistening the thin paper more delicately than a hummingbird's.

'It's like this.'

He looked at the pilot through the orange scraps of kerosene light. He massaged the rolled spliff between his thumb and first two fingers of each hand, coaxing it into a firm cigar.

'I figured it out while I was with the Brothers,' Hawkley continued. 'I noticed the small groups did OK. They knew each other, they didn't need to do a lot of rappin' and phonin'. But the ones that got bigger, suddenly they were spending close to ninety percent of their time just housekeeping. Sending messages back and forth: do this, don't do that. Bullshit.

'I parsed it out,' he continued. 'I had just enough stats training to do it. Once they got over a certain size, maybe nine people, their communications went through a paradigm shift, it happened at .667, on average, in terms of signal to noise. Point-six-six-seven is real close to .6653, which happens to be around the frequency (if you read Dr Zatt's research) where a lot of the world's behavior goes haywire. Serotonin receptor activity, the effects of crack on brainwaves, the rate at which you pick up your cup of coffee, the point at which wind shear becomes a tornado; below the .6653 ratio of events per minute, or second, whatever, you get normal creative energy, man, the orderly disorder of normal events. *Above that*, it goes into an unnatural order. A kind of organic facism. Like compulsive behavior. There's just too much info, and it gets funneled into channels it wouldn't go in when things were cool. It happens to people, it happens to smugglers' groups, when they get too big—'

Hawkley paused. He smiled, as if aware that, in going on too long, he had betrayed an obsession best kept to himself. He stuck the joint in his mouth and twisted the end in the sharpener of his pursed lips.

'Well, the rest is a couple pieces of intelligence. Got 'em through Cappy Hubbard – guy who flew the seaplane.' Hawkley flashed a Zippo. The end of the joint burst into flame, died into a coal, glowed red. Hawkley took a deep drag. The words that followed came in the squeaky, strained-bronchi rhythm of the life-long head.

''Mazin' dude, Cappy. He's eighty-five years old. Smuggled bombers north to Canada for FDR, before Pearl Harbor – Congress wasn't supposed to grok. Worked for the OSS. One of the first to get into acid – best customer, once. Real head for my purple. Went

455

Darkworld — few years ago — to work with me, still has friends in — what they call — "intelligence community."' Hawkley exhaled, finally. He offered the joint to the pilot, who took a quick drag and passed it back.

'CIA hates BON,' Hawkley added, by way of attribution. 'Territory thing. You really wanna do this, man?'

The pilot picked up the kava gourd again. He decided, even though he was getting heartburn from drinking it, that he liked the stuff. Kava made words flow easier. Feelings seemed more black and white, even when they really were laundry-gray, or deep mauve, like the mist.

'No,' he said, 'I'm not sure.'

'Why not?'

'Because I've lost friends.' The pilot's leg was going to sleep. He shifted uncomfortably. He looked inside the longhouse and noticed a man sitting at a bamboo desk, under a long pole. The man held a string to mouth and ears and spoke urgently into its frayed end. A small packing crate stood on its side on the desk. More strings linked the top of the crate to the top of the pole. Abstract dials and numbers were painted in merry colors along the face of the crate.

'I don't get it,' Hawkley said.

'It's simple.' The pilot spoke his words tense and sharp like spitting. 'It was fine while I was trading; walkin' the walk, talkin' the talk. But now this is all starting to hurt people.'

Hawkley's joint was two-thirds consumed. He sucked at it in little puffs, pulling it away from his lips with each inhale.

'You could hurt more people, you stop now.'

'How?' The pilot shook his head. 'No one would give a shit about us anymore, if we went home now.'

'We found a Yank tailing Daud Khan's caravan out of Chitral.'

The pilot frowned.

'Who?'

Hawkley shrugged. 'We lost him. But so what?'

The pilot shook his head again. 'That's not the point.'

'OK,' Hawkley said, 'what about revenge? Now there's a good, old-fashioned reason. The fact that BON has been offing your compadres, throwing 'em in Oakdale, least I assume it was BON – that doesn't matter?'

The pilot snorted. 'That's not the point, either.'

'The fact that, if you look at history, smuggling has always gone together with people trying to get rid of pigs, man – crawling out from under some goddamn jackboot or other – that's not relevant to you?'

'Jisi yomo don't exactly go to the underdog,' the pilot countered.

'It's not the cargo, man. It's the movement.'

'Oh. Hawkley-isms.'

The bearded man smiled and opened his hands.

'Sounds great,' the pilot told him. 'Don't mean a whole hell of a lot.'

'It's another *way*, man.' Hawkley leaned forward. The diffidence, the shyness were gone in a rush of exhaled java weed. 'Don't you see? Besides the ways of the state. It's not always copacetic. But when times get tough, smuggling's the only way the little guy has to get money, to get ideas. To get guns, or get out, if it comes to that. Why you think smugglers don't have the same rights as murderers and child molesters and rapists? Huh? Why can BON shoot us on sight, without warning? Why d'you think, under Anglo-Saxon common law, we're the only people who are guilty until proven innocent?

'I mean, I s'pose it could get out of hand,' he continued. 'You'd have total anarchy if it was all smugglers, no Coast Guard. There's definitely a balance to be struck. But right now the imbalance is on their side. Right now, the big organizations got the upper hand. Ninety-five percent of people's lives have to do with big organizations. Living creatures, man, giant bureaucratic godzillas! They eat, they grow, there is nothing people can do to fight them! Only us, man — only the smuggling nodes, the ones that can live outside the various 'nets. We're the only ones got an alternative.'

Hawkley flicked his roach over the porch into the water, where it sank and was eaten by a small yellow fish.

'And just for the record,' Hawkley added, 'Martha left me. Not the other way around. I mean, I'm not saying she was wrong. I don't think I made a very good husband, or father; it's why I didn't argue. But she was the one who split.'

'That's not what Ela says.'

'No.'

'You really hurt her, you know that?'

'It's not losing your friends so much is it?' Hawkley told him gently. 'It's losing Ela.'

The pilot did not respond. There was a second desk in the longhouse he had not noticed before. The man at this desk wore a uniform made of a policeman's hat, denim shorts, and black dress shoes. In some curious resonance with what was currently fashionable in the City, he wore a half-dozen watches, all Rolex, all fake, on both wrists. He was busy shifting large flat leaves of palm from a stack on the right side of his desk to a stack on the other.

'I'm sorry, man,' Hawkley said. He picked up the kava gourd, bit its rim thoughtfully, and shook his head. 'Listen, I'm gonna tell you what I know.'

'I don't need this.'

'It won't tie you—'

'I don't want this.'

'It's just info,' Hawkley said. 'Information is neutral. It's what you do with it that defines you—'

'Spare me the pop psychology, OK?'

Hawkley blew his breath out his nose hard. The pilot winced. Finally, after almost two minutes had passed, he said, 'There was a woman, in Chitral.'

'Zayid Shah's wife.' Hawkley nodded.

'You know about her?' The pilot could not keep the surprise out of his voice.

'Sure.'

The pilot leaned forward. 'What happened to her, Hawkley?'

'He sent her to Lahore for trial.'

'And?'

'And I don't know.' Hawkley looked at his seaplane again. 'Is that what's bothering you? It had nothing to do with the dance. Zayid Shah gets his cut.'

'It had to do with us.' The pilot picked up the kava gourd, finished the last drops. 'If it wasn't for me, if it wasn't for the Trade, she would never have seen Rocketman, she would never have gone to jail.'

'Oh, she won't go to jail.'

'How do you know?'

459

Hawkley laughed. It was almost the old laugh, full of juice and volcanoes.

'Her dad's a brigadier general in ISI. Oh, they'll do a court thing, maybe, so face is saved. But if anyone's goin' upriver, believe me, it'll be Zayid Shah, not his wife.'

The pilot upended the gourd again. He knew there was nothing inside but it gave him time to think. Hawkley took out his rolling papers once more.

'Look,' he said, 'you came to see me. You dropped in on my run without an invite. How come I feel like I'm asking you for a favor?'

There was room now, the pilot realized; in the area of his brain that, without his being aware, had been frozen because of what happened in Chitral, as well as by the pathetic arrogance of what he was attempting, there was now room for the data he had come so far to find.

Out of nowhere he found himself missing the ECM-pak. He wanted to do a scan; he wanted to run the sat-nav, and get the exact longitude and latitude, down to the decimal points, of where he now was sitting.

'What the fuck,' he said finally, 'hit me.'

So Hawkley told him.

He didn't know much, the smuggler said. Sometime in August BON had gone online with new analysis software. The program's code name was 'Control,' and it didn't fool with the traditional methods of tracking and tracing that the Wildnets – with their crippled Fedchips, their mobile uplinks, their codes and scramblers and cyphered algorithms – had been created to evade.

Yet somehow, after only a month in operation, the bigger groups started getting picked off, one by one: BON assault teams, BON fighters and cutters waiting for them at rendezvous points that were supposed to be absolutely secret; as if their plans and evasions had gone completely transparent to the electronic vision of Control.

It had something to do with the .667 ratio, Hawkley said, but what? He had lit up the second joint but was not smoking it. The wrinkles around his eyes looked deep as trenches in the kerosene light.

He did have one piece of specific info, Hawkley said: a name. The coal of the spliff glowed as he continued. The name was Peter Brodin, and it belonged to a mid-level nobody, a fifty-eight-year-old programmer who had put Control together. 'Supposedly a fan of Derrida, and Lacan, those University of Paris post-structuralist types,' Hawkley said, 'though what that's s'posed to tell you . . .' he shrugged. Brodin, he continued – a man no one knew personally – by virtue of his invention had become the most powerful individual in the enforcement wing of BON.

'There's a way to find this pig,' Hawkley grunted, scratching arrows on the planks with his Zippo to illustrate the point, 'but you can't do it virtual, all the best hackers have tried, they can't break through BON's immune-programs. So you got to do it physical. Which means you want to find him at his workstation, capish? That way you can see how it works, and figure out how to perpetrate his system. So you go to his office, which is in the BON complex at Fort Meade, Maryland; though most of the time he's at their science office at the TransCom Building, in New York.'

It took a second or two to sink in, in this context. But when it did the 'what?' came blurting from the pilot like a belch.

'The TransCom Building.' Hawkley glanced at him in surprise. 'You must know it, it's—'

'I know it. I used to live there.'

'Good. Then you'll know your way around,' Hawkley replied, comfortably.

Inside the longhouse the noise level was rising again. The emptied crates had been stacked to one side. The men and women gathered around the central pole, the one with the strings leading down from the top to the painted crate. The women were chanting and clapping. The smoky light reacted with the smoky tones of their skin and turned the whole longhouse into a show of fog and shadows.

'But why?' the pilot said without taking his eyes off the crowd inside. 'Why is he at the TransCom?'

Hawkley exhaled, a long feather of over-sweet smoke.

'Because it's all X-Corp software, man,' he said, 'and X-Corp belongs to TransCom now. BON uses Fujitsu-Cray 7300-series mainframes, all fornicated and copulated and parallel-processed together. X-Corp and BON worked together for years, pimp-'n'-hooker. X-Corp comes up with a new security network; BON buys it, tests it for 'em. That's how Stanley got to be called "Bokon." Bokon, it's Vodun for "Sorcerer", and "Taylay" means television, and by extension, electronic messages, even e-mail in Kriol; he tested his first system on the reefer-runners of Cap Haitien.'

'No wonder,' the pilot was saying, 'I used to get all that BON traffic so clear—' but at that point, inside the longhouse, a man with a snowy afro, dressed in cut-off jeans, climbed creakily to the top of the desk, and began to shout.

'Long long moontime we hangin' on for John Frum. Now him come again, hallelujah and by the way.' ('By the way,' the women answered in a sweet singsong.)

'Now John Frum bring us-bilong-cargo from German Town; straight from Time-before-tabu him come, hallelujah and by the way.' ('By the way.')

'Him come on mighty steamer-that-fly' – the old man's voice rose – 'an' soon cargo is bilong-men. Soon come cargo-bilong-Dakota, and Fokker, and De Havilland; yea, even come Boeing, hallelujah an' by the way.'

'Boeing-of-the-night,' the women chanted, swaying their breasts like orchids in a seawind.

'I speak finish,' the old man said. 'Now sing strong-fella, and no forget what I say; hallelujah and by the way.'

The women danced, and the men lifted up a couple of long black cases with fat square scopes and dials and eyepieces sticking out from the fiberglass, and all answered, 'By the way.'

'What the fuck,' the pilot said, 'is going on in there?'

'That,' said Hawkley, 'is "Cargo religion." '

The pilot just looked at him.

The people inside began to sing again. Their voices were strong; the bamboo of the porch swayed as they moved their feet in rhythm. Men beat on drums made of strong wood and carved to represent evil spirits. The complicated fiberglass tubes were set at a place of honor on the bamboo desks. Hawkley got up to fetch more kava.

'It illustrates what I meant,' Hawkley said when he came back. 'These people – the Watap – belong to an old culture, but they've always been real poor, and the Dutch, who colonized this island, made 'em even poorer. Took the good lands for copra, taxed 'em, beat on 'em. And the Watap would hear about the amazing cheung Whitney owned, like radios and ice-boxes and cars. And they would look up from their shitass manioc patch and see the airplanes and steamers bringing these goodies, and the airplanes and steamers always passed them by, "by the way," far away on the horizon, high up in the sky. They couldn't understand it so, like any dying culture, you name it, the Ghost Shirts, the Maji-Maji, the Moonies, this new Hoffa cult, whatever, they made up a story to explain it; in this case, the Myth of Cargo. Which was, that all the goodies actually are made in some distant Cargo heaven, and they are made by gods for the Watap, but somewhere along the way the goodies get hijacked by the whites. The Watap decided that paradise will come when the messiah of Cargo re-directs the cargo home.'

'By the way,' the Watap chanted, so loud, the kerosene lamp swayed.

Hawkley drained the kava gourd. His eyes glinted in the torchlight.

'Anyway, the Cargo witch doctors checked out the whites doing all the weird things whites do, and figured these had to be rituals to make the cargo come. So they copied 'em. They built fake airfields, in the jungle; they built bogus seaplanes and C-47s out of bamboo, to attract planes. They built fake wharves, like this one, to tempt in ships. They built "radiotelephones,"' he pointed at the pole inside, 'to talk to the gods of Cargo. They constructed "offices" and shuffled banana leaves back and forth, like they knew whites did. They searched the sky hopefully for planes. But nothing worked.

'The first time I came here, man,' Hawkley continued dreamily, 'I thought, shit, this is perfect – like, California's full of people like these.'

The pilot had been looking at the long fiberglass tubes, going from half-familiar detail to detail till it all suddenly came together and he said, 'Those are Blowpipes, Hawkley – surface-to-air missiles. Hand-held. Wire-guided.'

'You grokked it, man.' Hawkley chuckled into his gourd, a little embarrassed. 'Yeah, I figured – for the first time, they could really get their own cargo. 'Bout time, huh?'

'But they're gonna shoot down *planes* with that, Hawkley!' the pilot yelled. 'They're gonna kill pilots! We won't know what the fuck hit us, when those things go off.'

'Don't get so fuckin' sanctimonious, kid.' Hawkley's eyes grew hot and he looked at the pilot directly now. 'Djakarta's been wiping out these people for years. They want independence, but the Indonesians won't give it to 'em. The Indonesians use A-10 Warthog ground attack planes the Pentagon gives 'em. Eurofighters from the EU. They drop ball-bearing bombs, which are outlawed by the Geneva Convention, and napalm. It's self-defense.'

'Maybe,' the pilot said doubtfully. Looking at the Blowpipes, he thought about the terror in the pit of him when the AMRAAM flashed by the Citation's cockpit in the heart of the storm. It felt like years ago.

465

'So you're the Cargo messiah,' he said. 'You're some kind of god to these people?'

Hawkley laughed. 'They don't treat me like a god.'

'But you bring 'em the cargo.'

'I get paid for it, man. Not much, considering, but I do get paid. Actually these people kinda despise me. After all, I'm only returning what my people ripped off to begin with. And then I leave. Gods aren't s'posed to leave.'

'I found that out,' Ela said from the entrance behind them, 'twenty years ago.'

Hawkley swiveled, fast, like he'd been shot in one shoulder. His kava gourd rolled off the dock and, after two or three seconds, splashed in the water beneath.

Ela stood hunched at the entrance, staring down at her father.

'Pookie,' Hawkley said a whiny sort of tone.

'I'll split,' the pilot offered.

'No need,' Hawkley said desperately.

'I want to talk to him,' Ela told the pilot.

'Don't go far,' Hawkley said. 'We're dropping all of you off in the morning, near Manila.'

The pilot turned to leave, turned back. 'One thing—'

'What.'

'I want my ECM-pak. Abd el Haq — you — took it in Chitral.'

'I dig,' Hawkley said, 'it's on the *Silubloan*,' but his eyes were on his daughter, and his voice was already raveled in the complexities of what he was going to say to her.

The pilot climbed down the ladder to the beach. Above his head the Watap had softened their chant to a long, slow rhythm: by-the-way, by-the-way, by-the-way. The air was even more dense than before.

The coral sand felt warm underfoot. Foliage hung over the beach, over the lagoon, like a canopy bed. The mist still glowed in the death of moonlight. The water seemed to pulse, to shine electric under and beyond the small shafts of torchlight from the wharf. When the pilot took off his boots and waded in, he found his feet made ripples of light that illuminated the sand on which he stood.

Phosphorescence. He had never seen it so strong.

He took off the rest of his clothes and dove, heedless of the potential peril in waters unfamiliar as these. The lagoon was a perfect temperature – no shock, yet cool enough to stroke every cell of his epidermis. He was still weak from the flu, but the sea felt good, like a massage, pulling from his muscles strength that he could use for swimming. He dove deep, eyes open, seeing the millions of tiny piezoelectric plankton blooping softly past his face. It was like diving at a hundred m.p.h. the wrong way down a night-time highway at rush hour. Pressure popped in his ears. Enough light emanated from the organisms and torchlight and the mist for him to perceive his surroundings underwater.

The bottom of the lagoon appeared, shimmering up blue-green, studded with brain coral. A silver-blue cross hung beside a large clump of wavy coral to his right. The angle of the cross was too perfect to be natural. He kicked over. The cross seemed to recede, then magnify. As he swam deeper it grew into gigantic wings and a fuselage. Four bent props. He recognized the swept-back tail, the greenhouse canopy, from his model kits. A B-17.

Coming to the limits of his air now, he accelerated the kicks, sweeping water with great otter scoops of his hands. Down to the cockpit. The plane was unbelievably huge in the lens of water.

Holding on briefly to a round strut that once held glass, he saw the algae crusting thick over the round shape of dials, the empty framework of seats, the throttles. Kicking a little to stay in position, he disturbed plankton inside the wreck and they put out light in their unrest. In the added light he made out a patch of pearl in the jumpseat behind the copilot's position; and out of the scummy green darkness, in the directionless glow of micro-organisms, he discerned the sheen of cheekbones, and teeth, and long, graceful vertebrae, still laced to the backrest with some kind of webbing. Shreds of leather fabric remained belted around the ribcage; above it all, strands of hair, three or four feet long, waved just a touch in the corrupted water.

The last of the pilot's oxygen blew from his mouth. He headed for the surface, hands grabbing at the reflections above him like they were the last light left before darkness finally and irretrievably closed in around him.

33

'In each of these men . . . Mozart lies,
assassinated.'

Antoine de Saint-Exupéry
Terre des Hommes

Marco decided to hang around Pulau Karang. The
waterskiing possibilities of the lagoon were too good
to ignore, he believed. The Watap's code of hospitality ran too deep to refuse him.

Hawkley's Flying Boat dropped off the pilot, Ela,
and Rocketman the next day on an island thirty miles
from the Philippine capital. The headhunter delivered
the ECM-pak from the cargo bay shortly before landing.

Hawkley spent the whole flight locked in the cockpit with Hubbard. The pilot never got another chance
to talk with him.

He was disappointed, mostly because he'd been
going to ask permission to fly the giant seaplane, just
for a few minutes; it was something he'd been longing to do, at some level, ever since he'd woken up in
his bunk, after they were put to sleep in Nooristan.

They took a ferry from the island and boarded a

tired PAL stretch-747 the following evening.

Zayid Shah – so Hawkley said – had protected their UCC numbers from whoever was following. In any event they had no trouble at Customs when they arrived at JFK a day later.

New York seemed gray and bleached and shut-in after the rich smells and temperatures of Darkworld. Newspaper headlines spoke of an escalation of the 'Water War' between Iran and Azerbaijan. Brooke Denali had been spotted with a man she was not married to on a balcony of the Cipriani Hotel in Venice.

Light on choices, they went directly to PC's apartment from the airport, letting themselves in with PC's keys. There they slept, on and off, for two or three days as their bodies tried to catch up with the improbable hypotheses in space-time their brains kept insisting was the truth.

Ela's flu ran its course – got better, got worse, improved again. The pilot wiped her face, cleaned her body, helped her to and from the bathroom. He sat by the bed, leafing through *Shadow* magazine, watching while her temperature ran high. When the fever finally broke she was very weak. Her skin was almost translucent, like white candle wax; she would burst into tears without warning or provocation. The weakness went quickly and her skin regained its color in a couple of days, but the cough and depression remained.

Once, after Rocketman found PC's jisi yomo stash, along with the gleaming glass-bowled jis' factory, she smoked jisi for most of a morning, and spent the afternoon sobbing. Except for that one digression, all

470

she wanted to eat was popcorn, over-buttered and with too much salt; all she opted to drink was Zero Cola; all she cared to do was lie in PC's mammoth bed against a half-dozen propped cushions, her head half covered by a pair of PC's full-spectrum VR goggles, her finger twitching, during interactive shows, at the minute plastic joystick.

She refused to discuss what Hawkley said to her, or what she had said to her father.

She found a bottle of *Lebensraum* one of PC's women had left behind, and daubed some every morning behind her ears.

She almost never sang, anymore.

The pilot played classics of Shift-shin on PC's excellent inner-wall system – stuff like Clam Fetish's 'Geysir,' blending the rhythm gushes of volcanic water with raga riffs and Joe Tex bass lines.

She shook her head irritably when the sound penetrated her face-sucker.

On his third day in New York the pilot set up the ECM-pak, patching it into cables that led to a dish antenna on the roof. Strapping on the half-sucker he did a quick radar and radio analysis, picking up nothing unusual in the immediate area.

Then he punched in Wildnet scan.

At first he thought something was wrong with the software. Under the pulsing opalescent sky of the Web – so far above it was abstract, without meaning, impotent like an idea of God – the dense, matte nighttime of Wildnet space suffused the VR quadrant of his half-sucker.

Nothing besides remained. No light, no flashing arcs and pulses of information, let alone the busy gridwork of streets and highways of data he used to

471

see on the Wildnets when they were healthy. It reminded him of flicks that had scared him as a boy – the places left, after the holocaust, the nuclear wasteland; empty except for the skeletons of those trapped by a rampage of radiation.

Controling a sudden limbic-system panic, he joysticked forward, and down. The digits of silent SAPs flashed by as he traveled through the dead Usenets, but the digits were extinguished, like neon with the current cut, visible only as shadows.

The servers themselves were completely dark.

The feeling of devastation that he'd had before, doing this in Breslau, came back so strongly he could taste it like lye on his tongue. Now the silent servers seemed to him black tombstones arching hugely overhead against the electric night; the systems underneath were cavernous holes diving further into the arcades of the undead, and deeper still, into hell itself, the hell of killed Wildnets, cobwebs of bad info, crypt after crypt of messages lost, corpse after corpse of vampire-sucked phrases – 'Come in,' 'Skeeter, where are you?' 'I need,' 'I can't find,' 'Do you copy?' – all dried up and calcified around the horrible Gothic altar of silence.

Against the black vacuum in the corners of his 3-D vision, he made out one of the dark datalines he'd seen in Breslau, a dead line of silence marked only by the blip of blocked Fedchip from a server pinned just this side of brain dead.

The blip was thin, infrequent, regular. Carrier beam only.

Something moved. Down the subtle gray of maintenance, a dark shape swooped onto one of the dead servers and squatted there, silent, still.

As he passed the next server on the line a second search-engine appeared out of nowhere and settled, like a vulture, or a flying leech, onto the blocked code-matrix.

Deliberately this time, without panic, the pilot hit control-alt-delete. The half-sucker hissed. The image of desert, of sterile death, condensed to a bright spot of light — was gone.

This time, the cybernetic postcard, the blasted battlefield of gray that had flashed across his screen in Breslau, did not appear in that millisecond between shutoff and disconnection.

In a sense, it made no difference. As he pulled off the flying helmet the pilot felt in his bones the chill of ultimate control that had reached out from that blasted Webscape, and shivered. But the effect did not last, as it might have done a week or a month ago.

The 'nets were not as real to him anymore, he realized; their abstract topography had been thinned by the intense effort of concrete places and steel frontiers.

In the same way, he reflected, his former neurotic care for cyber-security was diluted in him by the solidity of a threat that could cause immediate damage — actual trauma of torn tissue and shattered bone — in Breslau, in the Northwest Frontier.

And that brought to mind Fat Chico Fong.

Now there was a threat of steel and fire or, more accurately, of sawed-off shotguns and Number 45. Chico must have seen through the New Mexico smokescreen by now, and he had to be pretty upset about being fronted off.

The pilot shivered again, thinking of the gray sludge of pork chow mein, Habana-style.

But while Chico had known of Carmelita, he had no skinny on PC. So they were safe in this apartment, as long as they stayed away from the haunts and old connections of their previous lives. In this one case, doing nothing was safer than action. And that was fine by him, for he was still deeply tired from the trip, and it seemed like a perfect situation when the option that led to more security was what your body wanted to do anyway.

Rocketman, on the other hand, was more concerned about their safety than before.

Specifically, he was terribly worried about the security in PC's building. He spent hours at the Micronta, watching Securicam monitors, hitting keys to change views, from black-and-white scalps and hats (downward shot) of people riding the elevators, to guests at the main doors, to deliverymen at the service entrance. He went out at random intervals, at all hours to check for Sour Lake Roustabouts or Bilderberg agents skulking down the adjoining streets. Sometimes he walked east and south to 35th Street to check if they were waiting for him at the Bellevue entrances as well.

On these visits he loitered across the street from the hospital, gazing up at the mental health tower where he used to live.

For all these missions he disguised himself in PC's clothes. Although the Safe People who lived in the building could not look at him without a twinge of anxiety, the building's doormen got used to the sight of a large, almond-colored man, with sad eyes and a worried frown, sloping in and out of the front door dressed in fashionable camel's hair chesterfields, worsted trousers, monkey jackets, and gaucho boots, everything two sizes too small.

The pilot, most of the time, wore nothing at all, or almost nothing. He had got used to walking around in underwear in the Flying Boat. He had decided clothes were psychologically as well as physically restraining. He thought better when he wore fewer clothes. When he went out for walks, he put on the minimum; a pair of jeans, his travel jacket, boots. He never wore glasses, or the fake moustache he'd bought after his apartment was busted. He took a scarf to wrap around his chin in case a cruiser went by. Nothing else. No socks, or underwear, or shirt.

He spent a lot of time walking, shivering, and thinking. He roamed Riverside Park, tramping the wild kudzu down as far as Television City, up to the latitude of Grant's Tomb, moving hard to keep warm in the eternal gray wind reaming the Hudson Valley. He sat out of the wind's pointed vector in the shelter of the Civil War carronades by the Soldiers' and Sailors' Memorial, watching the hedgehogs as they chewed at brake linings and sipped the sweet pink fluid, or the raccoons as they dug pitfalls to trap the marrauding coyote. Eating whole packages of extra-rich Brownie Chocolate Nut cookies. These, he had decided, were better than Double-Dark-Chocolate Milanos, or even the chocolate Chesapeakes.

He came to think of the Riverside statues as friends, and counselors. The grieving half-dressed widows and children of the Firemen's Monument on 100th Street; the two mounted soldiers – Joan of Arc, armored for winter on 93rd, and Franz Sigel, still musing over his military screwups on 105th – Sam Tilden, the also-ran of 110th Street; Louis Kossuth, the Magyar nationalist of 111th, sword ever unsheathed as a precautionary measure against the timeless treachery of Habsburgs; all seemed to have acquired human attributes by virtue of the character traits they shared with the pilot.

All of them were losers; Joan of Arc burned alive at Rouen, Kossuth in exile, Sigel a laughingstock, Tilden trounced by Hayes; but there was more to it than that.

Alone these forgotten statues held the line against the tazer-muggers, the pigeon shit, the tee-dees, and the eternal vicious wind off the river. It was that sense of last stand, 'The guard dies but surrenders not,' that brought out the empathy in the pilot, had him slapping their cold plinths affectionately as he passed beside; for solitude made them allies, all of them together in their hopeless defense against the cold that blew in from New Jersey, with its impossibly gaudy sunsets, its bitter rain, its taint of roasted coffee.

He got to know more than the statues. As the days wore on he became familiar with the ships that plodded up and down the river, the vessels that accomplished the day-to-day, bread-and-butter, in-tide out-tide business of the decaying harbor. He favored the utility boats – tiny harbor tankers like the *Jean Frank* or the *Northern Sun*. He admired them without reservation as they scuttled up and down the filthy water, churning stubbornly into head currents, coated with ice, grimed with diesel oil, stained with rust, heavy with the fuel that ran everything from boilers to trucks to the generators powering the subways.

He was fond of the tugs. He liked to watch them at night, reading their lights like port-pidgin; the two

476

vertical white mast lights denoting barges being pushed; the three lights indicating long tows; the red of flammable cargo, the blinking yellow at the barges' forward end gamely fighting the glare of a huge neon sign newly erected on the Palisades side. 'http://www.fix4god' the sign flashed, pink-red e-mail to Hoffa's heaven. Over the words, disembodied against the orange light-pollution, hung a neon like-ness of the prophet himself – pudgy nose, acid-eaten jowls, hand raised in pistol fashion, pointing at Manhattan.

He got to know the tugs during the day by the colors of their deckhouses, and their shapes. The *Buchanan 42* he recognized by her blue paint and flat riverboat bow; the *Mister Alan*, by her squat shape and her red-and-white trim; the *Ginni Reinauer* by her buff funnel. He could distinguish between the *Gulf Star*, the *Kate*, the *Mary DeFelice*, with their various loads of bunker-C or garbage, or crushed Adirondack stone, or twisted scrap metal from the Bronx and Bridgeport heaps.

Now, walking and watching the river traffic, he understood what had drawn Obregon to the traffic of the streets. If you became familiar with the patterns of traffic, you began to sense an underlying logic, a residual order, a general structure above and beyond the particular, as if this human expression of chaos were subject to the same laws of harmonics and period-doubling as more foreign agents like weather, or the boiling of water. The cargo of tugs and barges affected so many different levels of the city's life that their coincidences and delays had to have a ripple effect on both sides of their individual journeys. And that ripple must spread outward, in the movement of generators, of credit, of people, till eventually it came full circle and caused the tugs and tankers to change behavior, with downstream effects on future cargoes. And so forth.

He even fantasized that some Cargo cult – some version of the beliefs of the Watap on Pulau Karang – might one day spring up around the harbor of New York. Acolytes of tides and fuel slicks, witch doctors of subways and bus lines, they would plot schedules, delays, early arrivals. Clustering around VHFs, cell-phones, and CB radios, they would light communion flares at altars loaded with add-a-ride transfers and busts of Robert Moses. They would set up fake fuel terminals and commuter stops to influence the patterns that went beyond pattern, hoping one day to achieve some kind of hold on a structure whose mystery and omnipresence they could guess at but seldom grasp and never, under normal circumstances, affect.

But the pilot was careful not to let these thoughts get out of hand, even when he was casting around for something to dwell on besides Ela. He did not let himself become concerned, as Obregon had, about cars. Nor did he note the passing of traffic helicopters over the Henry Hudson Drive at rush hour, or the UAVs that flitted over Washington Heights, searching with VR-envirocams for the safe houses of Rwandan crack bosses. He ignored the choppers that went up and down the valley, ferrying Pentagon suits to north-ern bases, or flying the mayor and his Omega cronies to country estates in the Catskills.

Another factor besides walking and thinking was important in reestablishing a connection between the pilot and New York — for that connection was still tenuous, made marginal by the travel- and stress-induced fancy that his real self actually had stayed behind in Asian mountains or a South China Sea lagoon and New York itself was simply a bubble in the mind, a syndrome of disease, of brain-inflammation, something to be ascribed to malaria, or clawless lobsters, and dispelled by the appropriate medication and a good night's sleep.

That factor was TV.

The pilot took to coming back from his walks, removing his clothes, and sliding into bed beside Ela. He would wrap himself in what blankets were left and strap on the second of the paired shutter-goggles. He was conscious only for a short time of how lonely they must look, two living creatures with their heads mostly covered by plastic masks, together but not touching; staring at a seven-foot screen that sparkled with standby charge yet made no noise. Watching whatever Ela selected.

Entertainment and news, mostly, to the extent you could separate the two. He learned immediately of the latest in terror bombings, the Safeway atrocity in Brentwood (forty-three dead) and the sabotage of the Glen Ridge Canyon dam (casualties: a rancher, a tourist, and 437 cattle). He was fully aware of where the Truth Trust team, featuring Amy Dillon, stood in its quest to stamp out violent music pirates in Rio on the new VR serial, *Real Life*. He found out to the ounce the size of Brooke Denali's fibroid tumor (removed while he was away). He had at his finger-tips all the facts about the latest ATM hostage-takings, as well as about the restaurant (Tariq's Spa, Laurel Canyon) where Jason Rock, who played Chase

MacBride on *Pain in the Afternoon*, had thrown a waltz-mosh for his prenuptial.

When there was straight news, as Hawkley indicated, it barely touched on the continuing node-rebellion in Cartagena. In fact, the only mention of nodes was on the Entertainment/Fashion network, which aired a piece on calico kerchiefs, first worn in the Manila node, that were becoming popular in areas of Marina del Rey.

Once, as a feel-good kicker to an otherwise blood-soaked half-hour, XTV's Ned Reynolds aired a special segment on the mutating marsh on the western shore of Narragansett Bay.

'The federal government has declared a national security lockdown on this unglamorous piece of waterfront real estate,' Reynolds intoned. Over his head, Kiowas stuttered. A Predator UAV swooped dizzyingly near – so close that, sitting on their bed 150 miles away in full 3-D immersion, the pilot and Ela both ducked, knocking their heads painfully together.

The XTV camera panned. From overhead, they could make out splotches of spinach green spreading tendrils like mold around the cattails, the rusted piles of trash. The pilot extended his hand, the cattails looked so close, so real; he wanted to part the rushes to look for the swept-back crucifix shape of his Citation. But he did not see it. He saw no Jumpers, either. Only armed men in bodysuits with 'BON Piracy Task Force' across the back, rolling razor ribbon across access roads.

'Increasingly aggressive in its efforts to punish intellectual piracy, the Bureau of Nationalizations has cordoned off the entire former naval base against amateur chip-growers. At the same time it has committed more resources to finding out how the organic microchips got here in the first place.'

The cameras flicked back to Ned Reynolds. He had changed his haircut again, the pilot thought, turning up the volume on his face-sucker.

'But this may be a case of shutting the stable door,' the anchorman said, squinting to telegraph the building of tension. 'TransCom scientists have isolated strange attractors, repetitive patterns of energy flow, arising from background transmissions in a marsh sixteen miles away from here, near Fall River, Massachusetts. And these strange attractors *exactly mimic* the transmission patterns of this marsh in Rhode Island.' Reynolds leaned forward for the kicker.

'The organo-chips are moving, scientists believe, communicating as they move; and if this is the case, all the razor wire in the world will not stop them from spreading, taking root, and multiplying, wherever the tide floats them. And now this message.'

'TransCom must be really pissed,' the pilot remarked, in some awe at what he'd done.

'Shhh,' Ela hissed. Already she was engrossed in a commercial featuring Brooke Denali, from *Pain*, selling rectal deodorant. 'Flatter your fanny,' Brooke whispered as men with no definite sexual orientation pulled lace in waves over her buttocks. Brooke Denali was Ela's favourite TV star. After 'The News with Ned Reynolds' she flipped right back to a special season premiere of *Pain in the Afternoon*.

'That's what's-his-name, isn't it?' the pilot said, peeking out from under the face-sucker to steal some of her popcorn. 'The guy who just got engaged; in real life, he's really rich on the show?'

481

'Jason Rock.'

'And Brooke Denali's his wife?'

'Yeah. But she lost her memory. Some Japanese guys tried to steal her dog-video and locked her in the fridge, and the loss of oxygen caused amnesia. Now she's hooked up with an Adornista cell that wants to kill Chase MacBride, 'cause he's gonna turn Baja California into a whale theme park, which would be really good for Mexico 'cause of their unemployment, but she has no idea he's her husband.'

'And him?'

'Oh, he's Thorn Savage,' Ela continued, popping a new can of Zero Cola. 'He's the son of MacBride's biggest enemy. He just got elected Congressman, and he's got the hots for Simone, who's MacBride's illegitimate daughter, but no one knows that; he's about to ruin MacBride Software 'cause he knows that Chase's father bribed someone for their licensing rights, way back when.'

God scampered into the room in his freeze-bolt-freeze rhythm. The rat was still elated with all the possibilities of this apartment, after the confines of cages, and planes, and hotels. He sniffed around the skirts of the bed and touched the pilot's bare foot, hanging off the edge. The pilot lifted him onto the covers. The rat snuggled his way into the nest of sheets, searching for popcorn.

'That's their daughter?' the pilot asked, happy to talk to Ela about anything, even soap operas. 'Chase's wife's daughter, I mean.'

'Jessica. That's right. She just slept with a rollerblader in a green face-sucker, who I think is one of the Adornistas. She's suing Grant, Chase's son, because of a car accident – but I kinda think she's

482

falling for him. Of course he doesn't know she's pregnant, because of the rollerblader.'

'So she's gonna fall down the stairs, right?'

Ela hesitated.

'What do you mean?'

Her voice was suddenly devoid of relief.

'It's what always happens, on Pain. When someone gets pregnant.'

The bed rocked as Ela sat up from her pillows.

'You don't have to get so sarcastic. There's nothing wrong with Pain.'

'I din' say anything.'

The pilot lifted off his goggles and saw, as his vision adjusted to the gloomy room, that he had exactly mimicked the timing and nature of Ela's movements.

'It's your voice. I can tell. You think it's trash.' Ela noticed God, and her face screwed up. She dropped the shutter-goggles among the sheets, and threw her half-full can of cola at the bedroom door.

'I don't think it's trash. I don't—' the pilot struggled to remain neutral '— I don't think it's anything. It's like Zero Cola. It's like anesthetic. There's nothing to feel.'

Ela rolled over, away from him, into the popcorn bowl.

The pilot bit down on the defense, and the resulting anger.

'I can't help how it affects me, Ela. It just seems so – distant. Pain. Even the news. It's as if the real world didn't exist.'

'You're just making speeches.' She stuffed popcorn in her mouth, and licked at the dripping butter.

The elastic shock of a bomb blast gently rattled the windows.

He pushed one fist into another, trying to define exactly what he meant. 'It's not that people don't die, or kill, or have babies. On interactive TV, just like in the real world. But somehow here, well the 3-D is too good. It's as if we need clumsiness, and poor resolution to understand things. We need to make an effort so our brains can feel. On *Pain*, on the news, we get sex, death, luxury, a little social message in eight minutes before the commercial, so we don't have to work. We don't have to, well, *look* for anything. It makes everybody passive, on either side of the camera. And that's the definition of dead. Because we don't feel hard anymore, or understand, which is the same thing. Feeling too hard gets in the way of buying rectal deodorant. See, if we understood something we might be less worried about earwax odor. But we're all dead, and TV's there to help us forget we aren't living anymore.'

He tickled God's stomach, to take some of the weight from this discussion. But ever since the trip the rat had refused to do tricks. He just burrowed deeper into the sheets.

'That should be just about perfect for you, then,' Ela remarked, from under a butter-coated pillow. 'Seems to me you've spent your life hanging out with the dead. Your brother. Your friend, in the islands.'

The pilot got off the bed. He located his vodka flask and topped it up from PC's liquor cabinet. He put on pants, boots, his travel jacket and went out for a walk. Ela's words stayed with him. The image that had surged unbidden into his mind while talking with her also remained; the memory of Greenwood Cemetery, and the constant buzz of electronic voices rising ghostly from underground, where the dead watched TV.

He walked faster, away from Riverside Drive. Ahead, well down West End Agenue, a New Omega Plan district was rising over the Zabar's Salient. 'Old Vienna,' a sign blinked. 'Its *Kaffee*, its waltzes, its *Gemutlichkeit* – its SHOPPING!' For the first time since he got back the hangover of travel was vanished from the pilot's brain.

Eltonjohn was no more dead, he thought – even Eltonjohn, slowly tumbling at the bottom of the Gulf Stream somewhere, small crabs fastened to the last gray shreds of flesh, bones growing whiter as they were buffed and polished by the sand; even Eduard, whose bones had long ago bleached, splintered, granulated, and rolled down the Morava, into the Danube, and finally into the sturgeon-rich dung of the Black Sea; even that unaccountable woman in the jumpseat of the sunken B-17; were no more dead than how most people in a Liteworld society spent their lives.

Sirens moaned far downtown. A flight of Cobra helicopters followed the river to a Special Forces base. The pilot sucked from his flask, gently, like pulling at a nipple.

Smuggling might hurt, it might even be wrong, but wrong or painful, at least it felt. At least it was active, at least it tried. At least, he thought, it got up and took a poke at something.

He bought take-out goat curry from a Vicious Vindaloo, then – realizing that what he'd thought was hunger was ache of a different kind – gave it to a homeless family in Strauss Park.

Down 103rd Street, three men festooned with

broken headsuckers, cellphones, radios, and ancient tape players stopped to stare at him as he passed. They were dressed in cast-off clothes. The features of the men were abstract in the manner of all those afflicted with TDF, as if they were listening to the theme song of a faraway serial, as, most likely, they were. They turned and followed the pilot and he had to dodge into a bodega till the tee-dees had drifted off again. While he waited he bought a cheap Venezuelan kitchen knife, and stashed it in the top of his right boot.

He said nothing to Ela when he returned to the apartment, but she had heard him come in, and removed the shutter-goggles. She took one look at him and said, 'You're going to do it, aren't you? What my father told you about.'

He nodded.

'You're crazy. You'll get caught, for sure.'

He looked around for his ECM-pak. It was in the bedroom somewhere. He had not touched it since his last scan, almost four days ago. From Ela's shucked headpiece, the sounds of unfollowed drama emanated, like roaches singing.

'Please, Joe?'

He'd not heard that amount of crank in her since the Watap longhouse. He looked up. Her eyes were very bright. Her face was pale. Her hair was snarled, the multicolored ends greasy with popcorn butter. She looked more like an elf than ever.

'Please, Joe. Why can't you leave it alone? Look, I'll turn off the TV?' She pinched the remote. The screen hissed, and went dark. Silence, in all its richness, flooded the room.

'It's important, Ela,' he said. 'I do believe in the Trade. I know there's lots of things wrong with it. But—'

486

'He's using you,' she said. 'He won't do it himself.'

'It doesn't matter.'

'You'll get hurt!'

'I'll be OK. I've thought it out. I'll do a practice run first.' He sat down on the bed. He felt as if one hundred pounds of poisonous waste that had been sitting in his duodenum for the last week had suddenly lightened – a percentage bled off with hope for movement. 'Can't you understand that, Ela? I don't want to be stuck. I don't want to live a life where I can't move. I'm not good, that way.'

Her eyes were pink, from shutter-fatigue. They fixed on him as if he were a screen, out of focus, lousy picture.

'Draw me a sheep,' she said abruptly. She was deliberately harking back to *The Little Prince*, and the common ground of childhood; but he shook his head.

'You'll just say it's a hat,' he told her, 'like everyone else.'

Outside the window of PC's bedroom, illuminated in the glow from a hundred apartments, a peregrine falcon plummeted at eighty m.p.h., talons first into a pigeon flapping peacefully through the air currents surrounding the building. There was an explosion of feathers, turned yellow in the electric light. The falcon spread its pinions to brake its fall, then swept lazily up the darkness toward its ledge, the pigeon lolling in the grip of long claws.

The pilot saw nothing but movement, and a footnote of pigeon fuzz. The event, in any case, was not uncommon in the City.

'Then go ahead,' Ela said, flinging her hair back, bending hard to look into his eyes. 'Smuggle,

487

smuggle everything, everywhere. But don't go sticking your head down the dragon's throat!'

Rocketman came into the bedroom, silent, unnoticed.

The pilot stroked Ela's leg gently under the covers.

'Maybe we could get back together,' she said. 'Like we were in Breslau.'

'You mean, if I don't go?'

She nodded.

'You're being predictable, Ela.'

She flushed.

'Then I'm gonna come with you.'

'Now you're just being silly.'

'Just for the "practice run." '

Rocketman cleared his throat, making them both jump and twist to see him standing next to the door jamb.

'We all have to do something,' he announced lugubriously. 'There's a couple of dudes in a limo out front, and they're watching this apartment through nightscopes.'

34

'The patron god of smugglers is the Yoruban deity,
Exu. God of the absurd, of change and quantum
leaps, he is also the god of jokes; for the one thing
even BON cannot bust at checkpoints is a cool
sense of humor.'

Hawkley
The Freetrader's Almanac and Cookbook

Twenty-four hours and a series of hasty phone calls
later they all went down to the TransCom Building –
for different reasons, with different expectations, but
all knowing this was most likely the last expedition
they would ever embark on together, and deriving
some bittersweet pleasure from the fact – took
the Number 1 train to Times Square, changed to the
shuttle, then caught the Number 6 at Grand Central,
and got off at 28th Street.

Ela rode at first with her arms around both her
waist and the pilot's, then pulled back; to arm-in-arm,
to hands at her sides, to crossing her arms over her
stomach, as the realization of where they were going
came to her.

The pilot carried God, safely fastened in his cage.

In his pockets were a TransCom security passcard, his UCC-card in the name of 'Brian Veitch', six sacks of Korean deli peanuts, and nothing else.

It was just after eleven p.m., and the 28th Street subway stop was empty and hollow with vanished noise when the train had gone. The pilot led them down the steps at the end of the station, into the tunnel. A stigs victim, chased from his place of darkness by their passage, rose confusedly in the light of the emergency lamps, the wounds on his hands and chest gaping wetly, crying 'Aah!' Raising his arms in the classic crucifix position so that Ela, who had never seen stigs people in Lakewood, gasped and recoiled.

The passcard still worked, and they filed into the third basement of the TransCom Building and took the backup freight elevator to the 94th floor, two floors down from the penthouse.

As they rode upward, the pilot noticed, scrawled in marker on the lime paint of the elevator above the controls, the words: 'PILOT GO BACK BON HERE!' followed by the single initial, 'O'.

The pilot's chest tightened. Obregon had tried to warn him. As Roberto had, with his letter. He had a mental picture of the two of them, the big Cuban and the dark, small smuggler, marshaled in the violent sun and gleaming razor ribbon of Oakdale.

God, sniffing the carpet-cleaner and freon aroma of passing floors, twitched his whiskers mightily and sneezed. The pilot, relieved to be distracted from thoughts of his friends, bent to cage level.

'Almost home, boy,' he whispered, 'almost home.'

The 94th floor held the airco relay station that fed his former apartment. The pilot flicked the emergency stop switch, carried God's box onto the landing, and opened the tiny, hand-carved doors. The rat hopped out, whiskers still twitching, and sat up on his hind legs. He checked out all four directions, then scuttled over to sniff at the entry port to the airco complex. The pilot pulled it wide for him, and stashed the peanuts in the opening.

'Welcome home, old fella,' he said. He didn't make any promises about coming back; this was not something he was certain of. It struck him that he was getting used to dumping animals and people that were close to him, and the thought made him wince a little, but did not make him hesitate, because he did not know what choice he had. He returned to the elevator, flicked the emergency switch to 'off', and punched the controls, sending the elevator back down to the 30th floor and the air-conditioning relay for that part of the building. There he led them through the humming ventilation systems, up ring ladders in hidden airshafts to the 34th floor. They used successively smaller tunnels till they were all of them lodged in a square duct next to a plastic grate that, by the pilot's reckoning, lay directly over the hallway leading off the reception area of the only federal government offices listed in the building.

'You *sure* you don't want to can this?' Ela whispered. Her voice trembled a little. She cleared her throat twice.

'Yeah. You?'

She shrugged.

'It's just a scout, anyway,' the pilot added. 'The secretary said no one was around today. And nobody should be here at this hour.'

Minimal lighting and sound seeped from the grate underneath them. Just the hiss of climate-control, the moribund air of overinsulated space.

The pilot pulled up the grate, stuck his head down from the ceiling. He saw no trace of security cameras, or laser alarms. All of that would be at the entrance and in the elevator lobbies. He twisted himself around, lowered his legs and ass through the opening, and dropped gently to the synthetic pile below.

When they were all down they padded here and there along the gray corridors, reading the fake-wood signs that were glued to the various doors, sneezing from the dust. There were no windows off these corridors, no access to the outside. No horizon, the pilot thought, and shivered a little, mentally.

'Justice Department, Immigration and Naturalization, Office of Professional Responsibility,' Ela called quietly.

'Torts Bureau, Civil Division, Admiralty/Aviation?' Rocketman asked.

'US Trustees, Bankruptcy,' the pilot muttered doubtfully.

Finally they all collected around one door at the end of the long 'C'-plan of corridors.

Two signs were fastened to this door. The first read 'Department of Defense: NSA Regional Office.' The second said 'Bureau of Nationalizations: Technical Development Administration: Northeast Sector/ Liaison Office.'

'This is it,' the pilot said.

'Aah,' Rocketman agreed.

'I wish I'd brought the ECM,' the pilot muttered. The pak could have picked up the security wavelengths, the higher impedance that might warn of late-night activity in this office. Without it he felt like he was wearing no clothes – unprotected and cold.

He thought, This was how most people went through life, with no control over the forces that affected them, and maybe it was because of this he had taken to walking around half-naked at PC's, and earlier, on the Flying Boat; to regain contact with most people's reality. At any rate, it would have been tough to shlep the ECM through the airco ducts, although two weeks ago, he knew, he would have managed it, somehow. 'Ahh, fuck it,' he said, and took out his key card.

Ela said nothing. Her hands were twisted together in absolute nervousness. Her eyes were big and dark like a cat's. The pilot touched her shoulder, gently. She jumped, reached for him in turn, then pulled her hand back, just short of touching.

The pilot slipped the card into the slot beside the door. The handle moved. A tumbler clicked, the door opened. He raised his eyebrows at Rocketman, listened for a second or two, and moved inside.

The office was dark, except for the glow of video terminals. The splash of light from the hallway sketched out a wall lined with floppy files, hard-copy cabinets. VR workstations covered a long workbench. The screensavers moved in slo-mo, all similar, all showing a flat four-color landscape, with living trees and rolling weaponry, being stripped and ruined by an invisible force until nothing was left but bones and craters and blown-out battle-tanks and shapes quite foreign to what they once had been.

A faint hum rose from the massed machines. An even fainter odor, as of orchids left too long in water, tinged the close air.

The lights came on. The pilot glanced around, expecting to see Ela or Rocketman with a hand on the switch. Instead:

Three men sit in office chairs on each side of the doorway. One of them holds a small H&K MP5KS machine-pistol in his right hand. He is thick, short, in his forties. His eyes are a little hollow. The thin black beard does little to conceal a chin that is really no more than a slight rest-area between throat and nose. It is the engineer from Chitral; the one who hated *nan*.

The second man is in his late fifties or early sixties, with thin gray hair cut long enough to hang over the back of his collar. He is stooped, even when seated. He has very fleshy lips, red as liver, compressed downward. His eyes are light, coolly gray, exceedingly clear. He wears a fashionable green monkey jacket with a green paisley handkerchief folded in the breast pocket, and a green bow tie.

The third man is obese. His skin is without color. He wears a cheap anorak much too small for his giant gut. Under the plastic ski colors can be seen a filthy purple waistcoat that has no room to close. He slouches in the ergonomic office chair, arms crossed protectively over the anorak, watching the pilot from beneath eyelids that are so fat they fold, three times, like a lizard's.

The Cayman.

Time freezes. A great bubble of oxygen lodges in the pilot's esophagus, asking to be used. The pilot looks at Ela, who stands rigid in the doorway, willing her to sense what is going on, to back out, to run like a scared squirrel – but the second man, the older one with fleshy lips and the pistol, already has seen her. He glances sideways at Ela, the way a barracuda looks at another barracuda. His lips part upward, like a fish smiling.

'Thank you, Mrs Taylor,' he says. 'I never doubted you would bring them in — eventually.'

There had to be a threshold of psychological shock, the pilot thought; a threshhold that had just been bulldozed upward by the sight of these men; but even so the only shock, or surprise, came from the fact that he felt so little shock or surprise.

He looked at Rocketman, to share the vacuum, but Rocketman was not there.

Of course, the pilot thought. Rocketman had known. Even, or especially, through the filter of his paranoia, Rocketman had known, just as the pilot had known. Known this was the only resolution to the tension keen within her; this was the only bridge between the opposites in her mind. Betrayal was the one art that could unite opposites, he thought vaguely. Betrayal was an act of universal, as opposed to individual, love, because it brought together what could not be joined. Ela, in her own way, was trying to love him; love him, love her father, love the part of herself that sought escape from the living death of Lakewood — love the part of her that still ached to be a pom-pom football cheerleading girl at Lakewood High.

'I'm sorry, Joe,' she muttered, not looking at him.

'Don't worry about it.' There was a gentleness to his voice that surprised even him.

'I din' want to. I wouldn't have done anything if you hadn't come here.' She looked at the older man. 'I'm sorry,' she repeated.

The pilot shrugged. 'I'm only going to jail, I guess,' he said. 'You've got your own jail, all locked up inside you.'

'Very profound,' the man with the machine-pistol commented.

'And *you*,' the pilot said. 'You were in Chitral. You must have been in Breslau, too?'

The man smiled. 'We were behind you,' he said, 'the whole way. Till Daud Khan. Real cute, that was – faking a kidnap. Gotta hand it to you guys.'

'Excuse me,' the fish-faced man said. The sarcasm was heavy in his voice. 'I know I'm not as *important* as TransCom, but—'

The man with the beard made a magnanimous gesture with the muzzle of his gun.

'I haven't forgotten. BON gets 'em first.'

'TransCom?' Ela said.

'It's obvious,' the fish-faced man replied. He had a very light accent, the pilot thought. Not Czech; possibly Austrian, or even Polish. 'They didn't like Mr Marak's trick,' he told Ela, 'of bringing in the Korean organic chips. That got them really rather upset, no? Now there is a whole salt marsh system in New England that is breaking their monopoly every day. Free-growing organic micro-chips. The natural-growth patents don't matter a damn against free-growing algae. It will cost them billions of dollars – billions!'

'What for me hangin' here?' the Cayman interrupted hoarsely. He blinked, and his eyelids rolled over his pupils, folded back. 'I *mira* the man, *esta todo*.' He licked his lips.

'You *mira* him, Fawcett?' the chinless man said. 'You confirm he's the pilot of the pirate jet? *Trente Setiembre*, Rio Chingado.'

The Cayman hesitated, looking at the pilot now.

'Well?' the TransCom man insisted.

The pilot stared back at the Cayman. Looking at his leached features he felt he was smelling the jungle again; the centuries of rot piling up, piling up, covering the corpses that covered the corpses on the rain forest floor.

The Cayman looked away.

'*Claro*,' he said. 'dat's de raton run misuyunyu veggie-chips.'

The chinless one, without shifting the aim of his weapon, pulled a folded form and an inkpad from his shirt pocket, and handed them to the Cayman.

'Put your thumbprint on the line, there.'

'Enough,' the fish-faced man interrupted, 'you can finish your business later.' He got up from his seat in a bent, circular sort of motion and went over to the workbench. He punched a series of electronic relays, and unlocked a circuit with a passcard. Impatiently he handed Ela the pistol he was carrying, removed a shiny half-sucker from its stand beside the keyboard, and fitted it over his eyes. Settling into the chair, his body seemed to relax into the unyielding curves of it. Then he started tapping at one of the keyboards. On three monitors in front of him the ruined landscapes vanished in a phosphoric blink, as if finally vaporized by an ultimate weapon, and the realization shone in the pilot's brain with equal luminosity. This was Peter Brodin.

This was Bokon Taylay.

'Armored circuits to Fort Meade,' Brodin spoke in a rhythm, almost a little song to the snicky plastic percussion of his keyboard. '—encryption. Scramble. Control. Grid, phase-in? OK, OK.'

A web of patterns appeared on the three screens. The patterns shifted, flowed, rearranging themselves like colored glass in a kaleidoscope. The lines were green and black, as on the ECM's scan, but much finer and denser than the ECM showed. Most of the servers were unlabeled.

Wildnet.

Overhead, the lights and shine of the Web bubbled like a heavy cover of altocirrus with every molecule of vapor lit from inside.

Brodin joysticked forward, flying under, over, between the Wildnet lines, which grew bigger, flicked behind, like a chopper evading power cables.

'Eighteen-point-forty-six activity,' Brodin muttered. 'Way below average obviously, but within the margin for error.' He hit another series of keys and squares of text appeared on the right-hand screen. His head turned as he scanned the boxes. 'Activity on the 77 Pell Street SAP. No traffic associated with you. But that's the whole problem with you people, no? The indies. The little fellows. You have networks we don't know.'

'What are you talking about?' the pilot asked, ingenuously, thinking that if he could distract the two men he might just have time to reach for the shiv in his workboot.

'Don't tell him,' the TransCom man said quickly, 'it's Level Four classified.'

'What difference does it make?' Brodin replied.

'Si,' the Cayman agreed. 'Choo nail his ass anyway.' He chuckled, looking at Brodin for approval, but Brodin said nothing, and the Cayman licked his lips and shut up.

Ela shifted the pistol in her hands. She had both fists around the butt, FBI-style. She pointed it delicately at the pilot, without looking at his face. But he could look at hers, and wonder why it was so taut and pale, yet basically the same as always; wonder, if the sea rose in protest when the wind switched directions on it, if the air bubbled crazily when the land changed temperature, how the cyclone of human treachery could have no more outward manifestation than this.

'Here—' Brodin hit a few more keys. On the two left-hand screens, the point-of-view surged upward, following the wild lines where they straggled from secure access providers toward the jewel-filled clouds above; and then, just like an aircraft breaking cloud cover, Brodin had entered the overarching Web, moving faster by a factor of twenty, of a hundred, than the pilot had ever navigated before. Following the trail of a Wildnet data link, lights burbling around them exactly the way the phosphorescence had streaked past the pilot's eye when he was diving in the blood-warm waters of the lagoon at Pulau Karang.

Brodin pulled back on the joystick. Their speed slowed. Now a lozenge of dark neon flashed, on and off, in the screens' corner. 'CONTROL', it read, in deep pink letters.

The screens went dark. Suddenly, instead of the opalescent sheen of the Web, a half-dozen black sine curves bent back across all three terminals, undulating like snakes.

'OK,' Brodin continued. His voice was pleased, as if he'd just pulled a rabbit from a top hat. 'Here is the harmonic. Music, you see, a symphony of information, made up of billions of notes.'

'Why are you telling him this, Brodin?' Ela asked him, 'if it's so secret? What do you mean, it doesn't matter?'

The fish-faced man smiled.

'Because I think we owe him an explanation, after this chase. It is traditional, in English thrillers, no? But we own the subtext, so he cannot by some, ah, dexterous feat of heroism, turn the tables on us, the way they do in thrillers. The subtext is where control lies; that's what Lacan really meant.'

'The machine-pistols is where control lies,' the bearded man growled, patting his. Brodin ignored him.

'Also,' he continued, 'perhaps he can help us better, if he understands, when he goes to Oakdale.'

Ela looked blank.

'That is the other reason,' Brodin explained. 'Oakdale. The interrogation center. We need to get all the information on your father out of him, my dear. And we can't exactly let him loose after that, now can we?'

'But you'll get the information from me!'

'My dear girl,' Brodin said, 'you don't really think your father told *you* everything?'

He noticed the expression on the pilot's face. 'Don't look so sick, Mr Marak,' he added. 'It is the historical role of women, to switch sides. Helen of Troy, and so forth. Men fight for one side or another, yes? Perhaps it doesn't matter which. The balance is the point. It is women who keep the balance from getting too uneven.'

He looked at Ela with eyes that were interested, and not unsympathetic.

'He goes to interrogation tonight.'

'After that, we get him,' the bearded man muttered.

'TransCom were *extremely* upset with Mr Marak,'

Brodin continued. Then, going on as if he'd never been interrupted, he said, 'The notes to this symphony are what I call Fons. They are information broken down into the tiniest possible bits – tone, meaning, context, and so forth. English has an average of 4.7 bits of information per letter; each bit has approximately seven Fons. Then the Fons are broken down further, into Negons – Fons which have command value, as in imperatives, negations, orders – and Infons, which include all unweighted communications. Pure information, in the truest sense.

'You see—' Brodin tapped out another sequence. The sine curves split in two and multiplied, the data curves, the black snakes of information he was talking about dancing crazily, brightly on the three screens '—an organization that grows over a certain size always hits a singularity where the number of Negons in a given piece of communication suddenly jumps much higher than the Infons. That is because the organization, at this scale, all at once becomes much more occupied with regulating itself; it also spends less time processing information to and from its environment. Typically this threshold occurs at the level of 66.78 percent. Negons, that is.

'Now this jump in Negons is like a fingerprint. If you process it according to my algorithms, it not only identifies what type of organization has generated this piece of communication, but it identifies the organization itself. That is the beauty of negative information, you see. You can define yourself as easily by what you are not, as by what you are. And you can only do this with Negons; Infons are too volatile.'

'You wouldn't believe,' the pilot muttered, 'where I heard this shit before.'

501

'Shannon had an inkling,' Brodin replied seriously, still snicking at his keyboard. 'Zatt and Chomsky too; but they never perfected the algorithms.'

The bits of light on the screens began to sort themselves out, clustering around seven or eight points in different corners.

'Through NSA, we have access to all telephone, radio, cable, and video-broadcast communications in this hemisphere,' Brodin continued. 'Now, watch' (he hit a button), 'we ask the program to search for Negons that define a smuggling organization – Negons typical of concealment, travel, cargo, timetables, weight, foreign names, radio frequencies, chart data – and Bingo!' He hit another key, like Horowitz, flipping his wrist high in the air, gray locks flying. 'We get a TA, a traffic analysis, of all such organizations, by urgency, by depth, by sector.'

The bits of light fled their congregation points. They straightened, trembling, into several dozen broad lines.

More tapping on the keyboard.

'Then we correlate this with intelligence. Known names, locations, etcetera, and – Bingo again!'

The wrists flew.

'It's probabilities, really,' he said. 'Once we ID the group, and the urgency level, we fall back on human data. Like, when you ran the bodies from the Double Headed Shot Cays, that was a DeLisi contact. Once we knew that, once we sussed it would happen within two days, we staked out the Cays *because they'd used them before.*'

The lines on the screens flailed, whipped around like cobras being annoyed with a stick. Suddenly, they fused and became one long, regular sine curve with peaks and valleys very close together. Paragraphs of text appeared on one of the screens above the curve.

'Here we ID one particular organization,' Brodin said. 'The peaks and troughs are very close, indicating there will be action soon, I think.' He peered at a text box. 'Aha! Forty-six percent accounting traffic.' He pointed at the screen. 'Spirit Knives-Organizatsni, the computer says, they always have heavy accounting. Thirty-nine percent disciplinary, they disguise it as food orders.' He frowned. 'Although I must admit I thought we'd broken the tai-lo's network. In fact we almost caught you once, through his Negon—'

'Drop the gun,' Ela said.

Brodin switched to the joystick. The patterns shifted left, neatly. Gray hair fringed his half-sucker. His mouth pulled downward at the interruption.

The pilot swiveled away from the screens to face Ela – but Ela was leaning forward in the direction of the TransCom goon and she held Brodin's pistol in both hands and the pistol was aimed at the bearded man's head and its barrel trembled only a tiny bit.

'What the fuck are you doing?' the TransCom man said. His grip on the machine-pistol tightened, but the silencer was pointed away from Ela and clearly he was unsure whether he could line it up in time.

'Chingon,' the Cayman whispered. He looked less uncomfortable. Things suddenly had been reduced to a level he could understand, of threats, and potential mayhem, and how they balanced each other out.

'I'm counting to three,' Ela said. Her voice was tighter even than her grip on the pistol. Brodin looked around, finally, flipping the half-sucker up as he did so. His eyes moved back and forth, fast, efficient.

'You idiot,' he hissed at the TransCom man.

'You can do nothing,' he told Ela. 'I have people stationed at the entrances.'

'One,' Ela whispered.

'Stop this foolishness. Now, Mrs Taylor!'

'Two.'

The small ventilation fans inside the data-processing units were the loudest sound in the room.

'Three.'

'Do as she says,' Brodin ordered the bearded man.

The pilot spun left, his right arm hooking around the Cayman's elbow while his left pulled, from Fawcett's boot, a long thin knife with a handle made of jaguar bone.

'*Maricon*,' the Cayman hissed.

'Bad place to hide a shiv,' the pilot told him, stepping back but holding the knife ready for use, his thumb pressed against the flat of the blade.

'Slow, real slow,' Ela hissed in a tone she'd learned from VR serials. The TransCom man looked at the whiteness of the woman's knuckles, and laid his gun carefully on the wall-to-wall.

'What do we do now, Joe?' Ela whispered.

The pilot said nothing. His chest was exploding with new hope. Only part of the hope had to do with avoiding BON's interrogation and whatever TransCom was going to do with him. The rest — most of it — had to do with Ela, and the rescue of vital contact with her.

In one swift happy movement he slipped the jaguar-bone knife in his pocket, scooped up the machine-pistol, flicked off the safety and discharged half the magazine at the workbench with all its telephones, half-sucker interfaces, relays, satellite tuners, modems and scanners and video displays.

The silenced bullets made little cracking noises as they busted the sound barrier before plunging into the equipment. Silicon exploded into powder. The phosphor tubes disintegrated. Blue-green sparks arced in tiny fireworks. A fine green rain of chopped glass fell throughout the office. Chips of plastic, gold wire, and overworked metal ricocheted off the walls. The warm-broccoli stink of organic semiconductors suffused their taste buds.

'*Tchiot!*' Brodin screamed from the floor where he had dived for cover, and held out his hands at the broken machinery, as if in pain.

A Russian, the pilot thought. He felt an abstract sympathy; the man was in love with his machines.

'Fuck,' Ela muttered, astonished by the violence of the bullets.

'Come on,' the pilot said, 'let's get outta here,' and gestured at the door.

He held the machine-pistol on Brodin and the Cayman while Ela struggled to give the TransCom man a leg up into the air-conditioning ducts. As soon as he got into the duct the bearded man tried to scamper his escape, crawling fast for help, you could hear the metallic whanging of his knees. The pilot, sensing things about to veer fatally out of control, braced to jump after him – but just then the thudding stopped.

'Aaaah.' A voice came hollow and eerie from the grate opening. 'A scared little *rabbit*. I wondered what you guys were up to.'

'Rocketman,' Ela whispered. Her eyes warmed as she listened.

They shepherded the three men down the airco

ducts. This was not easy; the Cayman's bulk barely fit through the tighter passages, and he complained without cease, his dank breath and sweat-smell over-powering in the confined areas. Finally they reached the backup freight elevator landing. Both Brodin and the TransCom man seemed convinced that the build-ing was impossible to escape from. Their eyes were calm. At any rate, neither of them argued with the muzzle of Ela's pistol.

In the third basement there was a battery room for emergency power, and the pilot locked the prisoners inside. The Cayman and the TransCom agent argued now in Spanish. Brodin said nothing. The risks and possibilities of Oakdale and the massed threats of BON and TransCom were beginning to seriously raise voltage in the brain and sweat in the palms of the pilot and he did not spare a second glance or thought for the man he'd been trying to identify in one way or another since the Rio Chingado.

As they came out of the tunnel into the 28th Street station a gaggle of Safe People, late-night partygoers in Donna Karan black, moved nervously back against the wall. The three of them swung out of the dark entrance and loped quickly by, weapons clutched in filthy hands, eyes sharp with escape, faces and clothes smeared with soot from the ducts. The Safe People said and did nothing; the safest policy, then and always, in a subway station at night.

Plain gray vans were parked down the street from the station entrance. Thin-faced men with armpit bulges stood in polyester jackets under the sculpted electric 'T' logo at the TransCom doors.

The three of them ditched their weapons down a storm drain and took a cab downtown. Judging this to be far enough away from TransCom, they paid it off at 14th and Second.

Sirens howled in the distance. Smoke rose in gray dribbles from an oil-barrel stove warming the inhabitants of a Japanese compact in the bottom of a huge pothole on 14th Street. Ozone clouds teetered softly overhead. A quick sleet drew soot streaks down their features. The lights from shops and streetlights spilled long ribbons of yellow, green, red, blue on the wet tar. They stood around, not looking at each other.

'He found me three months ago,' Ela said finally. 'Brodin.'

'It don't matter,' the pilot told her. 'Not anymore.'

'I hated my father so much,' she said. 'I would have done anything to get back at him.'

'I know.'

'They wanted to find him so bad.' She was working her hands again, twisting the fingers around each other. 'They couldn't figure out, like, why his groups didn't get caught. They think he has a secret way of communicating with them.'

He reached out and grabbed her hands, to stop the finger-Houdini.

'But when I saw my dad,' she said, 'it all went. The hate, and everything. He's just a funny man. He's not too happy. He's getting old. *Really* old.' She shook her head. 'I didn't know what to do. I still don't believe in what he does. But.'

'Ela,' he said, 'it's OK.'

'I feel much better now,' she said.

'What you gonna do?' Rocketman asked.

'I'm not sure. I can't stay here. They'll be lookin' for me, now. I'm an outlaw too, I guess.' She looked up at Rocketman and smiled. 'Just like you.'

Rocketman moved off the corner, checking up and down Second.

'I thought maybe I'd go back to Chitral,' she said. 'Work in that hospital awhile, with PC.'

'You'll never get there,' the pilot said, 'with the snow. Not till spring.'

'There's always a way.'

'They'll be looking for you, like you said.'

'But I learned,' she told him. 'I learned from you. How to get across borders.' She pulled out her fake UCC-card. 'I'll need a new one of these, for starters.'

'Shit,' he said. 'Ela.'

Her face seemed to shine in his eyes. Now it had reacquired all the radiance, the light it had gained during their trip; all the fizz it had lost when they came back to New York. It made sense, at last, that the fizz should have evaporated so quickly.

'I couldn't go through with it, Joe,' she said. 'It wasn't only because of my father. I couldn't do it to you.'

For some reason he fixated on the little bump on her nose. It had become the focus of what he felt for her, the knot that connected all the little strings and gears and balances that were Ela, and the thought of that bump on her nose going out of his life seemed the saddest event that could happen to anyone.

An AGATE Apache thudded overhead, searchlights poking widely at the night. Above the chopper, a jet laid a bright contrail across the city's shine. The pilot felt a familiar lust for that jet; for taking off with no flight plan and heading toward a horizon that never ended.

But the lust, for once, was small. To fly well took energy, and he had none left.

'Ela,' he said.

'Yeah?'

'I'm sorry you never made that marching squad.'

'It's OK,' she told him. 'Maybe it was for the best.'

'I'll see ya,' he said quickly while his throat would let him.

'Yeah,' she said, 'take care of yerself.' She stood quickly on tiptoe to brush his lips with hers. Then she walked over to Rocketman and threw her arms around him.

'Goodbye, Tin Man,' she said.

'Aaah,' the big man replied. He hesitated a little. Then he hugged her so hard she came off the ground.

'You be careful now,' he told her. 'And if you get to Chitral—'

'I'll look out for her.'

Rocketman nodded. He put her down. She looked at the pilot once, briefly. She walked fast around the corner and into the steam and rain and funny colors all smushed and smeared into the New York night. A small bar of music wafted behind her – something hummed, something out of Cole Porter – and was gone.

A long black limo that had been parked a little way up 14th Street ever since the taxi dropped them took off silently from the curb and accelerated in their direction.

Rocketman sees the rear window slide open, the shiny snout of a big semiautomatic shotgun stick out, a Benelli. He jumps on the pilot and drags him to the ground behind a parked car as the street-sweeper opens up, huge 'booms' of mixed twelve-gauge, blowing shop windows and neon and car doors and streetlights all to hell but missing the two men rolling on the ground entirely.

'You got that, pilot?' a voice shrieks, dopplering down amid the whine of the limo's tires as it accelerates down 14th toward the FDR, but the voice is still audible as it finishes. 'You nevah welsh on me again, Gwailo moth'fuck!'

Korean voices spring from windows and fruit stands; nervous, uninvolved.

Thin men and women dressed in tattered blankets climb out of the Nipponese wreck, out of the pothole, to peer with dull eyes at the unquiet city.

When there was no more sound of tires and engine, Rocketman sat up and brushed shattered safety glass off PC's camel's hair coat. He stared down the lights toward the highway.

'What the fuck was that?' he asked wonderingly.

'Fat Chico Fong,' the pilot said. 'No one else calls me "Gwailo moth'fuck."' He started to laugh. It was the laughter of control-lost, of total absurdity, of situations where everything was possible and therefore nothing was on the cards. It was more than halfway to crying.

Rocketman looked at him uncomfortably.

'I forgot about Chico,' the pilot whispered, when he had got his breath back. 'He must have staked out Bellevue, because of Carmelita, and when you started hanging there—' He nodded to himself, as the bits of data supported each other in his mind. 'It was him at PC's, not BON.'

The pilot wiped moisture from his eyes. Suddenly he did not feel like laughing anymore. His stomach felt bad. Ela was gone and that made a big hole in which the sourness of being shot at washed like lye.

He shook his head.

'I'm getting sick of all this, Rocketman,' he said. 'Really sick of this. You know somewhere we can go, 'n' hide, 'n' just rest for a while?'

Rocketman thought for a couple of seconds. He smiled, gently at first, then harder as the thought nestled home.

'Aaaah,' he growled. 'I got an idea.'

35

'If you wake at midnight, and hear a horse's
  feet,
Don't go drawing back the blind, or looking in
  the street.
Them that ask no questions isn't told a lie.
Watch the wall, my darling, while the Gentlemen
  go by!'

Rudyard Kipling
A Smuggler's Song

Two days before Thanksgiving. A wind blew out of
the northwest at fifteen to twenty knots, bringing
with it occasional flurries of sleet.

The wind shook the spruces, already brightly lit for
the holidays, running down the spine of Park Avenue.
It swung the fifty-foot-wide turkey of yellow bulbs
dangerously suspended over the intersection of 57th
and Fifth. It stiffened the fingers of trumpeters playing Olde Romanov ballads outside the Warner
Brothers/Imperial Russia Superstore at 58th and Park.
It burned the ears of vendors selling the hard-copy
Post (*Midtown Mystery Shootout*, the *Post*'s subhead read,
under sixty-point type that spelled US INVADES
CHIHUAHUA); made them stamp their feet and

512

fumble as they swiped UCCs through credit-checkers. It stole the smell of roasting chestnuts and charring pretzels from street vendors and whipped it around the noses of Salvation Army bands three blocks to the south. It hurt the sales of Hoffa disciples selling 'Holy Lottery' tickets on the corner. It did little to deter the thousands of multicolored shoppers as they panted and hustled in the lust of acquisition and the comfort of fur-lined Argentinian gaucho boots through the gleaming shops and restaurants and hotels.

At 3:17 in the afternoon two men stopped outside the brightly lit windows of a famous jewelry store. Shoppers and sightseers from New Jersey and Venezuela and Austria crowded outside the windows, staring through transparent, bomb-resistant screens at the sensitively decorated displays inside. The displays all entered around the theme 'A St Petersburg Harvest'; they featured lovely little automated figures that drank spiced wine, were blown up by Anarchists, went on sleigh rides in blizzards, ran sweatshops, ate mountains of colorful foods, wore lots of expensive jewelry, and beat the recalcitrant mujik.

One of the two men was large, coffee-colored, and in his late forties. He was dressed in gaucho boots, and a camel's hair coat. The other was fairly short, and freckled, and very young-looking. He wore a faded denim jacket, a jumpsuit, and work boots.

The two men looked at each other. The younger man smiled vaguely. The older one nodded, and they both started to strip off their clothes.

The crowds parted around them like dishwater around a squirt of detergent. Women screamed. A pretzel vendor chuckled. A man dressed in Pilgrim clothes – a tall black hat, tight collar, shoes with buckles — shook his bell furiously as if to call down the vengeance of a Puritan heaven. The younger of the two men went up to the prettiest woman he could see.

'Let's communicate?' he suggested.

The woman backed away, giggling nervously. 'Oh my God,' she kept saying, between giggles. 'Oh my God!'

The older of the two men sat under one of the St Petersburg windows and sucked his thumb.

A squad car full of City cops drove by. The cops laughed and pointed and went on their way.

A homeless man scooped up the loose clothes and bore them off before anyone noticed.

Two Swedish station wagons pulled up in a squeal of hot tires. The words 'MANHATTAN SAFETY VOLUNTEERS' were stenciled on the side. A troupe of vigilantes piled out. It looked like the cars were vomiting button-downs, and Maine hunting boots. They subdued the naked men with kicks and nightsticks and dragged them into the wagons. They drove their catch, pink lights flashing, to the vigilante post.

The two men were booked, covered in blankets, and sent downtown in a paddywagon full of shoplifters to be charged. After four hours they were brought up before Judge Lawrence I. Levine of the New York County Court, known to friends and associates everywhere as Lil.

'What were you doing on Fifth and 57th, naked?' Lil asked the older, taller of the two.

'Waiting for my daddy, your honor,' Rocketman replied. 'He told me to wait till he got back.'

'You wan' I should take this down?' the stenographer said.

'Take it down,' Lil said.

Rocketman obediently dropped his blanket. The courtroom applauded, politely.

'No, not you,' Lil said, tiredly. 'Put the blanket back on, we got clerks here who this is news to. Get his name, Brenda.'

'George Armstrong Custer,' Rocketman said.

'You're makin' that up,' Brenda said suspiciously.

'So Sioux me.'

'Oh, lord,' Lil sighed, thinking it was going to be one of those days. 'What were you doing?' he asked the younger man.

'Just tryin' to communicate,' the pilot told the judge.

Lil looked at his booking sheet. 'He was harassing women,' the liaison man from the Safety Volunteers said, 'in an unsanitary way. No clothes, no underwear, who knows what kind of aerosol contagion? We got witnesses,' he added, nodding to himself.

'I was tryin' to communicate with 'em, your honor,' the pilot insisted.

'You're outta your mind,' the judge told him. 'You think you're gonna communicate any better with no clothes on?'

'I was only tryin' to reduce the barriers between us.'

Lil leaned forward to stare at the pilot's face. The kid was serious, he thought. There wasn't a trace of a smile in the mouth or eyes. He thought for a brief instant of his own wife, with whom he had last communicated around the time their second girl was born, about seventeen years ago. Lil shuddered. He remembered the thousand murderers, ATM-kidnappers, rapists, smack dealers, and child molesters waiting to be processed through his court, and leaned over toward Brenda.

'They got UCC-cards?'

Brenda lifted her chin toward the pilot. 'He does.'

Lil looked at the pilot. 'You responsible for your friend?'

'Always,' the pilot said, putting his arm around Rocketman's neck.

The judge raised his gavel and smacked the table with it.

'Remanded for psychiatric evaluation,' he said, 'Bellevue. Get 'em outta here. Next!' Lawrence I. Levine said, in a tone that betrayed a deep suspicion that things were only going to get worse.

The big black nurse let Rocketman and the pilot into the ward on the 29th floor of the South Tower at Bellevue Hospital.

'Well,' she said, and took off her headphones. A voice crackled thinly from the wires — *Jesus needs a kickback too!*

'Look who's here,' the nurse continued. 'The Rocketman! *Yah!*' she screamed in his face.

'Peace up, Linda,' Rocketman said gently.

She looked into his chin with her large yellowed eyes. She pressed a button and pushed him down the hall. Two green-smocked attendants popped out of the staff coffee room.

'Search him for matches,' she ordered, looking at Rocketman's admission form, 'then throw this Negro's ass in preventive. I don' believe it,' she added. 'George A. Custer my ass, they don' even know who he is! That's the guy set fire to the roof,' she told the attendants.

516

The attendants looked at him indifferently, chewing bluish gum.

Rocketman smiled. The neon in the hallway seemed to burn a little less brightly.

The nurse looked at the pilot. He looked back at her.

'*Wachoo lookin' at, weirdo!*' she screamed.

The pilot was searched, as well. He had to sign UCC-chits in triplicate, agreeing to reimburse Omega/Health Commitment Systems Inc. for psychiatric services for both himself and Rocketman. Then he was given a green smock and assigned to a room walled in orange plastic, with a man who was unable to stop watching television and who was suspected of being pre-TDF.

His other roommates were a man who could not stop mimicking the expressions of everyone he saw, and a former meteorologist who believed he could predict the future the way he'd foreseen wind and precipitation. He had written his secret equation on the wall in green non-toxic wax crayon. HISTORY = HUMAN WEATHER, it read.

The pilot almost smiled when he saw the words. They made him think of Ela, how she would have laughed, the way she always did at pretentious statements concerning history.

After he had put on the pajamas he went straight to the toilet and carefully extracted from his asshole a latex condom, well greased with K-Y jelly, that contained: fifty matches, with striking surfaces; two sets of skeleton keys; a fake physician's ID; a tiny emerald pendant in the shape of a dolphin; and one-and-a-half ounces of perfect lapis lazuli from the Panjshir Valley in Afghanistan.

The lapis sparkled in the yellow light of the lavatory. Its blue was the blue of macaw's feathers, the azure of the Aegean on a perfect fall evening, the indigo hue at the rim of the world, as seen from an airplane, where the planet was turning into night.

The pilot flushed the empty condom and washed his hands. He looked at the stones for a full minute. Then he wrapped the contraband in toilet paper and hid it carefully in the rough gray underwear the attendants had given him.

He found Carmelita in the rec room, sitting by the window, staring at the TV in a personal island of space that advertised like a billboard the fact that she still was not talking.

He kneeled down in front of her and gently laced the pendant around her neck. He took one of her hands in both of his. Her fingers were cool.

'Carmelita,' he said. 'It's me. I'm back.'

Her face did not change. The lines in it were, if anything, stronger than before; they made her look both more determined, and older. Her long hair — dull, without sheen — had been trimmed and strapped back with a cheap velvet hair tie.

Her eyes, locked on the TV, danced with the flat bright images of the products currently being sold. They did not look at him, but the left hand tightened around his fingers, just a touch.

He pulled a chair over and sat next to her. He put his arm around her shoulders, his cheek next to her cheek, and hugged her for a long time.

Below him the river ran, strong and black as Dominican coffee, in a rush of broken visions to the sea.

THE END

About the Author

George Foy is a writer and journalist. He has published five novels, including *Challenge*, *Asia Rip* and *The Shift*. He has worked as a commercial fisherman, a vacuum-molding machine operator, and a paralegal in New York City law firms. He has traveled into Soviet-occupied Afghanistan with an arms-smuggling caravan, acted on network television, and participated in the creation of a CD-ROM game. He lives with his wife, daughter, and cat in New York City and Cape Cod.

THE SHIFT
George Foy

'I can't remember the last time a novel had me
flicking forward several pages to check that a
character was still alive, or punching the air in
delight as the hero twists his way out of danger
and turns the tables on a villain... This is Gibson
updated for the '90s'
SFX

Divorced, disillusioned and drinking too much, television writer Alex Munn is on the edge. For two years
he's been working on the ultimate drama series, a
ratings-winning schlockfest of sex, adventure and
violence that uses Virtix, a virtual reality technology
so good the viewer won't be able to tell the difference
between real life and *Real Life*, the new show.

To get away from it all, Alex has written an altogether darker story of his own: a Virtix program he
calls *Munn's World*. It depicts New York in the 1850s,
complete with horse-drawn carriages and its very own
serial killer – the Fishman – who prowls the gas-lit,
poverty-stricken streets, disembowelling his victims.
His nemesis is a lone cop called Alex Munn.

What happens next is impossible, unscripted, and
utterly terrifying. For the Fishman has somehow
escaped his virtual domain and followed Alex into the
present, turning his world into a living nightmare...

A Bantam paperback
0 553 50611 0

LEONARD NIMOY'S PRIMORTALS: TARGET EARTH
Steve Perry

Sixty-five million years ago, aliens rescued a handful of promising species from a doomed Jurassic Earth. Today, one of our world's lost descendants is coming home.

Grad student Stewart Davies, working at a minor SETI station on Long Island, is the first to intercept the signal. It is not a hoax. It is not a freak burst of solar radiation. It would seem that this time it is for real.

And this signal hasn't travelled billions of light years to get here either. Its source is within our own solar system – a starship on a direct course for Earth. Who or what is on that ship? Why is it heading towards our planet and what are the consequences for humankind? Suddenly, all those old sci-fi films and TV series seem all-too terribly real...

Based on the celebrated comic book series created by Leonard Nimoy with concepts by Isaac Asimov, *Leonard Nimoy's Primortals: Target Earth* is a hugely entertaining and exciting galactic adventure.

A Bantam paperback
0 553 50666 8

TO HOLD INFINITY
John Meaney

'A cold fusion of post-cyberpunk tech noir with the expansive dreams of classic SF...dark, complex and glitters with brilliant strangeness'
Stephen Baxter

Devastated by her husband's death, biologist Yoshiko Sunadomari journeys to the paradise world of Fulgor to see her estranged son and bridge the gulf between them.

However, Tetsuo is in trouble. His expertise in mu-space tech and family links with the mysterious Pilots have ensured his survival. So far. Now he's in way over his head – unwittingly caught up in a conspiracy of illegal tech-trafficking and corruption, and in the sinister machinations of one of Fulgor's ruling élite: the charismatic Luculentus, Rafael Garcia de la Vega. When his home is attacked, Tetsuo flees to the planet's unterraformed wastes, home to society's outcasts and eco-terrorists.

So Yoshiko arrives on Fulgor to discover Tetsuo gone...and wanted for murder. Unnerved by this strange, stratified new world but determined to clear his name, she finds herself confronting the awesome, malevolent mind of Rafael...

A Bantam paperback
0 553 50588 2

THE RELIC
Lincoln Preston

'Right up there with *Jaws* or *Alien*, *The Relic* is a heart-of-darkness nightmare'
Fangoria

When a team of archaeologists is massacred in the Amazon, all that survives are several boxes of relics and plant specimens. From boat to boat, from port to port, the battered crates drift. They finally reach New York – only to be locked away in the basement of the city's Museum of Natural History, lost and forgotten.

However, the black heart of the Amazon never forgets. Just days before the Museum's massive new exhibition opens someone or something other than tourists is roaming the echoing halls and dusty galleries. And people are turning up savagely murdered. Forensic evidence points to a killer of terrifying strength and ferocity and rumours of a 'Museum Beast' begin to spread. But then graduate student Margo Green uncovers a link between the killings, the failed Amazon expedition and a strange figurine due to go on display in the upcoming exhibition. And suddenly it becomes a race against time and death and a horrifying adversary...

'Modern technology mixes with ancient lore and good, honest human fear...well-written, well-plotted and paced'
SFX

A Bantam paperback
0 553 50496 7

MOUNT DRAGON
Lincoln Preston

'A slam-bang medical thriller – swift, gruesome, and wickedly clever...a masterful story'
Richard Preston,
author of *The Hot Zone*

Mount Dragon: an elite desert laboratory belonging to GeneDyne, one of the world's foremost biotechnology companies. For scientist Guy Carson his transfer there is the opportunity of a lifetime – the chance to work alongside some of the country's most brilliant scientific minds on a permanent cure for a common, but dangerous disease. Success would guarantee enormous profits for GeneDyne – and a Nobel Prize for the Mount Dragon team.

But something very strange is happening at Mount Dragon. The hidden lab harbours a ghastly secret that puts the whole world at horrifying risk. And by the time Guy Carson makes his hideous discovery, it may already be too late...

'The writer that scared the willies out of readers with *The Relic* returns with a second, equally gripping novel of techno-terror...it's a grand and scary story'
Publishers' Weekly

A Bantam paperback
0 553 50438 X

RELIQUARY
Lincoln Preston

**The heart-stopping sequel to *The Relic* –
'A slambang horrific SF adventure'**
Locus

When two skeletons are discovered in the reeking
mud off the Manhatten shoreline, Natural History
Museum curator and anthropologist Margo Green
is called in to help out. There's something odd
about these remains, something dank and horribly
disturbing. The signs of foul play <u>and</u>
grotesque abnormalities can mean only one thing: the
awakening of a slumbering nightmare.

The mystery deepens with a string of brutal murders
and a reluctant Margo finds herself teamed up once
more with Lieutenant Vincent D'Agosta of the NYPD,
ultra-cool FBI agent Pendergast and brilliant scientist
Dr Frock. Their investigation takes them from crum-
bling warehouses and burned-out labs to the hidden
lairs of New York's homeless and on down to the long-
abandoned, long-forgotten galleries, tunnels and
sewers that riddle the bedrock beneath the city...to
the final hideous secret of the Museum Beast.

**'High on suspense and tremendous fun...
especially when exploring the city's nightmare
underbelly'**
Publishers' Weekly

A Bantam paperback
0 553 50633 1

A SELECTED LIST OF SCIENCE FICTION AND FANTASY TITLES AVAILABLE FROM BANTAM BOOKS

❑ 40808 9	STAR WARS: Jedi Search	*Kevin J. Anderson*	£5.99
❑ 40809 7	STAR WARS: Dark Apprentice	*Kevin J. Anderson*	£4.99
❑ 40810 0	STAR WARS: Champions of the Force	*Kevin J. Anderson*	£4.99
❑ 40971 9	STAR WARS: Tales from the Mos Eisley Cantina	*Kevin J. Anderson (ed.)*	£4.99
❑ 50413 4	STAR WARS: Tales from Jabba's Palace	*Kevin J. Anderson (ed.)*	£4.99
❑ 50471 1	STAR WARS: Tales of the Bounty Hunters	*Kevin J. Anderson (ed.)*	£4.99
❑ 40880 1	STAR WARS: Darksaber	*Kevin J. Anderson*	£5.99
❑ 40879 8	STAR WARS: Children of the Jedi	*Barbara Hambly*	£4.99
❑ 50431 2	STAR WARS: Before the Storm	*Michael P. Kube-McDowell*	£4.99
❑ 50479 7	STAR WARS: Shield of Lies	*Michael P. Kube-McDowell*	£5.99
❑ 50480 0	STAR WARS: Tyrant's Test	*Michael P. Kube-McDowell*	£4.99
❑ 40881 X	STAR WARS: Ambush at Corellia	*Roger MacBride Allen*	£4.99
❑ 40882 8	STAR WARS: Assault at Selonia	*Roger MacBride Allen*	£4.99
❑ 40883 6	STAR WARS: Showdown at Centerpoint	*Roger MacBride Allen*	£4.99
❑ 40878 X	STAR WARS: The Crystal Star	*Vonda McIntyre*	£4.99
❑ 50472 X	STAR WARS: Shadows of the Empire	*Steve Perry*	£4.99
❑ 40926 3	STAR WARS X-Wing 1: Rogue Squadron	*Michael Stackpole*	£5.99
❑ 40923 9	STAR WARS X-Wing 2: Wedge's Gamble	*Michael Stackpole*	£4.99
❑ 40925 5	STAR WARS X-Wing 3: The Krytos Trap	*Michael Stackpole*	£4.99
❑ 40924 7	STAR WARS X-Wing 4: The Bacta War	*Michael Stackpole*	£4.99
❑ 40758 9	STAR WARS: The Truce at Bakura	*Kathy Tyers*	£4.99
❑ 40807 0	STAR WARS: The Courtship of Princess Leia	*Dave Wolverton*	£4.99
❑ 40471 7	STAR WARS: Heir to the Empire	*Timothy Zahn*	£4.99
❑ 40442 5	STAR WARS: Dark Force Rising	*Timothy Zahn*	£4.99
❑ 40443 1	STAR WARS: The Last Command	*Timothy Zahn*	£4.99
❑ 40853 4	CONQUERORS' PRIDE	*Timothy Zahn*	£4.99
❑ 40854 2	CONQUERORS' HERITAGE	*Timothy Zahn*	£4.99
❑ 40855 0	CONQUERORS' LEGACY	*Timothy Zahn*	£4.99
❑ 40488 1	FORWARD THE FOUNDATION	*Isaac Asimov*	£4.99
❑ 40069 X	NEMESIS	*Isaac Asimov*	£4.99
❑ 29138 6	STAR TREK 1	*James Blish*	£4.99
❑ 29139 4	STAR TREK 2	*James Blish*	£4.99
❑ 29140 8	STAR TREK 3	*James Blish*	£4.99
❑ 40501 2	STAINLESS STEEL RAT SINGS THE BLUES	*Harry Harrison*	£4.99
❑ 50426 6	SHADOW MOON	*George Lucas & Chris Claremont*	£4.99
❑ 50492 4	HONOR AMONG ENEMIES	*David Weber*	£4.99